...is being
s . . .
...eller
...ETTERSSON's
SIGNS OF THE ZODIAC

"Vicki Pettersson is a new voice that needs to be heard."

Kim Harrison

"[Pettersson] blends fantasy, comic book super-heroism, and paranormal romance, but holds no promise of a happily ever after. . . . [Readers] will embrace Pettersson's enduring, tough-as-nails heroine and anticipate gleefully the next volume."

Publishers Weekly

"Pettersson's paranormal world is as original as it is compelling. The action comes fast and furious. Like Las Vegas itself, this is an adventure that'll keep you up all night."

Kelley Armstrong

"Unputdownable . . . with nonstop bursts of action and imagination."

Diana Gabaldon

"Passion and intrigue, heartbreak and victory. . . . Nothing is predictable . . . except the need to read more."

Melissa Marr

Books by Vicki Pettersson

THE SCENT OF SHADOWS
The First Sign of the Zodiac

THE TASTE OF NIGHT
The Second Sign of the Zodiac

THE TOUCH OF TWILIGHT
The Third Sign of the Zodiac

CITY OF SOULS
The Fourth Sign of the Zodiac

CHEAT THE GRAVE
The Fifth Sign of the Zodiac

CHEAT THE GRAVE

THE FIFTH SIGN OF THE ZODIAC

VICKI PETTERSSON

eos

An Imprint of HarperCollinsPublishers

This is a work of fiction. Names, characters, places, and incidents are products of the author's imagination or are used fictitiously and are not to be construed as real. Any resemblance to actual events, locales, organizations, or persons, living or dead, is entirely coincidental.

EOS
An Imprint of HarperCollins*Publishers*
10 East 53rd Street
New York, New York 10022-5299

Copyright © 2010 by Vicki Pettersson
Cover art by Don Sipley
Author photo © 2007 Derik Klein
ISBN 978-0-06-145677-0
www.eosbooks.com

First Eos paperback printing: June 2010

HarperCollins® and Eos® are registered trademarks of HarperCollins Publishers.

Printed in the U.S.A.

10 9 8 7 6 5 4 3 2 1

For Denise Rapuano—for exemplifying the grace and strength of a true goddess. Sola would be mad with jealousy.

Acknowledgments

Profound thanks go to my business and creative partners, Miriam Kriss and Diana Gill, whom I'm also blessed to call my friends. Immense gratitude also goes out to Jeaniene Frost, Melissa Marr, Kim Harrison, and Rachel Vincent for being ever-supportive allies and peers. Thanks to my readers as well, especially Dave Torres, Raven, and Joy Maiorana for early readings, and those other twisted souls on my message board who've used my books as an excuse to spawn happy chaos in cyberspace. I'm proud to be your mascot.

1

Dying isn't as painful as you might think. I've done it twice now, and each time the woman I thought I was fell away with relative ease, almost as if she was late for an appointment and glad to be gone. As hard as it was at the time, the only real casualty in my first death was my identity. Good-bye, Joanna Archer. Good-bye, strong and able and tough; hello to an exterior so sweet I might as well be clothed in a fucking candy wrapper.

But it was the second death, the one that'd cost me every foothold gained after taking over my sister's life and identity that really stripped me to the bone. In the ten weeks since, I'd been forced to rehab my blond, glossed, enhanced body as vigorously as a recently awakened coma victim, while hoping the work I'd already done on my mind would hold fast. It had, but there was no mistaking my losses. This time, good-bye twenty-first century superhero. So long to strength beyond a mortal's. Farewell even to what I'd fleetingly mistaken for true love. The kicker? After all those losses, dying had turned out to be just another life experience.

Which wasn't to say it got any easier.

"But third time's a charm," I muttered, gazing balefully down at the newly delivered letter as my driver rocketed past the multi-casino district, City Center. The doorman hadn't known who it was from, just said some courier—probably a kid off the street who was slipped a twenty and an envelope with my name on it—had given it to him an hour before. I'd have to talk to the buildings staff about allowing strange missives and packages up to my high-rise apartment. After all, Olivia Archer wasn't a mere celebutante anymore, or just a former Playmate and potential heiress. She was a mogul who effectively owned more of Las Vegas than any other living being.

"But I don't think that's why someone's threatening to squeeze my beating heart in their palm," I muttered as we flipped onto Vegas's most famous road, heading midtown. Pulling the note from my pocket, I read it again.

Stay home tonight, and you will be safe. Leave, and your organs will be sliced from your body one by one.

Not even a clue as to the sender, though that was no surprise. Nobody from the paranormal underworld had contacted me since I'd been cast from the troop. Despite losing every power that had once made me one of them, the leader for the agents of Light, my *former* leader, had ordered my once-allies to neither contact nor extend me any greater protection than they did the rest of the general population. This, despite the fact that if the Shadows learned of my now-human status, Las Vegas's mortality rate would see a precipitous spike.

You'll be safe. I had to laugh. God, had I even been safe the day I was born?

Of course, anyone who knew me—the real me, Joanna—wouldn't be surprised to find I went out anyway. My cat, Luna, had tried to persuade me otherwise, winding through my feet as I dressed, tripping me up like she thought the whole thing was a bad idea. But what could I do? Olivia's best friend, Cher—now *my* best friend—was throwing a bachelorette party for her stepmother, Suzanne, a woman who must have been born under the Universe's luckiest star. The loving relationship with her stepdaughter underscored that, but she'd recently trumped even herself by becoming engaged to a man who was both a billionaire and a prince. They were set to wed a week from now, on Valentine's Day.

Besides, I thought now, pulling to a stop in front of the world's tackiest party bus, I'd once battled in this city's paranormal underworld for the mortal right to freedom of choice. Now that I was once again merely mortal—after those who'd once called themselves my allies had tossed me in a desert wash with other broken, discarded, used-up objects—I chose normal. I chose those friends who chose me.

I chose to keep living beyond death.

Yet I still hesitated when confronted by the shining silver bus door. Sure, this was a part of Suzanne's month-long wedding festivities, a series of events that had set tongues wagging worldwide. Her fiancé had long been considered one of the globe's most eligible bachelors, an international textiles magnate who hailed from an Indian dynasty, and had homes on every continent.

But, man, a double-decker could hold a lot of trouble.

It's not too late to turn around, I thought, my too-smooth fingertips clinking unnaturally against the plastic. Their marblelike uniformity and pearlescent polish was one of the "tells" of my former involvement in a paranormal life, and should a Shadow see it, they'd know exactly who I was. Was an evening spent in a party bus worth risking that? I mean, there'd been a lot of recent nights when I'd kill for a glass of Belvedere . . . but to *die* for one?

"C'mon, Jo," I muttered to myself, straightening. "Can't turn down the promise of body glitter and temp tattoos, can you? Besides, how many people could say they've been on a bus with a disco ball before?"

But humor aside, a part of me was honestly worried. If the Shadows had discovered my identity, the bachelorette bus might turn into the lead car of a funeral procession. Yet some couriered letter telling me to bolt my door wouldn't help then. If anything, the missive merely underscored my continued need to convince the world I was my flighty, over-exposed sister.

But I took a moment before boarding the bus to look out over the city I'd once fought to protect, alongside a troop of supernatural beings I thought were my friends.

Fuck you—whoever you are—for being an armchair superhero, and standing on the sidelines while I shoulder this mortality. Fuck you for accepting the sacrifices I made for your world and then throwing me away like trash. Fuck you for bottling your power like it's your personal supernatural bong while I emptied mine out over this city and its people.

I didn't care if those in the Zodiac underworld believed fate was preordained. So what if my return to mortality had been written in the stars, in the dark matter between them, in advance, or in permanent ink? I gave up my life twice to save the collective asses of those who called themselves superheroes, so a letter intended to keep me safe after the fact meant nothing.

Besides, I thought, turning from the city. Here's what *I* knew of fate: it cared nothing about good intentions.

Becoming my younger, flashier, murdered sister had forced me to reconsider the way I moved through the world. After all, why use a deadly weapon when the crook of a manicured finger would just as well do? Yet I'd found a surprising strength in defying the world's relatively low expectations of Olivia . . . or at the very least in using them to my advantage.

I'd also found an unexpected strength in Cher and Suzanne. True, they'd actually once been my antifriends— women who didn't understand a woman who didn't understand women—but during my recent recovery from a sacrificial near-drowning, when all my superhero allies remained tucked safely in an underground sanctuary pretending I no longer existed, these two flighty, bright socialites had unerringly stuck by me. Yes, they believed I was Olivia, but their show of relentless friendship meant there was nothing I wouldn't do for them now. Even in my jaded postheroic state—even when I couldn't save loose change, much less a life—I'd willingly lay down my own for theirs.

"C'mon, Jo." I set my bare shoulders and knocked on the neon-trimmed door. After all, I was already here, defying a homicidal warning, and strapped into my big-girl halter top. If I could get through the first Jell-O shot, I'd probably be fine.

Then the door swung open. "Oh fu—"

A hip-hop/choir remix drowned out the rest of my curse, and my gaze caught on the turntable rising from the driver's seat. Cher stood behind it, decked out in curvy silver satin, blond hair set in seductress waves, her right hand pressed against headphones while the other scratched a beat. She was shaking her hips in time to the needle's drop, but she straightened and squealed when she spotted me waffling in the doorway. "Livvy-girl!"

She motioned me up the rubber steps, and I eased forward like a paranoid marine. No, I didn't expect to find otherworldly terrorists swilling Cristal, but the two lucite stripper poles arrowing out of the vehicle's middle were nearly as terrifying.

The bus's other dozen occupants caught my ascension through the mirrored walls, and greetings and liquor-infused smiles burst forth in raucous stop-motion beneath the fractured light of, yes, a disco ball. I waved back, hid my wince, and they resumed imbibing, applauding, and pole dancing. The bus wasn't even moving yet.

"Check out the old-school mixer!" Cher yelled, as I reached her side. "We're going to sing Bollywood songs on this here bachelorette bus. I swear, Las Vegas won't have ever seen a bash like this before!"

And the burnt-out party girl that was my beloved hometown had certainly run through a number of bashes. I glanced around warily. The lights, people, alcohol, music—a heap of sensory blocks atop already dulled senses. I began to reconsider the wisdom of coming at all. "I might have to leave early," I told Cher.

She finally fell still. "Why, are you sick? Is it fatal?"

Potentially. "Um . . . tomorrow's the big board meeting, remember? I've been preparing."

And I had. Binders scattered every flat surface of my living room like giant autumn leaves. Yet despite spending weeks studying the Company Bylaws, the Shareholder Agreements, and something called a Private Placement Memorandum, I still didn't understand half of them.

"Don't you have people for that?" she asked, scratching another beat with long, silver nails—acrylic across vinyl.

"*I'm* the one taking over Archer Enterprises." At her blank stare, I added, "And I want to, you know, make dear old Daddy proud."

May the cruel, greedy bastard rest in peace.

"Then it's all the more vital to your burgeoning business sense that you're out tonight." She tossed her hair authoritatively.

"How?"

"Because come tomorrow you'll be sucked into the corporate machine, never to don lucite heels at nine a.m. again. No more liquid lunches. No more 'Mimosa Mondays.' If you think about it, this is your last night of normalcy. Ever."

I snorted. Cher's idea of "normalcy" had never included disemboweling a homicidal supervillain as a prelude to Mimosa Monday.

A male voice sounded in my ear. "Finally."

Whirling to determine if this statement called for an air kiss or a death blow, I found myself within swatting distance of a pretty man wearing black wrist cuffs, eyeliner, and a fitted net for a shirt. Not kill, I thought with relief . . . though he probably wasn't angling for my kiss either.

"I'm Terry," he said, drawing close, then as if I didn't know, "You're Olivia Archer. I follow you in the papers. I've been wanting to shoot you for ages."

I reconsidered killing him until he held up a camera and looked at me expectantly.

I unclenched my fist. "Sure."

Terry shot off a quick series of photos as I struck poses meant to highlight certain body parts, unable to hear more than snatches of his chatter about celebrities he'd shot in L.A. before moving to Vegas. Unfortunately what I did hear included boastful accounts of erstwhile pop divas climbing from limos sans undergarments. "The society women followed suit for a while, but then they clued in to the upkeep."

Again that expectant look.

Not *this* society woman, I thought, gifting him with a closed-mouth smile. "I'll be by the pole."

And so I mingled, tossing air kisses, accepting a champagne flute, but painstakingly avoided the poles of iniquity. By the time the bus finally revved its engine, a professional had taken over DJ duties, Cher was at the side bar, surrounded by bottles like some glossy, gilded mad scientist, and her stepmother, the woman of the hour—or the past month, as it were—finally arrived.

"Ladies and gentlemen," the DJ said in a streetwise baritone, "please welcome to the par-tay, the future princess of the finest fibers, the westerner who won the heart of the East, our Texan treasure, and soon to be Mrs. Arun Brahma . . . Su-zanne!"

The packed bus rocked on its wheels as everyone rose to their feet, cheering as Suzanne ascended to a hip-hop version of the wedding march. Terry's camera literally went into spasms, though I couldn't fault his excitement. Suzanne, poured into hot pink leather cut both too low and too high, was the money shot. She milked the moment, flashed a diamond to rival the Hope, and draped herself against the first pole. Her eyes caught mine and she straightened before winking and taking a quick swing.

"Oops."

More cameras flashed.

"It's okay, Suzie," someone encouraged. "If you don't fall off the pole at least once, you're not really trying."

Suzanne pushed herself from the lap of a thrilled "husband of" and patted her hair back into place.

It was embarrassing to fall off a stripper pole when you were twenty, but when you were forty-something? You prayed for early dementia. I grabbed a shot glass from Cher and went to assist with the murder of a few hundred brain cells. "You okay?" I asked Suzanne.

She shrugged off the shame like it belonged to another. "Yeah, I'm just not warmed up yet. It happens to me in class all the time too."

"They have classes in pole dancing?" I asked, before giving myself a mental head slap. It was Vegas. They probably had classes in threesomes.

"It's good exercise."

I raised a brow. "You could go to the gym."

"Oh, no honey," she said in her trademark southern drawl. "Those weights are heavy. Here, help me out."

Reaching under the giant DJ turntable, Suzanne opened a mirrored trunk. A moment later bright fuchsia feathers flew my way. "Boas?"

She tossed me a half dozen more strands, and motioned for me to pass them out. "Arun, my one true love and future king, has arranged a scavenger hunt for us. He's giving away a world cruise on his private yacht as a prize." The women nearest us gasped, and the news spread like a brush fire. "We have to leave the bus to collect the clues, and this is how we're going to differentiate ourselves from the teeming masses."

I sighed, fingering my boa. Or I could just put a bull's-eye on my chest.

Suzanne swung a deep olive strand over her shoulders and smiled through the feathers as she led me into the throng, tossing boas left and right, and fighting for balance as the vehicle headed downtown. I watched her for a moment, wishing I could still scent emotion, though even in the dim light she glowed. She really was in love. Catching my look, she continued chatting about the scavenger's hunt. "These will help the guides we planted in the city know who to give the clues out to as well. They're customized for each person . . . though we're going in teams."

And just like that my paranormal bull's-eye expanded to include Cher.

"I really need more wine," I muttered, squinting up at the disco ball.

Magically, it appeared. Hanging out with a future princess had its benefits.

"Look, Livvy." Cher waved from the front of the bus, where I headed, barely managing not to spill into the same man's lap. His wife glared like I'd gotten up his hopes on purpose. Meanwhile, Cher was holding up a tiny gold ring. "Arun bought body jewelry for the party. It's all from his village in India. These are clip-ons, so you can try them on before committing. But the real deal is in the back with the piercer."

Which explained the lascivious looks I'd been getting from the guy eyeing my virgin nose. As well as that corner's intermittent screeches. "One badly timed speed bump and things could get very interesting at the back of the bus."

Nodding absently, Cher said, "Here, this loops around your eyebrow—sexy little center diamond, huh?—and this has a fancy magnet which attaches through your nose."

Cher kept the nose ring, so I gamely reached for the brow hoop. I squinted at the tiny designs flaring from the diamond like rays from the sun but couldn't make them all out in the dim, flashing light. I'd been having trouble with my eyesight ever since it'd reverted to 20/20. Meanwhile, Cher lifted my shirt without asking, a faux belly ring dangling from her fingertips, but she drew back in surprise. "Oh, you already have one. That's hot."

I glanced down ruefully. Maybe, but it hadn't been by choice. I thought about telling Cher where I'd gotten it, the story of a parallel realm called Midheaven, ruled by women who considered themselves goddesses, and fueled by the souls of those who entered there. But I didn't want to give her nightmares . . . or ideas. That underground world was a pocket of distended reality, like a bubble of poisonous, trapped gas. It offered a place for rogue agents to hide from whatever trouble they'd left behind in this world, but it did so at a price. It was a twisted place that twisted people in return, stripping them down, literally changing them at a cellular level.

Besides, tonight was supposed to be about safe and normal. So I wasn't going to allow in memories of my lost powers, my myriad mistakes, or other dangerous worlds.

Or of the man who'd betrayed me for one of those goddesses.

"Hunter," I whispered into my wineglass, the name lost in the bowl and the bus's growling technothrob. Then I banished his memory like a ghost and lifted my chin, determined to do the same with my thoughts. And be *normal*.

So as the rolling disco/revival got under way, I gave the pole nearest me a considering look. One foot in front of the other. That was how I'd re-embrace my humanity, my sister's life, and the sole responsibility for protecting my own. I'd forget about the Shadow and the Light soon enough . . . and that I'd once been both. Surely then, even the images dogging my recent dreams—of Hunter suspended amidst a star-studded sky, and wrapped in the slim, soft arms of another woman—would fade away as well.

2

The bus dropped the lot of us mid-downtown, and while the other partygoers scattered like frilly cockroaches in the bright lights of the Fremont Street Experience, I instinctively hunched in the night. My senses weren't what they used to be—I couldn't smell emotion, taste intent, feel violence approaching from behind—but still knew that feeling like prey meant you probably were. Besides, unlike the other mortals surrounding me, I knew what predators lay in wait in this concrete jungle.

So the bums and panhandlers resting in the cold night cavities near the spilling neon didn't bother me. They didn't seem to trouble the socialites and party kids much either. A world cruise was enough motivation to ignore both pedestrian and social ills, and had the participants moving in their Manolos. Watching a woman in a fur push the feet of a sleeping indigent off a park bench near Main Street Station so she could sit and study her map, I shook my head. I loved Suzanne . . . but sometimes I seriously questioned her judgment.

Meanwhile, Cher was shivering in short silver, her boa offering the only warmth, and her cute faux nose ring winking in the retro bulbs studding the Golden Nugget. She'd refused to don a coat, saying it would ruin her club kid vibe, though she darted covetous glances at her competitor's fur as she said it. I sighed. When I'd last been part of a team, I was paired with a weapon-wielding, building-jumping superhero who could lift fifty times his body weight. Cher, on the other hand, was a mortal girl who idolized Perez Hilton and thought caustic Twitter updates were the best way to inflict pain. And in this state, she'd be helpless to resist a pashmina, forget a full frontal paranormal assault.

"One of the clues is planted at a bar," she piped up, gazing at our clue sheet. We'd had a choice of three. Each, Suzanne had instructed, would lead us upon a different path with varying degrees of difficulty. So getting through the clues and back to the bus quickly was as much a product of fate as intelligence.

"Really?" I raised my brow ring. "A bar? In *Vegas*?"

She glanced back at the woman in the fur and bit her lip. "Hopefully their clues are just as challenging."

Challenging? This was like looking for a specific bulb in a sea of neon. "They're making us use our brains." I leaned against a billboard on the Nugget's brick face, searching for movement along the rooftops, while thinking it unfair to ask of a bus full of tequila-swilling boa wearers.

Cher blew a stray orange feather from her lip. "Envision the Mediterranean sprawled like a blue carpet before you."

"I can go any time I want," I said airily.

She cocked a hand on one slim hip. "Then think positive for my sake."

"Sure. I'm a glass-half-full kind of girl." Which is why I was jumping at the slightest sound.

But the Mediterranean comment caught hold. When *was* the last time I'd taken a vacation? Agents couldn't leave the city they were charged to protect, yet even before joining the troop last year, I'd rarely left Vegas. Why should I, I'd reasoned, when the world came to me? Why go—

I'd always thought with admittedly less reason—when the man I'd sought for over a decade was in this city?

But now I was an outcast, and that man was dead.

I was also so wound up the nearest slots were sending my nerves to clanking.

Straightening, I angled the map my way. The Mediterranean suddenly sounded pretty good. "It says here that the sky is our map. We have to correlate the right star systems to those above, which will give us the coordinates to our first destination."

We craned our necks back, but it was too bright on the ground to see any stars. Good. If I never read the sky's mysteries again, it'd be too soon. Fortunately, a year spent in a troop that practically worshipped the sky meant I'd already memorized the major star patterns.

"Here, give me that," I told Cher, holding the clue sheet eye level. The faster we did this, the faster we could get off the streets.

Squinting at the numbers again, I dug through the canvas goodie bag given to each team before we'd disembarked from the bus. In it were a flashlight, a detailed map, and the item I held up, a compass. "I'll chart it, you use the key on the map's side."

We spent five minutes bumping brain cells before coming to an agreement on which direction to head. Man, I missed the days when I could run down the block in zero to sixty. I'd have been back before Cher could vogue.

Cher slipped the canvas bag across her chest. "The corner of Ninth and Sandstone, then."

"I know a shortcut." I motioned for her to follow and we headed away from the canopied light show of not-so-subliminal messages and into the weed-choked environs of urban Vegas. Unlike the Zodiac agents who'd grown up hidden from the world's view until they metamorphosed into full-fledged star signs, I wasn't gifted with sanctuary when I was young, and by the time I hit the quarter century mark—the coming-of-age for the initiates—I'd been battling evil on Las Vegas's back streets for a decade. Sure, back then the demons I faced had been my own, but that hadn't made them any less formidable.

"Slum much?" Cher asked cryptically as I unerringly led her down another narrow alleyway. I turned to reassure her, but caught movement from a boarded-up convenience store behind us. My immediate impulse was to sniff at the air to scent out the cause, but that power had been drained from me along with all others. Besides, it could have been anything from floating debris to a shuffling homeless person, or nothing at all.

Immediate arrival at our destination provided distraction for us both. A neon sign heralded the spot, though parts of its tubing were burnt out and the remaining red glow muted by what looked like centuries of caked dirt. Yet the service it advertised was clear.

"A psychic," I said, feeling my gut sink. Anything having to do with astrology bumped too closely for my liking against the World that Could Not Be Named.

"Smells like cat pee," Cher said, bringing me out of my momentary reverie.

"We can hope it's a cat, anyway," I muttered, taking the lead. I had no weapon beyond my sharp tongue, but it was still natural for me to protect any nearby mortal. Old habits died hard.

Yeah, and sometimes they take you with them.

Climbing a narrow stairwell, we reached what in earlier, cleaner, more hopeful times might have been called a mother-in-law apartment. Right now it struggled to be a garret. I wouldn't have touched the walls even were I still impervious to disease, and Cher stayed to the stairwell's center, like the building was contagious. The thin hallway carpeting was torn and stained, and only one of four bald bulbs worked, but revealed a landing with a peeling green door dumped opposite us like an afterthought. Very bad feng shui. A no-longer-tufted stool slumped haphazardly next to it, bearing some long-dead plant in a shattered pot.

Since Cher had shrunk into the landing's center, boa damn near tucked between her legs, I sighed, folded my knuckles in the hem of my wrap, and knocked on the door.

Nothing.

Shrugging, I turned to find Cher already angling back down the staircase. She cringed sheepishly. "I don't think this is it."

"I bet they have butler service on that yacht."

Reluctantly, she rejoined my side.

"Let's look at the map again." We each took one side so we could cover our noses. The smell of urine was nauseating.

"This has to be it," she finally agreed, reluctance oozing from behind her palm. "But if this lady were a real psychic, wouldn't she know we were coming?"

Good point. I looked around, gaze catching on a shadowed alcove where too much of nothing lingered. "Hey, Cher. Swing the flashlight over there, will you?"

She did, and a stout, square shape took form. Not a guide, no. But not another dead plant either.

Cher inched closer. "What is it?"

"A wooden chest." It was obviously aged, but unlike the rest of this place, it wasn't battered. A closer look revealed a black silk lining between glossy if worn slats . . . something easily ripped, though this was pristine.

"Looks like a pirate's chest," Cher commented, and I pursed my lips. One with looping whorls and intricate designs that held centuries of meaning.

"Got that disposable camera they gave out on the bus?"

Cher's face turned into a shadowed amalgam of confusion and surprise. It looked distorted on the dim landing. "Why?"

Because the chest was too heavy to pick up and take with us, because doing so would be considered stealing . . . but also because I recognized some of those dark symbols. "It looks antique. I might want to get one like it."

"Honey, it looks satanic." She snapped off a quick shot.

"You might want to get some holy water."

It *was* foreboding. And if I had to open it, I'd prefer a little distance between me and whatever was beneath that lid. "Maybe we can use that broken broomstick to open it up." But the stick I'd spotted was as filthy as the rest of this place . . .

Catching myself mid-thought, I shook my head. I didn't use to be so precious about things.

"Here, give me the map."

Cher's mouth quirked in distaste as I wrapped it around the broom's splintered handle. "We'll have to sterilize it."

"Fine. Go boil some water. I'll just work on this latch."

Cher—savvy to sarcasm—stayed put, but after a few attempts I gave up on poking the thing with a blunt object and resigned myself to putting my opposable thumbs to good use. Fingers sinking into the silky lining, I lifted the lid. The hinges creaked.

Something moved inside.

"Shoot it!" I told Cher, jerking back, and I didn't mean with the camera. Cher just screamed like she was at a Madonna concert. A fat gray rat crawled from the chest and scurried away with the whip of a long tail. Shuddering, I caught my breath and, because we weren't already dead, picked up the flashlight Cher had dropped. Angling the beam back into the chest, I gasped, and tasted sweet victory despite the dank, rotting hallway. Two brightly plumed masks lay wrapped in clear plastic. "Look. Someone has thoughtfully provided waterless hand wash as well."

"I call dibs on the green one," Cher said, reaching in, revived by the sight of crystals and plumes. "That's totally my color."

And pink was Olivia's. I winced as Cher unwrapped it and handed it to me. Not exactly the sort of mask I was accustomed to in my role as a twenty-first century superhero. And just what I needed, I thought wryly. More feathers.

"So where's the guide to give us our next clue?" That was the point of the identifying boas, right? I searched the chest for an envelope, letting the flashlight beam fall over every corner, but there was nothing else. Yet when it centered on the open lid, I jerked back.

"What?" Cher asked, feeling me startle. She spotted the object strapped to the lid and bent for a closer look.

It didn't stir my blood as it would have a handful of weeks earlier, but I recognized the item instantly. A conduit was a weapon that could not only kill humans, but *super*humans—both Shadow and Light. This one was a silver dagger the length of my forearm, though the sole light caught on a depressed hinge. A trident, then, with two more lethal blades that winged out at a thumb's twitch.

Cher reached for it. There was only one thing to do.

"Cockroach!" I yelled so loudly my voice ping-ponged down the stairwell.

She fled down the stairs so quickly she could have medaled.

I waited until I heard her feet hit the landing, then leaned forward. Someone from my other life had clearly infiltrated Suzanne's scavenger hunt, maybe even the same someone who'd sent the warning not to go out. Seeing that they'd prepared for the possibility anyway, they also obviously knew me well.

Though my palm itched to hold a conduit again, I resisted. Mine had been stripped from me when I was turned out from the troop. This owner's weapon was probably long gone, as the silver was tarnished and clearly ancient, and I wondered briefly if he or she had been Shadow or Light. Then I recalled the sense of being watched outside, slapped my palm against the chest, and slammed the lid shut. "Fuck it."

I whirled, rapping on the door so hard my knuckles would bruise.

Nothing happened, though Cher did call up the staircase. "Livvy?"

"Open up, you rat-fuck bastard," I muttered under my breath, and the door ricocheted against the interior wall like a giant mousetrap. A clump of plaster fell from the ceiling, and I choked in the ensuing dust, covering my face with the mask and ducking at the same time. A figure swayed like a huge, opaque ghost in front of me, and I wished for the dagger behind me. When that figure slipped into the meager light, I wished for two.

It was a man, bald-headed, but with a black wiry beard twisted and forked into two sharp points. He stood barefoot and in tattered jeans, though his chest was bare. I began counting his ribs until I realized that, no, I was seeing his every *bone*—rib cage, chest, clavicles, shoulders and sockets, forearms and fingers. Their outlines sat tattooed atop his skin, fully inked, like his body had reversed its layering.

Yet his fingertips were the eeriest, nails an unnatural extension of all that bone, twining in and out of one another for a good foot each, effectively making his hands useless. Shellacked a shiny black, they matched his beard and, for some reason, reminded me of the dead plant lying next to the door.

"Yes?" he asked, like he expected me to offer him a magazine subscription.

"I want you to leave me alone."

"You knocked on my door."

"I mean all of you!" I hissed, and his smile spread like black syrup. "I gave everything I had to the world of Light and Shadow, and I want no part of it anymore. Leave me and my friends alone. Got it?"

"You should at least take the trident." His voice was a liquid warble, and though his eyes were sunken, his attention was locked on me. Just like the rest of that damned world.

"It's not mine," I answered with clenched teeth.

"I thought you'd be taller," he said, waving an envelope at me that was too pristine for hands with such gnarled knuckles. I wondered how he'd picked it up. I didn't even want to know how he went to the bathroom. But what he held was clear: the next clue on the treasure hunt.

Damn.

I didn't move to take it. He could have me pinned against the wall before I blinked, mask removed before I cried out, dead before I'd taken another breath, but I wasn't going to extend myself to him in any way. It was vital, I somehow knew, that I didn't do that.

"Warriors are supposed to have some height to them."

The inky divots where his eyes should have been remained pinned on me, and I shuddered, feeling my nausea return. For a moment it looked like the darkness was spreading from his body, like an airborne stain. I shook my head. "I'm just a girl now."

"Olivia?" Cher's concerned voice echoed up the stairwell. I swallowed hard. I did not want her back up there.

"Let me feel your fingers." He reached out with his free hand, palm up, his fingers five branchless black trees angling in tangled growth from his nail beds.

"I don't know you," I said, as an excuse not to touch him, not to extend or accept . . . not to reveal the smooth fingertips that would give away my past. My future lay somewhere else. Even if it turned out to be in the chest behind me, a coffin.

Cher's voice again. "Who are you talking to?"

I had to keep her down there. "Hold on! I'm coming."

"You don't know me yet," he corrected, slowly lowering his arm. The nails on his right hand clacked together. "But you will soon."

And he flicked the envelope onto the landing, backed up—arm straight out to the side—and slammed the door shut before I registered his first movement. Another larger chunk of plaster fell at my feet, and I dove for the clue, and then the staircase as the entire ceiling creaked. He wasn't the creepiest thing I'd ever seen, but that's why I moved so quickly. I couldn't combat even the slightest form of creepy.

Once outside, I shook chunks of dust from my hair, sucking in deep gulps from the crisp winter air. Now shivering in earnest, Cher sneezed next to me. I tilted my gaze to a boarded window, wondering if I only imagined seeing movement between the slats. Just in case, I kept the mask pressed to my face. Damn. Why'd I have to knock on that door?

"Oops. I guess we broke it." Cher sniffled as the old neon sign sizzled and abruptly snapped off. The house sunk further into shadows, the darkness a quicksand, and I took another step back. I could *not* get sucked back into that world.

"That's okay. I've got the next clue. Let's just go."

We scurried away at a fast clip, both happy to be away from the decaying house.

My glances around the hunchbacked streets were less furtive now than before. Whether I was just wired from the encounter with the psychic, or if we really were being followed, I waited until we found a brightly lit street corner without a prostitute on it to lower my mask and wipe my brow. That man had been expecting me, and as I'd never seen or met him before, it was unlikely he was working alone. Hopefully he would tell whatever allies he had that I refused their . . . what? Offering? Gift?

Meanwhile, Cher sneezed, pushed her boa feathers aside, and opened our next clue.

"Looks like a strip club," she said, studying it.

"Good," I sighed in relief, and turned toward Glitter Gulch and away from the house, its war chest, and its living skeleton. "I'm ready for something normal."

It took four hours, and a mixture of happenstance and luck, but thrice more we found our baubles, and thrice more weapons were tucked behind or beneath or beside the awaiting adornment. Each time I imagined breath on my neck, and had to fight not to whirl. Each time I felt eyes in the shadows.

And each time I cursed under my breath. I managed to distract Cher twice by telling her to look out for the guides handing us clues. I then ignored the conduits, and gingerly, hurriedly, picked up beads and bindis instead. Okay, so I paused to study the antiquated gun and its bubbling liquid vial bullets. And reaching for the saber with a firearm welded to its hilt was an involuntary reaction to such a fine piece of warfare. But by the time I spotted the cane with a pommel blade, Cher was over the fear she'd shown in the little shack of horrors, bored with the entire hunt, and sneezing uncontrollably in her sparkly dress. So despite the promise of a warm, tropical cruise, she only flicked an irritated glance at our fourth guide . . . thus catching sight of the last weapon before I could sweep up the studded bangles and shut the BMW's trunk.

Sneezing, she turned an accusing gaze on me. "What the hell is going on?"

I had no intention of telling her, and shot her Olivia's most stunning smile instead. She lifted a brow. I batted my lashes. She batted her own. I thought about lying, but even Cher wasn't likely to fall for something simple, and a complicated lie took too much time and energy. Not to mention you had to remember later what you'd lied about. What would happen, I wondered, narrowing my eyes, if I just told the truth?

You'd piss off any paranormal creature who might be lurking in the shadows.

What the hell? I was kinda tired of being pissed off all by myself.

"Okay. It's like this. There are, like, these people who believe I'm the savior of a paranormal underworld based on the signs of the Zodiac. See, they think my real mother was Light and my father Shadow, which makes me both, and *that* makes me the Kairos." I paused, but Cher only stared, and no one attacked me, so I continued talking. "Except it doesn't. See, I sacrificed all my powers ten weeks ago to save a mortal child's life, along with the entire Vegas population. So now I'm mortal, and re-engaging with that world, including all these weirdo weapons, would obviously be very dangerous for me. So let's just pretend we didn't see them, okay?"

Cher remained still for almost a whole minute, model-perfect face characteristically blank. Then, with just as much seriousness as I'd shown, she sneezed and said, "I think I'm allergic to my boa."

"Really?" Sympathetically, I linked my arm in hers as we headed back to the bus.

"I blew out my nose ring back there." She sniffled. "You didn't even notice."

"Oh, honey."

She remained stiff, and for a moment I was afraid she was going to bring up the weapons again. "It's hard to be a diva when you're allergic to your boa."

And as I murmured in sympathetic agreement, we donned our trinkets and masks and finally reboarded the party bus. To fanfare and music, but also to discover we weren't the first team back. Terry had beat us to it, reportedly mouthing the word "yacht" like a guppy gumming air right before he passed out. Bummed about the loss, Cher wrapped her boa around his neck, which I loosened as soon as she headed for the bar.

Good, I thought with a relieved sigh. Maybe alcohol would make her believe she'd imagined my explanation of Zodiac warriors and a woman who became a mortal to save the city. I certainly could use a drink after safely traversing the night. With any luck it would also blot out the knowledge of a man with a dead forest of fingernails and unwanted omens.

One, I knew, who waited inside a house of shadows for my return.

3

The other teams returned by midnight, exhausted from the hunt and disappointed by their loss. Those who could be easily bought by free booze and food—the majority of the partiers, it turned out—were appeased by the sight of the newly arrived caterers, though a few poor sports flounced off in sore-footed pique. I never understood that response to disappointment. If you didn't have a yacht before and you still didn't have one, what had you really lost?

Shaking my head as Suzanne hurried off the bus to coax them back, I turned back to Cher. "Who planted the clues for the treasure hunt?"

She was holding up a hand mirror as she fiddled with a replacement nose ring, while sitting third in line for a real piercing. Now that she'd taken off her boa, she'd returned to her healthy, mildly blitzed self. "What? Oh, one of Arun's people. He's got an army of them apparently."

"Apparently?"

A squeal sounded behind us, and she slid along the velvet bench, still gazing at her reflection. "Well, I've never actually seen any of them. They're like elves. They work in the night. Even when I stay overnight at the compound, my cocktails appear out of nowhere, or I'll enter the dining room to find my food set, and still steaming. But his servants? They're nothing but shadows. It's kinda creepy . . . in a decadent sort of way."

No, it was kinda creepy in a *creepy* sort of way. Was someone from my old life using Arun and his wealth to get close to *my* mortals? The coincidence was certainly uncanny, though I couldn't think of who it might be. As far as I knew, only the agents of Light were aware of the connection between Cher's family and me, and they were charged with protecting all mortals. Besides, if the Shadow agents knew, these bubbly socialites would already be sleeping in a shallow grave.

Still, my mind winged back to the feeling of being stalked while on the scavenger hunt. I looked back at Cher for signs of concern, but she was busy tousling her hair. I might have to warn her of impending danger later, but I decided against it now. She needed to be steady for her piercing.

Glancing over, I saw Terry holding statue-still, clearly waiting for a new earring. All I could see of the piercer was his hands and forearms as they rubbed alcohol over the area, but Terry was leaning forward into the light, his face ashen with anticipation.

"Are you sure you want to do this? Terry looks like he's going to pee himself."

"Terry's a wuss." Still peering into the mirror, she gave her newly tousled hair an experimental toss. "I have my Momma's strong constitution."

I thought of Suzanne running after a handful of spoiled debutantes, all huffy because someone didn't hand them a yacht. It made me want to order her into therapy where someone could talk to her about being a chronic people pleaser.

"I mean my real Momma," Cher said, catching my look and wincing in return. At least she recognized the disorder.

"She wrote me letters when she found out she was dying. Loads of them filled with all sorts of advice. I still have them."

"Wow." Cher's birth mother had passed away around the time Cher hit double digits, when a girl would need a mother most. Her father met Suzanne not long after, but because it'd been a May-December romance, he too had since passed. In all the years since, it'd been Cher and Suzanne going it alone, more girlfriends than mother and daughter, with Olivia a steady and welcome third wheel.

Slowly, Cher nodded to herself. "She thought of all the things I'd most need to know—the names of the best plastic surgeons in town, her personal shopper's home number—and wrote them all down. My father accidentally stored them with her belongings, so I didn't find them until recently."

"What a wonderful gift." Why couldn't my mother have left me with a treasure trove worth of knowledge and advice? I could have used a straightforward lesson on paranormal espionage and politics. "You're very lucky."

A high-pitched squeal sounded as Terry's earlobe came under fire. Cher glanced back and gulped, her Momma's constitution getting a test-drive. "Guess it's time," she said as a pasty-faced Terry wobbled past. The bus wasn't even moving.

"Want me to come with?" I asked as Cher shot him a finger wave.

"Accompanying one's best friend in all things that will eventually be attributed to a misspent youth is in the BFF contract. You know that."

"I misplaced my copy." I said, but held out my hand.

"I'll send you another."

We strode to the bus's dark back corner with as much boldness as we could while holding hands. The piercer was reclined, sucking back an entire bottle of water like he'd just run a marathon. Cher's brows pinched as she took in his scuffed boots, workman's jeans, and shiny black vest, but he didn't note it from beneath the low brim of his Stetson. My guess was that he came from one of the rougher ink parlors, and I whispered as much to Cher. "He probably has a name like Tank or Bruise or Bomb."

We giggled and she settled in the L-shaped corner. When I dropped down next to her, the piercer raised his head and my smile dropped like a stone.

"Hello, Archer."

Harlan Tripp leaned forward, placed his elbows on his knees and cracked his knuckles. I blinked twice, my mind needing an extra moment to catch up as I stared at the rogue Shadow agent I'd both mocked and left frying in another world.

Trapped there, I corrected, swallowing hard. His body set to a slow burn in a world closer to earth's core than this one. I wouldn't have recognized him as Shadow if we hadn't met before, but knew full well a charred skeleton lurked beneath his exterior of flesh, as did breath so rancid it could billow from hell's belly itself. I couldn't smell it now, but memory alone had my palms sweating.

My first impulse was to throw myself in front of Cher. My second was to run . . . though realistically I couldn't save either of us. Tripp could catch me, kill me, without breaking a sweat. Even a rogue, stripped of troop status, could blow a hole through a mortal's life with a rap of his fist . . . and Tripp was famous for loving to do just that.

I was fucked.

"Can't say I like whatcha done with the place," he said conversationally, motioning to the fat painter's splats of neon outside the bus, like he saw it everyday. Telltale neon bulged from the desert floor, but beyond that there was little that remained of the Vegas he'd left. As proof, he said, "Was that a fucking pirate ship settin' anchor in the middle of the Strip?"

"The light show's a nice touch, though," Cher said, oblivious to the tension between us.

He ignored her. "Even the grand ones—the Trop, Flamingo, Caesar's—they all look different. And what the fuck did you do with the Hacienda? And the little Glass Pool Inn?" Tripp still looked hard and mean, but also confused.

I shrugged . . . though I was melancholic about that one's destruction, too. "Eighteen years is a long time to be gone," I said stiffly. "Though not quite long enough."

Tripp shook his head. "Looks like a new Vegas got built up over the old."

"Can't stop progress." I shrugged.

"Can't stop much," he agreed.

"How'd you get out?"

Tripp's feral grin returned. "What you should be asking yourself is if I'm the only one who did."

No, I'd ask *him*, I thought, relaxing a bit. It looked like he was just here to talk.

"Now git up."

Or not.

"Let me put it this way, Archer," he said when I didn't move. "Throw up the sponge now, and I'll murder you gently."

Despite the deafening beats of my heart, I managed a sarcastic drawl. "Harlan, you sure talk mighty funny."

His sharp, black eyes darted from me to Cher. "Eighteen years of frying like bacon has made me a mite impatient. You'll come . . . or she will."

"Silly boy. I don't come for just anyone." The retort was classic Cher, though her voice shook as she spoke. No wonder Terry had been white-faced while having his lobe pierced. A mortal facing a Shadow was like a rat facing a hungry snake. Even if you'd never seen one before, you instinctively knew which side of the predator/prey relationship you were on.

Tripp knew it too. "Fine."

One moment I was seated, the next I'd been hauled up, neck trapped beneath an unyielding forearm. "You still stink," I managed before my eyesight grew spotty. I knew he heard me over Cher's screams because his clinch tightened. Would he really kill me in front of all these people?

He loves to blow holes through mortal lives.

Yes, he would.

The partiers nearest us took up Cher's chorus, a call-and-response of ascending fear. Terry flat passed out again. At least I think it was him. I was busy blacking out, so didn't note the finer details. Unlikely relief came in the form of Cher launching herself onto Tripp's back. His grip on my neck loosened enough for me to suck in one great breath before he resumed an even tighter noose as he angled from side to side. I let that last, lovely bit of air go in a futile warning. "Let go, Cher!"

He could dislodge her by throwing her through a window, squeezing her neck until her arteries popped, caving her head in against the minibar. Sure enough, after another second a thwack sounded before a soft limb fell into view, and Cher sprawled unconscious on the bench beside me. I had no breath left to scream.

The bus swayed, partygoers scrambling for the door in full riot. Tripp surprised me by stumbling as well, before body-slamming me onto the hard floor. My limbs were numbing but I still felt my face eat rubber as his full weight dropped atop mine. Pain arrowed through my right knee, tendons stretched and threatening to snap. Then he twisted again, loosening his hold on my neck. I choked on the fresh air, the soft tissue there already bruised and swollen. My larynx had either shifted to a place it shouldn't have or was missing altogether. The pain brought tears to my eyes even as the oxygen worked to clear my vision.

Then screeching metal joined the panicked voices, and the bus rocked harder. I was still trapped beneath Tripp's arm but glanced up to see the metal rooftop peeling open like an aluminum can. Tripp's partner, was my first thought, because such bold destruction was the mark of a Shadow. Then he cursed, and my hopes soared.

One of the Light? A former ally watching over me after all?

The thought gave me strength, and I decided to buy myself time for whatever they had in mind. I whipped my head back and his nose crunched beneath its weight. Another curse, then his forearm tensed in the tightest grip yet. My vision deteriorated into stop-motion, but I made out three terrifying things in the next few seconds:

A skeleton's face, wrapped in worn, leather skin.

The skeleton's rotted grin and bright, curved blade.

A scissored cry as the skeleton leapt.

Tripp yelled, terrified, but sunk one booted foot into the falling man's middle. The blade arced, and another scream followed, sounding red. Then there was more frantic jostling as Tripp fled with me, faster than a Chevy on drag night. On his way out, though, he thoughtlessly rapped my head into one of those sexy Lucite poles. Embarrassment flooded me as I thought, *Death by stripper pole*. Then I was out.

I'd been knocked unconscious enough times to be intimately familiar with the staggered return of hearing, the touch-and-go awareness of feeling returning to limbs, and the eventual need to open eyes and regain bearings . . . whether one wanted to or not.

"What fresh hell is this?" I murmured, even before I'd peeked. You were never bound to wake to something good after a violent kidnapping.

Despite a wave of dizziness, I recognized Tripp's stocky, hunched outline, though his back was to me, his desk lamp angled low. He didn't bother looking up.

Probably because of the Boy Scout/bondage thing he had going on. I tested my restraints, unsurprised when all I could do was tense my muscles. Overkill in restraining a mortal, but then Harlan Tripp wasn't known for his generous nature . . . and he probably didn't yet know I was mortal. I certainly wasn't going to clue him in.

Studying the narrow glass surfaces around me, I realized I lay atop an identical one like some pending sacrifice. I wasn't a virgin, though, so I reserved hope for escape. We were in a darkened jewelry store with bright surfaces and tiny custom cushions filling every available space in the glass interiors. I didn't know how Tripp had circumvented the store's alarm—the entire store was a vault, thus the jewels still safe in their cases—but there he was, relaxed as could be behind the jeweler's desk. I didn't ask what he was going to do with the cutters.

"Diamonds really are forever," I finally quipped in the elongated silence, though the scratch in my voice belayed the forced tone. "But if you're going to choke me, please use the emeralds."

"Don't tempt me . . . *Olivia*."

My purse was open next to him, my identification spread haphazardly over the desk. So he knew who I was, big deal. I was already mortal and bound like a rodeo calf. He didn't need my cover identity to kill me, just a reason and the flick of his wrist.

"How's the nose?" I asked cheerfully.

"Already healed. Bitch."

Sticks and stones, I thought, but stayed silent . . . and wary. It'd been weeks since I'd seen him, though to him it might have felt like years. Time moved differently in Midheaven. But on that first meeting Tripp had referred to the place as "Mid-hell," and I couldn't argue that. Midheaven drained a man's soul energy, using it to feed the desires of the chosen few—all women, and all with delusions of goddesshood.

I'd only been trapped there a short time, but Midheaven had served as Tripp's prison for years. He'd fled there as a rogue agent, banished by his leader, but it was the classic case of jumping from the pan into the fire. He'd attempted escape before, only to find someone had locked the entrance from the other side. So . . . "How did you get here?"

"You should damned well thank your stars that I did."

I didn't thank the stars for shit anymore. "Yeah. I'm always thankful when I get knocked out, tied up, and tortured with ring clamps."

He finally turned. The light even made him look marginally amused. "You could be dead."

"I'm sure it's on your to-do list."

He shook his head, features sunken beneath his wide-brimmed hat. "Nope. Mackie's the one lookin' to settle up with you."

Mackie. The name alone sent a shiver crisscrossing my spine. Also known as Sleepy Mac for his ability to fall into a comalike state to keep his energy from being drained by the women of Midheaven. A reported member of the Nez Perce tribe, he was the world's oldest living agent. I didn't know how he'd found his way into Nevada, or even if he'd started out as Light or Shadow, but I did know you didn't get to be as old as he was by being merciful. "I thought I'd imagined him busting through the bus's rooftop."

But I remembered the skeletal face clearly. I'd seen the leathery visage in recurring nightmares, the screaming mouth a sharp whir in my mind, the deadened gaze that could burn holes of decay in my body with a mere glance.

"Carving through," Tripp corrected, and shifted to reveal what he'd been working on. Himself. He'd been using a hand torch to cauterize a wound already festering with pus. He gestured with it, unnecessarily adding, "With his magic blade."

And when an agent of the Zodiac said "magic" like it was a special thing, it was worth fearing. Mackie reportedly stored the last bit of his soul—the small part Midheaven hadn't drained away—in his knife's blade. He kept it protected there, always on his person, and it did his will almost independently of him. That was why Tripp wasn't healing.

"What the fuck is Mackie doing outside of Midheaven? Who unlocked the entrance?" Someone who wanted me dead?

And why hadn't *that* list gotten any shorter?

Tripp resettled his hat on his head. "I thought it might have been you."

I shook my head.

Tripp shrugged. "Well, I didn't waste time askin'. I saw Mackie go through the lantern on that side of the veil and waited till I was sure he was gone 'fore diving out myself."

The pagoda lanterns were the exit on Midheaven's side, while a pinched taper buried in Vegas's underground sewer system marked this side. When the flame was extinguished, an agent's body was wrapped in a solid wall of smoke, ferrying them to the other world. But even Mackie couldn't have exited without someone removing the lock that secured the entrance on this side. And while entering Midheaven would still cost an agent one-third of their soul—the price of a round-trip ticket to another world, and no wonder there was no great rush—exiting meant freedom.

But who would allow that?

I bit my lip. "No one else got out?"

"You know how it is over there. No one even tried."

Hunter hadn't tried.

I frowned, but stopped following the thought when I realized Tripp was watching me closely.

"So how'd you find me?" I asked, clearing my throat.

Tripp's shrug allowed it hadn't been easy. Only true identities were revealed in Midheaven. I was Joanna Archer over there, my appearance reflecting the old me—muscular limbs on a slim frame, black bob and dark, unamused eyes—rather than this bubble gum, Barbie Doll packaging.

"I didn't," he finally admitted, lighting a strange little cigarette. He blew out the smoke, and though yards away, it choked my pores. I shook against my bindings, which seemed to amuse Tripp. "Mackie tracked you and I tracked him. After eighteen years, I could pinpoint that mean fucker anywhere. His power tastes black."

I couldn't help it. The opening was too great and inviting, and though I was all trussed up, Tripp had forgotten the gag. "And what did the power you stole from me taste like?"

I was referring to the chips I'd lost to him over a game of soul poker in Midheaven—two odd triangular symbols, their meaning still unknown to me. Not that it mattered much now.

Spitting a stray bit of tar from his tongue, he scoffed. "I won it from you."

"Then traded it away." For some alone time with a woman.

"Tell me you blame me." And he said it so defiantly I really wanted to. But I couldn't. Ruthless barter was the way of that world. Come to think of it, it was the way of this one. "That's what I thought. And now that that's settled . . . you're going to help me."

"Why, Harlan Tripp," I said, in my sweetest southern drawl, "why on earth would I deign to assist the likes of you?"

No amusement this time. He leaned forward, still seated, but far closer than I ever wanted him. In a voice rumbling like a far-off streetcar, he whispered, "Because I know who you are. Your father killed my entire family, outlawed me, and sent me on the lam. The only thing that kept me going in that seventh level of hell was the thought of killing him, his sycophants, and everyone else who done me wrong."

I lay silent for a long moment, trying to scent the heat of his bitter fury, and feeling only the warmth of that strange cigarette's smoke. If I could move I would have waved it away, though I had a feeling it would cling to my hands with its deceptive warmth.

"Tripp," I finally said, licking dry lips. "You and I are not on the same side, got it? Never have been, never will be."

I could appreciate the idea of a world unpopulated by the Tulpa and his Shadows—after all, my birth father had tried repeatedly to kill me, too—but even were I still an agent with powers beyond a mortal's, still in possession of a lineage marking me as special, I would never work alongside a man like Harlan Tripp.

A ghostly smile flashed on his ruddy stubbled face. "I will tear off long, precise strips of your flesh with these pliers," he whispered in a lover's voice, and holding up the sharp tool, "until you are."

I swallowed hard, but said nothing. Letting a Shadow know I was mortal was a direct invitation to the grave.

"I'll start with your eyelids."

I didn't need to smell my fear spiking, I could feel my heartbeat screaming. But Tripp's responding grin was short-lived. Inhaling sharply, head swiveling toward the glass door, he dove for me and began roughly working away my ties. They were belted around the entire case. Apparently he'd been serious about the pliers.

"Done it now, haven't you?" I said, as he cursed, my relief making me punchy . . . though I wasn't out of this yet. "What are they? Two blocks away? Three?"

I tried to remember how far off I could scent another agent. Three was my best effort. The most senior of agents could double that distance.

"I'm better than that, missy. I haven't smelled pure Light in so long, I could pinpoint them on a map."

It was a dig, but all I could think was, Pure Light. "They're not Shadows?"

He frowned, like I'd spit in his eye.

Even as my heartbeat bumped faster at the thought of seeing my old troop, the look gave me an idea. "Let me take care of them."

He was scrabbling at my ties, growing more anxious, and an edgy Shadow was a homicidal one. "Don't fuck with me, Archer."

"Just hide. I'll distract them. I'll tell them you've already left."

Tripp stilled, stared, and sucked in one long breath.

I held his gaze. "It'll be the fastest way to get rid of them, and it'll throw them off your trail too."

He dropped his odd, handrolled smoke on the floor and stomped on it as he angled his gaze toward the door. He either had to leave me there or kill me. Even I could tell there wasn't enough time to untie me. "Why would you?"

"I like my eyelids where they are," I said wryly. "Besides, they're not coming here for me."

Either the ticking clock or my genuine bitterness decided it for him, because he soon nodded. "Chisel me, woman, and so help me, I'll find a way to kill you. Even if it's my last act 'fore death."

"I know."

He backed away, disappearing into the shadows.

"Take my ID with you!" I hissed after him, because if Warren thought even a rogue Shadow knew my cover identity, he'd alter my memory, my mind, and my life altogether. It wouldn't have anything to do with my general safety either. He'd do it only to protect the troop.

So I took a steadying breath after Tripp and my belongings disappeared and resettled my head on the hard glass top as if napping there. Then I waited in silence, mere moments from facing an entire cadre of superheroes. The agent of Light. The troop that had abandoned me completely.

4

"What are you doing here?"

Warren's query, flat and suspicious, wasn't at all what I'd practiced responding to in the mirror of my barb-witted dreams. Still, I did my best work on the fly.

"Shopping," I said, turning my head to the wide-open door where eight agents of Light fanned out like a palm frond. Warren was centered like the sun, and the others were planets revolving around him. I gave them all a sweet smile from beneath my unyielding ties, then focused on my former leader. "What do you think, the pearl necklace or the choker?"

"Joanna." His impatience, immediate and unearned, had my hands clenching at my sides. I studied the craggy, sun-scorched skin I knew so well, and the hardness in his eyes I was beginning to know better. He was dressed in his favorite cover guise, a vagrant in a trench so tattered only his demeanor was more frayed. The last time I'd seen him was at the entrance of a swiftly flooding tunnel. He'd just locked a fellow troop member in another world with a calm ruthlessness, and had been thinking of abandoning me to the Tulpa to save his own skin.

"I'm thinking pearls," I continued, fighting the memory in order to keep my voice light. "Every high-powered female executive should own a set."

I glared at each agent in turn, the men and women who had once feared me for my dual-sided nature, who'd overcome it to accept me as one of their own, and who now regarded me as distantly as if we'd never met. Studying each carefully blank gaze, I tried to figure out who had left me the warning not to go out tonight.

Perhaps Vanessa, I thought, staring at the subtly exotic woman. We'd been the closest. She looked both beautiful and strong in her long black silken scarf, worn since her hair had been shorn weeks earlier. She'd secured this one with an antique silver brooch, an iron bolt pinning the black silk to the side. Other than the hair, which was still growing out, she'd otherwise recovered fully from the attack that claimed digits and limbs from her flesh. A sharp corner of the glass cabinet dug into one of my calves, and my sarcasm reared. *Good for her.*

Maybe it'd been Micah. Healer wasn't only his position in the troop, it was his calling. He might have an interest in preventing my injury . . . if he still cared. I found the seven-foot man standing to the left of Warren in shadows that so obscured his features I couldn't read whether any concern for me lie on them. But Riddick was next to him, and with a jolt I realized Micah wasn't in the shadows. They were in him. This time it was the physician who sported some kind of injury, a realization doubly shocking since agents always healed from attack unless struck by a conduit.

But how did a man as fair as Micah turn dark? Not black, no, because that was natural, and this was anything but. It was as if grit and soot strained at his pores, his skin acting as barrier, like a cement truck that had to keep moving so the ash or brick or burnt lime—whatever was inside of him—didn't still and set.

My gaze lingered too long, and he inched back. I jerked my gaze away, automatically wanting to give him privacy and to cover for us both, and studied the others instead. Riddick was ginger-haired, tight-muscled, and driven, but had yet to gain the experience that would make him into a dangerously seasoned agent. Jewell, next to him, was the same age, and they'd grown up in the sanctuary together. While she was a second daughter and had never expected to inherit her star sign, she almost wore the responsibility better. Having it unexpectedly thrust upon a person often made them more vigilant and serious, as I well knew.

I couldn't figure any of them keeping Warren out of the loop, though. If any knew about Mackie and his quest to kill me, if any *cared*—and I thought it likely there was at least that between us—they'd have told him. Unless one of *them* had opened the gateway to Midheaven, accidentally let the demon spawn out, and was too afraid of Warren to fess up. Though agents' actions were regularly recorded in comic book form, thus a matter of public record, this wouldn't be if it could upset the balance between Shadow and Light.

So had one of them planted the old conduits for me? Maybe . . . though wouldn't it have been easier to show up on my doorstep, hand me my crossbow, and bid me good day? I thought again of the fury I'd once seen blanketing Warren's face. *Maybe not.*

"Joanna." Tekla now, their Seer. Though the smallest, staturewise, she was arguably the strongest of them all. She watched me as carefully as I'd studied the others, her odd, birdlike stillness making me nervous, as always. She read the stars and skies, and carried the Scorpion sign fiercely in memory of her son. A mother wasn't supposed to outlive a child in any world, and since reclaiming the star sign, Tekla had been more daring and vigilant and aggressive than the others. Warren loved it, but I could have told him there was a fine line between nervy and nutty.

I continued on like I hadn't heard her. "Of course, there's high-powered like me, and then there's *high-powered* like you. There's a difference between mortal power and those who allow it, isn't there?" I struggled with the restraints any one of them could have broken through, and had the satisfaction of hearing someone moan. It sparked something dormant and dark inside of me.

"Riddick, untie her. Joanna, this isn't about you."

"Of course not." Gritting my teeth, I wondered what my anger smelled like. "If it was, you wouldn't be here."

Riddick, coming close, looked like he was holding his breath. It pissed me off even more. "Hello, 'friend.' How's life treating *you*?"

He didn't respond or look me in the eye, but his strong fingers fumbled at my ties. I snorted.

Warren cleared his throat. "Gregor, Jewell. Check the rest of the building."

"Harlan's not here, asshole." I added the insult because it would get his attention. "Don't you think I'd have said so first thing?"

"But he was," he said so accusingly it was as if I'd invited the attack on my life. "We can smell him."

That's the part I focused on. "Can you?" I replied sweetly. "How interesting. I can't."

And I didn't realize how furious I still was about that loss—about all of them—until the sharp words were out of my mouth. I'd been finely ground under Warren's ambitious heel, and I was as bitter as a glass of Campari.

"And you don't know where he went?"

I stared, buying time by taking in his scruffy hair—longer than when I'd last seen him—and the trench he'd abandoned a few months earlier, but had apparently reclaimed. Security blanket, I thought snidely. But I also tempered my emotions, knowing he'd scent out a lie as fast as I could tell it. So I scrounged up my annoyance as a cover. "I know where he *was*. On a party bus filled with mortals, including my best friends."

Warren's opportunity to turn a barbed phrase. "*Your* best friends?"

"Oh, that's right," I said, pretending to muse over Cher's

relationship to Olivia, not me. Never mind that I'd been forced to care for them and see to their safety over the past year. Someone here should have since taken up that slack, but in their efforts to avoid me, no one had. The memory of Cher's soft arm falling to the ground was what finally put me over the edge.

"What I meant to say was"—and here I yelled, muscles straining as I rose against my bindings—"he attacked the only friends who stuck by me after I lost everything!"

My voice was scratchy from the strangling, but louder than I'd raised it in weeks. And it felt good, using the only power left to me. It also surprised the so-called superheroes surrounding me. Even I had no idea this much raw anger simmered so close to the surface. Sure, I was resentful that every fresh morning brought with it a wave of renewed rejection, but this was the kind of fury that had once had my eyes burning black in my skull, my breath coming from me in waves of noxious hate.

It was my father's anger, and that, at least, I harbored still.

Felix's face was taut and drawn into the middle, as were Micah's mottled, sooty features. Tekla's remained unreadable, though she too had fallen superstill. Riddick's powerful hands briefly fell to his sides, and Jewell had begun crying, though she wiped away the tears before Warren whirled to see. Vanessa didn't bother. Though Warren gave her a warning under his breath, she defiantly continued to stare at me. I stared back as relentlessly, but didn't soften anything. *Sense my pain and your betrayal as I did. Scent it like a chalk outline stamping the air. Feel its abrasion erupting behind your eyelids at night.*

"Enough!"

I sucked in a deep breath, the air cool against my heated anger, and turned that hard stare back on Warren. "I don't take orders from you, old man."

He damned near hissed. "All mortals are subject to my whim."

I raised my brows so high they probably disappeared into my hairline. "So we owe you fealty, is that it? For your protection?"

He sniffed, regaining his composure. "Something like that."

"Then where the fuck were you tonight?"

His lips pinched reflexively and I knew he wanted to punch something.

My arms were still bound, but by now my legs were finally freed, so I decided to take my one-woman guilt trip on the road, slipping off the countertop, but staggering as pins and needles crawled up my limbs. I leaned against the glass case, refusing to fall in front of them as I hissed, "Where the fuck have any of you been?"

"We're not going to risk—"

"Shut up!" I fired back, because I'd heard the official statement, and wasn't buying it. "It was rhetorical. Riddick, are you fucking done yet?"

He mumbled what could have been an apology as the last of my bindings fell loose. I pushed from the counter to stand, and realized that my dizziness wasn't due to the change in positions. I was flush with the power of someone in full control of another's guilt. In this case, many others. And not just people. Superheroes.

Clinging to the power like a barnacle on a hull, I limped forward. "If you're done here, I'm going to find a clinic and get cleaned up."

Micah, ever the physician, stepped forward, sad eyes tucked into the smoky skin, voice strained with pain. "I can—"

"No!" Warren and I yelled in unison.

To ward him off, to keep anyone else from touching me, I swallowed back the lump in my throat and tried on a sneer I only partly felt. "It looks like you can't even help yourself."

Jewell gasped, as did Felix, but Micah just stepped back—which I took as a symbolic return to his betrayal of me—and Warren and I again locked gazes. I knew I'd hurt the big softhearted man, but I worked better with anger than pity, which was what I needed to get through this.

Warren made a growling noise in his throat. "Tripp did that to him, and if you know where he is, you need to tell us."

"I don't expect to meet up with Harlan Tripp again." A white almost-lie.

"But you might. And just in case . . ." He fished in his pocket, then held a cell phone out to me. "Use this if you see him, or hear of any other rogues hiding in my city. It's an untraceable number, you won't talk to a person, but you can leave a brief message. We'll only contact you if we must."

I fondled the phone, a one-way channel into my past. *Why was everything with Warren always so one-way?*

"Believe me," he said, mistaking my silence for acquiescence as I placed the phone on the counter beside me. "You don't want rogues leaking from Midheaven. They'll all be worse for their time there, even the Light."

Yes, he'd already told me. *A twisted place that twists people in return.*

"Even Hunter?" I asked coldly.

If I was a sore spot with the troop, Hunter was an open wound. Pain bloomed on every face, and Riddick even staggered. No one in the troop had experienced Midheaven the way Tripp and I had, but no doubt they'd each done their research into the world since discovering it really existed, a fact Warren had only recently and reluctantly clued them in on. I didn't know if they'd researched it with his now-blessing or furtively, on their own and behind his back—probably both—but from the collective look on the faces around me, they were actively imagining the horror their former troop mate and ally was enduring in a world meant to separate a man from his soul. *Good.*

Not that their imaginations could ever do the place justice.

An unreasonable pang struck me at their reaction—they *should* feel more for their lifelong troop mate than a woman they'd only known a year—but it was blunted by how clear it was that no one had forgotten. Not my sacrifice, not Hunter's banishment, not the way Warren had locked his Aries of Light in a world where men were used as batteries. They remembered all, no matter how much Warren willed it otherwise.

Meanwhile, Warren had closed his eyes, falling immobile. I fought not to step back, but after another moment he only strode to the room's center, gait powerful despite a pronounced limp. "The point is, it would unbalance everything. It wouldn't be good for you or us."

He just couldn't resist differentiating me, disparaging me, in front of them.

"I'm curious, Warren," I said, mimicking his indifference, right down to the placement of my hands on my hips. "Did you feel this sort of disdain for my mother too? After all, she was an agent who also became mortal by giving up her powers."

In a way, I'd simply expanded on the premise. She'd only done it for one person—me. Warren's gaze darkened, a look that said my mother's sacrifice hadn't been worth it. "Your mother never attempted to re-engage in our world after leaving it."

"I didn't re-engage! I was kidnapped!"

"By a rogue, right?"

His single-mindedness made me want to scream. "Don't ask me shit when you already know the answer! Harlan Tripp did this, and you'd better watch your ass because he's after you next!"

I said it for Harlan's benefit, to let him know that though I wasn't handing him over to Warren, I wasn't anywhere near on his side. If he thought I'd align myself with him against the agents of Light—that I was going to "re-engage" with this world at all—I'd disabuse him of that now. Getting a dig in at Warren's expense was just a bonus. "All the rogues in Midheaven would be after you if they knew what you'd done."

Warren lifted his chin, pulling the skin along his jaw tight. "Then don't open the gateway to Midheaven again."

"I didn't do it *this* time. Mortals can't. It hurts too much." Warren's gaze sharpened and I clarified, in case they'd forgotten: "The child I gave my life for in those fetid tunnels learned that the hard way!"

"Okay." It was a grudging murmur, but sympathy was on my side, so there wasn't much more he could say. And so as abruptly as he arrived, he turned back to the door, motioning to the others.

"Asshole," I muttered, and he paused mid-limp.

I winced. Of course he couldn't let it go, not with the whole troop watching. Pride was his personal Achilles' heel. I forced my gaze from the floor because now wasn't the time to back down, but when he turned, a rare flush colored his cheeks. "Remember your place, Joanna," he said softly.

"You never let me forget."

"But I can. With one command I can make you forget who you were, or that you were ever superhuman." He spun on his heel and spat his rejoinder at the same time. "Remember that too."

Survival instinct kept me quiet, but what stunned me into stillness was how the others followed without complaint, how Vanessa no longer met my gaze, and how not one of them said good-bye. Again. It's okay, I thought, biting my lip when the door finally swung shut. I didn't need to say anything. Let their shame speak for me. Let their guilt scream. Because after sacrificing my every power for their troop, I'd never be entirely absent from their lives. Not as long as I lived.

"You really got no power?"

I was slumped against the counter in sudden and complete exhaustion, but hastily wiped the tears from my face as Tripp drew closer. It was a pointless action. He could smell my every emotion. Besides, what did it matter if Tripp saw?

"I still play a mean game of tennis." The aftermath of the confrontation had my stomach twisting on itself, but I bit back the bile threatening to overtake my throat. I wouldn't allow them to turn my own body against me too. "But you'll have to find a different doubles partner for what you have in mind."

Tripp tilted his head and frowned. "So they kicked you out?"

I massaged my arms where the bindings had chafed. "I'm no use to them."

Which meant he now knew me as useless too. My greatest secret, my greatest weakness, in the hands of a Shadow. I glanced up at the clock on the wall, wondering exactly how many seconds I had left to live.

But Tripp remained where he was, faced off across from me like we were going to have a shoot-out. He nodded once. "So that's why you got no aura. I thought it was my eyes. They just ain't right over here."

He rubbed at them like that might change, but made no move yet to kill me. "How did it happen?"

I told him about Jasmine, the child I'd given over my powers to save, and how doing so had restored balance to the Zodiac at a time when the Tulpa had been on the verge of gaining it all. "I had to give her everything—my powers, my aura, all but the last third of my soul." I'd used the rest of it as payment to enter Midheaven twice. I sometimes wondered how I was still alive, never mind animate and able to stand upright. Wasn't the loss of your soul like removing your aetheric spine? What was left of me but a mind and shell? And was that enough to keep me moving through the world? "But it saved her, her younger sister, the city. And my tr—the agents of Light."

Squinting at me, he shifted on his feet. I braced for a blow, but he only said, "Like your mother did with you."

"You know that story?" He'd been stuck in Midheaven for eighteen years, and my mother had given over her powers to save my life when I was sixteen, only a decade before. But Midheaven's newest resident seemed to be angling for Mackie's position—trading in other people's stories for his own personal gain.

Yet I couldn't think about Hunter's abandonment right now. For some silly, stupid, girly reason it made me want to ask for that killing blow.

Tripp rubbed at his chin. "That's fuckin' crazy."

"Says the man who just went up against Death's blade." And he'd done it to keep Mackie from slaying me. I took a tentative step forward. "Warren doesn't know Mackie is here, does he?"

Because the leader of Light had spoken as if Tripp were this world's greatest threat.

Tripp leaned back against the glass case, favoring his injured leg. "Don't look like it'd matter if he did."

I hunched my shoulders because he was right. "So why is he . . . here?" Why'd he cross worlds to kill me? "I mean, I know I pissed him off by escaping Midheaven . . ." By knocking that soul blade from his homicidal grasp, I remembered, swallowing hard. "But that was the first time I escaped. He didn't even notice me the second."

"Ha!" Tripp shook his head, like I was the village idiot. "Ol' Sleepy Mac notices everything. He files it away. The knowledge lurks in his smile when he comes to kill a man later, like it's been carved on his teeth."

Carved like a marionette's toy, I thought, remembering the way Mackie moved; seated and slumped one moment, pulled straight and erect the next. Pouncing in a full lunge after that, the leather of his skin shifting over his skull in lieu of any real expression. It was like the cross section of an old oak renumbering its rings. There was nothing natural about it.

"But that don't mean he's here of his own volition." Tripp

lit another cigarette, though this one seemed normal. My skin didn't tingle, the smoke didn't press against my pores. Thinking of Micah, I couldn't help my relieved sigh. "No, ma'am. Mackie don't have enough of his own willpower left to make them sort of choices. That's what makes him so dangerous."

I shrugged. "And?"

Tripp huffed, a trail of smoke zinging from the side of his mouth. "It's Miss Sola wants you dead, girl."

"Solange?" I almost choked on the name.

"She ain't talked about nothin' else since you left."

Solange. The most powerful woman in that realm, and one who'd once dismantled everything inside of me—all the bits that made me "me"—without ever touching my body. I cringed, remembering the way my spirit had jigsawed free of my physical body before being thrown down a flight of stairs. Sure, it'd come back together at the bottom of the staircase, but had it been a physical repiecing, my thighbone would have been connected to my neck bone. I didn't know if I'd recovered or just gotten used to the feeling, but I did know that of everything I experienced in my year as an agent of Light, I'd never been so thoroughly frightened as I was by Solange's soft, gorgeous rage.

"Why?"

"'Cause when them divas and goddesses and matriarchs discovered they done released the woman with lineage divided equally between the two warring sides of the Zodiac, the uproar was cataclysmic. Even in that world, you're legend. The *Kairos*, both Shadow and Light, the Zodiac's 'chosen one.' It's a great loss for the females who care only for power."

I shook my head, but it didn't stop my mind from spinning. Sure, I was still technically equal parts Shadow and Light. Believe me, if I could change my parentage, I'd have done so long ago. But why would Solange want me dead? I was no longer the Kairos. The woman who could bring to life the portents that would have one side of the Zodiac asserting dominance over the other.

But you once were, I thought, trying to remain reasonable. And only one person could have told Solange all that.

My God, Hunter. Will your betrayals never stop?

Tripp studied the air around me, trying to match it up to the emotions unraveling from me like a knot. He gave up, gaze landing back on my face, implacable. "I don't know why Miss Sola hates you so much. I ain't seen her so riled up 'bout a person before. Not that I envy you the distinction. But if you help me, Joanna, I'll keep you from Sleepy Mac." He paused, his next words sounding near a vow. "And anyone else who moves to harm you."

I thought about it, automatically repulsed at the idea of working with a Shadow. Even if he was the only person with a hand extended to me now.

Except for the one who sent you that note.

Yeah, I thought, biting my lip. That anonymous do-gooder had been a *huge* help tonight.

Angling my head, I gave him a quick once-over. "You're really trying to kill the Tulpa?" He nodded, and I immediately shook my head. "Helping you will put a bull's-eye on my chest, Tripp. From both the Shadows and the Light."

He shrugged. "Don't make you different from any other rogue agent."

"Except for the whole mortality issue," I said, but he shrugged again. Near fuming, I ticked some of my short-comings off finger by finger. *Maybe I should drawl 'em.* "I can't fight with you, protect you, or travel the world as you do anymore. I'm not fast. I've no strength. I have nothing to offer you."

"You can give me your blood." He waved his cigarette in the air. "I mean your bloodline."

I shook my head, swallowing hard. "What does that mean?"

"The Tulpa doesn't know you're mortal yet, right?"

"Right."

"So we use you as a lure. Ask him for a meeting, then fake anger over Warren treating that ex-boyfriend of yours—"

"He wasn't my boyfriend," I interrupted, giving the phone Warren had left me a hard glance. Hunter and I hadn't gotten that far before our mutual pasts had reared up to trample the present. As for Warren? I wouldn't have to fake anything when it came to him. Though, in a move as inexplicable as a woman who went back to an abusive husband, I pocketed the phone.

"Whatever. But we get him to meet you alone, which will probably take more than one conversation. He'll be willin' to, though, 'cause you're his daughter and the Kairos . . ."

The Tulpa cared only about the latter. Outside of his initial shock in learning of my existence, he'd never given a shit that I was his daughter—but I didn't interrupt Tripp again. He couldn't see past his need for vengeance to converse about this intelligently or see anything other than his own bloodred obsession.

"And once he lets down his guard . . . bam! I'll be there. We'll make sure you're out of harm's way, of course. Then I'll paint the walls with his blood." He puffed out his chest, drawing heavily on his cigarette.

And despite myself, despite the danger in playing chicken against a being who could kill me with a look alone, my heart skipped in my chest. Sensing it, Tripp almost smiled. I saved him from cracking his face with a brisk shake of my head. "No."

His eyes narrowed and he licked his lips, then ran his tongue along his top teeth before slowly nodding. "Okay."

I drew back in surprise.

Shrugging his broad shoulders, he flicked his cigarette to the floor. "I'll let you think on it."

"Listen, Tripp—"

"No, Archer, you listen!" And he was suddenly inches from my face, his wide with fury and animate with hate. He jabbed his finger into my chest and I stumbled backward. The smoke of both cigarettes was on his breath, the first one trying to lasso me back. "I aim to kill that motherfucker, understand? Him and Lindy Maguire and every other Shadow agent who helped kill my family. I'm going to pull their veins from their limbs like straws, then suck 'em dry. I'll hang their muscles in jerky strips, and if you stand in my way, I'll fucking kill you too."

He was breathing hard, and I glanced back at the closed door, my own heart racing. Any agent within a five-mile radius would be able to scent the sudden rise in his emotions, and they'd follow it right back here, to me. I didn't know what was preferable. The Shadows, the Light, or Tripp. But he caught my worried glance and calmed himself, his will tugging hot rage back into his physical shell. If I could still see auras, I bet he'd have been rimmed in black tar. But I saw nothing.

Which rather underscored my point.

"Look, you saved me from Mackie, so I won't tell the agents of Light of your quest." It was the best any reasonable person could expect from me under the circumstances, though it remained to be seen if Tripp was reasonable. "But I can't get involved. You're a rogue agent, Tripp. That means you're free to flee the city. You can get away from Warren and the Tulpa and anyone who might know of your story and past. You can start a new life elsewhere. Don't underestimate the power of a new beginning."

Tripp's anger evaporated so quickly it was like clearing an Etch-A-Sketch. "Well, I'll take that under consideration just as soon as you do, Archer."

That wasn't the same at all, and I put a hand on Tripp's chest to push him back. Annoyed when I couldn't budge him, I ducked around his frame and peered into a tabletop mirror to fluff my hair. "Las Vegas is my home. I'm not going to let them take that from me." I'd been stripped of enough.

Tripp loomed behind me, gaze lost beneath the brim of his Stetson. "I might not be able to save you next time."

I glanced at his leg, already festering with pus, though he'd just cleaned and cauterized it.

Which settled things pretty handily for me. I wasn't going anywhere near the underworld. If Tripp kept my identity to himself, and the agents of Light continued ignoring my existence, I could live in peace, in my city, as casino magnate Olivia Archer. I'd use the phone Warren had given me to tell them when Mackie showed up, and then they'd do what I couldn't . . . and what I seriously doubted of this lone rogue agent.

I'd also avoid the damned party buses.

"There won't be a next time."

Tripp snorted loudly. "Girly, I've seen some scary shit in both the worlds I've lived in, but Mackie's willpower has been fired in Midheaven's kiln. His mind will not, cannot, be changed. And don't forget that knife. It's imbued with his soul so it damned near does his will all by its lonesome." He pursed his lips in worry, clearly thinking of his leg, though he didn't glance at it again. Instead he eyed me. "So the 'next time' you're trying so hard not to think on is just a matter *of* time."

Tilting his hat my way, he then limped back to his hiding place at the back of the store. It was another few seconds before I realized he was leaving.

"Wait!"

He turned, smirking like I'd confirmed our partnership by calling out. *You can give me your blood.*

"I mean, you heard Warren." I cleared my throat. "There's no place for you now."

"There's the *cell*." He grinned widely at my returned frown, but didn't elaborate. "I'll be in touch."

"Don't bother," I said petulantly, causing Tripp to snort as he disappeared into shadows.

"So easy to say, ain't it? I mean, when Mackie is already gone."

No, I thought, shivering once I was alone. Because Mackie *was* still out there. So it wasn't easy to say at all.

5

I left immediately after Tripp. Warren hadn't been exaggerating when he said he could tell the rogue agent had been there. What he'd probably smelled was a combination of brimstone and sweat, a strong enough aroma that I could conjure it from memory alone. Add to that the residual emotion from all of us that now tainted the place—my own injured fury included—and I had no doubt it would soon attract the attention of a Shadow.

Or Mackie.

God, I thought, rubbing a hand over my face. Sleepy-fucking-Mac.

Legend had it he was the oldest living agent in our hemisphere. Rumor claimed he was the most vicious too. History and hearsay aside, I knew he was as crazed as a hatter sucked down a rabbit hole, and he'd literally taken over my dreams just weeks after I lost all my powers. Only recently had I been able to reclaim my night hours for this world.

And faced with the responsibility of taking over Archer Enterprises, I had plenty in this world to keep me busy. Yet Mackie's attack made my last dream appear more ominous than nightmarish.

In it, the saloon those in Midheaven called the "Rest House" was just as I remembered: the shining bar, the poker tables, the "most wanted" posters featuring every agent who'd dared to enter pinned at the far wall. Even the haze that made the entire room look like a cameo browned with age had been there. Who knew you could dream in sepia?

Mackie was there too, skinny hook nose visible in profile beneath his bowler hat. Yet slumped in his usual stupor before his battered piano, he couldn't compete with the real star of the show. Because perched on the center poker table like a prize was the woman I'd been turned into through a crafty combination of medicine and magic: my dead sister, Olivia.

"Mom is looking for you," she said, glancing up from filing her nails and sending me a prissy little finger wave, utterly nonplussed to see me emerging from an opaque wall of smoke.

Yet I was dumbfounded. I'd rarely dreamed of Olivia since her death, and while early on my reaction was to flee to wakefulness, in the latter stages of my grief I'd clung to her visage like a security blanket. Maybe that was why I'd ceased having them. My neediness was likely too weighty for the dream state. So, surprise kept me flat-footed in this dream, even as I edged away from Mackie.

Yet he remained slumped inertly over his ivory keys, bowler hat and piano top all covered in a thin layer of dust. Had I actually entered Midheaven, he'd have straightened like a marionette's toy to compose a jaunty tune . . . flattering, true, cryptic . . . and one that would mark the last third of my soul's siphoning into Midheaven.

Since Mackie didn't seem inclined to engage in any macabre jam sessions during my dreamscape, I ignored him, and turned back to the women I saw every day in the mirror, yet missed so much. "You shouldn't be here."

Olivia lifted a perfectly waxed brow and motioned with

one hand, pointing out two things: there was no one else in the room, and it lacked its usual furnacelike heat. So like me, she was in no real danger. Besides, even Sleepy Mac would struggle to murder someone who was already dead.

And, in spite of *that*, Olivia looked great. A dress I recognized as Chanel cupped her catwalk body, and the understated gold on her neck and ears was fine, though it dimmed in contrast to her bright blue eyes, fixed on me with unconcealed amusement. She swung her legs like a child, showing off her Blahniks.

"I like your hair that way," I told her, and she preened, straightening her back so all the bits boys liked protruded in perky agreement.

Then she frowned. "But you haven't done a thing with yours since I . . . left, have you?"

I glanced at my image in the bar's smoky mirror. A person's true physical form was always revealed in Midheaven, and so there I was again, the Joanna Archer of old, the appearance I'd been born with, though disconcertingly less familiar than it had once been. I was dark-eyed and -haired, where Olivia had been light. I was longer and lanky, as obsessively muscular as I could make myself in a slim, feminine frame. Olivia's curves, by contrast, were a battleship boom that hit you dead center, a bull's-eye in the gut.

Yet I was no longer comfortable weighing our differences, no longer felt wholly like either of us. These days, I was a mash-up of the women we used to be. So I turned from the mirror. "Where's everybody else?"

Because the green felt tables were empty of players, the chips representing personal powers and soul slivers all neatly racked before the empty dealers' chairs. Even the bar was barren, which was good. No bartender meant no drink, and imbibing was what drained one of the willpower and ability to leave this place. Again, the absences helped confirm this as a dream. The real Midheaven would never pull its guards.

"The only people you need to worry about are in this room. They are the ones who will affect you most in these next months."

My turn to raise a brow. My dead sister and a comatose psychotic with a soul blade tucked beneath a bowler hat? Yeah. They were going to be real effective.

Hopping from the poker table, Olivia tossed me a knowing look as she sauntered to the bar. Once there, she lifted to her tiptoes, floated to a seated position atop the length of polished mahogany, and recrossed her tanned legs. "They're coming now. They had to wait until you got here first."

"Why?"

"Because it's your dream, silly." Smiling, she gestured to the wall behind me, and I turned in time to see the paneled oak begin to smoke, then backed away until I was pressed against the bar. I felt better with Olivia at my side, and as if intuiting that—and who said she couldn't in the dream state?—she rested her hand atop my shoulder. "There they are."

And I was suddenly standing across from three of my former troop members: Warren, Tekla . . . and Hunter. Their gazes were cautious, and they shifted away from Mackie as a group, but didn't look surprised. They also didn't look any different than they did in the real world. Warren donned his favored hobo gear, though the authentic limp in his injured leg was even more pronounced. Tekla was wrapped in a traditional salwar kameez, favored for movement and ease. And Hunter was borne forth in the shape of the man I'd begun to love, even though his arrival in Midheaven meant he should be taking his true form as Jaden Jacks: bigger, both blonder and darker, and completely unknown to me.

"Why haven't your appearances changed?" I blurted,

and immediately tried to settle. Why should I feel panicked? It was my dream. But they all ignored me, continuing to stare at Olivia, expectancy on Tekla and Hunter's brows, wariness upon Warren's.

"They can't see or hear you," Olivia said, and they all cocked their heads. "I have to translate."

"Why?"

"Because for the intents and purposes of this dream, I get to be your T-Rex brain."

She smiled down at me, and unexpected laughter burst from me. T-Rex brain was something we'd coined years ago when discussing a friend who refused to believe her boyfriend was cheating. She'd told us she wanted proof. But T-Rex brain was a primitive knowledge, a fact or piece of information that lay between two people in spite of denial or proof. It was knowledge at the cellular level—he's cheating, the secretary can't be trusted, the maid took the money—and whether both parties openly admitted it or not, they *knew*.

I'd told Olivia then that some people called this their lizard brain, and she'd wrinkled her nose before informing me that she personally drew the line at anything that slithered, thus the new moniker—something that was large, primal, and strong.

In glancing at Hunter again, I wondered if that was why I was having such a hard time forgetting him. I hadn't ever felt he'd been lying to me . . . though it could be hard to tell. Emotions clouded the T-Rex brain.

But at least I understood Olivia's purpose here. She would allow me to step over that emotion, and learn what I needed to from the safety of this dream. So at least *something* was making sense.

"Of course, there's another reason you're invisible," she said, before gesturing to the mirror behind her. "None of *them* see you for who you really are. Not yet."

"And you can?"

"I'm dead."

It was the first time she'd said it so bluntly, and a look like storm clouds passed over her face. I winced. "I'm sorry—"

"Shh. We're beyond all that, you and me."

Yeah, we were. And while I was still tortured by her death, and that it'd come indirectly because of me, the actual memory of it was rubbed out, a blueish line drawing more than a full-colored panel of pain.

"Besides, we're bound as sisters, no matter what realm we inhabit." Including Midheaven, apparently. Olivia gestured at the others. "So what would you have me tell them?"

The words "Fuck off" blasted through my head, and though I didn't say it, Olivia shook her head. "One by one. Address them each honestly, have your say, and you'll thereby forever banish them from your thoughts and dreams."

If only *life* were that easy.

"Once you decide a person has no control over you," Olivia continued, "they no longer do."

I sighed. "So tell them what I really think, and they'll disappear?"

She shook her head, curls bouncing. The trio across the room watched, mesmerized. Meanwhile, Mackie stayed slumped. "You say it, but I'll tell them. Then they'll go away . . . as long as it's the truth."

Hesitating, I sighed, but not because I found it hard to tell the truth. I often told a hard truth. Yet voicing what I really wanted to say to these people was painful . . . so also why it would be so powerful. I turned to Warren, who was leaning on his good leg, arms crossed, and took a deep breath.

"I trusted you, Warren, and you treated me as badly as you would a Shadow. Even when I proved myself willing to give my life for you, for the troop, for a mortal, you still believed the worst of me. Why did you just throw me away?" My voice cracked, and I was glad he couldn't hear it. He remained impassive, looking at Olivia with the cool detachment of a person who knew his place in the world . . . and everyone else's too.

Olivia lifted her chin, and in a voice as fragile as bone china, said, "Your days are numbered, old man. You're going down so hard the earth will quake."

I gasped, whirling on her. "That's not what I said!"

She shrugged. "But it's what needed saying. See?"

And I spun back in time to see Warren fall backward without taking a step, the smoke reclaiming him and his shocked expression like an incinerator.

"Now you can live your dreams your way."

I shook my head. "I'm confused."

"Life is confusing. It's also messy and has no reason outside that which you impart to it." Before I could respond, she jerked her head. "Okay, what about her?"

Biting my lip, I eyed Tekla. I didn't know. Olivia had said she was one of the people most directly influencing me now, but I didn't see how. As far as I knew, she'd turned her back on me as wholly as the rest of the troop. I glanced up at Olivia. "Well, what does she have to say to me?"

"Hmm, no one has ever asked that before. Yet as it's clearly a question that demands a true answer, I think it'll do." Olivia nodded, then turned back to Tekla. "Speak, traitor!"

I gaped, automatically taking a step back. I'd seen Tekla reduce a man to shards with her mind alone, and while I hated the way she'd gone along with Warren's wishes, abandoning me, I still respected her. Even in a dream state. "Um, Olivia . . ."

But Tekla, normally so stoic and sure, began to weep. "Not everybody has abandoned you, Jo. Remember, you're not the only one doing the best you can to survive in a hard world."

And the wall of smoke loosened its fingers, reached forward and reclaimed her too.

"There . . . see? Even questions can reveal truths and provide peace." Olivia then frowned. "And now for him."

Hunter. I turned back and stared at him for a long while before speaking. It was easier when he wasn't looking at me. He continued to gaze up at Olivia with that Lost Boy look, soulful and bad and repentant all at the same time.

"Your betrayal was the largest," I told him evenly. "I let you into my heart and my body, and now I can't get you out of my mind. So, please, be a man about it and remove yourself. Because you've hurt me enough, and I need to be free."

That was it. I swallowed hard, proud of myself. I'd practiced so many variations of that speech—outraged, sad, defeated, and depressed—that when the simple truth came out—*I loved you, you hurt me, and now you have to let me go*—it was like a baptismal. I felt renewed. I turned to Olivia and smiled.

She smiled back, sweet and with tears moistening her eyes, before turning to Hunter. "You are a part of me now, and I will love you forever."

A relieved smile overtook his face, and he faded like a ghost. I whirled on her. "I'm going to kill you!"

Olivia laughed merrily. "I believe I have the advantage here."

"Ugh, God!" I pulled at my hair. "Olivia! What the fuck?"

She laughed some more. "Yep. That's about as T-Rex brain as you can get."

I lunged for her, and in my dreams, she evaded. I gave chase, wanting to shake her and yes, just touch her, but she sidestepped once she reached the wall studded with pagoda lanterns. I swerved, reached forward to brace myself against it, and instead fell right through it, to the sound of Olivia's fading laughter, muted by a thickening wall of smoke.

I knew the difference between reality and a dream, of course. There wasn't going to be any heart-to-hearts between me and my former troop mates, never mind Hunter, who was lost to Midheaven and another woman's arms. Olivia was truly gone, her only message to me a flash of guilt whenever I caught her face staring back at me from the mirror. Some wistful dream wouldn't change all of that.

It also wouldn't change the fact that Sleepy Mac had crept over into my waking hours. I could no longer pretend he was locked securely in another world, slumped before a piano, and waiting for me to offer up the last third of my soul. He was here, after me, his soul blade already poised in my direction.

I quickly shut off the thought, my fear of Mackie strong enough to bloom into scent. Besides, it wasn't thought that was needed now, but rote movement; robotic limbs, a cold heart, and a quiet mind.

Yet shutting down emotionally somehow seemed a step backward. Hadn't I just gotten over relying only on myself? Hadn't I worked hard to become a part of something larger than me, earning a place in a troop and proving they could trust me? Even before Olivia reappeared in my dreams, when I was rehabilitating in Xavier's mansion, I'd decided no one was going to strip me of my hard-learned lessons. I was determined to drive forward on the twin turbines of belief and faith. I would live, I would love again, dammit, and find others to trust . . . but I would do it on my terms.

Meanwhile, I needed to put one foot in front of the other, and stay ahead of Mackie. Maybe a former ally, like Tekla, would help me. Maybe not. But my sister was waving at me from the other side of death, and Mackie had breached the barrier between my world and his. I didn't need my T-Rex brain to tell me that Harlan Tripp was right. It was only a matter of time until Mackie found me again, and next time there might not be anyone standing between me and his blade. Next time I might not get away so easily.

After all, there were only so many ways to cheat the grave.

6

I had to return to the bus, of course. Or the "scene of the crime," as Terry whispered when I came up beside him, not looking over as he mentioned he had been there, seen everything . . . and survived. I glanced at him askance, then realized he thought I was a spectator, and he'd positioned himself behind the yellow police tape for just this purpose. Prima donna.

But there was quite a crowd for him to play to. Even my cabbie was standing alongside his open door, smoking and gossiping and staring at the destroyed party bus now surrounded by the yellow tape and flashing sirens. It was an abnormal sight, even for Vegas.

A handful of ambulances made a U shape in the center of the street, back doors flung wide to administer aid to the lightly injured, which helped me feel momentarily protected. Mackie wouldn't return as long as there were this many people milling about. He, like all agents, operated in the shadows.

". . . not everyone else was so lucky."

I glanced back at Terry as he closed his eyes, a tear slipping from beneath one tarred lash. The mesh of his shirt was torn, his eyeliner smeared, and the new piercing in his ear was bright pink against his sallow flesh. I bet Tripp hadn't even sterilized the piercing gun before sticking a hole in the poor guy. For some reason, that made me feel sorry for him. I returned my gaze to the destroyed bus, its top peeled back like a tomato can. *With a blade alone.* I shivered.

"We are lucky." I shook my head, but immediately regretted it. It was as if Tripp's infective, tapering smoke had slid past my earlobes and into the fragile drums to clog my thoughts like swamp water. I raised a hand to my head. "Though my hearing feels funny."

There was a gasp beside me, and I turned in time to watch Terry's eyes widen. "Concussion!" he screamed, pointing at me.

Three EMTs surrounded me like bees on a hive. *Great.*

"The cowboy knocked her out as he carried her out of the bus," Terry said as someone started feeling up my skull. "She shouldn't even be standing here now!"

Well, that was true enough.

A female tech tugged me in the direction of the nearest ambulance, but I was practically bowled over halfway there.

"Suzanne."

The bear hug tightened. "Oh, darlin'! Oh, dear! Oh, honey—are you okay?"

She punctuated each exclamation with a smacking kiss, but I managed to nod in the middle of the gentle mauling, which earned me more bracing hugs and heavily accented endearments. The female EMT, clearly used to such emotional displays, disentangled me from the distraught woman and her seemingly eighteen limbs, but when Suzanne pulled back, I noted the knots in her hair and circles under her eyes. She looked a decade older than when she'd trailed a bunch of disgruntled socialites off the bus.

My heart fell cold and plummeted to my toes.

"Cher?" I asked in a small voice. The last I'd seen *her,*

she'd just been tossed none-too-gently from Tripp's back. Where she'd only been because of me. *Just like Olivia.*

Oh God. If something had happened to the vapid, shallow, softhearted ninny because of me . . .

As I searched Suzanne's swollen red eyes, the fine lines of worry around them crinkled, belying her age. "She's in the hospital, but she's fine. They're making sure the bump on her head is no more than just that."

"Like we should do with you," the tech put in, blotting out Suzanne as she shone a light into my eyes.

I let out a breath I hadn't even known I was holding, and blinked away the spots and threatening tears. Suzanne gave me a watery smile when I again met her gaze, while a stethoscope was pressed to my back. The tech had the endless pockets of a circus clown.

"But what happened to you?" Suzanne asked as I was dragged to the bright interior of one of the ambulances and pushed onto a stretcher despite my obvious fitness. I concocted a story about being woken by the sound of sirens, alone in an alley, sans pocketbook. I was halfway through an explanation of the alley's other inhabitants when a man sidled up next to Suzanne.

"Excuse me." He had a cop's inflection, though he wasn't wearing a uniform. I sat up, ignoring the EMT's protests, eyes flicking to the badge at his waist. "Can we finish your statement now?"

Suzanne looked at me with injured eyes. "They won't let me go to the hospital until I finish telling them everything I know."

Like she was a criminal.

I turned a cold eye on the cop. "Her daughter is there."

"Stepdaughter," he clarified, and Suzanne and I both narrowed our eyes. "And if we get this over with now, we can find the man who did this to her much faster."

I put a comforting arm around Suzanne, who'd begun softly weeping. "You clearly don't have children."

His brow lifted. "And you *do*, Miss Archer?"

The professional tone altered into derision. I leaned forward, slipping a fraction inside of his personal space. "I have people I care about, if that's what you're asking. I was with one of them when she got knocked unconscious by . . ." *A Shadow agent. A rotted man. A grave-dodger.* ". . . a cowboy."

"Then maybe I should take your comments as well."

"I don't think so," I said, matching the arctic chill in his voice, and before he could protest, I sat back. "I'm suddenly feeling a little dizzy."

The EMT glommed onto me like she'd been waiting for those words, and my arm was cuffed before I blinked. The officer shifted into view over her shoulder, mouth thinned. "Then maybe I should contact you at your workplace instead?"

"Sure," I said lightly. I pointed with my free arm into the distance at the tallest, brightest building in the sky. Valhalla Hotel and Casino. Which I now owned. "You know where it is."

His eyes narrowed into pinpricks. "Yes, being a casino heiress seems to pay very well. Though even the loftiest job can't keep you safe all the time, huh?"

He dug out a business card and handed it to me, and one to Suzanne as well. "You ladies contact me if you manage to think of anything useful."

Suzanne, missing the slight, just sniffled as she deposited the card in her purse. I crossed my legs and gave him a carefree smile, letting it fall when he joined a handful of other officers across the lot. After a moment they looked over, shaking their heads and muttering under their breaths. I knew how Suzanne and I looked in our designer wear and bleached hair—like two fireflies trapped in a bottle between the late night neon and harsh ambulatory lights. I didn't need superhearing to know they thought us frivolous and useless, our brain matter as thin as tissue. Everyone made judgments based on first impressions, and police officers were most often proven right. Besides, how could those men know that beneath this waxed, perfumed, sculpted frame was a former heroine with a vigilante's heart?

Then again, most people had some form of street smarts lurking beneath their chosen exteriors. Even Suzanne had some iron to her spine. She ran marathons, had raised a teenager on her own, and navigated the annual sale at Nordy's with a warrior's instinct. I glanced over to find her cleaning her nail beds.

Well, a shark's instinct, anyway.

But Suzanne's sort of savvy, as well as Cher's, was harmless. Admittedly I hadn't always felt so benevolently toward them, but after being turned into Olivia, I'd lost the ability to sum a person up based on their skin alone. I no longer judged them for using their looks to shape their realities. Besides, it wasn't as if they were operating a Ponzi scheme. Their need to shellac, color, and buff every possible body part was a bit obsessive, but it didn't hurt anyone else. So big deal.

"Don't pay attention to it, Livvy-girl."

I hadn't realized I was glaring at the clustered men until Suzanne spoke. I shook my head, my hearing taking a momentary dip until equilibrium returned. "They're jerks."

"Well, that's as obvious as Terry's need for attention," she said wryly, causing both me and the tech—clearly the one to treat the distraught man—to snort. "But what did I tell you years ago, when you were broken-hearted for your sister and embarrassed about your runaway Momma?"

I frowned, not knowing. Olivia had never shared it with me. "Um . . . hot pink is the new black?"

She kept her gaze even and didn't smile, that iron spine peeking through. "That it ain't your business what other people think of you. Especially assholes."

"But they're *wrong*."

"Which is their right." She shrugged and started playing with some cables, letting them drop when the tech cleared her throat. "Can't change it. Might as well ignore it."

"Is that what you do?" I asked, then cringed when I realized I'd just told her people thought she was a bimbo.

"Yes," Suzanne said resolutely. "I ignore the gossips and naysayers and, yup, the assholes, and just go about doing what I gotta do to claim my own life."

I glanced back at the party bus containing booze, boas, and stripper poles.

She followed my gaze, pursing her lips. "You know, people criticized me when I married an older man, first saying I was a gold digger, then sayin' I was the one who put him in his grave." She swallowed hard at the memory. "But we shared a powerful love, even if it was short-lived." She lifted her chin as she returned her gaze to me. "So I was never embarrassed about it. After all, I knew true love . . ."

"And how many people can claim that?" the EMT put in, sighing. Suzanne nodded.

Frowning, I thought of my childhood sweetheart, Ben, whom I'd outgrown through time and experience. Then of Hunter . . . who'd thrown me away.

"After Cher's daddy died," Suzanne continued, oblivious to my silence, "I was also criticized for tryin' to raise a girl closer to my age than not. I neither had kids nor knew the first thing about 'em, but I knew something those assholes didn't."

"What?" asked the tech, wrapped up in Suzanne's story. I wondered too.

Suzanne's responding smile was fierce. "I needed that little girl's love, just as I'd needed her daddy's. And my little Cher-bear needed mine."

Olivia had too. She'd escaped to their home after our mother abandoned us, and while I shut down—thinking I'd caused the abandonment—Olivia could only find ways to endure it.

Suzanne addressed the tech now, chatting like friends over tea. "So now people are talking about Arun like he's a golden egg. Like I laid a trap and he slipped right in. But I'll just chin up and ride through that too. Ride all the way into my late years like I'm straddlin' the sunset. And you know why?"

The tech, unblinking, shook her head.

"Because I choose love again. And no gossip or naysayer—certainly no ass*hole*—is going to keep me from love."

The tech slumped, leaning back on her haunches. "You're so right."

"Yes I am." Suzanne put a hand on the woman's leg. Only she could bond with another woman under such circumstances. I'd have rolled my eyes were it not for the force of her words. "True love never dies. Even when it's gone, its memory keeps you safe."

Even the loftiest job can't keep you safe . . .

Asshole, I thought again. Though the officer was right about one thing. "Love can't keep you from getting sideswiped by a bus. Like tonight."

We'd almost lost Cher.

Suzanne turned back to me, the knowledge stark in her eyes. She finally nodded. "But it isn't love that's dangerous. Every life gets sideswiped at one time or another. Sometimes more than once. The question is, what do you do after that? Build something new out of the shrapnel . . . or just stay safe?"

The now-sniffling tech put her hands on me again, and I squirmed, suddenly tired of being touched. Having lone wolfed it for years after the attack on my life, I still got twitchy with too many people around me, too many hands on my body, even if they were soft and reassuring and supportive. I simply fared better emotionally when my knuckles were wrapped and I was punching something heavy. Having something to beat against loosened tension inside of me, enabling me to drop my worries behind like fallen foes until I was the last woman standing. I shut my eyes, mentally sparring.

Double jab. I am not weak.

One-two-three. I keep myself safe.

Push for space, front kick . . . take out a fucking kidney.
I protect my friends too.

But I *was* weak. I was not safe. And Cher and Suzanne
were not safe around me. Mackie now knew what they
looked and smelled like. If he thought I really cared for
them, he'd use them to get to me.

I sat up quickly, ripping off the cuff, and pushing the
tech's hands away.

"I have to go," I whispered, clamoring from the ambulance, tears cutting through the words. I added something
about Cher and the hospital, though I had to stay away
from her too. Especially now.

Head lowered so my hair hid my face, I picked up my
pace, ignoring the EMT's calls, the watchful cops, and
the rubberneckers snapping photos and video to upload to
YouTube. *Look what I saw on my Vegas Vacation.*

"Olivia! Wait!" Suzanne rushed to catch up, her mouth
already open in protest. Yet whatever she saw in my face
had her mouth moving soundlessly before she managed,
"Do you have a ride?"

I jerked my head curbside, where Kevin waited. My
driver had practically arrived before I'd hung up the phone.
After all, I *was* Olivia Archer.

Suzanne's lips pursed, and I could tell she wanted to say
more, but at last there was only a teary smile of her own,
and a final hug enveloping me in her custom perfume and
soap and shampoo. All signature Suzanne. Then her phone
trilled from within her handbag, and she untangled herself
with a sob.

"Arun—" she was already saying as she lifted it, hands
shaking, to her ear. I turned away to give us both privacy,
but glanced over my shoulder once. She was curled around
that phone like it was a lifeline, arms wrapped around her
slim body as if holding herself up. But she wasn't keeping
herself upright, I thought as I turned away. It was Arun.
Because she chose him, and love.

And they chose her.

* * *

Suzanne may have been right about true love never dying. I didn't think so, but the things I didn't know had turned out to be more varied than I'd ever imagined. Still, her determination to hang onto love—and Cher's Disneyfied dream of it—didn't match up to my own experience. I couldn't put my faith in a fairy tale. Sure, I believed in the wicked witch and the fire-breathing dragon parts, but the happily-ever-after? True love?

I scoffed, and pushed the thought away.

Misgivings about love aside, there were a shitload of other things I didn't understand, all of them more pressing than finding some elusive Prince Charming. For example, who had removed the lock on this side of Midheaven, letting out Mackie and Tripp, and effectively any rogue who still had enough willpower and soul energy to attempt the crossing?

What was this "cell" Tripp was entering—a place to keep him safe? Surely not another lockup. And could I be safe there too? Because how the fuck was I going to dodge a homicidal agent with a soul-stealing knife when my own protection was skin-thin?

"I could use a fairy godmother about right now," I muttered, and I didn't mean a rogue Shadow agent fond of shit-kickers and strange cigarettes. Even had I agreed to help Harlan Tripp, he was no match for Sleepy Mac. He'd already been wounded, didn't seem to have a conduit, and besides, I'd seen the fear in his eyes when he mentioned Mackie.

Cautiously, almost furtively, I reached into my pocket and fingered the phone Warren had given me. I'd been able to count on him and the troop to cover my back in the past, but Mackie had ruled over agents like him in Midheaven. The strongest agent of Light I'd ever known was over there now, though hoping Hunter Lorenzo would rescue me was as reasonable as believing in fairy tales about princes on noble steeds.

Because Hunter *hadn't* come after me. And with Mackie and Tripp's disappearance, he had to know the entry between the two worlds was open . . . and my life was in danger. His girlfriend—no, his *wife*, I remembered belatedly and bitterly—had sent Sleepy Mac.

And that brought me to Solange. Ah, beautiful Solange. I sighed, thinking of Midheaven's queen bee. Sola, Hunter called her. Other women adorned themselves in clothing to entice, makeup to enhance, baubles to catch the eye. But Solange *was* the adornment and enhancement and enticement of her world. Her appearance was a private thing, a bottle you'd found and rubbed. The answer to anything you could wish. At least, that's how she appeared there.

But she'd originally been a Shadow agent, also from the Vegas valley, escaping to Midheaven a few years earlier for some unknown infraction against the Tulpa. She and a man named Jaden Jacks had met here, unwisely beginning an affair that was a paranormal mixing of oil and water. When Warren discovered it, he forced J.J. into a new identity—Hunter Lorenzo—and ordered him to forget the Shadow he loved.

Except he never did. Hunter spent years searching for Solange. He donned a new cover identity and kept it from Warren. And sought her even after we became lovers.

As for my would-be rival, all I knew was this: Solange was the most beautiful woman I'd ever seen, but it was a beauty gained by raping the souls of others. She used alchemy, magic, and a uniquely savage mean streak to turn those valuable bits into gems, which she then strung into a recreation of the night sky. So beneath her soft, inviting exterior was a beast as vicious as a rabid hellhound, and that was the type of woman who thrived over there. In short, Solange made Mackie look like a pet rock.

And Hunter was in love with her.

So I'd helped him get to her. As hard as it was—and it'd been as acute as being struck with Mackie's blade—what else could I do? Even learning of his past—discovering I hadn't known him at all—I'd wanted good things for him. Besides, Warren had thrown him from the troop, essentially declaring paranormal jihad on his ass, so there wasn't anything left for him here anymore.

There was you.

I shook my head, stopping when the smoky feeling hit me again, though I was grateful to note it was marginally less. No, Warren had been clear on the terms of Hunter's banishment. If he'd stayed, Hunter would have been a rogue agent, driven from the city to live somewhere not yet populated enough to warrant a troop. If he remained in Las Vegas, or tried to contact any of his former allies, then the people he'd been raised with in the sanctuary of Light would kill him. So, either way he was an outcast. At least in Midheaven he'd have the love he'd so long searched for.

But he'd betrayed me, not by leaving me for his version of true love, or even because he'd failed to warn or protect me from Mackie. But *he* had been the one to tell Solange who I was, so that she could whisper it into Mackie's ear. *Go after Olivia Archer,* I could practically hear her purr. *Joanna's alias in that parallel world.*

I shut my eyes and leaned my head back on the buttery headrest. Whomever contacted me that afternoon had been right. I should never have gone out tonight.

True love never dies . . . even when it's gone, its memory keeps you safe.

"Bullshit," I whispered, though I didn't believe love, once felt, just disappeared. My first love, Ben, still influenced my life, though our love belonged to a different place and time. No less meaningful, but no longer relevant to the woman I was today.

Yet my burgeoning love for Hunter had been different. We were two fallible people with scarred pasts that had springboarded us into the same passion. I might have been wrong about the permanence of both relationships, but they had shaped me. Love, truly felt, really did leave a mark.

But so did getting whacked with a tire iron. And in my experience, *that's* how love marked a person's life. It was as random as violence. As senseless as an early death. And Suzanne was dead wrong about one thing in particular, I thought, a lone tear slipping over my cheek. Love *could* be dangerous.

Mine was fucking killing me.

7

Las Vegas actually dozes in the early morning hours, resting up from the roughshod night, and catching its breath before it rides again. Unfortunately, you don't fall asleep after a night like I had. You drop into a pool of exhaustion, and land in restless half-consciousness. But only after locating a place of relative safety, where demons wearing bowler hats can't plow soul-stealing blades through your innards.

For me, that place turned out to be a bright conference room streaming with morning sun, espresso fumes, and the disapproval of twelve board members constituting the whole of Archer Enterprises.

"Ms. Archer?"

Too late I realized my head had lolled on my neck again. Snapping upright, I checked for drool. Seriously, these blue bloods were so boring they could send Mackie back into his coma. Still, it was my first board meeting of Archer Enterprises, where I'd just replaced Xavier Archer as chairman of the board. It occurred to me that maybe I should make an effort. I yanked off my oversized shades and shielded a *ginormous* yawn.

"Sorry. You lost me at the bit about that vesting thing." They'd drawn the subject out so long I think oceanic plates had shifted.

The man to my left, six feet away but still seated closest at the long, glossed table, studied me drolly. "Late night?"

"It was a killer," I replied huskily, and reached for the water.

The man beyond him—indistinguishable but for the three feet separating them—placed his pen down and folded his hands in front of him. "Yes, word is your traveling disco got hijacked. It must have been terribly traumatic for you."

I let my water glass dangle dangerously from two fingers just to see him squirm, and discarded the idea of detailing what "trauma" really meant to me. "It was more of a rave than a disco," I said, angling my glass in a halfhearted toast.

He stared at me with undisguised disdain, and though I hated to do so, I blinked first. Olivia Archer didn't "do" stare-downs, though I quickly followed up with another gaping yawn. At least that didn't have to be faked.

"Perhaps we can get back to the business at hand?" One of the eleven identical twins intoned. It was John, Xavier's attorney, whom I'd apparently inherited as well. "The compensation plan again, then?"

I replaced my water glass with a pen and waved down the table with my free hand. "That would rock."

He began his monotonous intonation again . . . and I began to doodle. Catching the words "strip" and "straddle," I perked up a bit, then realized he was talking about how they intended to keep the money I paid them this year. Oh well, I thought, broadening my pen stroke along my pad. Someone would go over all this with me later, I was sure. Ad nauseam.

As John droned, a shape formed beneath my pen. I jolted upon recognizing it, marring the precise whorls, but was back at it before it could escape me. I began sharpening the outline more consciously, scrollwork leading up to a pair of wings. It wasn't just familiar, it was somehow *mundane*. I pulled back my pen, frowning. It was also the symbol I'd spotted on the giant chest from in the previous night's treasure hunt. Cher's report that Arun's servants were the ones to arrange the hunt and plant the clues initially surprised me, but it was now clear that someone with unnatural powers had infiltrated Arun's little cadre. Maybe, I thought, pen stilling, Arun Brahma himself. Could he be an agent? A rogue newly arrived in the valley, and using Suzanne and Cher to get to me?

Or, if the weapons were left for me, could he actually be some sort of ally? My pulse leapt at the thought, not because it was particularly likely, but because the idea of an ally in a world rife with enemies was shiny enough to draw even a magpie's attention.

It was worth looking into either way, if only because of Suzanne and Cher. I might not be a superhero anymore, but I'd die before I allowed another attack on someone I cared for, like the one that'd taken Olivia's life.

Making a mental note to research Arun Brahma when I wasn't being bombarded by balance sheets and cash flow statements, I started drawing the emerging symbol again, trying to remember where else I'd seen it. *And what did it mean?*

"Excuse me, Ms. Archer?"

Blinking, I startled into awareness. "What?"

"You said something?"

Shit. I'd spoken aloud. "Um, I said . . . what does that mean?"

"Which part?"

"Um. The last part."

John lifted a brow.

I waved my hand. "Just the bit before I interrupted."

He sighed, and started over.

I tapped my pen. Maybe the symbol was benign. Or meaningless alone. Stripping it of context might also have removed its significance. But I'd had Cher take a picture of the chest. I could study that and try to make out the surrounding carvings. A quick Internet search might yield the information I needed.

Yeah, but will it keep you alive?

I sighed heavily, and the attention of the room shifted my way. I ignored it. Let them think I was shallow, hungover, and ineffectual. A death-dealer on a mission took precedence over stock options any day.

Then the door to the conference room opened. *Or maybe not.*

Dropping my pen, I crumpled the paper with the strange symbol between my palms, and slid my hands—with their printless fingertips—into my pocket. Then, touching the phone Warren had given me, I watched the leader of the paranormal underworld, my birth father, enter the room. His flinty gaze roamed the length of the suddenly silent conference table before landing on me, at its head. My mouth went dry. He sensed it . . . and smiled.

Here's the thing about the Tulpa. You never knew when or where he was going to turn up. The agents of Light had long known he'd been Xavier Archer's benefactor, and the one who actually ran Archer Enterprises, but his appearances were as random as tornadoes. As far as I could tell, even his own troop didn't know when he'd drop in. Grasping the phone tighter, I slid lower, like I was again nodding off.

You could never be sure what physical form he was going to take either, and clothing was the least of it. While agents could be given new identities or take over others—like the way I'd been transformed so convincingly into Olivia—his body literally shifted and morphed depending on what he needed to present, and to whom. I'd seen him as a mafia don, a mild-appearing professor, and a monster pulled directly from Stephen King's dreams. As you can imagine, it made him rather hard to track.

It also freaked me out. This man was my *father*. A

mutant being that had somehow taken on enough cells
and atoms to impress a genetic code upon me. It made me
wonder how I'd have turned out if he'd been wearing his
horns at the time of my conception.

I'd seen him in this current guise once before, at Xavier's wake, so it was clearly the personage he wore when
taking care of any Archer-related business. His skin was
unmarred by freckle or line, his limbs deceivingly slim
and long. Yet he was still seated as he made his way into
the room, the benign exterior framed in an electric wheelchair. That was the difference since we'd last met. Were I
still able to sense the power swirling around him, I'd have
realized it sooner. Yet even in the absence of that ability,
one thing was achingly clear.

The Tulpa was exhausted.

The thin skin beneath his eyes was powdered in gray,
and though smooth as clay, his mouth turned down at the
corners. His lids were heavy, and his right hand trembled
slightly at the control panel. Despite the careful attention
paid to what had to be a three-thousand-dollar suit, one
side of his hair was mussed, like he'd just come in from
the wind.

Or he'd just come out on the losing side of a battle.

The men at the table recognized him, and the way John
stiffened told me they didn't care for him either. I remained
prettily slouched. Better to observe the dynamics of power
from Olivia's usual position. Window dressing.

"Don't tell me I'm late." The whiskey-strong voice was
as smooth as ever.

"Almost an hour," said one of the men meekly, earning a
hard look from the others.

"You're not on the board," John said shortly.

He *was* the board, I knew, eyes racing over every face.

The Tulpa smiled, unperturbed. "Xavier never seemed
to mind. He rather appreciated my advice. Benefited from
it too."

"Xavier's dead."

"So severe, John." The Tulpa rolled up to the opposite end of the table, one corner of his mouth lifting so a dimple flashed. "You should be more sensitive. His grieving daughter is sitting right here."

Silence rang, and I pretended to startle awake. "Sorry. Are we done?" I ran a hand through my hair, but paused halfway through a stretch. "Who are you?"

The Tulpa inclined his head. "I was your father's consultant in all matters of business. We met at his wake, remember?"

Clearly. He'd been at Xavier's bedside, keeping vigil with the corpse. *Seeing if there was any lingering soul energy he could suck out and use as personal power.*

"That day is a bit . . . fuzzy," I said lightly, looking down at my hands.

"Understandable." His voice smoothed out even further. Backing up, he pushed a couple of finger levers and headed my way. "Mind if I sit to your right?"

I'd rather pull my own tooth. Fortunately, John minded as well.

"This meeting is for board members only."

"Xavier never minded as long as I helped make him money." The Tulpa's pale face took on a new shape, almost menacing, as his brow quirked up. "If I recall correctly, neither did the rest of you."

"Well, I'm the senior board member now." John sniffed. The others looked back to the Tulpa, like it was his volley.

I tilted my head. Wasn't *I* the senior board member?

The Tulpa rose from his chair slowly but steadily, catching the eye of each board member, who gazed back as if mesmerized.

"Maybe," he said in a liquid whisper, "we should vote on the matter."

And like machines, everyone lifted their pens. I felt a pull too, and looked down, horrified to find the hand previously gripping Warren's phone snaking toward my gold pen. It wasn't done as quickly as the others, but the impulse was still there. Shit. I looked up to find the same confusion marring some of the men's faces, while others had hands already poised over their pads as if waiting for dictation. I followed suit and pretended to wait as well. It wouldn't do if Olivia Archer were seen as strong-willed. The Tulpa found anyone in control of their own mind an irresistible challenge.

"I love democracy," I quipped, though it might have been overkill. The Tulpa's gaze left John's, who I saw slump out from the corner of my eye, and locked onto mine.

"Then you, as the controlling partner and figurehead of Archer enterprises—not to mention the only lady in the room—should vote first."

Heads swiveled my way. They should form a synchronized swim team, I thought, though even my dry humor fell away when I saw the blankness shellacking their gazes. I felt that pull again, the Tulpa willing me to press my pen to the page, and let my gaze gloss over as well. I didn't know why I had partial resistance to this—perhaps because he was my father?—but I wasn't complaining. And yet, I hesitated. "But, sir, I don't even know your name."

It was a sore spot, not one I could afford to push even were I still an agent, but I couldn't help it. The Tulpa didn't, and would never, have a name. So even though the words were delivered with the sweetness of pure cane sugar, I knew they stung. Leaning forward, he pressed his palms flat on the table. "Sir is fine."

The mental pressure urging me to write increased. To hide my worry, I bent my head, and decided to listen. Just a little.

My hand automatically began to scribble.

Yes.

And John is out.

With deadened eyes, I pushed my vote forward for all to see. I might be a figurehead, but as the Tulpa had said, I had majority interest. Even I was interested to know exactly how much power that would yield me.

"Read it, Brian," the Tulpa said, so smoothly the words were almost slurred.

The man closest to me—the one so offended by party buses—pulled the page in front of him, and gasped. His mouth worked silently until the Tulpa's amused voice encouraged him to pass it along. Apparently board meetings were just like middle school, I thought wryly. Pass notes, form alliances . . . and always keep an eye out for the big motherfuckers.

John froze as he gazed down at the paper. "I'm your father's attorney," he finally said, leaden-voiced.

"My father's dead." I returned his earlier words, my feathery voice gone flat.

He sputtered in a mixture of indignation and poorly concealed disdain. A corner of the Tulpa's mouth rose slightly, and words rose in my mind with it. I knew them as his will, like a collision between his spirit and mine, and also knew I had a small ability to control them, but I didn't.

"And I don't like you." My mouth moved oddly over the syllables. It was like licking Braille, tongue catching on the individual hooks and sounds.

"Listen, Olivia—"

"It's Ms. Archer," I said sharply, this time my voice all my own. "To all of you. Now vote."

The Tulpa sat back in his wheelchair, as if a mere observer, his will withdrawn. Moments later the votes were counted, and John was out. The bombastic attorney remained motionless a time longer, eyes fixed straight ahead, brows bunched, though he didn't bother arguing. He'd obviously seen, felt, and *done* this before. Finally he stood. "This is not over."

And he left. Weighty silence returned to the room, punctured only by heavy sighs.

"Well, that was very uncomfortable." I pushed back from the table, my chair thudding behind me. "Let's try this again tomorrow, and see if it doesn't turn out better."

Picking up my handbag, I patted my pocket to make sure

the phone—my lifeline to Warren and the troop and *help*— was still on me, and made my way down the table. "My secretary will schedule something. Oh, and don't forget to invite . . ." I waved in the Tulpa's general direction. ". . . him."

I was almost out the door by then, and proud of how airy I sounded while sharing a room with a man who could insert his thoughts into my mind.

"Ms. Archer?"

These words were voiced and not merely thought.

"Olivia." I turned slowly and inclined my head. "Please."

"Olivia," the Tulpa purred, wheeling closer. "You dropped something."

I glanced down and found the crumpled paper with my carelessly drawn mythic doodle in his hands. He smoothed it out for me, then jerked and stilled.

Should I wait for him to toss me from the fifteenth floor window, or just throw myself from it now?

His voice betrayed no emotion. "This is . . . interesting."

When dealing with a man constructed of lies, truth was always the best policy. "I saw it last night. It was on a box used in a treasure hunt, a game we were playing. For some reason I couldn't get it out of my mind."

The Tulpa held the paper out to me, though he didn't release it when I took hold. "Perhaps I could take you to lunch and we can discuss it further?"

"Kiss-ass," Brian muttered lowly. The Tulpa, facing me, whirled in his chair unnaturally fast. The room fell silent again.

They fear him without knowing why, I thought, as Brian's face went ashen. It didn't matter how frail he seemed. Never mind the paranormal battles forcing him to conserve energy. A whisper of quiet madness told them he'd willingly pin them to a board, dissect them like frogs, and do it while they were still alive. And for just one moment that madness screamed.

Despite my own survivor's instinct, I stepped closer. "Perhaps, Brian, you'd like us to take another vote?"

As the Tulpa and I looked at him together, a thought raced through my head.

The Shadow will bind with the Light.

It wasn't the Tulpa's thought. It was a prophecy, but I told myself it had nothing to do with me, or this. I was no longer Light.

Brian, meanwhile, couldn't seem to catch his breath. "N-No. You're right. You two go have your lunch. We'll finish up here."

"No." I tucked the wrinkled sheet of paper in my bag, just to get it out of sight. "You are finished. However, I'd be most grateful if you'd catch *my* consultant up to speed on that . . . stuff you were talking about earlier." Turning to the Tulpa, I forced myself to meet his eyes. Tar black, their intensity made mine dilate, and time unexpectedly slowed. Blinking fast, I managed, "A rain check for lunch?"

My father's voice was schooled again, his features as smooth as mine. "I'll call for you soon."

And he said it like I'd come running.

8

After beaming some overly cheery farewell, and donning my shades, I took a private, recessed elevator down to my personal garage, where Kevin was already waiting. I had to admit, certain aspects of Xavier's lifestyle were easy to get used to . . . and after the last few moments spent holding it together, I was grateful not to have to single-handedly battle rush hour traffic.

Instructing Kevin to head to the hospital where Cher was recuperating, I dropped my head back against the soft leather seat. I waited until we'd flipped onto the boulevard . . . then I began to shake.

Mind control. Holy shit.

I guess I shouldn't have been so surprised. A tulpa, in the traditional sense of the word, *was* a thought-form. Where the rest of us poor sots had to crawl into this world through blood and bone, a tulpa was a being birthed from another person's imagination. This tulpa, however, developed enough free will to loose himself from his creator's reigns, and then took over the Shadow side of the Zodiac. That he'd done so with barely a dust-up was a testament to his brutality and power. Unfortunately for that still-growing power, his creator had died before providing the Tulpa with a proper name, so "Tulpa," though meant only as a title, was what he was called, and what he'd forever remain.

Thus while being a tulpa granted him extraordinary abilities, like adjusting his appearance depending on the viewer's expectation—and friggin' *mind* control!—it also hamstrung him. Without a proper name to cement him in the real world, to ground him and allow him to manifest permanently, there was a limit to his power.

One that might yet lead to his downfall.

Because there was another tulpa in town, this one created by my mother specifically to battle him. And the work she'd begun, sinking the past decade into visualizing his enemy into existence, I had recently finished by giving the creature a name: Skamar. In doing so, I'd redoubled her energy, and her power.

So you can imagine how peeved I was when, entering the hospital, Skamar appeared from nowhere, sneaking up behind me to give me the equivalent of a paranormal wedgie. Squealing as she sniffed at my neck, I put a hand to my thudding heart. "Damn it, Skamar! You trying to kill me?"

"Not anymore," she murmured, remaining close. Thin, small, and pale, she'd have been plain too, were her features not so sharp. Her short hair was blunt and red, her matching lashes so light they made her look bald-eyed. Yet her lips were defined even without color, and her nose arrowed between cheekbones so high you could hang laundry from them. She looked like a Victorian lady who'd been misplaced in the ages, which was deceiving. Skamar had once been so hungry for life, she'd been willing to take mine. And right now she was inching forward in a liquid glide, still impossibly and preternaturally graceful . . . and still sniffing at me. "You've been with *him*."

I smirked. "That's right, Sherlock. He waltzed into my conference room at Valhalla this afternoon. Where the hell were you?"

"Permanence has its limitations." Meaning she could only be one place at a time.

"Okay, then how about a warning next time you sneak up on me?"

"Well, I would have called first," she said sarcastically, "but I didn't know I was tracking you. I thought I'd found *him*."

She wouldn't say the Tulpa's title, I knew. Every utterance about another being gave them a degree of energy, reinforcing their position in this world, and their right to move about in it. Skamar's raison d'être was directly opposed to that.

"Nope. Just little ol' mortal me." She averted her gaze, and I let my tone turn sarcastic. "How's Mom?"

Skamar shrugged. Sure, *now* she clammed up. As the only one who knew of my mother's true identity, she also knew I—like everyone else in the Zodiac world—was angling for it. Obviously she'd been instructed not to tell me who Zoe was, but knowing my mother was in the valley, watching me, and actively augmenting the agents of Light in whatever capacity she could manage as a mortal, I couldn't help myself. Sure, the woman had given over all her powers to save my life a decade earlier. I knew better than anyone what that felt like. But I had trouble understanding why she hadn't contacted me once in the years since. At least Warren had thrown me a fucking phone.

"Valhalla, huh?" Skamar sighed, mind already working on how to approach the fortress without the Shadows noting it. "Fine, I'll start there."

"Wait!" I put my hand on her arm before she could leave. Another second and she'd be a fistful of miles away. That's how powerful she was. "I—I need help."

Her expression immediately shuttered. "I can't."

"But—"

"It'll put you in danger." She raised her voice, her tiny nose stubbornly upturned. "You should get on with your . . . life."

"I know, I'm trying—" I rambled quickly, so she'd hear me out. I hadn't slept in two days, and everything I owned was at Olivia's midtown penthouse. Sending someone to pick up things for me was like handing them a death sentence, yet Mackie would have all of Olivia's information by now so I didn't dare return alone. I needed to grab private disks and journals, and retrieve Luna as well. Funny how the wealthiest woman in the Las Vegas valley valued only a few small, priceless items. "Please. I'm blind here, Skamar. There's a man, a monster, looking for me. He could be behind me and I wouldn't know it."

Her eyes flicked over my shoulder. "He's not."

"Give it another minute," I retorted wryly.

She said nothing, which caused me to tilt my head, a hand cocked on my hip. "You already knew about Mackie, didn't you?"

She widened her eyes in innocence. "Only since last night."

I stepped forward. "Then you know what I'm up against."

My mother conceived of Skamar in Midheaven because the Tulpa couldn't access that realm without a soul. When Skamar was actualized enough to take on a personality and self-will, yet still malleable enough to pass through the threshold between the two worlds, she relocated here . . . and found me.

After I'd named her, she was free to take on her own identity and life, and had been battling the Tulpa ever since. With the small exception of once being pinned to a makeshift cross, she'd mostly prevailed, and now, with her name recorded in the Zodiac manuals, she had the additional power of mortal minds behind her. The manuals, seemingly innocuous comic books, were critical to the Zodiac world. They recorded each side's actions in graphic titles, both Shadow and Light, putting it in print for young, nubile minds to read, dream about . . . and, in turn, provide the energy fueling their chosen side's battles. So if anyone could protect me from Mackie, it was Skamar.

I opened my mouth to say as much, but she cut me off with a jerk of her head. "And you know what I'm up against as well."

"The little ol' Tulpa?" I scoffed, fisting one hand on my hip. "You're winning, Skamar! He was in a wheelchair today. He's conserving energy like a starving python."

"That's right. I'm winning!" She punched her chest so hard *I* felt it. "And I intend to keep on winning. I know who he is, what he is, and how he formed. I know what it's like to hunger for more substance in this world, and I can anticipate what he's willing to do to get it. But Sleepy Mac?" She shook her head. "I don't know how to fight him."

I didn't blink, and I remained silent until she again met my eye. "I'll die, Skamar."

She just looked at me.

"Oh." I got it. It wasn't her problem. I was no longer the Kairos, or a part of the world she considered her own. I couldn't help her . . . therefore she saw no reason to help me.

Seeing my realization, she shook her head. "That's not it. I need to conserve my energy too. The Tulpa may be weakened, but he's resourceful and established. I can't rest until his last cell is stamped from this earth."

"You wouldn't be able to tap your fucking toe if not for me," I whispered lowly. And though I hadn't known the sentiment was there until it was out, my fury flared with it. "*I* gave you a name. *I'm* the one who fought to get it recorded."

"And so I owe you?"

"Fucking right, you do."

It was a stupid thing to say to someone who could pulverize me with one fist, but if she didn't help me, I was dead anyway. We locked gazes for a full raw minute, visually arm-wrestling, the one area where I was as strong and willful as she.

Finally, she sighed. "Once, but then we're even."

It didn't feel even. I had sacrificed all and she had gained all, but with the Tulpa closing in on the only remaining Archer in his dynastic cover, and Sleepy Mac determined to carve me up like holiday meat, I could only nod. Right now, I thought, leading her back to my car, I'd take whatever help I could get.

Skamar fell into sleep as soon as we settled in the car. It was hard to impart a sense of paranoia in a being with no equal in power. Yes, she understood the gravity of my plight on one level, but it was like a virgin's understanding of sex. The textbook explanation could only get you so far.

When we arrived at the Greenspun Residences, Skamar roused herself enough to scan the perimeter of the highrise condo. She returned in time to place herself before me when the lobby's elevator doors opened, moving ten times as fast as a mortal. The doorman hadn't even known she was gone.

"What do you remember about Mackie?" I asked, fishing Warren's phone from my pocket, thumb hovering over the panic button.

Skamar snorted. "What do you remember of your birth, Archer?"

"What do you mean?"

"I mean, my gestation in Midheaven was like your evolution in the womb. The right components in the right environment leading to a rising consciousness. But I had no words to put to my existence while there, and without words, images are meaningless. Without meaning, they fade. I simply can't remember."

I blinked, momentarily forgetting my fear. "Then how did you know about Mackie? You weren't a bit surprised when I said he was after me."

She quirked a fine brow and waited.

"Because my mother knows." Of course she did. Zoe Archer had been in Midheaven long ago, and Sleepy Mac was the oldest semiliving being there. But if she'd known of his escape, why hadn't she alerted Warren?

Why wasn't she helping me now?

"Don't ask me," Skamar said, reading my thoughts. "I can't get involved."

"I'm mortal too." I hated how injured my voice sounded. I hated to beg for information about my own mother.

"She knows, and she's still working on your behalf. She still . . . believes in you." While Skamar's tone said she clearly did not.

"Then why won't she—"

"She doesn't tell me why."

"So make her!"

She turned her gaze back to the panel where the floors ticked by. "I don't care enough to make her do anything."

I angled myself before her, putting myself in potential danger when those doors snicked open. "If you thought I was the Kairos would you care?"

"If you were the Kairos," she said, using one finger to push me aside, "I wouldn't be here."

The bell chimed at our floor and the doors opened. The hum of empty air stretched, and trailing Skamar, I thought maybe this would be a nonevent.

That hope died as soon as the giant French doors swung open. "Oh my God."

The phone nearly slipped from my hand as I stared at the gleaming foyer, the remnants of Olivia's physical life strung over it like confetti. Skamar whizzed from room to room, leaving a whistle in her wake, but I simply pushed the door shut and slumped against it.

Every item Olivia had collected on vacations, sprees, and whims . . . destroyed. The Swedish crystal she valued for its thickness and curves was smashed on the marble floor. The built-in shelves housing them were carved up, symbols scratched into the surfaces, though it was mostly a cross-hatching of random, furious scrawls that left wood shavings scattered among the broken glass.

The antique scrolled daybed in the room's center was dumped on its side, the gorgeous wood equally blade-raped.

Its silken throws and pillows hadn't been spared either, and soft down, cotton, and wool lay in destroyed puffs and strips. Graffiti marred the entire room—glass tops and walls, ceiling and marble floor—though it wasn't paint scrawled over every surface, but the mark of that deadly blade. Each score was a warning even though the damage was already done. I didn't know what sort of strength was needed to make marble scream, but knew if Mackie had his way, there was a death cry waiting in my body too.

Lifting my head, I stared at the floor-to-ceiling windows revealing the penthouse's money shot—an unobscured view of the famous Strip. It was an even better view now, I thought sadly. Because every plate-glass window bore a jagged hole the size of a doorway in its empty middle. Cold air rolled in uninvited, though that wasn't what had me shivering as Skamar returned to my side.

"Check the ledge outside, please." Mackie could literally be hanging there, waiting in ambush. I'd once traversed that ledge as well.

While Skamar investigated, I repocketed the phone and forced myself into action, stepping over shattered picture frames, littered flowers—already wilting—and vases near impossible to replace. Every step forward was an invitation to panic, so I deliberately slowed my breathing to match my footsteps, not daring to release any strong emotion. Mackie could be close enough to scent it. He'd return eventually, and of course Tripp was right. The monster wouldn't stop until I was dead.

Something inside of me lifted its head at the thought. It was as if logs were being thrown on a newly lit pyre, and each one choked back a scream. I held my breath even as my heartbeat quickened—panic attack, I realized, bracing my weight against a wall. That's what people had when they were up against something far stronger than themselves. Shuttering my eyes, I tried to ignore it, but it flared behind my lids in a blinding orange-red, and heat struck at my heart.

"Joanna?"

Skamar's voice was as airy and far off as she'd once been, like she was still stuck in another world.

I rubbed at my eyes, the fire in my chest building. My rib cage began to ache, and I stumbled into Olivia's bedroom. Not a whole lot more to destroy there either. The same definitively careless lacerations scored every surface. I bumbled through the upturned furniture, tripping in my blind panic, and cut myself on the fragrant perfume bottles littering the floor.

"Joanna!" This time a hiss. My blood and panic must have reeked.

I ripped at linens and sheets, searching, the fire mounting, before I clamored over a halved mattress to the closet I'd fitted with a false back. Clothing—ripped, slashed, slit, torn—designer labels, and remnants of beauty mocking me with false value. I pushed it all aside, along with leather shoes and boots now made of fringe . . . and finally found Luna, wide-eyed, in a corner.

"No."

Was that my voice? I wondered. Or an echo too from another world?

"No, no, no . . ."

Ah, that was keening. A death wail that straddled worlds. I recognized it because I'd lost loved ones to violence before. But never a being so innocent and small. Never a pet.

I hadn't thought wardens could be destroyed. Conduits only made them stronger, larger, and fiercer. Mackie's soul knife wasn't a conduit then, because Luna had faced a reduction—her form removed along with her life. I only recognized the feline face because of those great, unseeing eyes. Gathering the rest like kindling in my arms I folded over the fur and bone, wrapping it around her like a blanket, trying to put her back together.

And then she blinked.

"Oh God, oh God . . ." It wasn't me this time, but it was

just as unnatural. Beings imagined into existence generally didn't pray. "Come. Let's get you out of here."

But I couldn't leave my warden. After all, she had never left me. I curled my own body around her as I was lifted in turn. The pyre in my chest flared, Luna and me caught in its center, bloodied fur and raw emotion mingling like our biology and spirits were one. Yes, I thought, a small piece of me dying.

"Hold tight," Skamar whispered raggedly, but instead I tucked into myself and just let go. She jumped from the rooftop, Olivia's condo dropping away in a roller-coaster dip. Then the air pressed me back against the tulpa, her flight a shuttle takeoff. I curled in tighter. Burning on that pyre, I let go all the fear and sadness and horror I'd been trying so hard to keep from being scented by those in the underworld. The wind whipped away my screams before doing the same, eventually, with my manic laughter. I imagined Mackie crazed on the ground, trying to track those cries, but only stopped when my throttling gasps extinguished the fire behind my lids. Gradually the air lessened against me, and I slumped in those slim, tenuous arms. For a moment I could almost imagine Luna was warm, curled in my arms, purring and whole. Then Skamar landed. And the world was cold again.

My mind was clenched, registering only *tunnels, darkness, beneath the city* . . . but eventually a face appeared. Again, just eyes, though unlike Luna's, these weren't framed in a broken body. The skull housing them wasn't crushed. And they remained fixed on one spot, willing me into coherence.

"You could crush me like that," I said, voice so flat it could've been ground beneath Mackie's boot too.

"Anyone in our world could crush you," Skamar replied, truthfully. I winced, but didn't hold the lack of sentiment against her. She wasn't born like me. She didn't have a past, so how could I expect empathy to be part of her makeup?

It had to be learned, gained through experience. Skamar had never been weighed down with a personal history. No family or allies to betray her, while I'd had both. "But not like that," she added, almost to herself.

So keeping a being alive beneath a pulverized body was a skill unique to Sleepy Mac. I swallowed hard, and though Skamar didn't move, imagined her doing the same.

"Help her." My voice came out knotted. Hearing it, I had the urge to resume my wailing, but I squeezed my lips tight. That's how I held myself together.

"I already have."

I frowned, and the glyph on her chest lit in response, delivering those deep-set eyes back into a face I'd helped create. Her mouth was rimmed in crimson, like she'd been smoking blood.

"What did you do?"

"Separated her soul from her body. Took her awareness out of that already rotting mess. I helped her," Skamar added quickly, though she didn't sound happy about it.

I thought of the Tulpa leaning over to suck life from Xavier's body, and of the magic candle leading to Midheaven that yanked out soul bits along with a blown breath. I lunged for the darkness.

We remained silent long after I finished being sick.

"If it's any consolation, her fear and pain eased at the end. Her consciousness thanked me."

A tear rolled down my cheek. "And now?"

"She's gone."

Silence again, but I couldn't hear it over the screaming in my head. Finally Skamar sensed my panic settling. "I will watch over you when I can." Reluctance edged every word. "I was built to battle the Tulpa, it is my reason in all things, but if there's enough left over . . ."

Meaning there were no promises. I might yet end up a bleeding sack of slivered organs and crushed bone, consciousness trapped in a postmortem stain.

Hours earlier I might have retorted smartly, but now I

only nodded and swayed. Skamar's arms steadied me, but I remained unaware of my body, so numb the command to wiggle my feet didn't register. I'd seen and even caused gruesome death before. People pitched into the afterlife with limbs wheeling to fight the inevitable. But I'd never seen something living reduced to such abject nothingness.

I angled my head to face her. "Do I smell like fear?"

Skamar hesitated, then shook her head.

"What, then?"

"Despair."

"Will it encourage him?" I asked, because I knew Mackie would scent it eventually. That's why Skamar had taken me here, into the tunnels beneath the city, where emotions could be temporarily crushed between two worlds.

She glanced up like the answer was scrawled in graffiti on the tunnel's slope. Then she sighed. "It will fuel him."

Another truth. I nodded woodenly, mentally chaining myself to it.

"Come," Skamar said, holding out a hand.

That was the prod I needed to feel my body again. But I recoiled, lost my footing, and slid into a crouch against the curve of the tunnel wall. "Five more minutes. Just a little longer in the dark."

Her hesitation was silent argument, but then her glyph lessened until it soundlessly snapped off. I heard a slide, Skamar reclining across from me, and we both disappeared again, drawing the thick silence around us like a quilt. I sat in the long ticking minutes without any idea of how to fight this, or even if it would help to turn and run. Mackie had crossed worlds to find me, and city limits meant nothing to rogues. I could flee to another continent, and he would still be able to track me. If he had the will.

I thought of what he'd willfully done to Luna's body, and swallowed hard.

"Goddamn Hunter," I said. His name tasted like bile. I cursed his other one. "Goddamn Jaden Jacks."

"That's right," Skamar murmured in the dark. "Anger will help."

And I'd need all the help I could get. I frowned, then scrambled to my feet, holding out my hand this time. I saw and sensed nothing, but knew Skamar's hyperkeen eyesight had me flooded, as though in a spotlight. Her loose, dry hand wrapped around mine, leading me forward, and together we headed out of the darkness, back into the city, hauling emotions strong enough to stoke an inferno.

9

I drove. Specifically, after Skamar dropped me at the guard-gated compound my not-so-dearly departed stepfather had left to me, I had the estate guard let me into the garages, left my black Porsche there, and took Xavier's gold-toned Bentley. I'm sure *that* had him squirming six feet under.

Sailing from the gates and out onto residential streets stained with neon and oil, the Continental GT was the opposite of urban camouflage, yet I didn't think Sleepy Mac knew the difference between a Bentley and a Buick. I figured he was aware of Olivia's possessions and routine, which was why I didn't head to Valhalla. Despite the army of security at the casino, I wouldn't be any safer there than at the death house. It would also be the equivalent of thrusting innocents into his homicidal path. Besides, companionship was an illusion. Despite Skamar's reluctant promise to watch over me when possible, I was as alone as when Warren had abandoned me on the shallow bank of the Las Vegas wash.

So I drove through the bold, bleak city, a landscape colored by my own problems, wanting to at least make

Mackie work to find me. And though still shaky from losing Luna, still horrified at the nature of her death, I was steadying. I'd long faced my personal demons head-on, and merely running made me antsy. Even if I did have a good reason for it. To temper my unease, and at least feign proactivity until I figured out what to do next, I pulled out my smartphone and surfed the Web for info on Arun Brahma. I hadn't forgotten that either he or someone around him was angling for me, or that they were using Cher's family—my only remaining family—to do so.

Rich as the proverbial Midas, untouched by even a remote whiff of anything resembling a recession, the international textile magnate Arun Brahma was also the kind of handsome some would call devastating. As someone with a good deal of experience in real devastation, I wouldn't go that far, but I could understand Suzanne's attraction. He had the gold undertones of his Indian descent, with the strange light eyes that relatively few in his culture were blessed with—which was why, I decided, they were so desired. People always valued more that which the masses did not possess. Stick the same eyes in the face of a Swede and they wouldn't be remarkable at all.

Yet combined with the dusky skin and perfect thatch of ink-dotted hair, they *were* remarkable. The photo I pulled up with his Wikipedia entry showed a man who knew it too. His smile was cool and wide, smug with the knowledge that he'd been born with reservations tapped out in his name. *Here is your palace, Mr. Brahma. Here is your empire. The world is your garden, everything in it yours to be plucked like fruit.*

I wanted to hate him. My knee-jerk reaction was to dismiss a man born to the lucky sperm club. Yet I caught the envious thought like a fly between two fingers, and just as swiftly flicked it away. Who was I to talk? From the outsider's perspective, Olivia Archer was a bubble-headed debutante with an entire empire also thrown at her rose-petaled feet. Everyone had some sort of substance to them, even if it was only the clay that made up all of humanity. My purpose in studying Arun now was to find out what lay beneath the slick, playboy exterior.

Because there was more to Arun Brahma than that. Either he was an agent masquerading as a mortal, or he was a rogue agent who'd somehow made his way into the valley. I leaned toward the latter explanation, if only because he could travel so freely between countries and continents, something a real agent, Shadow or Light, could not do. But why his interest in me? And why now?

I looked up, and realized with a start that nearly an hour had passed. I'd been driving in circles both mentally and literally—getting nowhere on the streets or in my search for any real information on Arun. I also found myself skimming the warehouse district, and did a quick U-turn without stopping. The troop owned a building not fifty yards away, though the place had essentially been Hunter's. He had set the security system, laid the booby traps coiled inside, and run the tests to develop weaponry for the troop's battles with the Shadows. But now he was gone and there were only unfinished sketches inside, foam mock-ups for conduits he'd never make, and a ceiling of mismatched stars above a bed we'd once made love in. Everything he'd left behind in this world locked up tight. Everything but me.

"Damn him . . ." Running from the thought, the Bentley's engine growling like a low-slung predator on the streets, I wound up at another unexpected destination. It was probably just my research on Arun and the mysterious trunk left by someone in his party, but it was as if my subconscious was touring all the places haunting me. Idling before the dilapidated house Cher and I had visited the night before, I willed myself to keep driving until I either found a safe place or ran out of gas, whichever came first.

The neon green sign spelling PSYCHIC flickered on while I idled. Leaning forward, I peered through the windshield at the boarded-up building. Nothing moved, and after another moment I slid from the car's high-tech womb and into the chill night. A man's harsh, rattling laugh sounded from the nearby apartment complex, an answering hoot rocketed into the night, and if I squinted, I could imagine myself in a bombed-out country with rubble and lean-tos competing to hide the most menace.

Sidestepping a stain that looked like it could rear up and bite, I fought the impulse to turn back. I'd done my best to honor Warren's wishes and stay away from the Zodiac world, but what he should have done was tell the Zodiac world to stay away from me. If he wasn't going to protect me, then I'd do what I'd always done . . . as Joanna, as the Archer and Kairos, and now as Olivia: arm myself.

My eyesight, always dim these days, adjusted slowly, but I spotted the spindly form of the clay pot and dead plant upturned next to the door.

And the man who wore bones on the outside of his skin was waiting.

Again, he was not dressed for company. The same torn, grubby jeans—too loose for the thin white body painted black. Thank God for the slivered light angling through the boarded-up windows like lines on a music sheet. If not for that, he'd have looked exactly like the skeleton he was pretending to be, the tattooed bones inky in relief, his sunken eyes twin voids of dark knowledge. His nails, living dead things, writhed slowly as he considered me.

"No mask this time," he said, though I didn't know how he could tell with eyes sewn shut.

"You're a Seer." I fought not to cross my arms. He'd know it for self-protection, not defiance, and I needed defiance. "You already know who I am."

"And why you're here." He swung the door wide to reveal a room bare but for the dust. And, I thought, the ornate chest marking its middle like a black hole. Holding my breath, I edged past the Seer, pretending not to hear his inhalation, or his nails clacking as he shut the door behind me.

"That where the psychic part comes in?" I asked, struggling to keep my back to him. I wouldn't be able to stop him from killing me now. And why would I want to see death coming anyway?

"It's merely obvious. Question is, do *you* know?" He appeared in front of me. Just like that. One sharp clack of toenails like talons and his breath was on my cheek. He angled his head, his beard forking right. "Quick—what do you most desire?"

"Protection," I said, sighing deeply. There was a relief in speaking openly again with someone about the underworld and my former place in it. It was like the first breath after taking off tight clothing worn too long. "To arm myself. I need help."

"Then you shall have those things." His lacquered nails glinted in the slanted light as he gestured to the chest. "We all manifest our true desires. As long as we name them, of course."

Because desires were the emotions that most heavily controlled our thoughts, and the Zodiac world had taken the "it's the thought that counts" principle and turned it into a religion. Thoughts—precise, applied, fixed—determined action. They could create living beings and walls and plant life out of nothing. Our minds were our might.

I smiled wryly as I crossed the shadow-drenched room. I should have gone for the man, the munchkins, and the picket fence. I'd have made a kick-ass soccer mom.

Dismissing the pipe dream, I traced the symbol centered on the chest's carved and silken top. The one I'd drawn from memory and that had so interested the Tulpa. "May I?"

"Do you believe you are the Kairos?" he asked.

Jerking my head, I flipped open the lid. "I believe I still count."

He made a considering noise in the back of his throat. "That's a start." Then a pause. "My name is Caine."

I nodded to acknowledge I'd heard, but the odd arsenal before me was a shadowy attraction, like death beckoning. All four weapons I'd seen before were here; maybe Arun Brahma was an ally. I tested the hinge on the trident, a thrill reverberating up my arm as the blades winged open with a definitive snap. It was older than me by at least two lifetimes, but still sharp, which was all that mattered.

It's also magical, I thought, retracting the blades and tucking it into my oversized bag. Conduits were allegedly taboo for me now. Most often they turned impotent in mortal hands, though in some cases they backfired. Seeing the gun with the coolly glowing liquid vials again, I was too juiced to care. It felt like a part of me, long buried, had just lifted the casket lid. Better to die armed than stand flatfooted against a magical blade.

I placed that into my bag too, though the saber with an additional firearm was too large to tuck away. Good thing it was winter. It could be concealed in a long coat. I decided to leave the cane, with a blade at its pommel, out. Carrying it as Olivia Archer would either be attributed to affectation or need. It was well known I'd only recently rehabbed from a near drowning. As to actually using it, or any of the conduits, I guess I'd test the backfiring theory when the time came.

"Don't forget the additional ammo," Caine said, jerking his head. His beard did the pointing for him. "That's all there is."

Because the weapons were so old. Their controlling agents were long dead . . . as were the weapons masters who'd created them. Every paranormal weapon was made for a particular agent, and most effective in its original owners' hands. However, they could also be inherited, which was how I'd once gained my palm-sized bow and arrow.

I sighed, still wishing for my conduit. Nothing else was so perfect an extension of my body, as if my skin wrapped around it to draw it closer to my bone. I glanced up to see Caine's attention on me, despite his sunken gaze. He would know of my losses. No reason he couldn't tell me about his.

"What happened to your eyes?" I asked, with the same directness most Seers used. People who could intuit others' designs and deeds before they occurred had no need or patience for pretense. I'd learned that from Tekla.

"Ironic, isn't it?" He shifted so his face fell into the fractured light. "My visions are gifts from the Universe, but a great gift requires a great sacrifice. As you know."

I did. Tekla's gift had taken a good chunk of her sanity. She slept sporadically, mumbled to herself, obsessed over her charts. Screamed in the night. I used to feel sorry for her. Lately I'd found myself thinking, So what? She had more than enough power to compensate, and so did Caine.

I turned. "I don't want to give any more."

"That's your problem."

"My problem," I snapped, "is that no one will leave me alone."

He shrugged. "And that you wallow in self-pity."

"Fuck you," I said, drawing it out. It felt good to say to a person who could snuff me like a cigarette. I muttered it again, even lighter.

"Thank you for confirming it." Caine's tone was taut, like it was threaded with a thin strip of wire. "But don't dare say that again. Your losses have nothing on mine."

We had losses in common? Doubtful. But it'd been a long time since anyone wasn't patronizing me. "I'm sorry."

"I understand your wish for less weight on your life," he said, inclining his head. "But what you should really be wishing for is more strength to bear it."

"Wishes don't mean shit."

"True." He closed the distance between us again, his nails clicking like children's jacks against the scuffed wood floor. "You must take action. Which is why I sewed my eyes shut as soon as I began to See. I knew the narrowing of my sight would make me stronger than the distractions' full vision would allow."

"You . . . did that to yourself?" I shuddered at his nod. Tekla had nothing on this guy's madness. "Let me rephrase my earlier statement. It's not that I don't want to give any more. I don't want to lose anything more."

Including my eyesight. I turned quickly and headed for the door.

"Better to know what you *do* want than what you don't." Caine clacked over to the window, and I wondered if he'd counted out feet from one side of the room to the next. Without touching the wall, he pointed between one of the boarded-up holes like the view was a good one. "Like him."

My hand slipped from the doorknob. "Who—"

The homicidal whine started up then, a long, loud throat-burn that made me wonder how he, it, breathed. "Mackie."

Caine stepped aside as I ran to the window, hunching to peer through one of the fist-width slits. Caine remained still, head tilted, the nails of his right hand clacking lightly against the wall, like mice fleeing up its sides. Meanwhile, Mackie tore into the Bentley. Face hidden beneath his inky bowler hat, he hunched on the shining hood, knife plundering sheet metal like scissors slicing rice paper. Ripping strips of the hood back with one hand, he then dropped inside, his guttural whine pitched high as he went to work on the oiled leather seats.

Shit. How'd he get there so fast? I'd never even driven the Bentley before. From the way Mackie was shredding it, I wouldn't do so again. "He wants to kill me."

"More than anything."

Caine's nails snapped louder, and I glanced down to see the black bone tattooed on his forearm flex with his fingers. I didn't think he was doing it consciously, but the motion proved mesmerizing. In the dim room I could almost believe the bone moved, inky against the skin, defined and liquid all at the same time. Looking up, I saw his nostrils widen, opening and closing like fish gills, seeking to discover exactly what sort of monster Mackie was. He was also sensing Mackie's destructive rage in a different way than I ever had.

One, I thought, looking back down, I'd never even conceived of before.

The bones on Caine's body continued a sinewy, almost sexual dance that traveled up and then back down the length of his body. Yet all the energy was derived from and concentrated in his fingertips. They vibrated finely, black nails banging into each other like wooden wind chimes. He almost appeared elegant, feeling out the world not through sight like everyone else, but through little implosions of movement on the air. I tested the theory by waving my hand at my waist, as if motioning him away. His pinky darted in my direction, taking on an unnatural angle before twitching and falling back into the reading rhythm of his other fingers.

His head was still upturned, but if he had eyes, they'd have been closed. A moment later he finished this vibrational reading and dropped his arms to his sides. "Oh. He's *new*."

Why'd he have to sound so damned impressed?

"No, he's old," I said on a long sigh. Mackie's head shot up, his long neck craning from the destroyed car like the tourists in their moon roof limos. His feral grimace went wide and he snarled into the air. Rabid wolves might make that sound. People didn't.

Caine raised his brows. "You may want to call the police. Tell them vandals have your car."

Shaking my head, I pulled out my single-use cell. "He'll mow down the mortals."

Warren could very well take care of this. I'd saved his ass enough times, and besides, he'd told me to let him know of any other rogues. "I'm calling the Light."

"Wait!" Caine reached out, no longer elegant as he scrambled to grab at my wrist. I still didn't understand the purpose of the nails. They seemed more of a hindrance than help. "The attention from the mortal population will be enough to scare him off. He'll want to remain under the radar as long as he can. Besides, other than Tekla, your former allies have never been mine."

Other than Tekla? I drew back, distracted that this man would know the powerful Seer. It made sense, I suppose, as they had the same gift. But *how* did he know her? "Aren't you Shadow?"

"Born free, here in this valley. Same as you."

Not exactly an answer, thus all the answer I needed. I stepped back. Despite his blindness, he smiled. At least I now knew what we had in common. "A rogue," I said harshly.

"I prefer the term 'independent.' "

"So do I," I said, and turned away. I had what I'd come for. I'd exit the wooden house, guns blazing, punch holes in Sleepy Mac while he was gnawing on the steering wheel, then run like crazy. If he caught me? Well, maybe it was a blessing. Maybe a girl wasn't supposed to spend her lifetime on the run.

"Please," Caine said as my hand hit the door. "Remember why you're here."

Protection. Armor. Help.

I looked down and considered the phone, still clutched in my other hand. I'd asked those same things of Warren and he'd turned his back. "The mortal police are no match for Mackie."

"That's why I'm here. Destiny has provided me with this choice. Our choices bring us relevance."

I laughed bitterly, and Mackie heard all the way outside. A homicidal cry spiraled into the air. "I'll settle for surviving the night."

"I can give you that wish."

Wishes don't mean shit.

True. You must take action.

I put the phone away and squinted across the room, the meager light colorless against all the room's shadows. I didn't know what Caine sought from his destiny, but he waited, a motionless monster, for my answer. Just waiting. Letting me have a choice, when choices had been a diminishing commodity in my life, was almost too much responsibility to bear.

But Caine did see me. Despite his blindness, or because of it, he was offering his power to me now, when Warren and everyone else refused to give even an inch of respect or acknowledgment. How could they not know, when this man clearly did, that it was all anyone really wanted out of life?

"Fine. I'll allow you, a *rogue*, to be my protection." Then I pulled out the saber and pumped its attached firearm. "But I'm going to do it armed."

Of course Caine was a Shadow. He said independent, yet everybody came from somewhere and had an individual lineage as clearly drawn as the lines on their palm. But when up against something as destructive as Mackie's blade, those things ceased to matter. Race riots were quelled when it was the entire human race thrown into the fray.

A Shadow helping me. I shook my head as I backed into the center of the room, giving Caine access to the door. It was an awkward thought, like someone poking me in the brain.

"So don't think about it," I muttered to myself as Mackie's war cry ricocheted up the staircase. Just aim.

But the building shook under Mackie's ascent, and when his blade pierced the wooden door, I wished I'd run. Then I thought of Luna, eyes moving within a ruined body, and widened my stance. The scent of my defiance made Mackie squeal louder.

I waited for Caine to get in front of me, but glanced over to find him peering back out the window instead.

"The problem is over here, Skelator." I probably shouldn't let my nerves—and thus my mouth—get the best of me when someone was actually trying to help, but what was he doing by the boarded-up window? He couldn't even see the moon he was gazing up at!

"A lovely evening, really," Caine said, like we were meeting for a midnight cocktail. He stuck his fingers through the slats, palms disappearing out the window, as if feeling for the night. "I can smell the spines on the yucca."

A scrabbling on the floor, like Mackie was trying to sneak underneath. But when I whipped my gaze back, his blade was still actively sawing through the door's center. "Caine?"

"I love the tarry wood scent of the creosote bush."

"I don't fucking care!" More scrabbling, more cutting. Caine was playing touchy-feely with the night sky and I was trapped inside a collapsible fire hazard across from someone who made him look sane!

Glancing at the floorboards as the sounds ran along the scarred planks, I wondered if Mackie was down there. For all I knew, the blade imbued with his soul energy could cut all on its own. I backed up, heard more scrabbling behind me, and altered direction. It was like playing hot potato with the floor, trying to avoid getting burned.

Until I tripped over something and fell on my ass. Pushing to my feet, my fingers slipped alongside something abrasive, like an exposed extension cord. Odd, I hadn't seen it before. Usually hyperaware of my surroundings, especially in a battle, I knew my mortal eyes had failed me again.

Gaze and gun focused on the knife at the door, I used my foot to tap out the dark space on the floor. I found that strange ridge again, and followed it backward . . . all the way to Caine. More specifically, to his foot.

"Ew!" I jumped again. Mackie howled in the hallway. Caine continued to lean against the wall, breathing in the moonlight, hands outside. I bent, squinted, then my eyes widened as I held back a squeal. Caine's talons had lengthened into black spears that cut shavings into the floor as they slithered all around the room. I followed the one I'd first encountered back to the room's center, realizing it had cut a path around me on its way to the front door.

Caine *was* standing in front of me, I realized. At least, his toenails were. And what allowed all that forward extension? I lifted my gaze to find the tattoos on his body pulsing like individual hearts—two hundred and six of them, I bet—one for each bone in his freaky body. I also realized I was having trouble seeing, like the skeleton drawn atop that malleable skin was pulling in all the light. Opaquely, the tattoos burned.

A tremendous crash sounded at the door, then Mackie's howl slid around the frame. I shook and fired off a round, wincing from the sound and in belated anticipation of losing a limb. Yet the conduit didn't misfire, and after another cry from Mackie—this one steeped in pain—I knew my bullet had struck home. I aimed again.

"Please don't put holes in my door," Caine said calmly. "I've got it from here."

And he did. His ten nails had made their way across the entire floor like roots, planted like they were born of the wood grain. By now they'd disappeared beneath the door's frame, and whatever they were doing, Mackie didn't like it. With a furious grunt, the knife disappeared, and then the pounding began. The building shook with each blow.

"He's cutting them," Caine said unnecessarily. I refrained from telling him I thought they could use a good trim. The lacquered bone-nails were the only thing keeping Mackie from this room. Caine leaned against the wall like he had a listening glass pressed there, and I heard a sinuous slide making its way over the roof and the building's sides. "It's okay. My fingernails are almost there."

Mackie seconded that with an infuriated howl.

"Are you hurting him?" Not that the idea bothered me. But if those nails turned into spears, it was something I needed to know.

Caine angled his head once in negation. "They grow too slowly for that. I've often wished for a nice swift jab, an exact thrust. Alas, it's not my gift."

"So . . . you're just holding him there?"

"No, he can move, but it takes effort. Every time he frees himself from one nail, two more replace it."

Or *nineteen* I thought as the building shuddered over and over again.

"It's like trying to escape an octopus. Mind, it's pure defense, but it allows me to touch others without them ever touching me."

"Awesome gift." Minus the foot fungus.

"He's fast, though." Then he muttered to himself. "Can't crush this one . . ."

"It's the blade."

Caine nodded. "Let me lead him away from the door. Then you can run for it. Mind, I can hold him the night, but no longer. And he won't fall for the same trick twice."

So I waited, marking Caine's progress by the scrabbling of nails over the rooftop and the occasional blade piercing the rotted wood. I wanted to run when Mackie hit the apex—I wanted to pump the entire round of glowing ammo into his stomach, but Caine asked me to hold my fire until I was outside, and it was the least I could do. This was his home, and despite the sparse interior, I got the feeling he'd been here awhile.

Finally, Mackie was entrapped in the web of nails on the house's side, Caine pulling him near, ostensibly so the new growth could reach Mackie quickly every time a nail was cut. The nearness to those long, strong fingertips also increased the likelihood of crushing the raging man. I began relaxing, readied by the doorway, when something unexpected happened.

"Ouch."

For a moment I thought I'd misheard. But Caine's face was black with wild and soundless shock, and I squinted at him warily. "Ouch?"

"He touched me."

That was a severe understatement. Caine pulled his right hand—the higher one—back inside to reveal bloodied fingers . . . cleaved at the first knuckle. Blood poured down every digit, causing a macabre bracelet to appear on his wrist, but the nails continued to grow from their centers, black coils unfurling like licorice. Mackie, now close to his captor, had launched another, apparently new and untried assault.

"Never felt that before," Caine said with a disturbing lack of concern. Then, inexplicably, he stuck his hand out the window again. Though anticipating the next blow, he jolted when Mackie struck, and I jumped with him.

"I—I could just run, you know."

"Not yet." He licked his lips, the slow swirl of his tongue at odds with the grunts coming from his throat. Mackie was relentless. "He'll catch you."

But these were like Tripp's wounds. Something in that blade infected the agents Mackie struck, so while mortals died, agents were left wishing they had. "You have to cauterize it," I said, remembering Tripp's work at the jewelry shop.

Caine sniffed, nostrils going so wide it seemed he could take in every mote in the air. His nose was angled toward his outstretched arm, though, and after another moment—and three more strikes—he shook his head. "It won't help."

And yet he held his hands out there still. He even leaned closer, turning from me to press the front of his body against the wall. "I've never been touched in this way before."

And suddenly I got it. He wasn't offering protection from Mackie from purely altruistic purposes. No. He wanted to see what Mackie's blade felt like. It had nothing to do with my fate, or our commonalities—few that they were. He didn't feel a kinship with me beyond the here and now.

The bones atop his body seemed to sharpen with my realization, the full body bleed of tattoo work now making sense. So did the piercings along his ears and brows and spine. And the eyes. Oh my God. The *eyes*. This man had a love affair with pain.

"But what if I need you again?" I meant only to think it, but somehow whispered it aloud.

Caine's head alone swiveled, ecstasy etched on his pained, pierced brow. "All you needed from me was imparted once you walked in the door. Walk out with it, and in a way, I will too."

He knew he'd die here, hugging the wall in this crumbling shack, another victim of Mackie's poisonous blade. "I'm sorry."

"Ah but it's such a novelty to finally be touched." And Mackie reached the digits on his other hand. Caine gasped, sewn eyes bulging, but when he'd finally regained breath, he rubbed his cheek against the splintered wall. "Do you understand? Being untouched is the price anyone in possession of strong defenses must pay."

I raised a brow. He was imparting a life lesson? *Now?*

"One should feel the pain as it comes. Losses aren't bad things in themselves. Not as long as you remain open to new sensation. Be careful," he said, nodding at the forgotten treasure chest, "Or your defenses might wind up being your prisons."

I wanted to say that only someone who'd never been touched could give such advice, but his sudden cry didn't back me up. "Thanks for the weapons anyway."

"Oh, those aren't from me."

"Then who—"

But before I could wonder about Arun, or voice my new suspicions about Tekla, he gasped. Mackie's face appeared, sliced on the diagonal between the mismatched slats, and when his gaze landed on me, he opened his jaw wide and hissed. Caine turned his head to me, face etched in an orgasm of ecstasy and pain. "Go . . ." he moaned.

I lunged for the door. I avoided as many of the hacked nails as I could, stepping on and snapping the ones I couldn't, then practically threw myself down the stairwell. Mackie screamed, and his guttural war engine cries chased me into the creosote-laden, moon-hung night.

10

I left the destroyed Bentley in Caine's front lot. Let the scavengers drawn by Mackie's cries take whatever remained. It was amazing how little value there was in something worth so much money. Because sometimes, I thought with a shudder, a person would simply rather be touched.

Mackie continued to wail behind me, his rage sailing like a disease through the night. When a second, agonized voice joined his, it set off a nearby car alarm, and had a woman in the apartments I was cutting through muttering, "What the fuck?" as she peered through her steel screen door. Hastening my steps, I hoped Caine's restraints held.

I remained in the downtown area, mostly because I had no other safe place to go. That was okay, not all of it was bad. A revitalization project had been going on for years, more successful in some areas than others, depending on whether the locals got on board. I spotted an alcove next to a loading dock amidst a cross-hatching of narrow streets, where young entrepreneurs competed for the title of hippest local bar. I'd appreciated the friendly rivalry in the past; it was always a novel thing to enter a place absent of the Vegas shuffle, but even those were too desensitizing and busy for my needs tonight. I wouldn't be able to avoid propositions in there, never mind attacks.

So instead of burying myself in the rich scent of smoke and warring perfume, I camped out against a cold metal door, where spent fuel, dust, and the cracked blacktop ruled the night. Were it summer, the scents would be stronger and the ground would burn my ass and palms despite the deep night. The entire city soaked up the sun's heat like it was hoarding it, but like any good desert rat, I preferred that to the cold. The only way I could get less comfortable on this winter night, I thought bleakly as a gust of wind whipped up the street, was to slip beneath the actual loading dock next to me.

Though it might not be such a bad place to hide if Mackie got away before the sun's rise. I bent and peered underneath. There was a frantic scuffle at my approach, but the movement was too small to be a person. A cat, I realized, as it mustered courage to bolt. Watching it streak away—thinking of Luna—I tried not to take it personally. Though it was difficult not to imagine the hard flash I'd spotted in the feline eyes as somehow knowing. Like it sensed what happened to living beings when they got too close to me.

Yet somehow the damage done to Caine had calmed me. Nobody and nothing—not even an old, powerful Seer—could stand up to that blade. So while the reminder of Luna saddened me, I was no longer consumed with fear. In fact, I was getting pretty pissed off. I'd been driven from my home, was a fugitive in my own city, and anyone who aided me ended up dead.

I was also a tad distracted. Chalk it up to fatigue—mental relief that Mackie was, literally, tied up for the night—or just plain laziness. Whatever, when the man passed by my alcove the first time, I remained seated with my back to the steel door and didn't really note it. My mind was spinning with deepening questions about Arun Brahma, mushrooming ones about Tekla, and flashing visuals of Caine's rapturous death. So when the man backed up, I dismissed it as drunkenness or forgetfulness, and closed my eyes. But when he came to a stop in front of me, so close the gravel under his boots pinged off mine, I sighed and opened them again.

He was burly, wide-legged, and bald. His pocketknife swung open with a resounding click. "Give me your pocketbook, bitch."

I reached into my handbag and pulled out the heavy iron gun. "Give me yours."

He backpedaled, tripping once, until he'd returned to the mouth of the intersection. I shot the wall to his right, spraying red brick just because I could. I probably shouldn't have wasted the ammo, but his holler was gratifying as he disappeared in the same direction he'd come, footsteps fading like slap shots. Survival in the land of mortals, I thought, crossing my legs as I dropped the conduit to my lap. "Like a day at the spa," I muttered, closing my eyes.

And that's when something changed in me. It was like a caterpillar cocooning up in a self-made shell, or a woman's gestating body. I didn't move at all on the outside, but inside there were subtle shifts, excess cells altering to make room for something new. I realized then it wasn't Warren or the troop or even the Tulpa I'd been struggling against. I was simply a woman who took up arms. Even before the Zodiac troop came along, I was someone who shoved back harder when pushed. I felt the pain of all the things taken so incrementally from me, and piled them like bricks to build my defenses in this world.

I wasn't like Caine, that was for sure. I wasn't so unfeeling that another person's touch was a novelty, or that it made me seek out sensation in an abnormal manner. I was a city girl who'd been attacked at a young age, who survived it only to be caught up in more violence. Yet I'd survived that too.

Time to start acting like it.

No one else stopped by, but an hour later *my* phone trilled next to me. I pushed to my feet like I'd been waiting for it all along, and maybe I had. Because even before I lifted the phone to my ear, I knew who it was. And the new me, the old me, the *only* me, answered back. "When and where?"

The "when" was immediately. The place? A plant nursery where overzealous residents used mulch and shovels and hard labor to fight the desert's natural inclination to starve every resource from the soil. Climate be damned, we wanted our petunias.

In the morning hours the corner adjacent the nursery was occupied by day laborers, mostly Mexican, willing to work for cash with a landscaper or resident in search of someone strong and willing to haul colored rock into pretty formations. Xeriscape was environmentally responsible, but the installation was a bitch.

But in these hours before morning, the street front was empty, the silence broken only by a car whizzing by on the interstate. I had a cab drop me across the street at a modest shopping center housing a hopeful independent coffee shop, a doomed independent bookstore, and a thriving nail salon. After the cab left, I crossed the street, circled the building once out of habit, then tried the giant iron gate at the nursery's back. The green paint was peeling from the cold bars in strips, and though the gate was closed and chained, its padlock hung free. I unwrapped the chain, dropped it to the ground, and entered.

The bulk of the nursery sat in darkness and shadows, the damp and greenery making it even cooler than the surrounding night air. I didn't try to hide—an agent's hearing was as good as their sight—and it would have been hard to slip in unnoticed anyway. Gravel crunched like beetle backs with every step. Yet it was still a good place to meet. The rioting scents of competing flowers and fauna masked errant emotions, and the green netting draped above like an oversized mosquito net held it all in.

I followed the main trail to the front of the building

where the cashier's stand and dark office were locked tight. Squinting, and whirling around myself, I then took a smaller path through the annuals, the section putting on a bright, brave face despite the scarce winter showing. Then, from a nearby stand of Italian cypress . . .

"A bit petite, isn't she?"

A second cypress answered. "*I* thought she'd be larger than life."

"Nah. Just in the manuals."

The cypress shifted. "How can you look taller in a comic book?"

I leaned closer. "Hello?"

"It's because she's not a real superhero," the first cypress explained. "She just plays one on TV."

Snickers rose, and I crossed my arms. "Can you guys please stop talking about me like I'm not here?"

There was silence, then shuffling, before two men appeared. The first was bald, and had eyes like black opals and skin to match. He was the more wiry of the two, and his partner was as bright as he was dark. So blond, in fact, he damned near glowed next to his counterpart. Together, they were an eclipse.

"Sorry," said opal eyes. "We thought you'd be taller."

It was the same thing Caine had said. I glanced down at the cleavage busting from my business suit. "Yeah, it's my height that people usually comment on first."

"Heard you were a smartass."

I shrugged. Better than a *dumb* one.

"I don't care what she looks like," announced cypress, the bright. "Or if she's smart. I can still smell *it* on her."

"Leave her be." Tripp emerged then, an unlit cigarette hanging from his lips, hat drawn low.

I resisted the urge to smell myself, and angled toward him. "Well, it's been a long day and I had to wait for your call under a loading dock."

"It took time to secure this place first," Tripp explained, but the second cypress was still inching my way.

"Not that," he said, his voice deep, but oddly warbling. "The *Light*."

He said it like I had leprosy.

"Fletcher is right. You still smell like one of them."

I looked at Tripp meaningfully. "You're *all* Shadows?"

"Former," he said, knowing exactly how I felt about that. "This is Fletcher. That's Milo."

Milo raised his chin. "Like you're a *former* agent of Light."

"Discards, then." I glanced at the two men, not a bit like each other . . . but not like me either. And not like Caine, born independent. These men had been raised in a Shadow troop, and if Las Vegas's, then they were old enough to have once worked for the Tulpa.

Shaking my head, I turned back to the gate.

Tripp caught up, closing the expanse between us in one step. "Where ya think you're going?"

"I don't know." But I wasn't bedding down with Shadows. I kept walking.

"Ain't nowhere Mackie can't find you."

I said nothing.

"And Warren won't help." He pulled the strange cigarette from his lips, licked them, replaced it. I shuddered, remembering how the smoke felt pressed against my pores. "If he even knew you were talking with us, he'd kill you himself. That's truth."

Hastening my pace, I reached into my pocket for the phone Warren had given me. I had a brief, insane urge to dial his number to ask him. *Hey, Warren. If I took up with a splinter group of rogue agents, would you slay me on sight? Oh, they're all Shadows too, but they told me that no longer counts.* I laughed, humorlessly, imagining his response.

"So would the Tulpa," Tripp continued, easily keeping pace.

"And Mackie and Helen—and still every Shadow agent in this city." I halted and pointed back at the ones watching me. They'd held back, but I knew they could hear my every word. "So many ways and people to kill me. Why should I give them the pleasure?"

"They're not the ones swingin' at you."

I angled a hard glare at Fletcher and Milo, then glanced at the mesh roof obscuring the winter sky. I felt like one of the plants trapped beneath that net, caught someplace un-natural, and likely to wind up in the hands of someone who would treat me carelessly.

"Skamar said she'd help," I said, but the promise sounded hollow even to me. At some point Mackie would be too close to me, she'd be too far, and by the time she finished her death-dealings with the Tulpa, it would be too late.

And the other agents of Light? The ones I once counted as friends? Tekla had some sort of dealings with Caine, the Seer who'd just sacrificed himself for me, for relevance. She'd appeared in my dream, saying not everyone had abandoned me. But that was just a dream. It remained to be seen if she'd lift a finger for me in real life.

And what would Vanessa and Felix do, the couple that'd gradually become my closest new friends? Or Micah, who'd healed me more times than I could count? How about Gregor, who had a warden like Luna that was as protective of him as he was of her? Would their in-difference to my mortality turn into aggression, just on Warren's say-so?

Feeling unsteady, I leaned against a giant green machine called the Mulch Master. "You said before I could leave the city." Maybe it was still an option.

Tripp said, "And go where? You got paranormal contacts elsewhere? Someone who knows how to deal with ol' Sleepy Mac?"

"Do you?" I snapped back.

"Yup." He spat something black and nasty into the green bin. I imagined it working like cement, binding the mulch together. "Why do you think we're here?"

"You lie, Shadow."

"I'm *rogue*," Tripp corrected. "A *free* agent, though I still know a brethren Shadow when I see one."

"I'm Light."

"Goodness *and* Light," Tripp taunted, scattering ash.

I ignored his sarcasm. So he was here on someone else's orders. Not to save the petite mortal girl from a magical blade. *Fucking Shadows.*

"Did you tell this someone about Mackie?" I asked. "His quest?" His blade.

Tripp nodded.

"And he's still willing to side with me?"

"He's been waiting to do so for years."

Options bounced around my skull like superballs. Slowly, dreamlike, I pulled Warren's phone from my pocket and stared at it, trying to anticipate a conversation that had me explaining about Sleepy Mac and asking for sanctuary. That was the one place, I knew, the man from Midheaven couldn't go. Hidden underground, protected by a security system even the strongest of Shadows couldn't breach, and located on the other side of reality, it was home to the agents of Light.

And inaccessible to mortals, I thought, sighing. I couldn't enter even if he did relent.

Which was what Warren would argue without even trying to find another way. I sighed. He'd then probe me for everything I knew about Mackie and Tripp, but what then? Would he have a sudden change of heart? Offer the troop's protection if I agreed to work as a mortal beard or spy for the troop? Or would he kill me, as Tripp suggested?

"Sleepy Mac killed my warden," I told Tripp, tilting my head, watching carefully for his response. "He killed a Seer too, a man as powerful as any I'd ever seen."

Tripp only removed that strange cigarette again and slowly licked his lips. "Do you want to live?"

Was it wrong that I had to think about that for so long? Fletcher grumbled as he plucked leaves from a topiary, but Tripp shot him a silencing look over his shoulder.

If I wanted to live.

I glanced again at the phone Warren had given me, remembering how afraid I'd been before of losing it. Of losing, I now knew, anything else.

Losses aren't bad things in themselves. Not as long as you remain open to new sensation.

Irritated, I huffed. Like working with Shadows?

Then again, Caine had been of the Shadows. Maybe he'd been born "free," as he put it, but his lineage was stamped on his disposition as clearly as postage. And yet he'd sacrificed himself to Sleepy Mac's blade for my sake.

Maybe, while I wasn't looking—while I was getting reaccustomed to my mortal skin—my old defenses *had* become my prison. With the agents of Light turning their backs, and the sanctuary closed to me, the city I'd always found refuge in did suddenly resemble more of a tomb. But what had me pushing upright and turning to the mulch machine was that unanswered question, and the full comprehension of a niggling I'd already sensed. My T-Rex brain, I thought with a small laugh. Sparking to life.

Because though I didn't know what Warren would do to me, I knew I didn't trust him to protect me, not as I once had. Mortal or not, I no longer counted in his worldview, and he'd like nothing more than for me to disappear, become part of the woodwork . . . at most a bit of scaffolding on which to build his own idea of the way the world should be. To him, I was just someone to run down with his ambition.

Once you decide a person has no control over you . . . they no longer do.

And Warren's mind didn't create *my* reality. I would not be overrun because, all-powerful leader of Light or not, I mattered. I counted. And would as long as I lived.

"Your days are numbered, old man." It was my T-Rex brain talking, pitching my voice low, my lips barely moving. No matter that he wasn't there to hear it. Tripp heard, and one corner of his mouth lifted as I tossed the phone over the side of the mulcher, waited to hear it clank on the steel bottom, then laid my palm against the red button on the panel to my right. "You'll go down so hard the earth will quake."

The mulcher started up with a screeching roar, blades battering my only remaining connection to those I'd once counted as allies in the paranormal realm. Now, like Olivia said, I could live my dreams—or at least what remained of my life—my way. So I left the mulcher running, ensuring that if found, Warren would know exactly what I thought of his treatment of me. Then I nodded and left the nursery the way I came, through the back gate, under the cover of night.

But flanked by Shadows.

11

The supernatural community at large could move around in ways mortals couldn't, but we just took a cab. Yet when Tripp directed the driver to an address on Main, I couldn't hide my surprise.

"El Sombrero? Seriously?"

He shrugged, indicating it wasn't his first choice. Of course, he'd spent the last eighteen years living in an environment about as comfortable as a deep fryer. A mom-and-pop shop with tonsil-dissolving salsa was probably well behind his vote for Ben & Jerry's. However, Milo and Fletcher were already debating the merits of a verde relleno versus a red enchilada, while the cab driver—also a fan—put in his vote for the menudo. I just wondered what a handful of rogue agents were doing at the oldest Mexican restaurant in town.

We hopped out on Main Street, and I stared at the neon green and red sign. El Sombrero Café was a hole-in-the-wall if ever there was one, in the best possible sense of the word. It'd been in the same location since the fifties, and the interior was as dated as the exterior, both adding to its charm.

"You sure it's open?"

"Well there's open," Tripp replied, as I gave the door a fruitless tug, "and then there's open." He pulled on the steel handle, and the entrance swung fluid and wide.

"Show-off."

"You should see me two-step."

The Big Hat was definitely closed. Every surface wiped down and reset for the next day's crowd, the kitchen quiet and dark, the scent of rice and beans faint as a memory. Yet a sole man sat in the room's center, as if stranded there. Posters of matadors and raging bulls surrounded him, and giant hats were pegged indiscriminately to each of the four walls. Tripp motioned me forward with a jerk of his head, though he remained behind with Fletcher and Milo, making like the mafia of old. It helped me feel at home as I wove my way to the center table.

"José. *Mescal por mi amiga.*" The man lifted only his voice, the rest of him utterly still and fixed on me, as if he was a lizard I'd surprised in Red Rock Canyon. Or, I thought as I sat, a rattler. "Unless you're a margarita girl?"

I was. Rocks and salt, but when in little Baja . . . "Tequila is fine."

José, obviously the owner, brought the bottle. I studied his fingertips as he filled my shot glass, and he smiled— either missing the direction of my gaze or pretending to— and replied in soft Spanish at my nod of thanks. I waited until he'd disappeared to wince at the fat pink worm floating along the bottle's bottom.

Glancing back at Carlos, I lifted my brow, an invitation to explain why a mortal would be serving a rogue. His lips were a soft heart beneath a thin, Errol Flynn mustache, and he licked them before giving me another answer entirely.

"My name is Carlos Fernandez. I became a rogue at age fifteen by entering the city of neon with my mother, an agent of Light in La Ciudad de Mexico until the Shadows overtook it in the nineties."

I remembered, though obviously not in the same way

Carlos did. World events and paranormal activity were invariably intertwined. Victory by the agents of Light or Shadow made its mark on the mortal population, though all the humans knew was that in 'ninety-four the peso had plummeted, sending the country into despair. The chasm between the haves and have-nots widened like the grandest of canyons, and things had only worsened since then. I'd be surprised to hear if there was even one agent of Light left in any major Mexican city.

Carlos spun his shot glass in his hand, making no move to drink as he watched me from across the table. His dark hair was cropped close, but you could still see a bit of a Caesarean curl. His eyes were light brown, the simple table-top tea light catching deeper flecks of color like grains trapped in amber. Though darker, with long sable lashes, his gaze put me in mind of Hunter. The same patience lurked there.

Or maybe it was the same calculating spark.

"My father, determined to fight the enemies of Light to the last, sent us ahead without him. He was forced out a year later, finally leaving that dangerous place to travel to us, and this safe one." Another slow slide of his tongue over his bottom lip, like he was trying to seduce me, before he blinked. "He lost his life in the weedy meadows after which this city is named. Almost immediately."

I froze, unsure what to say. I sensed a drama involving me, but like a person wrongly accused, wasn't yet sure how. Carlos, still reclined, pulled a card from his shirt front pocket as he spoke and slid it toward me. I leaned forward, frowning as I recognized the small square format. It was a trading card so old the stock paper was thinned and frayed at the edges, and worn so finely in one spot I could almost see the grain of the paper.

The black and white photo showed a man wearing tight jeans and an unstructured blazer winging open to reveal a mesh tank top as he leaped through air. Very eighties. His conduit was some sort of mallet, and his name, troop number, and city were scrawled in Spanish across the card's bottom. His vital stats were on the back, similar to a ballplayer's, and identical to the cards featuring superheroes sold in comic book shops all over the world. Gently, I handed the card back.

Carlos took it between two fingers and tucked it back in his pocket. It was probably the last of his father's trading cards in existence.

I glanced back up into his face, noting the resemblance now, especially those darkly expressive eyes. "I'm sorry to hear that."

He inclined his head, and lifted his shot glass from the table, allowing the edge to kiss his lips. I echoed the movement as he said, "Your mother had him killed the day after he arrived."

I sputtered homemade tequila over the glossy tabletop. Wiping my mouth with the back of my hand, I bent my head and cleared my throat of its burn before letting out a huge sigh.

"I guess here's where I say I'm sorry, and while I have no control over my mother's actions now, never mind back then, I'm sure none of that matters. You've clearly been planning your vengeance for a long time. I expect you'll kill me in the same way she murdered your father. You latinos have deep poetic leanings."

"We do?"

"Yeah. Ever the closet romantics." I shrugged. "So what will it be? Decapitation? Pull out my guts? Boring ol' slice of the arteries?"

His amusement vanished and I was sorry I'd asked. The reminder of his father's death was obviously still painful, and it only occurred to me belatedly that it might be better not to know how I was going to die. "He was ambushed while seeking sanctuary in the Strip-front cathedral."

"The Guardian Angel?" I'd heard it'd once served as a place for rogues to connect with one another, but that was long before I'd come along. Warren had made sure of that.

"That's right." Carlos drummed his fingers on the tabletop. "She could have warned him not to enter, but she didn't. Two agents of Light chased him out. They ambushed him in the brush surrounding the springs. Let his blood run where the natural streams once had."

I swallowed hard. He made the Light sound as brutal as Shadows.

Carlos pursed his lips as he stared through his glass of amber liquid. "He was impossibly fast, my father. They'd never have caught him if he'd known Las Vegas like you . . . or me."

"Is that how you've evaded Warren for so long? Because you know the city?" Its pockets and hidey-holes. How else could a rogue survive?

"That . . . and I'm even faster." He slumped lower in his seat, but the movement didn't look sloppy. His long— apparently speedy—legs sprawled like a desert spider taking hold of a rocky crag, and the top of his white shirt flared to reveal the hard lines of a smooth, honeyed chest. If I wasn't currently so put off by male agents of Light, I might have been moved.

I turned in my seat, glancing back at Tripp and the others, but they hadn't moved. Swiveling back, I found my glass again full. Carlos smiled. "Um, just so I can firm up my plans for the evening . . . you're *not* going to kill me?"

"No." He sipped.

So did I. "Why?"

His soft lashes curled up as he lifted his gaze, making him look angelic as he nodded at José. The owner silently crossed the room, lifted a bright orange sombrero from its peg, and removed a picture box hidden underneath. He then presented this to me as he would a menu, and the two men exchanged words in the smooth cadence of their native tongue while I flipped a clasp on the shadow box's side and opened it up.

"Cuidado," Carlos said, but the warning was unnecessary. My gasp told him I knew exactly what I held. Knew too who was depicted on the inside cover: me, my image drawn upon the manual . . . and done so long before I'd ever been born.

The book wasn't inked, only penciled, and wasn't even a proper comic, having been drawn well before the format's Golden Age. The pages were bound together with a peeling yellowed glue, and every brushstroke had a sense of age to it, a style as easily discernible to the modern eye as a Pixar movie versus Bugs Bunny's debut.

At least the subject matter was familiar. A woman cloaked in shadows, running through a tunnel while glancing over her shoulder. Her face was indiscernible, her body long and muscular and absent of the pinup features commonly associated with females in comics. Despite the shading, I knew this was me. The old me, though, Joanna, before my transformation into an action figure with body parts more important than the whole. The drawing perfectly captured how I moved, or at least how I felt when I moved.

Adding to its accuracy, and its mystery, this had clearly been sketched by someone used to the strong, serious lines of cartography or botanical drawings. I felt like I was holding a piece of art worthy of Sotheby's, and flipped through it quickly to find the attached story. A jagged tear interrupted, though, and disappointment ripped through me as well. Some point in the manual's storied past had found it rent in two. I glanced up to find Carlos watching me with sympathy, and knew he'd felt the same loss upon seeing the tear.

"How old?" I managed, my voice a mere creak.

"Closer to the first manual than anyone I know has ever seen. My father must have had it for years, maybe since he was a boy. He obviously knew what it was." Carlos rubbed his bare chin thoughtfully. "He hid it under a pew in the cathedral just before the attack which took his life. It was an agreement between my mother and him. Her idea. She wasn't as fast, but she was smart."

I reached forward, unable to resist running my finger over the images. "What does it say?"

"It foretells the Kairos's birth in this city. That here she would be raised, survive attack, go into hiding, and discover her true destiny upon metamorphosis in her twenty-fifth year." He waved his hand over the open pages. "This legend on these pages was why he sent us here when our own battles were deemed lost."

I shook my head, and the mescal took hold. I shook it harder to regain my vision. I couldn't play savior to this man, or anyone, anymore. I'd tried it before, and look where it had gotten me. "Look, I did some of those things, it's true. The commonalities are even uncanny . . ." How many other women in Vegas *had* done all that? And how could every depiction on these panels ring so true and right in my marrow? "But you're too late. Maybe if he'd had the full issue, or the one printed after this, he might have seen that."

"You are the Kairos."

"I am a mortal."

"You underestimate your strength."

"Understandable . . . since I have none."

Carlos remained unmoved. "Did you read the text on the final full panel?"

"It's in Spanish."

He held out his hand. "Then I will read it for you."

Cradling the manual like a prayer book, Carlos cleared his throat and began to read from the blurb on the inside cover in a strong, clear voice, his accent transposing beats in the sentence, like it was music. " 'Light returned to the valley, where the meadows had long been falsely lit, to lure and fool the unwary. But with this true light came genuine hope. Balance seemed possible . . . right up until the Great Sorrow. This event marks the onset of the Fifth Sign: the Shadow binding with the Light.' "

His deep, dark eyes blazed expectantly.

"More fucking signs," I muttered, and poured myself some more fucking tequila. I took another sip of my liquor, holding it in my mouth so long it numbed my gums and swelled my tongue. Carlos obviously thought the fifth sign was my willingness to work with the yahoos making like Tony Montana behind me, but that wasn't possible. I swallowed the warm tequila with a grimace. I was no longer Light. Or Shadow. I was no longer Joanna, or really Olivia. I was not a daughter. I was not a weapon. I was not the Kairos. I leaned my elbows on the table and said as much to Carlos.

"And that's where I come in." Carlos finally leaned forward, forearms on the edge of the table, fingers twirling his shot glass, though not a drop spilled. "I can teach you the tricks and trade of being a rogue. The power in being powerless. The Kairos is not meant for only Shadow or Light. She is preordained to be the deliverer of us all."

I leaned forward as well, meeting his dark, pretty, zealous gaze with a cynicism earned by listening to too many zealots. "Carlos, you seem like a . . . nice man. Fairer than any I've met in my recent past, that's for sure. But you're too late. Even if I were the Kairos—obviously untrue—I'm not anymore. I gave up every drop of my power and aura and life force—*chi*, whatever you want to call it—to save a mortal child. There's more power left in the bottom of this bottle than there is in my entire body."

"I have total confidence in you."

"That manual did nothing in my hands," I pointed out, important because they once had. All written histories burst to life and color, "Pow!" and "Bam!" exploding from the panels in brilliant bursts when in the hands of an agent. Carlos shrugged, unmoved, and even in my increasingly drunken state, I knew why before he spoke.

"Because you've become an independent." It hadn't come to life in his hands either.

"You mean a rogue," I said, raising a brow, testing him.

"I mean a part of this valley's prophesied revolution. The woman who will rise from ash to become the leader of a new world order."

"Gee, why does *that* sound familiar?" I tapped my chin like I was really considering it, then brightened. "Oh, yeah—because I already did that. And failed."

Carlos only lifted a dark brow. "Tell me. What is Warren's stated agenda for the agents of Light? Defeat the Shadow agents for good? Annihilate them from the valley?"

I shook my head. "Balance. He said a true and continual balance between the two sides will allow mortals the greatest choice in their own lives."

"Yet he continues to seek the Shadows' destruction."

"As they seek his."

"There is no balance when destruction is the goal. It's like adding a fat kid to your end of the seesaw. The other side is forced to overreact."

"There's no other way with the Tulpa." The leader of the Shadow side had long made it known that any Light in the valley would be exterminated. His position was as inalterable as Israel versus Palestine. The only way to stand firm against attack was to preempt it yourself.

"Ah, but there is. True balance in life comes only when there is total freedom of choice . . . from either side." Carlos sat back so suddenly my mortal eyes only picked the movement up in panes. "Let me ask you something. What do you see when you look at me?"

My eyesight blurred as it trailed his features; cinnamon face, hair a soft, black blot. "You're the Latin archetype. The one they write songs about."

"Thank you," he said, beautiful smile widening. "But I meant, what do you see of my intent? My nature?"

"Oh." I flushed, but then chalked it up to the drink, and shrugged. The idea of a flirtation or romance was about as attractive as a harelip. "Well, you're Light. I'd be able to tell even if I hadn't been an agent. I bet even lifelong mortals flock to you." Especially the women.

His smile went closed-lipped, modest and knowing, and he lifted his chin, angling his eyes over my shoulder. "And what about Tripp?"

"Clearly Shadow. Even Fletcher and Milo would have been easy to spot."

"Once, you would have been right. But things are different when you're reduced to gray, and that's what being a rogue truly means. We walk the line between both sides, accepted by neither. We are all gray." He laughed then, which made no sense to me until he explained, "That's what we call ourselves. Grays."

"So what about me?"

"Born gray," Carlos replied immediately. "A natural blending of Shadow and Light."

"Natural?" I laughed so loud and long that disapproving mumbles rose between my decidedly unfeminine snorts.

"What, you had to work for the ability to enter the sanctuary of the Light? Or bring to life the glyph on your chest? To leap to rooftops? To survive man-made weaponry?"

"I had to learn," I remembered, thinking specifically of the way my glyph, a bow and arrow, burst to life in glowing brilliance upon my chest when in danger. That didn't happen anymore.

"A different thing altogether." He waved the protest away. "And now you have the added ability to walk the line between superhuman and mortal."

I began to scoff, but he cut me off with a lazy flick of his wrist. "Oh, I can tell you think you have nothing by the way you carry yourself. There is a fatalism about you that says you expect to be attacked and killed and there's nothing you can do about it. But do you know what I see when I look at you?"

"A pin-up with attitude?"

He didn't smile. "I see a woman with *everything*."

"I'm not the Kairos." I said flatly.

He surprised me by agreeing. "Not right now."

"So what can I be to you?" What exactly was Carlos after?

"You can be saved. Join our cell, or at least consider it, and I promise our full resources in protecting you from Sleepy Mac."

"You're rogues. You have no resources."

He lifted a brow. "You didn't know of our existence until now, right?"

I bit my lip. True, nobody in the troop had mentioned it. And Warren was obsessed with the subject. If he thought a splinter group of former agents was living in his domain, he'd blow the whole place up.

I glanced back at Tripp, Milo, and Fletcher. These people—Shadow, Light, gray and *super*—still had a *use* for me. Sure, they'd bred chaos the world over, but they were already working to change that—at least if Carlos was to be believed. And while I wasn't sure I did believe him, I could go along with it for a while, at least until Mackie was subdued. Then I'd get back to my mortal life.

"What about Mackie? True death to the monster, or just a one-way ticket back to Midheaven to get him out of your hair?" I thought about the men in Midheaven, and what Mackie's absence might mean to them. Each would have a better chance of escaping that twisted world without the knife-wielding piano player there to intercept. That Hunter was over there still had nothing to do with it.

"Oh, no." Carlos's dark brows creased low. "Most of the men in Midheaven are rogue agents. Tripp wasn't able to tell us about them"—because what happened in Midheaven stayed in Midheaven, I thought wryly—"but he could tell

us of Mackie's purpose there once he began interfering
with this world's mysteries."

He meant once Mackie came after me.

"Okay. Get rid of Mackie," I said, turning back to Carlos.
"And I'll try to keep an open mind."

Carlos allowed only a small twitch to his lips. "And may
I ask why?"

I thought about my drowning, about being abandoned in
a desert wash along with broken bottles and stripped tires,
and left with a body too weak to hold its own weight. Yet I
spoke of my most recent loss. "Because the bastard killed
my cat."

12

I stood, my chair bumping over the aged floor, wondering if we'd leave via one of the cabs at the neighboring yard or if we'd walk. Or, I thought, amused, maybe one of these grays would pick up their new "amiga," fling me across their shoulders and vault into the night. Mackie was probably free by now. He'd start tracking my scent as soon as I was on the street. He could be tracking it now. I shuddered . . . then shuddered again when I saw what Carlos, still sitting, had done.

"You're joking, right?"

He leaned back, a full smile branding those soft wide lips as he motioned toward the last of the mescal he'd poured into my shot glass . . . along with the worm. "*Gusano rojo*. It's the ingredient which lends the true complexity to the drink."

I crossed my arms. "I'm more than happy to keep it simple."

Carlos nodded, but I could see he was enjoying this. "It's a delicacy."

"It's a fucking worm."

"Larvae, actually." He laughed at my grimace. "But don't worry. It's nonparasitic."

"I don't want it."

Carlos fell still. "This one is . . . special."

I studied his smooth face like a map, then picked up the stunted glass for a closer look. The worm looked like a moth with no wings. It was bloated and soft from marinating so long in the alcohol, its destroyer and preservative all at once. I wondered if it'd sunk to the bottom of the bottle thrashing and alive, fighting in inelegant bends and sweeps, or if it had sunk resignedly to its fate. It might have been palatable stewed with some garlic or sweet onion, but sushi style? I didn't think so.

I followed the length of its velvety sides, which ribbed outward and wide, until my eye caught on an unnatural bulge in the middle. Some sort of device. "Tracking?" I asked, glancing back up at Carlos.

He nodded. "It's old technology like most of our weaponry, but it works surprisingly well. The sensors inside react to adrenaline and body heat, so even if we're not near you, we'll know when you're in trouble and be able to swiftly pinpoint your location." He motioned for me to drink again. "Please. I've been saving this bottle for a long time."

I stared at his hands, the liquor I'd already consumed making them appear larger than they were. Yet they tapered nicely, almost elegant in their jointed shape and warm skin. Not at all like the worm.

"Trust me, Joanna," Carlos said, somehow both composed and imploring, strength and vulnerability living in the same melodious tone. "It will open your eye to things previously hidden."

I sat the glass back down. "I'd prefer my taste of the forbidden in the form of an apple. Tradition, ya know."

He pursed his lips, eyes lowered on the small glass containing the large worm. *Larvae.* I shuddered again.

"Did you know worms have been around for more than 120 million years?"

"This one in particular?"

Ignoring me, he leaned forward to explain. "They evolved along with dinosaurs. They have no brain, eyes, or feet, yet they have burrowed through centuries while those greater, grander, and larger around them have fallen."

The bigger they are . . .

Which was the not-so-subtle point he was trying to make about the troops—the Tulpa and his relentless pursuit of power, Warren and his equally determined fight for the same. I sat down again, keeping my eyes averted from the glass. It was an invite to keep talking, but I still wasn't biting.

"Night crawlers travel underground, hunkered deep and unseen by those who walk the surface. They help with decomposition, eating away the dead, aerating the earth with their movement, enriching the environment through this lowly work. Ask any biologist, and they'll tell you everything on the surface thrives because of them. They ingest the old so the new can be born."

I slid lower in my chair and eyed the drink warily. "All right. I get the analogy." Worms and rogues, both underground, both working beneath the sight of those who ran the world. I'd have still asked if I could skip it, if not for the tracking device. Why couldn't they have planted it in a chimichanga?

Carlos was gazing at me, dark eyes luminous in the tanned face, beautiful hands still as artwork on the tabletop. I knew he could force it down my throat, but he was waiting for my acquiescence. Not running me down with his desires and demands. "First rule of the cell. Do not underestimate the lowly."

I see a woman with everything.

Why? I wondered, biting my lower lip. Because I was on my heels, back to the wall, helpless as a being without brains or eyes or feet, but somehow surviving still? The comparison didn't repulse me as much this time around. Not with Carlos's gaze on my face and his dark head dipped toward mine. He was a realist, rogues had to

be, and my weaknesses were already laid before him like
burnt offerings.

It made me feel more seen than at any time since donning Olivia's flesh. My flaws were my only defenses now
that I had none, but I suddenly felt myself lowering my
guard willingly. Maybe they weren't defenses after all, but
pretense. Like a child sticking her fingers in her ears and
saying she couldn't hear.

I picked up the glass, eyed the death inside. Would sucking on it draw out the power to burrow to safety as well?
If I chewed it into little pieces, could I then ingest the discarded bits of this world, pump life back into them, and
create something new?

In the end, I swallowed it whole. Carlos was right about
one thing. It was delicate, but for the device buried inside.
That stood out like a wire ball of fury. It pierced the worm,
took root in my throat, and stuck there like a metal spider
until I forced it down. The tears along my esophagus were
cold when I breathed. When my eyes had ceased watering,
I looked up.

Carlos smiled, holding out a hand. I pushed to my feet
again, then lunged for him as the room began to spin. I was
in trouble, a teetering dreidel on the inside, but all Carlos
did was hold my hand. Remembering the myth about tequila worms having hallucinogenic properties, I slurred,
"Is this laced?"

And weren't drugs supposed to make you feel a high
before you hit a low? This one pulled me down to my knees,
like a slap from on high. Right before my limbs numbed
out, Tripp reached my other side. I imagined I could scent
him as I once had in Midheaven, when he'd been sweaty
and defiant and smelling of old burnt cedar.

Carlos, so forthcoming about the rogue agents and their
desire to help me, about being the one to give me a chance
to become "who I was meant to be," not to mention a detailed history of the worm, simply dropped a silken kiss

upon my lips, setting them to buzzing as he braced my arms. "Repeat after me, one word only: Midheaven."

He whispered it into my opened mouth, his breath touching my tongue, tickling my throat. My lips moved around the sound, briefly touching his as they formed the word. Then my eyes crossed, there were three of him before me . . . and then there were none.

I hadn't dreamed since Olivia's lesson in trusting the T-Rex brain, and the knowledge that I was doing so now would have surprised me awake were it not for the narcotics sizzling in my system. They caught me like a firefly in a jar, and there was nothing I could do but wait until they wore off. So I opened my dream eyes . . . and found myself facing an endless ocean of desert terrain.

Not my beloved Mojave, I thought, looking around as the drug-induced sizzling increased. Blood was snapping in my veins, but the foreign landscape of sand sheets and shifting dunes was enough to distract from that. Ridges and mountains of filmy grit angled hard in the spotlight of a red sun. I shielded my eyes and took a step into the ever-shifting softness. I'd have felt weightless if each step didn't shuffle beneath my feet. Licking my lips, I tasted lead, as if my body was made of metal.

Then a sound as bright and faint as a rainbow stretched overhead. I looked up, twisting as it whipped by, but it was gone as quickly as it came. "Hello?"

My voice echoed, but unnaturally so. Less of a reverberation off canyon walls than a CD that kept skipping until the volume was turned down. Meanwhile, the sand continued to snake around my feet, each fine, pretty grain winking as it shifted. Every once in a while I'd hit a sinkhole and was forced to flail just to remain standing. Was it possible to be buried alive in a dream? If I died here, would I still wake?

I slipped, abandoning the thought to catch myself with

my palm, the imprint blending into nothingness as soon as I'd scuttled back to my feet. A moment more gave me back my balance, and I held very still, though individual grains still threatened to give way beneath my weight. Then there was the full pregnant sound again, like ghosts whispering over the dunes.

"So you're back."

Whirling at the scratchy echo, I found a Chinaman perched directly in front of me. Blinking, I rubbed at my eyes.

Yes. Chinaman.

He was dressed in silk, a green brocade that lay sallow against his skin. His wide-brimmed conical hat hid most of his features, but the brown skin at his neck and jaw was wrinkled with age, his braided queue shot through with strands of thick silver. He was curled tightly over himself, a walking question mark, and jutted his chin to peer up at me.

"You!" I accused once he did, but fear rushed me all the same. I'd left this man in the Rest House the last time I'd fled Midheaven, neither expecting nor especially eager to see him again. Shen hated me.

Panicked, I turned again, searching for a way out—and succeeding in only sinking some more. Though the desert terrain was unique, the magic in this place was known to me. Only Midheaven took something normal and turned it on its head. "I do not want to be here. I don't, I don't . . ."

I pinched myself as my voice scratched the air, but the chemicals in the worm kept me under. My bloodstream was burning, while my thoughts were vicious jabs, needles trying to wake me up. It wasn't the first time my dreams had been invaded this way—and I didn't mean my mind's hopeful conjuring of Olivia either.

No, the Tulpa had visited me in my dreams before too, months ago, also under the influence of sleep-inducing drugs. Something about the altered state made the mind more susceptible to influence and suggestion. And, apparently, gave the spirit the ability to travel between worlds.

"I don't want to be here!" The echo married with the metallic taste, and I bit my lip to keep from screaming.

"Of course you do. One's truest desires are always revealed in Midheaven." I'd have thought the sand would mute Shen's soft clipped voice, absorbing it like a sponge, but his dismissive tones stood up well, bright as bells. He hadn't liked me since we sat together at a table of soul poker and I accidentally gambled away some of his personal information.

That's what Midheaven ran on. Names, desires, attributes, powers and skills—all the building blocks of a viable life-form. I had to admit, I'd probably still be irked too. But I'd paid him back with a chip of my own, and the power he'd taken was more than a revealed name. Shen had stripped me of my ability to heal quickly, like a superhero.

Not that it mattered now.

I could tell it also didn't make us even in his eyes. He scuttled over to me like a bug, a sourceless wind catching the sandy dunes behind him, making them shimmer and slide in the cold red light. "If you didn't want to be here in some small part of your thieving heart, then you wouldn't be . . . and neither would I. So just tell me what you want. I have to get back to my game."

"I'm the reason you're here?" I asked as he came to a stop in front of me.

"Men are never allowed into the elemental rooms without invitation."

Because women ruled Midheaven. Gazing around, I wondered which element this room represented. The last time I was here, I'd visited only one of the four rooms upstairs—Solange's fire room. It'd been remarkably absent of fire, but for the stars burning up the night sky of her makeshift planetarium.

Yeah, makeshift. Comprised of people's friggin' souls.

But what could a vast expanse of arid desertscape be? The earth room? Or was that too straightforward?

"Am I really here? I mean, I was drugged. I didn't cross here via the line." I swallowed hard, hopeful even though my body continued to buzz like a live wire, and the question rebounded back at me.

Shen tilted his head, looking at me like I'd just gotten off the short bus. "Your ignorance is appalling. Drugs allow incorporeal passage for those with the ability to interact with this world. If you didn't want to be here, you shouldn't have taken the drug. Or called forth the world in your mind."

Carlos, I thought, gritting my teeth. That's why he'd had me repeat the word he whispered into my mouth. But why? What was I supposed to do here? And, more importantly, how the hell did I get *out*?

"And you're going to help me?"

"I am a man. You are a woman." Shen rolled his dark, jaded eyes. "And the task would be infinitely easier if you actually told me what you want."

But I had no orders to give him. I had no idea why Carlos would send me here, or what I was supposed to do now.

Then the other sound rolled over the sky again, not in the tinny tones of my voice's echo, but the whipping arch from before, like the bright sweep of a lionfish's tail as it sped along the ocean floor. It sounded like color, and moved like it came from within me. I followed it, neck craning from one side of the "ceiling" to the other, though the room sat like an island between red horizons. "What is that?"

"Finally," Shen muttered, as if I'd made a wish. He reached into his robe, and I braced for the appearance of a weapon, wondering if he could go Jet Li on my ass in my own dream. The question became moot when all he did was pull out a forked branch and held it in front of him.

I palmed my hip. "What are you doing to do, poke me in the eye?"

He shot me a look of ill-concealed disdain, gripped one side of the branch in each hand, palms down, and pointed it in front of him. Head bobbing beneath his conical hat, he began muttering as he circled me. I frowned, then straightened. "Wait—are you dousing?"

I tried to recall what I knew about divining rods and dowsers. They were used to find water. Only seconds after this great mental leap, the rod took a dive of its own, seemingly flying from Shen's hands to bury itself, single point down, right between my feet. It found a soft, or softer, spot, and sunk straight down, though the sand around it, and beneath me, remained unmoved. Relieved, I glanced back at Shen.

He lifted his head, the giant hat sliding away to reveal a mocking grin. Then he flipped me off.

A whirring sound started up underneath me, growing louder as the grains began to drain between my feet. The rod's handles became propellers, blowing sand outward in a whipping blast to sting my bare skin. The ground altered elevation, and I backpedaled as if balancing on a rolling ball. I did a fair job of remaining upright—my dream, remember?—until a pair of rough hands found my lower back and gave me a good hard push.

"You little—"

Flailing, I slid in a roller coaster arch down the waterfall of sand, the light of the red sun disappearing like it'd been swallowed in one bite. Or maybe it was me. I thought of Carlos's worms, burrowing through the years, existing underground, ingesting the old and birthing the new in the gritty darkness. Was Shen right? Had I called all of this to me? I waited for the drugs to wear off, and—as I continued to fall—prayed for a soft landing.

Sliding to a surprisingly easy stop, as if flowing off a large silk veil, I spit grit from my mouth, wiped it from my eyes, and tried to regain my bearings.

"Here." An unsurprised voice—one that didn't echo—sounded next to me, before a cool, damp cloth was pressed against my cheek. I wiped the sand from my face, noting the sound of running water as my dirtied rag was replaced.

As I wrung water into my eyes, another voice, farther away, piped, "If you hadn't fought it you would have arrived as you were meant to, clean and on your feet."

I sighed, because I knew that voice. It was both chipped and singsong, with a light tone and dark smoky texture. I'd left its owner, Diana, in Midheaven too. "Ah, but this makes such an impression," I muttered, then squinted, gazing about. "Where am I?"

The metallic taste was worse down here, weighed down and compressed like a silver bar in my mouth.

"The water room, of course." Her voice didn't echo either.

So it *was* one of the elemental rooms. Squinting, I looked about. At least more of one than the dust bowl upstairs. It had glass sides and a sandy rooftop, yet it tinkled and flowed, its perimeter completely awash in clear water that fell over the walls in a steady rush. Slate shelves caught the musical liquid, spilling it to the ground in beautiful, almost balletic, designs.

The room's center was dotted with basins: black marble, clear crystal, hammered copper, and rose glass. Each bubbled in competing heights, and where there wasn't water, there were mirrors, including underfoot. Straw-thin streams backlit with firefly lights filled in the blank spaces, and behind all the watery reflection was the constant movement of white sand shifting against crystal walls. It added to the eerie movement of the room, so that I felt caught in the middle of an hourglass.

There was no music, but the various pools sang as though charmed. The thought kept me alert as I turned my attention to the room's occupants, three in total. The one with a waist comprised of dangerous S-curves still loomed above me, but two others lounged in webbed hammocks winking with gold fringe. None looked particularly surprised to see me, and the voluptuous one even offered me a hand up.

"It's a water vein," she said, pulling me to my feet. "Both

the water and the electromagnetic current from our bodies allow the dowsers to measure our depth and location."

"And time," Diana added, swinging in her hammock like a bright, overgrown black widow. She wore voluminous skirts in layers of taffeta, and black fishnets studded with crystals that flashed when she kicked her heels. The venomous spider analogy, I thought as she smiled, was something to keep in mind. "They can also douse for a specific place in time."

And time didn't pass the same way in Midheaven as it did in the real world. Here it bent and twisted upon itself, eating large chunks of a lifetime even in a blink. I hoped that wasn't also true when visiting in your dreams.

"How would you prefer to die?" The woman next to me tilted her head prettily. "Fire or ice?"

"You giving me an option?" I said, returning the dirty cloth to her. My echoing voice made the question sound more forceful than I intended, but she took the cloth without moving to harm me. I remained wary. The women in Midheaven, powerful to the last, were never exactly what they seemed.

This one seemed to be a forgotten flower child, with dried blooms woven through her hair and light brown curls streaked with gold and red. Round cheeks dimpled beneath a cheerful spotting of freckles, but the sweet visage changed drastically below the neck. Cleavage bloomed over a black bone corset, covering the sinuous slide of those hips to end in a skintight pencil skirt. The outfit, and the body it encased, was totally out of place beneath a face of such abject innocence.

She took the cloth, smiling, and folded it in the crevasse between her milky breasts. "It's only a question."

But in case it was a trick one . . . "Old age. In bed."

She shifted, causing gold flecks to spark from her limbs. Musk, like a tobacco rose, wafted to strike me in the gut. I hadn't scented anything so heady and delicious since losing all my amplified senses. Though fully clothed, the sight and scent and sound of her were a promise of pure sex. The men in the Rest House, like Shen, and Tripp when he'd still been here, probably fell to their knees in front of her, begging for a taste of all that softness.

"In seven and a half billion years," she said, breathy voice filled with wonder, "the earth will be dragged from its orbit by the sun, and spiral to a vaporous death."

I blinked.

"Fucking cheery, Trish." Diana rolled her eyes at me, then turned to address her companion on the hammocks. "Does she know how to bring down a party or what?"

That woman said nothing, her silence a rebuke after Trish's bubbling friendliness. She could have been either white or Asian, porcelain skin almost translucent atop chiseled cheekbones and piano-black lips. I thought about checking my reflection in them. Her hair was a severe bowl cut in the same glossy ebony as her mouth, but the thick bangs cutting straight across her face obscured her eyes, rendering her expressionless.

Covered from neck to ankle in form fitting black, she reminded me of a severe Audrey Hepburn without any other adornment beyond long dark nails. Yet every bit of her skinny body was revealed in a way even Trish hadn't dared. Her ribs could be counted, her elbows jutted sharply, her nipples looked set in concrete.

She reminded me a bit of Mackie, I thought, shifting uncomfortably. Alert even without the use of her eyes. I glanced at Diana, who was lazily swinging a leg just above the ground, and when I looked back, the woman's long, elegant fingers were tucked beneath her chin. A mannequin striking a different enticing pose, not moving into the position, but simply there, rigid and aloof. I frowned.

"I'm stating fact, right, Nicola?" Trish said, breaking me of my study as she whirled to join Diana, curls flying to emit another whiff of sweet muskiness. "Just because you don't talk about it doesn't mean we're not all going to incinerate as the globe is engulfed by fire. Though we won't even make it that long," she turned, saying to me, "the sun will be ten percent brighter in just a billion years, causing all the oceans to boil away. No water, no life. Want a drink?"

"No." Taking a drink was how I'd gotten into this mess. Or was it? Shen claimed I'd called him to me, and these women were acting as if I'd stepped in from another room, rather than another world. I blinked again. "I am dreaming, right?"

"Of course," Nicola said. Amazing, because her chrome mouth never moved. "But that doesn't mean you aren't really here. You're a part of this world now, or didn't you know?"

Maybe giving up two-thirds of the *essence de vie* gave me free admittance for the rest of my natural lifetime. If only Disney had the same policy, I thought wryly. "So I need a drug to induce some sort of deeper level of sleep "

"The theta level," Trish said helpfully.

"And then I call the world to me just as I go under."

"So telling someone to go to hell at that moment isn't probably the wisest course of action." This from Diana, hers a more mocking helpfulness. I scowled, and she smiled prettily. "Hope you have someone to pull you back out, though."

"What?"

The smile widened. "You know. In case *she* finds out you're here."

But then the arching sound was back, bursting through the room like a low-flying phoenix. Ducking, I studied the cascading water walls, but the sound was already gone, lost in the rush. I held still, eyes darting, waiting for it again.

"So *that's* why you're here." A slow smirk finally curled at the corners of Nicola's black lacquered mouth. "Should have figured."

"Solange was right," Trish singsonged.

The name alone sent shivers along my limbs, and apparently Diana felt the same way because she shushed Trish with a harsh glare. Maybe she'd done something to anger the woman too. Too bad for her . . . for us both. Solange's was the sort of anger that blotted out entire planets. Basically, the difference between her and God was that God didn't require the breath from your body, the bone from your marrow, the white from your eyes. Solange did.

Fuck the sound, I thought, and began looking for a way out instead. The other women chuckled, but didn't look like they blamed me. "She sent Mackie after me," I told them.

Trish shrugged, smiling sweetly. "He probably just wants to talk."

Yeah, and porn stars just wanted to cuddle.

"Carlos?" I called the name tentatively, looking toward the ceiling. It echoed in that mix master's scratch. Water continued to pour down the glass walls. I sighed.

"She sent him because you're a danger to us all," Nicola said, still stiff and autoerotic, like everyone else was incidental to her existence.

Diana flicked her fingers at me. "Joanna's no danger to me."

"She is if Solange catches you with her."

"Stop saying her name!" This time Diana curled her delicate hands into fists, squeezing tight before forcibly relaxing them. "Besides, she doesn't rule me."

"She rules everyone whose soul has been melded into her sky!" Nicola said bitterly. *Her* sky, I thought, shuddering, remembering the planetarium.

"So you've all had parts of yourself put in her sky?"

Diana snorted. "It's the first thing she does when someone new arrives. But you protected yourself from it somehow, and she hasn't forgotten it. She thinks you're after her power."

"I don't know why she wasn't able to touch me." I'd come awake while she'd been fashioning my gem, somehow deforming it and keeping her from using it. "Besides, not everyone is after power."

Nicola and Diana scoffed, but Trish lifted her chin. "Maybe Joanna just wanted to watch, like us." She turned to me, wide-eyed. "Is that why you chose the water room?"

"I've no idea why I'm here."

Yet even as I said it, the bottom dweller sound echoed again. Arching my head, I followed its path as it vaulted overhead, then fell like invisible rain into the basin sitting between Diana and Nicola and their four hammocks. I strained toward it like I had gills. What *was* that?

No, not a basin, I thought, frowning as I took a step to follow. A well.

Trish motioned me forward. "Come. Look."

"No!" Nicola hissed.

Ignoring her, Trish slipped into a third hammock, and pointed to a fourth. I inched forward to peer in the thick crystal basin.

My anti-Olivia self was reflected in the water—dark eyes and choppy, blunt cut. Strong, lithe limbs, and a severe expression to match my mood. But I stared past my reflection, wondering where sound could go. Unlike the rest of the room, it was ice still. I waved my hand above the small pool.

"Not there." Nicola was back in slideshow mode, bowl-cut fringe still perfectly arranged over the bridge of her nose. Her face was upturned, the shifting sands of the mirrored skies sending light to dance over her profile. She looked like a Roman bust, hard edges cut and sliced into soft curves.

"The water is merely a conduit for sound. You have to relax into the hammock, and once you've caught the rhythm of the room, look up."

So I did, leaning back carefully, gaze on the blurred ceiling as I began to rock.

"You have to wait for it, since you are attracted to it, and not the other way around."

Whatever "it" was, I thought sullenly.

"It's not fair," Trish sighed as we waited, airy voice rising, flowing upstream. "When are we going to get a turn?"

Diana hummed her agreement. "She gets to do whatever she wants."

"Shh," Nicola chided harshly. "She'll hear you."

But then I heard *it*, coming at me like it was shot from a pistol, but also from another room, another world.

"Ready?" Nicola turned her sharp chin my way, and this time her fringe parted enough for me to momentarily glimpse a startling blue eye before the hair fell back into place like a curtain. "Say hello to your mysterious sound."

The sound buried itself in the basin. Then the haze above us parted like curtains, and light from the basin beamed like a projector onto the ceiling.

He lay in a skiff shaped like a lily petal, made of glossy teak and edged with imposing symbols. Immediately recognizing one of them, the same as that carved upon the treasure chest at Caine's, I gasped. *He* stirred in his sleep, rolling his head on the red velvet tufted pillow until his body positioning mirrored mine exactly. I lifted my hand to my mouth in shock. He did the same. I ran it through my hair. He echoed the movement in his sleep. Meanwhile I took in the sight of him—white-blond cropped hair, thick neck, wide shoulders, skin as dark as Carlos's—committing to memory how vulnerable the fierce man looked. Hunter . . . but laid out here in his true identity: Jaden Jacks.

"Oh, this is interesting." Nicola's reluctance veered to interest as our movements synched again. I dropped my hand to my chest. He did the same. "It really is a soul connection."

"Solange is going to be pissed." Diana.

Singing again, Trish. "Something tells me she already knows."

It's Miss Sola wants you dead, girl.

"But that one would almost be worth the risk," Trish

murmured, shifting luxuriously. "I mean, since we're destined to be incinerated anyway."

I swallowed back the metallic taste in my throat, ignored the drugs crackling like sparklers in my bloodstream, and lifted my hand in the air. Still asleep, Jaden Jacks did the same. I'd kick myself later over how lovesick I was acting in front of women who would have no qualms about using it against me, but for now my heart pounded in raw beats, my body knowing what it wanted despite my mind's holler to cease and desist.

"Hunter—" I whispered, the scratchy echo of my voice clanging clumsily against the ceiling. I winced . . . and his eyes rocketed open.

His gaze burned with the same honeyed hue I remembered, though it was alive with horror as he found my face. He lifted his head from the red pillow, lunging for me, but his head banged against our ceiling like glass.

I strained upward as well, echoing the movement, but the hammock wouldn't release me . . . and neither would his shocked gaze. "Hunter?"

"Jo?" The strange face with familiar eyes went rigid. "Oh my God. What are you doing here? I've been trying—"

"No!"

No warning. Just that one strained, screeched word. The women around me screamed and scrambled as a face of feral beauty filled the sky, looming, thrusting forward to distend the sky. The others fought to untangle themselves from their hammocks, yet caught in Solange's gaze, I couldn't move.

She didn't scream again. She didn't have to. Her original cry never ceased as she too strained forward, unfortunately with greater result. Her face broke against the projection, the reflected water wrapping around her bulging eyes, like Saran wrap. Rage carved her brow, and pressing harder, she leered. Her teeth went black. Her eyes white.

The singing streams shifted into raging rapids, and my hammock began to shake. The other women were free—

Nicola, unsurprisingly, had moved the quickest—but they couldn't find an exit to the room. A sound like nails over a chalkboard etched its way over my spine and a hairline crack formed along the walls. Sand began filtering in, slowly at first, then pouring and pooling as the walls began to shake and splinter.

"What have you done?" Trish cried, ducking low, staggering against walls as Solange's face pressed closer. The hourglass was being tipped. Marble basins cracked, and the crystalline walls shattered. Sand poured from the borders of the sky. And I still couldn't move.

"Carlos!" I yelled as loud as I could, the taste of tin and sand flooding my mouth, while my pounding heart sizzled as though in a fryer. Willing myself awake, I screamed again. The sound clanked against shattering glass.

Then Solange took a deep breath, and in her mad gaze was a reflection of my grave: crystal shards and sandy dunes. "He's *mine*!"

The ceiling burst, the scream blowing me backward in a deafening heat. I turned my head to the side, body scorching like a marshmallow over flame, and somewhere, faintly, Hunter's cry rippled in my mind. Then, like debris, it was swept away in the torrent of sand and water that mixed to cover my burns, soothe my skin, shield me from Solange . . . and bury me in the shards of the destroyed room.

13

I awoke to a heavy wet rag being dragged across my face. A foul heat and the stench of the unwashed dead accompanied the sensation, and though there was intermittent relief—brief moments when the rag was removed and my air passage freed—I'd barely filled my lungs before it started up again. It was a slow torture, and a terrible way to die. I was so concerned with catching my breath, I didn't realize I'd been feeling disembodied until the tingling started up in my limbs. Immediately, and clumsily, I lifted my arms to push the rag away . . . which was when I touched the attached teeth. Jerking back, wiping forearms over my eyes, I squinted into the face of a dog as large and black as a tornado. One come to eat me whole.

Screaming, I scrambled backward, though since I was lying down, there wasn't really anywhere to go. The mutant animal jolted, shook his muzzle back and forth, and advanced on me again.

"Now now. Don't go and scare the baby girl." An arm, just as black, came out of nowhere to calm the now-whining animal. I squinted around splayed fingers—puny defense against nail-head fangs—in an attempt to see who the arm belonged to. "Interesting, though. She don't usually like you mortals."

"Th-That's a warden," I stammered, lowering my arms, staring into the dark. I was laid out like a sacrifice beneath a black light, which wasn't as blinding as a bulb's full glare, but still made it virtually impossible to see beyond the soft ultraviolet bubble. The last time I'd run into a Shadow warden—dogs, as opposed to the cats serving the agents of Light—the rabid bastard had tried to rip out my throat. Actually, there'd been two of them . . . though neither had been this big.

And because I'd made the mistake of releasing an arrow from my conduit into the first beast's gaping maw, I also knew wardens grew instantly stronger and larger—not to mention really pissed off—when struck by the magical weapons. It seemed this fiend had seen plenty of battle. She ambled closer and I shielded my eyes and tried to sit up. "She probably doesn't like agents of Light either, right?"

"Oh, she loves them." Those strong dark hands reached through the violet rays and pushed me back down. A wide, round face followed them into view. "Bone in, still warm, and medium rare."

Wincing, I tore my gaze from the dog to study the now-cackling woman, so dark she seemed kiln-fired, like some glossy, smooth-faced fertility goddess. Her curves were nothing like Trish's. Those had been inviting, whereas these were daring. She wore ornamentation like Diana, but the true adornment was her skin, shoulders shining over a strapless orange dress, muscles thick and defined like giant ropes of black licorice. She had nothing at all in common with Nicola's goth glamour. Her hair was a wild black moon, and hid nothing of her exotic face . . . including eyes like disks with onyx pupils filling the whole of the socket.

I'd only seen depictions before of such women in the manuals. She was, or had been, a ward mother, but unlike those I knew, she had reared the Shadow children. She cared for them until they reached full maturity at the time of their metamorphosis and left the Shadow lair. "I always wondered what one of you would look like up close," I told her. I was mortal, naked beneath a black sheet, and obviously under her care. Why mask my words? I didn't have a whole lot to hide.

She smirked, motioning down her body, and stood back, caressing the head of her strange pet as I took a closer look. "Just as you thought?"

"Not really," I admitted, though the eyes were more disturbing than expected. Where the "mothers" who raised the initiates of Light had a sunken and violent crosshatching of scars over their eyes—a product of raising children whose glyphs were as powerful and unpredictable as a solar flare—the ward mothers for the Shadows lived a rayless, shaded existence. Exposing them to the smallest amount of natural sunlight would be like forcing their face into the core of the sun. It would kill them outright.

I thought of Carlos's worms, burrowing through centuries, hunkered deep and unseen, their work impacting the entire world.

"Why do my hands hurt?" I finally rasped, leaning back. It didn't look like either of these Shadowy beings were going to kill me. In fact, the ward mother brought me a clay tumbler of water.

"Oh, I worked on those first. I was hoping they'd be done before you woke." I finished sipping from the cool, fresh water, and studied my throbbing right hand. Prints had somehow been applied to my fingertips. I used my thumb to try and flick one off—that was an old trick—but they ached too much, like individual hearts lived in each tip. The woman shook her head, tsking as she pulled my arm away. "Hold on, now. You don't want to undo all my handiwork. Let it set. Another hour and it'll look like the real deal."

I swallowed hard, dropping my head back again. The light was a vibrant purple halo around her dark cloud of hair. "What are you doing to me?"

"Giving you the tools you need to live, my girl," she said, and shrugged, one large shoulder moving up and down. "Or at least to hide in plain sight. Rules are different when you're gray."

That's right. That's what the rogues called themselves. I'd have to get used to it. I looked at my body, laid out beneath a black sheet and the dark light. Get used to being gray.

She must be like Micah, I thought, which made me wonder how the physician was doing. I winced, thinking of the damage Tripp had caused him, and how odd and pained he looked with soot roiling beneath that first layer of skin. I would have never wished that upon him. Micah had only ever been kind . . . right up until the moment he turned his back on me. I sighed.

The dog took it as a sign to resume licking my face. After three wet smelly licks, I got up the nerve to push it away.

"Back off, Buttersnap." The woman tapped one finger on Buttersnap's haunches, and the animal sat. Four times larger than a Great Dane, dozens deadlier, and it responded to this woman's index finger. I shook my head.

"Was it you who pulled me back?" I asked, noting the scratchy echo of my voice was gone as she nodded. My blood once again moved about in my body unfelt. The water and wakefulness had washed the metallic taste from my throat. I was home again . . . wherever home was. "You guys drugged me."

"In more ways than one," she said, not bothering to deny it. "We also have you on a drug that coats your organs and larger arteries like armor in case you're assaulted, though there's only so much we can do since you're mortal." Reaching forward, she inserted her hands beneath the dark sheet and stared into nothingness with those strange disc-like eyes. Her fingers, warm and strong, began to work along my abdomen, touching me in long strokes like she was smoothing out my skin. "Still, we can use other means to help stimulate your cells so they rebuild faster. As long as you don't receive a life threatening blow by a conduit, or this so-called soul blade, you should be fine."

So I was only vulnerable to the most dangerous weapons on the planet. How comforting.

Her massage turned circular, fingertips just short of painful on the sensitive flesh of my stomach. I glanced over to find Buttersnap gazing at me with apparent pity. Dogs didn't like their underparts exposed to probing fingers either.

"I'm Io, by the way, and thank you for asking. Mine is the gift of touch, if you haven't noticed." I jerked my head upright at the chiding tone, catching an eyeful of ultraviolet. The wide fingers pressed me again into stillness, before resuming their circular probing.

"I'm sorry I just it was just . . ." *The dream and then the dog and then the woman without eyelids.* "Where am I?"

"Just outside city limits. In a burnt-out crater off of Frenchman Flat."

Anticipating my reaction, she pushed me back down—again, using fingertips alone. "The friggin' Test Site?"

Io saw my reservations. Shit, with those eyes, she probably saw my tonsils. But Frenchman Flat was famously the first detonation site for the nuclear facility. Back in the day, they had mushroom cloud parties, the lethal explosions used as their fireworks sequence before they knew you could *die* from the exposure . . . or the radioactive waste left behind.

"I understand your concerns. Brought it up to El Jefe himself." She grinned, flashing me a row of square pearly teeth, "He said that sort of fallout is the least of your worries. Besides, you'll learn right quick, a rogue takes sanctuary where they can find it." She gestured around the jet void of the room like it was a plutonium palace.

"The cell has been in this sink for a good decade, and I can tell you straight up there's no freer place. Certainly not in the fiery world you just journeyed from."

I braced my elbows behind me, refusing to be put down again. Staring with eyes nearly as wide as hers, I shook my head. "So I was really there?"

"Of course. It's all here, I can just follow your body to see where you've been." And she grabbed. I made a strangled sound as those tensile fingers pinched something *vital*, rubbing the organ like it was a spa specialty. Whatever massage she'd done had turned my skin to putty, stretching and pulling it to allow access by those strong, knowing fingers. I dizzied as she slid her fingers along the kidney-shaped mass, and though it didn't technically hurt, it was as foreign as first time sex. Then I burped up a surprising dry wad of sand, right onto the cloth covering my chest. My mouth remained hanging open, though shock kept me from letting out the scream leapfrogging through my brain.

"I can tell from touch whose daughter you are as well." She grabbed for another internal organ with those searching fingers, but I blocked, pushing her away. I didn't like my insides being fondled like cuts at a butcher's shop. Yet Io was as strong as she looked. She nailed me with that unblinking gaze, held both of my hands over my head with only one of hers, and found my pelvic bone with the other. Damn near wrapping her fingers around it, and far less gently this time, she gave it a little tug. "This tells me you're Zoe Archer's daughter, born of both Shadow and Light, also of deceit, which is the real shadow clouding your life."

She let go and, just as abruptly, resumed the gentle massage. Sweating, I dropped my head back and whimpered. Buttersnap slobbered all over my right cheek.

"You know my mother?" I asked when I finally found my voice.

"Felt your imprint in her once," she confirmed. "Along the backside, though." And this time, when she slid her fingers under me, she ran one right up the connecting vertebrae. "Right there, see? That's her."

And an entire concert of near-forgotten scents filled my

nose. It was the mixture of emotions one would expect when remembering an absent mother, lemon-bright happiness accompanying a memory of bouncing on a knee. It was herbal also, fresh as green paint, as she instructed me on how to ride a bike. Then ginger hair swung over one shoulder as she bent over my homework, taught me to thread a needle, tie a knot . . . make a fist.

Make a fist? Where had that memory come from?

The question, though, was chased from my mind by an earthy musk, almost masculine, my mother's strength as I recalled her standing up to others—teens who drove too fast on residential streets, women who snarked at each other over tea. Xavier, when he dared to malign me.

"God." I was surprised into tears. It'd been so long since I breathed in that scent. Of course, I'd never experienced it so strongly before, but Io was right—sometimes the body knew what the mind did not, including how very much I missed Zoe Archer. I nearly lunged for another whiff, but the dog was back, bearskin breath obliterating the lemon-herb musk.

"And here, just below, is *your* daughter." And she scooped up my womb firmly, but gently, still encased safely beneath my skin, which wrapped around it like warm stretched dough. I opened my mouth to object . . . and another scent and memory I'd not had in over a decade careened through my consciousness. A newborn's wail, unmasked before they whisked her from the room. It was accompanied by a simple scent—wet and without hooks, just a smooth slide into my gut. *Ashlyn.* The accompanying memory, buried like a time capsule, was of perfect hands and legs flailing, a brief brush of warm pink skin against my thigh as the umbilical cord was cut. Experiencing it again was so powerful I almost said her name aloud.

"Stop," I whimpered. "Please stop . . . doing that."

Her hold lessened, though she didn't release me entirely. "What? Making your mind remember things your body holds as its secrets?" She shook her head, pressing more firmly again. "A woman should know her own body, at the least."

A burst then, powdered rose blooming as her fingers inched higher. "Feel this, where the base of the fallopian tube sits? That tells me the whole world is going to know about your hidden little gem pretty soon too. You were late to your second life cycle, but this one here takes after your Momma."

The second life cycle. Puberty. When the rest of the supernatural world scents a future agent coming into the first of their powers. It was what had caused the first attack on my life as a teen by a Shadow agent.

I shook my head side to side, causing the dog to wag his tail. "She's not my daughter."

"Oh, *okay*." She pushed with her pinky finger. Again I heard the newborn wail.

"She's not. Never was. She was placed with another family at birth."

She pulled her hands from beneath the sheet, then cocked them on her hips. I wrapped my arms around my middle, not daring to touch my stomach, feeling hollowed out, and strangely empty. "Baby, that child was comprised of your cells, conceived in your body, and nourished with your blood. Once she's been in you, she's always of you. Same with you and your Momma. You see the connection? That's why our world is matriarchal. Every person, no matter how powerful, is dependent on the matriarchal link."

"Not the Tulpa."

"Which is why he's so hard to kill."

Hard? I thought, with an inward scoff. Impossible was more like it. More impervious to attack than the beast next to me.

Io leaned forward, so close violet light sparked in her hair. "And it's also why he hates us all, Shadow *and* Light."

Now that was a new thought. Was that why she, a ward mother of Shadows, had left the Tulpa's compound? But I couldn't follow the thought to conclusion, not right now. I was suddenly a stranger in my own body and surprised to find those links Io spoke of, ones I'd tried so hard to forget these long years—were still there. No matter what I did, their mark was inside me, like some sort of injury.

Same as everyone else, crybaby. I thought again of the first Shadow agent I'd ever met and battled, Ajax. His mother had defected to the Light side, leaving him embarrassed, outraged, and haunted by the betrayal. But if what Io was saying was true, he'd been dependent on the link as well, as attuned to his mother as a concert violinist's ear to the string. He'd used it to find her, and when he did, killed her. I glanced back at Io, shuddering and wondering if she'd unlocked those secrets in his body, and somehow helped him.

Io was holding her palms over me, not touching my skin, though heat from her hands radiated into my body, like flat lasers searching for signs of life below a bleak sky. She tsked, shaking her head. "Your chakras are blocked. Your spleen is almost entirely comprised of black bile. How do you even walk upright? You need to start allowing yourself to feel the things that have shaped and formed you, my girl. The ones that have *de*formed you. Once you accept them, you can present your new shape to the world."

My mind winged over my long ago rape, my mother's abandonment, my sister's death, my ejection from the troop. My deformities. I paused a little too long on the thought of Hunter, probably because of his appearance in my not-dream, and whisked a tear away. Disconcertingly, Buttersnap ate it from my new fingertips.

"You need to make this old world conform to your new curves." She tilted her head up at me, even though she was working below, and gave me a conspiratorial wink. "A confident woman's body . . . a most dangerous terrain."

I nodded like I understood, but I really just wanted her to look away.

"By the way, *he's* over here. Want to feel him?"

"The Tulpa?" I shook my head. She could feel my father in me. How gross was that? She'd probably wrap her hands around the organ telling his story and come away with acid fingertips.

Io stared at my face, observing every pore with those unblinking eyes. "Well yes, him too. But I meant the other. The one you been trying to tell yourself is not meant for you."

And she pushed without permission, moving aside ribs and lungs with a necessary gentleness. She could kill me, I realized, with a mere twitch of her thumb. My heart pulsed in her palm, faster when I realized she was cradling it, and then it expanded, opened to her. Opened to me too.

I smelled a doused campfire, wet wood and tobacco, soapy suede, sunset heat. I closed my eyes, dizzied, and breathed in Hunter—the way he was when he moved inside of me, when he bent his head to mine, when he met me halfway, then kept coming. My heart beat faster, my palms begin to sweat, my mouth parted, and I swallowed hard.

Then I thought of him pursuing Solange. "Dreams are the only place that man, that scent, exists."

But even as I said it, I heard his dream voice—wrapped in hot tobacco and suede—calling. *Oh my God. What are you doing here? I've been trying—*

Trying to what? Say he was sorry? Forget me, maybe? *Trying to come back to me?*

No. I'd seen his face before he left for Solange, and Midheaven. He was resolute in what he wanted, and that was *her*. What he'd probably been trying to do ever since was sever this so-called soul connection the other women had been taunting me over. We'd shared a unique magic once, called the aureole. For a brief time he'd known my thoughts and I'd shared his. Swapped them as if we'd lived them. Took individual experience and made them our own.

Solange was obviously angry about this, so he was working to appease his *wife*.

Fine. I'd happily agree to cutting the cord if it meant her calling off Mackie.

So I didn't care if he resided in my body like Io said. Like I'd just scented. Those campfire logs were really driftwood disappearing around a river bend. The heat of sunset was the end of our affair, and my job now wasn't to remember, but to excise him. If I just kept moving, maybe he'd work his way out like a splinter under the skin.

Io finally put my heart back in its place, like tucking an egg in its nest.

"Are we done?" I asked. This emotional prodding was worse than the dream. Buttersnap licked a tear from my cheek. This time I let her.

Io smoothed damp hair from my forehead and offered me a surprisingly kind, and yes, motherly, smile. "I know you feel weak right now, but you know what Carlos would say?" She straightened and donned a perfect Mexican accent. "Don't underestimate the lowly. You're a night crawler now."

And a gray. Frowning, I glanced back up at Io. "What does that mean?"

She smiled, and held out a strong hand. "Why don't you come see for yourself?"

14

Much of the Zodiac world was hidden beneath the known one. Midheaven was locked in the water and sewage system built to relieve our bowl-like valley of the seasonal floodwaters. The sanctuary where agents of Light were born, raised, and trained to battle Shadows was hidden below the Neon Boneyard, where the famous signage of Las Vegas's yesteryear was put to rest. The Shadows too had a place of sanctuary, though it had yet to be revealed to me. Following Io, I wondered about that. Surely Warren knew, or at least suspected its location. Had he said nothing to me, and ordered the others to do the same, because of the Shadow in me? Had he trusted me so little from the beginning? Did he think I'd go knocking on the door and ask to join their troop after he so thoroughly tossed me out of his own?

I wouldn't, of course. Accessing the sanctuary of Light had nearly killed me the first time I tried it, and the only way I could safely pass the security system unharmed was by donning a mask Hunter had designed to shield my Shadow side from the system's defensive light. The undoubtedly painful necessity of trial and error aside, I had no desire to experience the Shadow side's equivalent, or hang out with a bunch of rotting, homicidal demons in my copious spare time.

But it was obvious from Io's unblinking, wide-eyed stare that the Shadows made their home belowground as well. A mutation like hers wasn't created in a vacuum. Basic biology demanded a reason, use, and purpose for everything in the world, and following this former Shadow ward mother—alongside a warden that would have eaten me whole a scant few weeks earlier—I couldn't help wonder at mine.

"What do you think?" Io asked, motioning with one great arm at the remnants of nuclear fallout like it was her own Buckingham Palace, half turning to me as she continued walking.

I thought it looked like the place had been bombed, but kept the snarky comment to myself. "You said the cell has only been here a decade?"

Because despite the postapocalyptic feel, the bunker was rather homey if you didn't mind living like a mole. Though the passageways were narrow in some places and wide in others, hollowed out shelves housed scentless white candles, and the walls beneath these were caked in mounds of wax. The ground was worn smooth, and looking up, I noted the ceilings had been sanded into roundness. It was as cool as a wine cave, though not cold, which I found surprising. Winter nights were as fierce in the desert as the summer's heat, the flat Mojave terrain welcoming of extremes.

In addition to the candles, cables ran along the passageways, metal hooks securing them into place, though where they started and ended, I didn't know. There were also objects cemented in the walls—pens, stones, medallions, broken pottery, silver rings—certainly nothing that would be out of place in a trash heap, though each was fastened with obvious care. I wiped my sore fingertips along a Scrabble tile caked in what was probably fallout, and Io paused, answering my unasked question.

"Every rogue carries a sort of talisman from wherever it is they've escaped. That's Melania's. She . . . she wasn't here very long."

I frowned at the tightness in Io's voice, but she'd moved on. "This is Cedric's. He fled the valley last year. And you know who this one belongs to. See the flag?"

A patch from an item of clothing, the colors dropped vertically in green, white, and red. An eagle devouring a snake atop a prickly pear cactus. "Carlos."

I felt rather than saw her nod. "Most agents don't even know they're carrying around pieces of the lives they've fled. It's an unconscious impulse, a way of staying connected to the home and family they've always known. But when they truly become a member of the cell, they're able to give up the old."

She looked sharply at me here and I looked sharply back. I had no such object to release. I was still home.

"Don't worry," she finally said. "Carlos doesn't force the issue and there's no ceremony to mark the occasion. When the time is right, each rogue simply picks out a spot on the wall that feels right and claims it as their own."

I gazed along the length of rough hallway, gaze catching on dozens of talismans. "How many rogues are here?"

Io shrugged. "The cell shifts as people come and go, though each member changes the makeup of the whole. Even when they're gone, they leave a bit of themselves behind."

"Are there really that many displaced agents in the world?" Warren had made it seem there were only a few . . . and those were alone, broken, dangerous, or crazy.

"As long as there've been societies, there've been people on the fringe of them." Io motioned me forward and we entered an anteroom that dipped dangerously in the middle, blown out rubble still trapped in the bottom of the bowl. A wire net crisscrossed the opening, ostensibly to keep people from falling through, but I shuddered, thinking it could just as easily be someone, or something's, cage.

"A sink within the sink." Io jerked her chin at the hole. Her tone was dismissive, so I relaxed enough to turn my attention to what was by default the most interesting part of the room.

"More talismans?" I asked, though the objects in here weren't embedded in the walls, just piled along them. The wall candles were planted haphazardly by necessity, and the shadows they cast caught the strange objects in bumpy relief. It was light enough to see that everything was burned, twisted, melted, or savagely mutilated, and would have been unrecognizable if they hadn't been so patently mundane.

There were car doors, ripped from their hinges, with shattered windows and bubbled, peeling paint. A scorched tabletop missing all of its legs. Steel gliders so gnarled they couldn't support their own weight. Giant slabs of concrete, plaster, an airplane propeller, front doors, and a mishmash of smaller debris caught in jars like fireflies made of rubble. The place was packed, floor to ceiling, with the scorched remains of every material known to man.

"It looks like Ali Bubu's junkyard."

Io snorted. "Welcome to Doom Town. And Survival City . . . at least what remains of them." She shot me a wry smile as she reached atop a teetering pile of scrap metal and punched blackened keys on an old fashioned cash register. "Atomic cities. Fictional, except that they were real, down to the smallest detail. They used to piggyback on the nuclear tests, building homes, military operations, shelters . . . all in varying distances from ground zero. Then, boom!" She made an explosion with her strong hands.

"They built entire cities just to blow them up?" I asked, running my hand along what looked like the front of a train.

"Survivability testing."

Looking for the rest of the engine, I peered around the train's nose before jerking back, letting out an involuntary squeak. A charred face stared back at me, the skin bubbled and blackened on one side. A single blue eye locked on my face, and Io chuckled behind me.

"I see you've met Marge. She was reading the paper and listening to the radio at the time of attack. The scientists wanted to see what a thermal pulse would do to a human being, depending on where the bomb was dropped."

"So they used mannequins?"

She picked up her pace as she crossed the room, no novelty to her. "And pigs."

I shuddered, thankful I'd run into Marge instead of the pig. "But why is all of this here?"

"Shits and giggles, mostly," she said, placing her hand on a perfect iron door. "It was Roland's idea to start the collection—he's inside—but we all joined in. Let's just say it can get monotonous on Yucca flat."

And with that she yanked the iron door open. Carlos's voice reached out to wrap around me even before I saw inside. "She did it?"

Io nodded once.

"Fantastic!" Carlos clapped his hands once, then held out his arms as I ducked through the doorway. "Welcome."

I said nothing, noting eight other pairs of eyes studying me. Tripp, hunched in an outcropping of the circular room was one of them. Fletcher and Milo sat together at a wider sandy bench, also outfitted with dark hemp pillows. The room was as sparse as the other had been cluttered. Yet five other men sat in similar alcoves. Some of the seating areas looked like they'd been blown away, while others like they'd been dug out with a spoon. All appeared positioned around an invisible round table. I met each gaze boldly, memorizing faces, trying to intuit thought, but it was useless. The men were naturals at hiding their emotions—both the physical expression and the accompanying scent. I wouldn't be able to scent them anyway, but if I were a betting woman, I'd pin them all as Shadows.

Former Shadows, I corrected, with some effort. Grays.

Tables made of barrels and flat-topped sawhorses sat to

the side of each alcove, topped off by actual china settings, mismatched but shining. I'd clearly interrupted dinner, and my stomach growled, recognizing carne, tortillas, beans and rice.

"Come. Your meal is waiting," Carlos gestured, indicating one of the empty alcoves. "As is your place in our circle."

The other men remained silent as I eyed the seating more closely. The benches weren't just smoothed out, but sported glyphs and symbols as mysterious and meaningful as those I'd seen in Midheaven and on the chest at Caine's shack. And someplace else, I thought, furrowing my brow. *Why couldn't I remember where?*

"This drugged as well?" I asked sarcastically, pointing at the food as I sat.

Carlos shrugged, unapologetic. "I took the opportunity to see if you could return to Midheaven via your dreams . . . even without your powers. This proved you can."

"Is that why you said gnawing on your little night crawler would open my eyes to 'that which was previously hidden'?" I lowered my voice an octave, and put on an accent as I picked up a tortilla. Warm, fresh . . . delicious. Okay, so they lived somewhat better than moles, I thought, settling back, surprised to find the natural dirt alcove comfortable.

"*Sí, mon.* I needed you to stay under long enough to determine you were still a part of that world. And you are. Entwined in its fabric, you have changed it as much as the knowledge of it has changed you. What do you expect when you gave up a portion of your soul to get there?"

Two-thirds, to be exact, I thought, chewing. Not that the remaining third was a worry. I was never going near the real entrance again. Especially after that dream. "And why would you want to see that?"

Why had he given me a tracking device that reacted to body heat and adrenaline? Why return prints to my fingertips? Why coat my organs with an armor that made them impervious to all but the most magical of weapons? *What* exactly, I now wondered, did Carlos want out of all this?

He didn't pretend not to know what I was asking. Instead he smiled so broadly, teeth blinding against his honeyed skin, that I was momentarily startled. Could the leader of an underground rogue cell, with a past tailored to bitterness, really be so guileless? Even as I had the thought, he spread his arms, as if inviting me inside. "First, let me introduce you to your fellow grays.

"You know Tripp from before, and you've already met Milo and Fletcher." Carlos strode to the center of the room like a lion tamer in a cage. "To their right are Alex and Oliver. On the other side we have Gareth, Roland, and Vincent."

"Not Vinnie," the last man said, in a voice that screamed old school Bronx. I let my gaze pass over him with disinterest before landing on Roland. The collector. He looked at me like I was the one who blew up Marge.

I looked back. "Met your girlfriend outside."

Oliver snickered from the other side of the room, and when Roland's gaze returned to me, it was as narrow as not-Vinnie's had been. "Pretty, ain't she?"

"I think you make a beautiful couple."

Carlos cleared his throat, a too-bright smile widening his face. Well, what did he want? Pom-poms and a spirit song for waking up in a nuclear crater with a bunch of leukemia breeding trash? Not that it mattered to the *non*-humans in the group, I thought wryly.

"There are currently four more of us," he said, "but they've gone on a recruiting trip to Salt Lake."

I nodded to indicate I'd heard, but took my time looking not-Vinnie over, then did the same with each man in turn. Alex was obviously Mexican, like Carlos, though shorter and rounder. Oliver's genetic background was indistinguishable, probably some Americanized bastardization of British and German and Irish. Roland was as black as Io, while his tablemate was what one would expect from a not-Vinnie from the Bronx. I paused on Gareth, who was lanky, not even into adulthood, and sported spiky dishwater blond hair that reminded me of a rooster's comb. I'd wager he was less than a handful of years past his second life cycle. Obviously used to the speculation about his age, and sensitive about it, he thrust out his chin and took a menacing step forward. I ignored the implicit challenge and studied each face again. *Interesting.*

Carlos anticipated my question as I turned my gaze back upon him. "There are no female rogues in the cell. The nature of a matriarchal world means women are the first and most targeted of us. When a female rogue is discovered, both Shadow and Light dispatch as many agents as it takes to destroy her. We lose them as quickly as we gain them, so you're the only one."

"Um, I hate to bring up the obvious—" Wasn't joining the cell going to make me even more of a paranormal pariah than before?

"You're already targeted," Carlos interrupted, with less concern than I'd have liked. "You already know the history of the struggle between rogues and agents in this valley. You know the laws as laid down by the ruling troops, and the dangers we face as independents. We've also given you some of the tools to survive those dangers, and trust me, they'll come to good use."

"When?" I asked warily, not entirely sure I wanted to know.

"When we overthrow the current regime of Shadow and Light, of course," Gareth snapped, still stinging from my earlier observation.

I'd have told him to chill, except his words stalled me cold. "Overthrow?"

Carlos cleared his throat, then ducked his head as he shot me that beautiful, and now sheepish, smile. "That is the purpose of the cell. By unifying the independent agents into a third, larger troop, we will wage our battle for the right to live aboveground. We will fight for the right to live as we choose. And this emerging troop, Joanna Archer," he said grandly, gesturing at the ragtag men again, "is your army."

My eyes went almost as wide as Io's, and I waited for someone to laugh. Roland and Gareth only scowled more deeply. I sighed. Well, of course they were an army. What else could they be?

"Surely you're joking." I had swallowed a worm because Carlos promised to stave off Mackie's attacks if I'd keep an open mind. But an open mind to what? Leading my own troop against those I used to count as allies? In my mortal flesh?

"You're right. There aren't enough of us yet. Only fourteen with you," he said, shrugging as I opened my mouth to protest. That wasn't what I meant. "But once we open the threshold to Midheaven and free the others from their bondage, we'll outnumber both of the existing troops, two to one. Maybe more."

My mouth stayed open. Holy shit. An entire army of rogues. "What about individual star signs?"

In the existing troops there was only one agent for each sign of the Zodiac, twenty-four in total between both sides. Rights to the star sign were guarded fiercely, passed down through the mother's lineage.

"Fletcher and Milo are both Pisces."

I glanced at the two men, sharing a bench and alcove. A meal of meat and beans. From the way they touched, lightly and comfortably at the knees, probably also a bed.

I crossed my arms. "Okay, so what about Warren's lock?"

He'd placed it over the entrance to Midheaven as soon as Hunter crossed over. Though Mackie and Tripp had since escaped, I knew there'd be another barring the entrance by now.

Carlos shrugged. "We'll break it again."

Because he was no longer worried about the valley's agents knowing what they were up to. *Building an army.*

"Don't worry," Alex said, misinterpreting my silence.

He lacked Carlos's discernible accent. "Between the defenses we can offer you and the weaponry left to you by your mother, you'll be well protected while in this world."

While in this . . . "My mother?" My head jerked up and I swallowed hard.

"Why, yes." Carlos glanced at Io, whom I now realized was more of a den mother than a ward mother. "The treasure chest. Didn't Io tell you?"

Io held her hands in front of her, an uncharacteristically defensive motion. "She didn't even know I could feel the past living within her."

"She's disconnected," Tripp said. I couldn't tell if it was accusation or excuse.

"Bet she never even knew she possessed a sixth sense!" Fletcher dragged from a long necked bottle.

Milo hit his leg. "That's not the problem. I told you. She's chased death before. She has a taste for it now. She'd rather die than live."

Carlos held up a hand, halting the discussion. I took the opportunity to jump into the fray, ignoring the comments of men who'd never known me. "Let's go back to the part about my mother."

"She's the one who set it up so we could find you. Told us where you'd show up, when, and to leave the weapons until you found them. Once she learned of Mackie, she knew she could no longer protect you on her own. She's never involved us in her affairs to this extent before, so she must realize it's time."

My mother had left me weaponry. I was willing to bet she'd left me the warning note on the day of Suzanne's bachelorette party too. She'd also created Skamar to rival the Tulpa in power. *Before that, she had taught me to make a fist.* I shook my head as all this new knowledge flooded it. "Time for what?"

"The Shadow to bind with the Light."

The fifth sign. I'd stumbled right into the portent . . . just by trying to avoid it.

And Zoe had known what happened to me too! How could she not, when she knew all this? That I'd given up my powers as she once had, the pain and struggle in that . . . and how Warren had left me in the world, alone. Yet she remained hidden, waging a solo war on the Tulpa, her sole obsession and care. I mattered . . . but only if I could help her with that goal.

Io, who had touched me on the inside, took my hand with her own. "You've got your own vigilante guardian angel. Always have."

I gritted my teeth. All I'd wanted was a *mother*.

"Let's go for a little walk," Carlos said, and I realized the rest of the room had fallen silent. I wondered belatedly what my bitterness smelled like, and tried to dam up the emotion before these strangers learned anything more of the woman who was supposed to somehow lead them into a new existence. Yet holding it back was like trying to stop floodwaters with a single sandbag. Besides, my dreams had been invaded, my insides fondled, and my body told the secrets I'd long denied to myself. I had a daughter in the world. She would need to know about her fate. I had a mother too.

And though absent from my life, she somehow unfailingly continued to manipulate mine.

15

I emerged from the rogue's lair hesitantly, squinting like a newborn into a blinding winter day. For some reason I'd expected nighttime, but the sun rode high above the desert, sprawling around us like a forbidden planet. I felt like a cactus thrusting up through the crusty terrain, surviving despite the harsh climate, eking out an existence with only the barest of necessities. Not too far from the truth, actually.

Looking at Carlos—busy not looking at me—I wondered if he felt the same, emerging from an environment no one knew existed. Looking *past* him, I saw something else residing on the desert floor. Like the cactus, like me, it too was built for survival. And like most things on Frenchman's Flat, it was also built for destruction.

"Go ahead," Carlos encouraged, as I took an involuntary step toward the cache of weapons . . . those I'd just learned my mother had left me. "I always feel better about things after I hit something."

I did too, I thought, gazing down at the trident, gun, cane and saber. They'd been returned to the original black chest, retrieved at some unknown point from Caine's destroyed home. Its lid was propped wide and, in additional invitation, a bull's-eye was set up across from it in the distance.

I reached for the saber, stroking its small antique firearm. Though still upset about the drugging, I wasn't unaware of the faith Carlos was putting in me by bringing me here, revealing not only his location but the bulk of his plans. There was nothing keeping me from going back to Warren with the information, trying to insinuate myself back into the troop . . . or even to the Tulpa in efforts to exact revenge on my former allies.

Though Carlos wasn't entirely without protection. The agents wouldn't be able to destroy the bunker beneath Frenchman Flat because they couldn't leave the city, unlike the rogues—and now me—who could travel freely. And right now, I thought, leaving didn't sound half bad.

Lifting the saber, I tested its heft. Two months ago I'd have been able to propel the thing across the desert floor like a javelin, striking dead center ten out of ten times when standing still. Squinting, I sighted down the silver barrel. I'd be lucky now if my mortal eyesight would allow me to hit the thing at all.

I squeezed the trigger. There was a swift chuff, as if I'd shot air instead of a bullet, then silence. A miss. Gazing in the opposite direction, I sighed.

"You could do it," Carlos said, reading my mind. "You could just start walking, head northeast toward Salt Lake. Use Olivia Archer's money to alter your appearance, draw up new personal documents, build credit under a new name. Even enterprising mortals have managed all that."

It wouldn't be so different than how I was living now, I thought, reloading. All my possessions and habits dependent on the woman I was impersonating. Going through each day ever conscious of appearances. I sighted again.

"But—"

"There's always a but," I muttered, firing. Damned sun. Its glare was relentless, even in winter. I immediately reloaded.

"You can't unlearn what you know. Your experiences this past year have shaped you into a different person entirely. Even with a full memory cleanse, there will be dreams. I know . . . because there was a time when I tried to forget as well."

"What I need to forget," I said, squeezing air—whoosh! "Is that last shot."

Yet Carlos's words made me think of my old boyfriend, a mortal and my first love, who'd recently undergone a memory cleanse. I wondered if Ben had dreams featuring him in the arms of the woman he'd known as a boy? Or of watching the daughter he never knew he had playing in her yard, his own dark curls lying damp on her forehead?

Had I done him any favors in allowing his memory to be erased? The idea had been to free him from the knowledge of the Zodiac world, and keep him from being targeted by the Shadows. Maybe the cleanse worked better on those who'd always been mortal. I propped the saber back in the chest with a sigh, picking up the gun instead. I sincerely hoped so.

"You know I'm right. You've tried to forget the past before."

I looked up at Carlos, a breeze shifting long strands of hair across my face. He meant the attack that had claimed my innocence, and nearly my life, when I was a teen. Brushing my hair back, I again turned away. "I never forgot."

"No, you fought." He joined my side, arm brushing mine. "But you cannot fight who you are. You must accept it, let the knowledge wash over you, and allow it to change you. The truth forces you to become who you are meant to be."

"I'm not Shadow, Light, a rogue agent, or a leader. I don't have any power and—as you might have noticed—I don't really play well with others." Relaxing my shoulders, I sighted the target. "I'm human, and nothing else."

He snorted next to me. "So you're exactly like all those who are unaware of beings who fight to control this valley and every person in it? Is that what you really want? A return to ignorance despite the truth tunneling beneath your feet?"

Sometimes. It would be infinitely easier to believe people acted of their own volition for both their good and evil deeds. Like the guy who'd tried taking my wallet while I sat alone and defeated on the cold winter ground by a loading dock. Could he take responsibility for the impulse . . . or had a Shadow once whispered in his ear? Had a not-so-coincidental series of misfortunes sent him spiraling into self-indulgent madness, making him prone to exert his control over someone who appeared weaker? Or was he just a prick?

I fired. A bubbling green vial shot forward, the barrel burned. The target stayed intact. My shoulders slumped.

"Face it, Joanna," Carlos said, moving behind me. "You'll never be blissfully ignorant again, wish it as you may."

Wishes don't mean shit.

You must take action.

"I want to be normal."

"That's different for everyone, isn't it?" He put his arms around me, guiding the gun back to the target. Sighting for me, he guided the weapon higher than I would have. The liquid vial gleamed in the sunlight. "You, *mi weda*, will be normal when you accept your destiny as Kairos."

Warren once believed that meant working on behalf of the Light. The Tulpa had been hedging his bets toward the Shadows . . . though if what Io had told me was true, he hated agents on both sides of the Zodiac. And now Carlos thought I could represent neither . . . and both. *The Shadow will bind with the Light.*

And do what? Create gray?

We fired together. The target's center exploded . . . and disintegrated in an acid burn. I lowered my arm. Satisfying . . . though not as much as if I'd done it on my own.

"Well, I still don't understand why it has to be me. You're *El Jefe*," I said, giving Io's words a bite she hadn't. "Those men look up to you, they're *your* army. So why don't you unlock Midheaven? Fight your own war."

I'd had my share. Turning, I held the gun out to him. He ignored it.

"We need more than just the lock removed. We need a woman to enter and free our men."

Because Midheaven was ruled by women who could move about freely, while the men were slaves. I thought of the abject bitterness living in Shen's gaze. Even in dreams, even unwittingly, I'd told him what to do with my will alone. Wishing might not mean shit in this world, but in an entire realm created from thought? It was everything.

But Carlos knew nothing about Solange, or Hunter, or the way I'd been treated the two times I'd managed to enter. If possible, Midheaven was more dangerous to me than this world. "Let my mother do it."

Since you're so buddy-buddy and all.

"Mortals can't get near Midheaven."

"*I'm* mortal." And I was exhausted. I dropped the gun back into the chest.

"But you won't be."

I turned at the smile in his voice. "Really? Got a phone booth I can change in? Maybe an invisible plane and bulletproof bracelets while you're at it?"

"No. Only the opportunity to help you achieve what you've already done twice before . . ." He paused for an imaginary drum roll, smile widening. "Gain the aureole."

And even jaded, tired, and mortal, I could see how well that could work. The aureole allowed a person to wander the earth like a ghost—no one could sense, touch, or even see them unless they willed it. Yet to acquire such power, you had to kill an agent with his own conduit, turning their own magic against them. As Carlos had said, I'd done it twice, something no one else had managed. I swallowed hard. The whole plan was starting to make sense. "Look, if I don't convince the Tulpa that I'm Olivia Archer, he'll take me out. And if Warren suspects for one instant I'm working with you, he'll do the same." As much as I'd like to believe otherwise, I knew that much to be true. "There's no way I can just hide out here, or take time off to go traipsing off to another world to gather an army meant to usurp them both."

Surprisingly, Carlos didn't disagree. "So continue being Olivia. Attend your meetings at Valhalla. Live in the mansion as the Tulpa expects. We will watch for Mackie . . . as well as a chance for you to gain the aureole."

A chance to kill a Shadow agent. And then re-enter Midheaven and usher every last trapped rogue—men who'd gone there to escape something unsavory in their past—back out into the Vegas valley. Yeah, *that* sounded like a good idea.

But I thought of Tripp, and how he'd been the one to step up against Mackie. I thought of the men I'd spent time with in Midheaven, washed out lithographs of their old selves, sweltering in heat no living thing should have to bear. Even Shen, as much as I disliked him, deserved to be free of a tortuous place that slowly siphoned his soul.

But how unlikely that they'd follow me, that I'd succeed, or even manage to escape once I was there.

How much that would piss off Solange and her ilk, who fed off the souls of the agents trapped over there.

I was smiling faintly at the thought when I had another. Looking at Carlos, I said sharply, "I'm not killing one of the Light. I know you're all one giant paranormal Woodstock lovefest here, but that's not how this is going to play out."

"*Sí, mon.*" Carlos shrugged one shoulder, recrossing his legs on the desert floor. "Only Shadow. *The* Shadow."

I jolted, self-preservation jump-kicking in my gut. "Which Shadow?"

"The one you're closest to, of course." Carlos squared on me, filled my vision, causing the desert and all other worries to disappear. Replacing them with a new one. "The Tulpa."

* * *

I swayed, but shook off Carlos's steadying hand. "The Tulpa can't be killed."

That's what made him so effective and dangerous and powerful. Even conduits were useless against him. In fact, the energy spent trying to bring him down made him even stronger. He fed off the intent of his attackers. Even Skamar, another tulpa and the most powerful being to ever challenge him, hadn't found a way to kill him outright.

"That's because nobody ever tried to turn his own weapon against him."

"But he doesn't have . . ." I stuttered into silence under Carlos's weighted stare. A magical weapon, a conduit, was as much an extension of an agent as a limb. Once made and bestowed, it was a part of them, and by striking them down with it, you turned their own magic against them. It was a natural law in any world. No person could stand divided, or in conflict against a part of themselves. And true, the Tulpa didn't have a conduit forged in a smithy, and fitted to his attributes, abilities, or whim.

But he did have a daughter. Someone who was a part of him. Someone who, over the past year, he'd simultaneously courted, feared, and wanted dead.

"You *are* that weapon," Carlos said, supplying the thought's end for me. "Better, now that the whole of the paranormal world knows you're mortal, he will never suspect you might be his downfall, blood against blood."

Io's lesson about the body's connections was still fresh in my mind, as were the scents it'd brought to life. Coupled with her warning about Ashlyn's fast approaching second life cycle, I realized there was more at stake in the immediate future than my life. So regardless of what Carlos said, I didn't have a choice. I needed to do this for her. But damned if I wasn't going to get something out of it too.

"Maybe," I finally conceded, nodding slowly. "But if I'm going to kill the Tulpa, then enter Midheaven and free an army—"

"Then lead it," Carlos added, seeing no reason to hold back now.

"Right," I said dryly. "If you want me to do all that while still running from Mackie and hiding it all from my former troop, then I want something in return. Something equal to the risk."

He finally looked wary. I let him think about it, and it didn't take long. He shook his head. "She won't like it. She may even stop working with us. Helping us."

"*I* may stop working with you," I said testily, and turned back to the weapons. "Look, Io said she worked on my mother before. She probably gave her the same protective coating for her organs, right? What else did she give her, Carlos? What else do you know?"

"Nothing. Zoe Archer is infamously paranoid and secretive. She trusts no one."

"But you've been in contact with her." Pulling the ancient trident from the chest, I flicked the blades open. They winked sharply in the full day's light.

"She's in contact with us. That's how it is with her. I go along with her whim."

Because he hoped she'd lead him to me. "I thought she had your father killed?"

"I don't blame her. She was newly mortal, had no defenses against attack in the Guardian Angel Cathedral. Besides, she has done many helpful things for us since. While others merely sit around and talk, her actions are proof of her intent." He pursed his lips and locked his dark, serious gaze on mine. The lone wolf act, coupled with a tragic past and dark good looks, was a heady mixture. His expression alone could gain a hundred beds. If I wasn't already actively avoiding dangerous men, I might have inched closer. "But I can't find her, no more than the Tulpa, or Warren. We've all looked, you know."

I hadn't known that about Warren . . . but it didn't surprise me. He did a lot of things without the rest of the troop knowing.

I straightened, still determined. "But they don't have her lineage and bloodline living inside of them. I do. I just need you and Io to help me develop my hereditary gifts."

He continued gazing into the distance, breathing in deeply before allowing a slow nod. "It may be possible to redevelop your senses. With time and study and Io's help."

"That's all I'm asking."

Then I'd go after my mother myself. Because with her granddaughter's second life cycle approaching fast, she'd be sticking close to Ashlyn. Thanks to a Shadow agent named Regan DuPree, the Tulpa knew of his granddaughter's existence, and was gunning for her too. A feminine triptych, I thought wryly. He wanted us all.

Yes. My mother would be very close.

So with that alone as incentive, I would have agreed to help Carlos. But Mackie wouldn't stop until either he or I were dead, and I certainly couldn't take him on by myself. But with the grays' help, an *army* at my back, it might be possible to survive.

As for a return to Solange and Midheaven and the special horrors awaiting me there . . . well, that was a worry for later. And I owed Carlos enough to try.

So he smiled when I nodded, a heady look bringing out new angles on the beautiful face, and I glanced back down at the conduit in my hand. It was archaic and not even my own, but my fingers twitched with the need for action, to once again take my fate into my own hands. Sure, I made mistakes—I had never pretended otherwise. But I did it armed. "Let's try that gun again."

16

So they took me back to Vegas to do what was previously thought impossible. Kill the Tulpa.

The opportunity wouldn't come immediately. I was hosting Suzanne and Arun's rehearsal dinner at the estate that night. Though far less crowded than the eight hundred wedding guests due at Valhalla the following day, it was still a big undertaking. Making sure there were enough hors d'oeuvres would be challenging. Killing the Tulpa might be a little too ambitious for cocktail attire. Which meant I had to stay alive at least until the next day.

Valentine's Day, I remembered with a frown. Silk-lined boxes of chocolate. Intimate candlelight dinners. A body studded with weapons in order to kill a friggin' tulpa.

Just like every other girl on V-Day, I thought wryly. Dressed to leave an impression.

I shook my head. Weaker than I'd ever been in my life and I was going to attempt to murder a being birthed through calculated thought and mean ambition. One who had taken over the Shadow organization with a virtual snap of his fingers. If it was really the thought that counted, why couldn't I just *wish* him away? As it was, I had no better plan than to leap and lunge at the opportune moment.

Speaking of leaping and lunging, I glanced to the back of our stolen van to find Gareth, Vincent, and Roland all eyeing me speculatively.

"No," I told them all. "I won't go to the dance with you."

Gareth and Roland shot me small smiles, and while Vincent didn't offer me a promise ring, his scowl didn't deepen either. Guys who looked at you and smiled, or at least didn't frown, always wanted something, so I waited. Gareth finally held up a comic book . . . a manual depicting the last days of my time in Zodiac troop 175, and as an agent of Light. I assumed that's what it was anyway. The cover art showed me drowning.

"You were the Kairos," Gareth said, jutting out his pockmarked chin.

"So they said."

"But you gave up all your powers for a mortal child. Someone less than even a rogue."

I shook my head. "She wasn't lesser than anyone."

"And that's why I will follow you." Vincent crossed his arms over his beefy chest, his nostrils flaring. "Not because Carlos tells me to. Not because you're a female and you can enter Midheaven and increase our numbers."

"'Cuz the only number you care about is one," Gareth snorted.

Vincent punched the kid's shoulder so hard his entire arm went limp. I winced, but Vincent's eyes were back on me. "Because I'm independent, and I am honorable. I don't mask my deeds, good or bad, with lies. I won't deceive you like that." He jerked his head to the manual where the story of Warren's trickery was literally spelled out. "I won't betray you like the *other* one either."

I'd wondered if Hunter's story would show up. I swallowed hard. Now my personal life was splayed along those pages in the comic book equivalent of a gossip rag. And all these men had read it.

"Nor will I," Gareth added solemnly, which had me

glancing up despite my embarrassment. He seemed to have forgiven me for questioning his experience. Meanwhile, Oliver muttered his agreement from the driver's seat. Carlos beamed. Tripp, gazing out the window, said nothing.

"I've a gift to seal my oath," Roland said, rising from his seat. Oliver stretched to see through the rearview mirror, and Gareth leaned close. Vincent rolled his eyes before leaning his head back and closing them.

"What is it?" I asked, accepting the object. It looked like a fork that had gone head-to-head with a Roto-Rooter.

"It's from the original Doom Town," he said, returning to his seat. "I found it buried closer to ground zero than any other artifact to date. I want you to have it."

How sweet. He was proving his loyalty to me with radio-active rubble. I could practically feel the ions banging against my palm. It was like the entire city of Whoville was jammed together in a metal mosh pit. Yet looking back up at the three men, I found their expressions as open as I could expect on people I'd known for fewer than twenty-four hours.

"And I want you to have these," Gareth added, lifting a small duffel bag over the seat.

"Nah, man!" Vincent came to life then, making a grab for the bag. "I wasn't done with the last issue!"

Showing his quickness in spite of—or because of—his size, Gareth dodged, ending up next to me before the larger man could swipe again. "She needs them more than you, bro. More than that stupid fucking cancer spoon too."

Not a fork, then.

The van rocked as Roland lunged.

"I love the cancer spoon!" I yelled, wanting to prevent being squashed by an errant fist while trapped in a moving vehicle. I held out my hand for the manuals. "And I'll read the issues backward, and return them as I go, okay?"

That calmed everyone sufficiently . . . except for me. Now I had a bag full of manuals detailing what the troop had been doing since my absence. I swallowed hard, and tucked the bag beneath my feet. Truthfully, I didn't know when I'd get to them. My feelings were too raw where the troop was concerned. Seeing them on the pages of a comic book—even if the action no longer lifted from the page, coming to life before my eyes—might pull the scab from that mental injury before it'd fully healed.

Still, glancing over at Carlos, I found Alex, Fletcher, and Milo all smiling at me from behind him. He inclined his head, like he'd known all along they'd accept me. I turned back in my seat, and found that despite the day ahead of me, I was smiling too.

Yet, just like the clouds that'd once dotted Frenchman's Flat, another worry immediately mushroomed. Harlan Tripp. Unnervingly silent since learning of Carlos's plan, he was gnawing on one of those strange brown cigarettes he'd brought back with him from Midheaven, running his tongue along his teeth as he stared out the window of our stolen van. Carlos had paired us up, so while the other rogues were to observe and protect me from afar, Tripp had instructions to never leave my side. If spotted, we'd act in tandem to make either Shadow or Light believe we were together against my will.

"Is this it?" Oliver, in the driver's seat, pulled me from my thoughts, and I leaned forward to see around Tripp's bulk. The building was immediately recognizable, and I instinctively glanced around for signs of the Light.

"Yes." I answered softly, and the vehicle fell oddly silent. I'd just told a band of rogue agents what building the Light used to fashion weapons and train for battle against the Shadows.

Buttersnap and Tripp flanked me as we disembarked from the stolen van, looking less for signs of the proprietors of the building than for Mackie and his unstoppable knife. That, after all, was what had made me think of the warehouse. Inside was a compound Micah had created for the Light, which effectively acted as a barrier to any conduit's blow. A spray solution that adhered to the skin, the defensive preservative only lasted against one strike, but the time it would buy the rogues from a first strike to a second might make the difference between life and death . . . and God knew we needed every advantage we could get.

The only problem? The warehouse was booby-trapped to the teeth.

"Sure you 'membered all the obstacles?" Tripp asked as we skirted the building, kicking rubber strips and broken bottles and concrete from our path.

"No," I said honestly, blowing out a breath, and rearranging Gareth's duffel over my shoulder. He'd handed it to me again when I'd oh-so-subtly tried to leave it in the van. "But you only need to dodge the poisoned bullets to get to the alarm panel, and I remember the pass code."

"They coulda changed it."

"I don't think so." Hunter had set up the alarm system and the lethal backup methods, and told the code to no one but me. My bet was the warehouse hadn't been used in the weeks since his disappearance, which meant the defensive preservative was still tucked safely inside.

"A smidge more certainty would be nice," Tripp muttered. "Since it ain't you who's gotta run the gauntlet."

What could I say? He had a point. I wasn't fast enough to dodge the poisonous missiles on the way to the panel, which left it up to my surly southern wingman. The bullets weren't the only issue either. If he failed to disarm the system within a minute of gaining access, the place would blow. And wouldn't *that* make a nice lead for the six o'clock news?

Alas, the perky local newscasters would have to fixate on another headline. Tripp picked the lock, and raced inside amidst the whiz of two-dozen bullets striking concrete. Buttersnap's gaze fixed on the darkened doorway, ears pricked, and it was only when her tongue lolled from her mouth and those great, humping shoulders relaxed that I knew the alarm had been deactivated. Tripp appeared a moment later.

I waved backward, and a moment later the van, idling

behind the warehouse block, ambled away. They'd canvass the perimeter by vehicle—with Fletcher and Milo on foot—while I showed Tripp where the protectant was.

"There should be a giant tool chest in the room's center," I told him, ducking past to take the lead. It wasn't real power, but pretending made me feel better. "The solvent is in there."

And it was so easily found I half expected a trap. Yet why would the troop hide it? It wasn't a weapon, and until now no one else knew the warehouse's location. This had been the safe spot when all true safe zones were inaccessible, though because of what I'd just revealed, it would never be that again.

Snatching up the canister and its spares, I whirled to find Tripp examining a template of a weapon Hunter had recently designed. It had a long slim chain with an attached leather wrist loop, though it was tied to a foam dagger—a most lethal lasso. Tripp was comparing it to the sketches laid out atop the drawing board. "Put it down," I ordered sharply.

He did . . . and immediately picked up another.

"Stop it! Let's just grab the protectant and get out of here."

"No." He sounded like a school kid with a new toy. "I'm curious."

And the chances of convincing a curious former Shadow to leave a refuge of Light unexplored was next to nil. I rolled my eyes. "You're smearing your scent all over the place," I protested.

He responded by picking up a foam cross section of a four-headed axe, and I made a warning noise in the back of my throat. He looked at me like I was a gnat and he was tempted to swat. "Why don't you git. Go check on Buttersnap. Make sure she don't eat nothing."

"They're waiting for us."

He turned the template over in his hand, then began searching for its drawings. "They'd do the same."

So much for taking the lead.

I glanced around, then wandered a bit. Other than its purpose as a martial headquarters for a troop of paranormal beings, the warehouse was unremarkable. I poked my head into the panic room, which was as utilitarian as a librarian's desk, cabinets pressed against the wall, fluorescent lights off, doors closed. I touched nothing, knowing it would leave prints.

I slipped around a floor-to-ceiling plastic partition separating the combat area and shooting range from Hunter's workshop to find Buttersnap inspecting the wide-open area like she was on patrol. I sniffed but smelled nothing, though if I closed my eyes I could imagine the martial dance of the agents of Light the last time we'd trained for war.

Which brought my mind around to what else I'd done with Hunter in this room. My gaze swept right, to where he'd had me pinned to the wall. Granted, I deserved it, as I'd just thrown him across the space moments before. What lay between us had always been charged; our joining elemental, like planets banging together to create a scalding eclipse. I closed my eyes and could still picture our silhouettes, sharply edged. I could hear the frenetic need of our undressing. I could taste his breath. It didn't matter that he'd been planning to betray me even then, not in my heart's memory. Just because a love was made up didn't make it any less real. Illusion had its own reality.

"The weapons, Joanna. Think about the weapons." My voice, though low, was like water splashed in my face, and just what I needed to banish the past. Because not only could I still touch another agent's conduit, I could also handle the antique ones left by my mother, and as a mortal I shouldn't be able to do either. My fingers skimmed the trident at my hip, which steadied my breathing. Once I was sure my emotions wouldn't leak from me, I slipped back around the partitions, leaving Buttersnap to patrol the memories in the shooting range. I simply wasn't up for it.

But then I spotted the secret passageway. Recessed, the alcove was practically invisible to the eye's quick scan, and as yet unseen by Tripp. Glancing back at him, still studying Hunter's drawings like they were key to discovering the

Ark itself, I quietly crossed the room, pushed on the hinged panel, then slipped inside.

The small stairwell was as claustrophobic as any other narrow, dark space, the trapped air pressing in on me to amplify my footsteps and breath. I chided myself for having the nightmarish thought of something waiting for me at the top of the staircase, and climbed as quickly as I could, ignoring the noise I made as I clamored to the top. Feeling around blindly at the passageway's end, I pushed open the simple shuttered door and stepped into the crow's nest, a tiny alcove overlooking the entire warehouse.

"Masochist," I mumbled, shaking my head. Because if the room downstairs was a reminder of how much I'd opened myself to Hunter, this one was head-on collision. It was small, holding nothing more than a bed beneath a slanted roofline and a cheap press-wood desk. I sighed, then slumped to the edge of the bed, giving up any pretense of strength . . . or interest in anything beyond what was left of Hunter in this world.

Were I still an agent, I'd be able to scent him everywhere, as Tripp undoubtedly could. As it was, I pressed my face to the pillow propped atop the unmade bed—a pathetically girly, lovesick, and patently unexpected thing for me to do.

"God, Hunt." And I allowed myself a moment to do what I previously hadn't when thinking of the man who'd abandoned this world for another: grieve.

So it is a soul connection.

Was it? I asked myself, remembering Trish's words, uttered just before Solange annihilated the water room. And if so, how could he leave me for her with so much remaining between us? I'd dodged the thought for weeks, cringing every time it poked its head into the light, but I couldn't dodge it now. I had fallen in love with the man, perhaps on first sight . . . most definitely in this workshop. I'd been so sure he felt the same that the shock of his betrayal still crashed over me in unexpected waves.

I leaned back and gazed up at the roofline angled close

over the simple bed. Stars shone there, glued, but still glowing in his rendition of a makeshift sky. "Fucking pitiful."

I hated looking at what I'd lost instead of what I'd managed to save. I had life. I had a troop again . . . or at least a pseudotroop. I had a purpose, and if not a real chance of killing the Tulpa or avoiding Mackie's blade, then at least hope. If I began counting my losses, my mind could quickly become an endless game of Russian roulette.

Sniffling, I lifted Gareth's bag from my shoulders and rifled through it until I found the manual I wanted . . . the one I knew would be there all along.

Dark Matters. With my heart caught in a syncopated beat, I stared at the cover featuring Hunter as Jaden Jacks. Funny, but if you'd told me even two months ago that Hunter was tiny, I'd have scoffed. Maybe it was just his presence; he was a man who knew his own body and mind, one who took over rooms just by entering them. Or maybe it was that he was a superhero, one the other agents of Light had looked up to . . . until they'd looked away. One thing was sure . . . my unswerving attraction to him had been there from the first.

In any case, Jaden Jacks was a Wrestlemania sort of giant—bronzed skin, bulging biceps, bleached military hair, squared jaw. The man I knew was all of that, though coiled in a tighter frame, along with straight mocha hair and eyes like honey over toast. Though the eyes had been the same, I realized, staring down at them now. I should have caught that when first encountering Jacks, but had been so overwhelmed by his physicality I hadn't.

I pushed my back against the wall, but got a flash of Hunter reclined in the same place, covers draped across his naked thighs so artfully he should have been sculpted. Clearing my throat, I shifted back to the edge of the bed like some prim old maid and opened the manual to find out if becoming Hunter had been as unwilling a transformation as my own into Olivia.

But *Dark Matters* didn't begin there. Instead it began with what had made the makeover necessary, and that began with the death of his parents.

I knew it had been violent; it was a death I'd experienced as though it were my own via the power of the aureole. However, what that shared magic hadn't shown, what it'd neglected to play out in my mind like some sort of mental horror flick, was the brutality of the attack upon them. They'd been beset by the entire Shadow troop one fateful Fourth of July. They'd done well for themselves until the second wave of Shadows hit. Then they'd gone under, fighting back-to-back, until they were flattened. Hunter had watched the whole thing from his hiding spot beneath a car. He was five years old.

The Shadows left. The child emerged. And so did another one—one who was three years older, one from the shadows. One who was *of* the Shadows. And Solange spared his life.

Holy shit. A relationship begun in childhood? A life-debt that practically predetermined a connection? I scoffed, shaking my head. I'd never even had a chance.

Flash forward more than twenty years after that tragic beginning, and those eyes I'd recognize anywhere were dull and brittle, like burnt-out bulbs in a man ready to tune out, turn off, and shut down. The thought bubbles blooming overhead indicated he was jaded about humanity's desire to be helped, and bitter over giving his life over to people who rarely lifted a finger to help themselves. This, more than his appearance, made him alien to me. The Hunter I'd known was a hero through and through. His life was spent in service to humanity, preserving choice for them through unceasing battle with the Shadows.

But you hadn't known him at all, had you?

I resumed my reading, feeling like a voyeur but unable to look away.

Solange first approached him in a bar, intent on com-

pleting the task she'd neglected when they were both
children: end his life. She seduced him at the height of a
desert storm, but whatever she saw in the final flash of heat
lightning, as her tomahawk was poised overhead, had her
withholding her killing blow . . . and had him doing the
same. They made love instead, and then they made a pact
. . . public enemies, private lovers. For months he'd had an
affair with a mortal enemy, one this manual revealed in
embarrassingly erotic detail.

Was that why he could accept the Shadow in me? I
thought, flipping pages faster and faster. Was it how he
could look past my father's mean influence and unwanted
lineage, and say there was nothing wrong with me? And
why he believed my Shadow side could ultimately be overcome?

I blinked, shocked to find tears staining the pages, and
slapped the manual shut. I knew the rest of this story
anyway. They'd had a child together. She'd fled to Midheaven.

And I was wrong about the connection between us.

My soft thoughts of us together weren't memories . . .
they were recurring deaths. I hadn't been made love to him
like the woman on these pages, like a goddess. The time he
spent with me had been a lie and dream. And when I was
awake? I was alone, trapped by mortality.

I tucked the manual back in the duffel, glanced back
up at the stars scattering the ceiling and reaching to touch
what he'd called a frozen star. They were really black
holes. Dead stars. He tracked them along with the others,
he said, because they had the shortest lives. For some
reason Hunter had been attracted to dark things. Like me.

Like Solange.

I've been searching for Sola for a long time, he'd said,
before leaving me for her.

It was enough to harden my thoughts to him once again.
Because he'd admitted this *after* making love to me, after
convincing me that being vulnerable wasn't synonymous

with being weak. After I'd allowed his voice to wash through me, filling crevices and hollows I hadn't even known were empty.

I gazed at the wrongly marked sky, the version of true love *they* shared, until my vision blurred. Then I pushed from the bed and rejoined Tripp downstairs.

17

"I'm going to take a few of these for you," Tripp said, gathering together drawings, careful not to look at me. Buttersnap nudged my elbow, and I knew they both scented my pain. I wiped at my eyes and face, also content to ignore the obvious. "If we ever get a real weapons master, they can fashion more conduits for you . . . maybe even some for the rest of the rogues."

A rogue weapons master forging tools for rogue agents. There was a thought large enough to eclipse any other. But Tripp wasn't finished.

"Look what else I found." He opened a satchel I immediately recognized . . . one I'd stashed in the bottom drawer of the tool chest the last time I'd been there. Reaching inside, he withdrew a handful of poker chips embossed with illustrations of my former powers.

The currency of Midheaven. Tripp and I had once battled each other over a green felt poker table over chips like this. I swallowed hard, having forgotten about them, then reached forward to touch one. The powers represented on these chips were abilities like regeneration and speed, each of the five amplified senses as well . . . things everybody in the Zodiac world possessed. Yet others represented individual gifts.

"I had no idea you could slip into the sanctuaries of both Shadow and Light," he said, fingering through the chips curiously. "Or that you could leave the valley even before you were thrown from the troop."

Neither had I.

"Oh, lookie here. You got Shen's sense of smell. And the albino's aether."

I glanced at the two new chips he held. "What?"

"Their powers. I heard you cleaned up at soul poker once I was off the table." He tossed one of my chips, my speed, aside, muttering, "These are all useless."

Yeah, this warehouse was just rife with my losses. I sighed . . . and my emotion clearly bloomed into scent. Tripp blew out a chiding breath and readjusted the big, black Stetson on his head. "Man, what a double standard. You won't allow others to feel anything soft for you, but you wallow in your own pity. Know what your father would say?"

"He'd be happy to relieve me of the problem?"

He picked up the canister we'd come for, a modified fire extinguisher holding the fortifying preservative, and motioned for me to hold still. "He'd say just 'cause you got something doesn't mean you got the *right* to it."

"Swell guy." I shut my eyes, and a soft mist enveloped me, falling over clothes, hair, and skin in an even invisible webbing. A conduit could now strike me once, and the effect would be the same as trying to chop through petrified wood. It wouldn't even make a dent. Opening my eyes, I motioned at Tripp, and he handed it to me.

"But he's right," he said, inhaling so deeply his black vest moved against his great belly. I misted him, then handed back the canister.

"Easy for you to say when you've got all your strengths." I swung away to leave, but Tripp was suddenly in front of me, aptly illustrating the speed I didn't possess.

"Stop." I jerked back when his hand fell to my waist. But he wasn't touching my flesh. He was fumbling for the trident secured in my pants pocket. There was a faint hum when he found it, a vibration rising from the pocket and up his arm. He gasped, his face scrunching in pain, and when he pulled his hand away a second later, his palm was mottled, red at the edges, black in the center. The smell of burnt flesh filled my nose.

"Oh my God." Dropping my chips, I reached for his hand, but he flipped it over, grasped mine and pulled me closer until my gaze returned to his face.

"Ya don't know what you can do till you try," he growled through clenched teeth. "Or if your talents are unique until compared with someone else's. So just stop underestimating your damned self. Now, come on. The others are waiting."

I followed Tripp, dumbstruck by what he'd just done and unsure of what it meant. So he *couldn't* touch the old weapons? Was that the same for all rogues? Thinking back, I hadn't seen any conduits in the bunker, any of the grays armed, or heard anyone speak of their conduits.

"I'm thinkin' we should leave the alarm off," Tripp said, interrupting my thoughts. "Locking the door should be enough to convince the Light nothing's amiss. They already know the place will blow without the right security code."

And none of them had it.

"That'll allow us to leave Buttersnap too, since we can't exactly show up with her to your big bash tonight." He put his hand on my back, guiding me to the door.

We then paid a visit to the complex's Dumpster, where Tripp tipped in the protectant, the foam templates, and most of the drawings, though I had a feeling he'd tucked a few away in the inner pocket of his leather vest. I too had the soul chips tucked away. They might be useless, but they were still mine.

The thought had me giving the cabdriver we hailed an

address far from the Archer estate. I leaned back, trusting Tripp wasn't yet familiar enough with the city to object . . . at least not until it was too late. Meanwhile, the driver's log would contain the account of this trip, one easily traced were someone so inclined. Which was the point. Someone, I knew, was very interested in the activity in and around this neighborhood. I waited until the cab's taillights disappeared, then headed the other way, jerking my head so Tripp would follow.

"This ain't right," he drawled, clearly uncomfortable. I smiled. Good. Let him be the one in the dark for a change. "Don't you have a rehearsal dinner to attend?" he finally said, sidestepping a fledgling anthill. How cute. Just like a Buddhist. "And a tulpa to kill?"

Or a Buddhist's polar opposite.

I made a humming noise in the back of my throat but kept walking.

Our destination was a flat-topped single story, neither the nicest home in the neighborhood nor the least attractive. This was not only anticlimactic for Tripp, but probably a downright disappointment. As we halted before a sprawling patch of lawn, I knew he scented nothing of the Shadow or Light around this house. After all, great pains had been taken to keep anything related to that world away from the people inside this home.

I studied the simple residence, looking for a place not easily visible from the driveway and front walk, but not exactly hidden either. A place the vigilant would easily spot. The hose spout might do the trick, though the silver cassia planted before it would obstruct its view if someone were driving by in the dark.

Fuck it, I thought, pulling out the gun with the glowing green liquid vials. I needed a guaranteed reaction.

"What're you doing, girl?" Tripp hissed, his natural instinct to run from mortal attention clearly warring with his need to remain next to me.

True, it was five-thirty, and people were headed home

for dinner after a long day's work—the perfect time to draw the attention of the Neighborhood Watch—but I might not get another opportunity to return before my next near death experience.

I fired at the living room's giant glass window. Mortality didn't affect my aim this time, and I hit the pane dead center. The tempered glass exploded into a million glass pebbles. A light flipped on, and panicked voices filtered through the curtains. A moment later one lace panel parted hesitantly. I kept watching.

"Come on!" Tripp was ready to bolt.

"Wait," I said, eyes angled the other way. A woman yelled for someone to call the cops. Still, I stood in open view. "Wait," I whispered again.

And there it was. A shifting at the window opposite the first, a wide parting of girlish curtains, then a bold, defiant stare. Locking onto a gaze similar to mine, I watched a little girl's eyes darken. My eyes used to blacken in the same way.

Tripp gasped. "Holy shit!"

His nostrils widened as he scented the girl's anger . . . and her heritage. He turned to me with eyes as wide as I'd ever seen them. "You're baitin' her. Darin' Zoe Archer to come after you."

"She'll come after you too," I said coolly. "Because that girl may not know who we are, but she obviously knows what we are. She'll tell Zoe there were two people here."

He swallowed hard as he realized I'd just bound him to me in secrecy. If something happened to Ashlyn, Zoe would have no problem finding out Tripp was the one standing next to me today. And if she knew it, so would her creation, the most powerful being in our world, Skamar.

Tripp whistled through his teeth, shaking his head as sirens sounded in the distance. "You best be careful, forcin' that woman's hand."

It was about time someone did. "I'm just shaking things loose a bit. See how she reacts."

Tripp blew out a breath and shook his head. "She's gonna lose her God-given mind."

Good. Because the days where Zoe could hold back, stay safe, and pull strings behind an impenetrable curtain of anonymity were numbered. If I had to be out here, actively risking my mortal ass for a world that wanted to crush me, then she could very well join me.

18

I was back at the Archer estate a half hour later. Tripp was right; I did have a party to throw—more specifically, a rehearsal dinner Olivia Archer would be thrilled to put on for her best friend's mother on the night before her wedding. Despite the threat of Mackie's attack, I still had to keep Warren from being suspicious, all while trying to draw the Tulpa in close.

So when my driver arrived, I'd shoved Tripp into the trunk of the Town Car, along with a paper bag filled with the incriminating weapons. He eyed the bag warily when I placed it next to him, but Kevin—getting a "forgotten" bottle of wine at the store—would be back soon. Tripp also wasn't happy about having to leave my side, but he'd never blend with tonight's tony crowd, and we couldn't be seen entering the mansion together.

I exited the car, using the gigantic front steps along with the earliest guests, already arriving. My rumpled appearance earned me a few surprised stares, but I just smiled and waved as I headed up the winding front staircase. I'd pop upstairs for a quick shower—or maybe a splash bath, since scenes from Hitchcock's *Psycho* were winging through my mind—then pull my hair back into a slick chignon for the evening. Olivia Archer's body was *her* weapon, and it didn't take a whole lot to pull that trigger.

"Your friends are waiting."

The voice came from behind, and I jumped so high I half expected someone to score it. Whirling at the responding chuckle, I saw a figure slip from the shadows. The smirk that met my gaze wasn't a look any housekeeper should use on their employer.

Then again, Helen wasn't just any housekeeper.

She also wasn't really named Helen. Lindy Maguire was her given name in the Zodiac world, and she was the Tulpa's most loyal, lovesick lackey. Placed in this household years ago to look after the Archer interests on his behalf, she'd contributed more than a little to Xavier's death. Sure, he'd been mean-hearted, greedy, and got what was coming to him, but humans were walking squeaky toys to her. She'd have no problem sending me to an equally agonizing fate.

"You're late." She held a flat gift box in one hand, vaguely familiar. She was also dressed for the occasion in crisp black and white, an old fashioned kerchief holding back her hair. Her skin was still sallow, her face long, but there was something additionally off about her today, I thought, tilting my head. I inhaled, but scented only drugstore perfume, and cleaning supplies. Still, it was something aggressive and predatory, because even with mortal senses, I instinctively tensed.

She tilted her head from one side to the other, like an insect considering its next meal. I half hoped Mackie *would* strike tonight. Maybe cleave her in two on his way to me. Then again, if she knew he wanted to kill the Zodiac's former so-called savior, she'd lay a red carpet at his feet then ask for his autograph when he was done.

"I brought this for you." She held the box out, so close to my chest I had to take it. I shook it, straining for a rattler's shake or a bomb's tick. Nothing.

"What is it?" I asked suspiciously.

"Well, your little friends told me you had plans to reminisce about mothers and families. I thought you might want to join in the conversation."

She smiled, sweet as saccharin, and I forced a smile in return. No doubt this was some item that would have Olivia tearing up. I merely inclined my head and tucked it beneath my arm. "Thank you."

Helen frowned, obviously disappointed I wouldn't be opening it now, then recovered, lifting her chin. "By the way, Xavier's private consultant called here this afternoon. He said you have plans for a lunch meeting?"

She was fishing. The Tulpa had told her we'd met, and her job was to make sure we did so again as soon as possible. Meanwhile, the question marks stamping her retinas were jealous green swirls.

Schoolgirl crushes, I thought wryly, not just for schoolgirls anymore.

"Yeah, I might not keep that." I shook my head. "Like, I don't even know his *name*."

In my defense, I *was* screaming at myself inside to shut up.

"I'm sure if you take some of your precious time out of all-night keggers you'll find he's a font of valuable information."

So was the encyclopedia, but it didn't try to suck out your soul in return.

My response was airy in contrast to her hiss. "It is a rather hectic life."

"Well it ends tonight."

"My life?" It was a flippant comment . . . but I wasn't so sure that wasn't what she meant.

A small sneer lifted her top lip, and her pale skin was mottled red. "You'll be staying here from this night on. It's time you shouldered more responsibility as the sole remaining member of the Archer dynasty."

Even Olivia wouldn't have let that pass without comment. "You don't even like me, Helen, so what's it to you?"

She lifted her chin. "Your father wanted it this way."

She referenced Xavier, but the Tulpa was the one she meant. And "Helen" was so blindly in love with the Shadow leader I doubted she even saw her own reasons for it anymore. The spark igniting those feelings all those years ago had probably snuffed into long-cold ash, and she just held it so tightly inside of her it had yet to come apart. Not that she could afford to let it go. Everything around it, all her insides and reasons and feelings, would crumble if she did. It defined her life. Without it, I bet she wouldn't even know how to live.

"You miss him, don't you?" I asked softly, ostensibly referencing Xavier too. "I understand, you know. You think you can count on someone to always be there, but sometimes they're gone even before they leave. Sometimes," I said, shaking my head sadly, "they've been gone for years."

"I don't know what you're talking about."

"Then let me clarify." I stared at her, tried to regain a sense of deference, and failed. "Fuck my father and what he wanted from me. I'm not a belonging, and no one claims me. Got it?" *Pass that along to your schoolgirl crush, you bitch.*

Helen's face was sandblasted shock. "Olivia . . . ?"

"And fuck you too for being such a goddamned sycophant." My mouth was dry but my tone never wavered. "He never thought of you as anything but a tool. So keep dusting, Helen. Because you and I both know you're just here to keep things clean."

I pushed past her then, and wondered what I'd smell if I could still manage it. Shock like an acid burn? Sorrow like stale air freshener? Then I forced myself to stop wondering, to cease caring if I ever smelled emotion again. There was no point in lamenting that loss.

And, I thought, shutting the door behind me, there was no pity for Shadows.

19

"That is one nosy twunt," Cher said, cocking her head at the closed door. Helen could be heard stomping down the hallway, and Cher's rude amalgamation only increased the effect. I smiled and looked for Suzanne, before hearing water running in the adjoining bathroom. "She'll probably offer to bring up some cookies and milk just so she can spy on us. We can't let her ruin our sleepover, okay?"

Shit. I tossed the box Helen had given me on the dresser, then flopped on the bed next to Cher. I'd entirely forgotten about the sleepover. It'd been a sound enough idea in the monotonous safety of my sickbed, at a time when I believed the supernatural world had abandoned me altogether.

Cher, misinterpreting the wince on my face, smoothed the hair back from my forehead. "Don't worry. I've brought enough alcohol and chocolate to last the night. We'll bar the door with a chair back like we did when we were kids."

"Sounds great," I lied, because it sounded dangerous. I couldn't allow Cher, or anyone else, to remain in this house any longer than necessary. If Mackie knew I was here—

and odds were he did—he wouldn't wait long before trying for me again.

Suzanne appeared just then, and clapped like a schoolgirl upon seeing me. "Oh, good! I was starting to get worried. And hungry. Arun flew in his personal chef from Delhi. Get ready for some Tandoori to-die-for!"

I momentarily wondered what it was like to live in that brain.

Cher, used to it—a party to it—reached over the bedside to hoist an overnight duffel. "I brought the letters too."

"Letters?" I asked absently, watching Suzanne apply poinsettia lipstick.

"The ones I told you about before?" She crossed her arms, piqued. "On the party bus, remember?"

"Nah. It kinda fell out of my head when you got hospitalized," I told Cher, though I did remember now—the letters her birth mother had written when she found out she was dying.

"I thought tonight would be a good time to reminisce."

I glanced at Suzanne. Weren't we supposed to be celebrating? Looking forward, not back? But Suzanne shrugged as she caught my gaze through the mirror, seemingly more concerned with her updo than anything else. "Oh, I think it's a wonderful idea. We're products of our pasts, after all. And of the people who shaped them. I'm not jealous when it comes to love. I want my baby to feel as much love as possible."

Cher teared up. "Aw, Momma . . ."

"Besides, my psychic told me it's not too late to have another baby with Arun. Fingers crossed that your replacement is on the way!" She did just that.

"Momma!"

"What's in the box?" Suzanne asked, pointing at whatever Helen had left in there to flatten me.

"Nothing," I lied, but she was already lifting the lid. Her movement slowed, then froze altogether, though her eyes darted to my face and away so quickly I knew I'd been right. Helen's intent was to sully the celebratory mood. I held out a hand for the box, wondering why some people thought making someone feel bad would make them feel better.

The only blessing was that it wasn't Olivia really opening this box. Had to give it to Helen, I thought, shaking my head. She sure knew how to hit below the belt.

Cher had told Helen that tonight's gathering was about mothers and family . . . but the photo I held was devoid of either. It was of my college graduation, three people glaring into the afternoon sun with false smiles plastered over sweating faces. Olivia's had been bright and eager, almost frantic in her hope to wring some happiness out of the occasion. Mine was as stiff as the cardboard in my graduation cap. Xavier's wasn't even that, just a half squint, and a meaty-jawed scowl as he gestured for the photographer to hurry up. Of course, my mother was absent entirely . . . just as she'd been for nearly the entire previous decade. And that was what Helen was so clearly pointing out.

Yet even before my mother left, we hadn't been the Cleavers. Xavier was only present on this day because it was expected. He'd hopped from his limo, posed for this moment upon Olivia's request, before tossing me this sterling silver frame and an unsigned graduation card with the down payment for my own house, then disappearing again. Both his absence and the money were readily accepted. We all knew he wanted me out of the mansion as badly as I wanted escape.

I filled that new home with items that spoke to the person I'd become—photography equipment and a darkroom, modern pieces with Asian accents—taking nothing from the mansion, including this frame. I shook my head again. Olivia had been so desperate for a normal family life that even a farcical photo of a broken, unsmiling family had moved her.

"What's that say?" Suzanne asked, pointing to the frame's lower edge.

I read the inscription. " 'Making an impact is easy. Making a difference is hard.' "

I scoffed at the irony, musing how he'd only ever accomplished the former, but halted in mid eye roll. "Huh. That's funny."

"Really?" asked Cher, tilting her head. "I think it's profound."

"No, I mean I know someone who used to say that."

"Xavier?" Suzanne guessed, pointing at the quote's attribution.

"Someone else," I murmured, biting my lower lip. Someone I hadn't known when this photo was taken.

Of all the agents of Light, I'd spent the most time around Tekla. She wasn't comfortable with me at first, nor I with her. Though sparrow-slight, she was too powerful to induce relaxation, with a sense of the otherworldly about her that set her apart from even those in the Zodiac. As the purported Kairos, I'd been much the same. We were also mutually indebted to one another, having saved the other's ass more than once.

So we were an unlikely pair, the Seer and the reluctant new Star Sign. I wondered now if she'd taken me under her wing because she'd seen Fate's plans for me—my fall from the troop's grace, my restored humanity, my lost loves— and wanted to prepare me, or maybe even provide a soft spot while she could. After all, with the murder of her son the year before, her mothering instincts had no obvious outlet, and I doubted it could just be turned off. Perhaps she saw me as the daughter she never had.

We had certainly butted heads like mother and daughter.

"Goddess damn!" she'd said once. "You're birthing plant life from thought and giving it roots in the world. You're not smashing sandcastles. Try to use a bit of finesse!"

And Tekla waved her hand over her own giant pot of soil,

the gesture so elegant it was probably Kabuki-inspired. I'd looked down at my pot and given it the middle finger. Tekla scowled.

"Well, maybe it's the Shadow in me that keeps life from growing," I said, shrugging. Bringing living things to life was a skill particular to the Light.

She'd lifted her sharp chin. "Maybe it's stubbornness of spirit and a prideful mind."

"Maybe it's indigestion."

But despite all the maybes, she did teach me. We spent hours in the sanctuary's dojo together, sparring with our bodies and minds and words . . . and occasionally smiling. We never talked about our losses on or off the mats. I think we both dwelled on those too much when we were alone to indulge when there was a task at hand, and another person in view.

And then one day she took me into her astrolab. It was more geek dome than observatory, a den detailing her obsession with the stars, and piled high with the mathematical tools she used to read the sky. It may as well have been a space station *on* the moon for all I could tell. She'd dimmed the lights, and the night sky appeared above.

"Can you point out the twelve constellations that comprise the Zodiac?" she asked imperiously.

"No."

"That's okay. I only want to show you one." She pointed to a constellation west of my own, Sagittarius. It looked like just another clump of stars to me. "This is Ophiuchus, and its brightest star is a white dwarf. It's feeding on matter from its neighbor, a red giant, and quickly approaching its maximum possible size. It's highly unstable."

Like you, I remember thinking, as she craned her neck upward. "Maybe it should go on a diet."

Tekla's mouth firmed, but she otherwise ignored me. "It will go supernova soon. It will be a violent explosion, one that will outshine entire galaxies for a time."

" 'Soon' meaning thousands of years from now, right?"

She shrugged. "Or tomorrow."

I'd eyed the star nervously because there was a reason she was telling me this. Tekla didn't waste energy on trivialities.

"Don't worry. It won't affect earth in the least. And after it goes supernova, turning into the thing it was meant to be all along, all that will remain of it will be a little pulsar. Just another tiny neutron star freckling the face of the night sky."

"So it just disappears?"

She shook her head. "It's displaced, dispelled. The matter comprising it simply goes somewhere else, and all that work, all that energy and violence, really amounts to nothing."

"So?"

"So it shows that against the palate of the universe, making an impact is easy. But making a difference . . . that's what's proven to be hard."

And no matter how much I huffed, puffed, teased, and taunted, she'd refused to say more than that. Apparently I was supposed to look at ol' Ophiuchus and be a Seer too.

Making an impact is easy. Making a difference is hard.

As Cher said, how profound. How telling that it could have such disparate meaning depending on who, Tekla or Xavier, was saying it.

"I have something too," Suzanne said. Her cheerful voice was strained with the need to get this party back on track. I smiled, grateful for her concern, though it was unnecessary. I wasn't Olivia, and held no soft spot for Xavier. She pulled a small jewelry box from her black clutch, handing it to me with a shy smile. "It's a thank-you for throwing the rehearsal dinner tonight. Arun wanted to show his gratitude for allowing the wedding to be held at Valhalla too. We know how much work you've put into this."

"It was no problem," I murmured, taking the box. Opening it, I found a bracelet in gold so yellow it was almost orange. It was studded with multicolored precious stones, obviously antique and very expensive.

"It's called a hand flower. It's been in Arun's family for five generations."

"I have the matching ring, see?" Cher clamored from the bed to join her mother and me at the mirror. "They're kundans, one of the most popular motifs in Indian jewelry. Isn't that right, Momma?"

Suzanne nodded. "Arun said they're good luck. Protects against the evil eye."

"Arun said that, did he?" I murmured.

I thought of Tekla giving me lessons and knowledge she thought would protect me, and of Caine, another Seer who gave me weapons and his body as armor. And now this woman—or more accurately, her wannabe baby-daddy—was giving me a pretty, hopeful little bauble with mystical meaning from a country I'd never visit. I lifted the bracelet to the light.

"Why would Arun give these to me?"

"I told you. He's grateful. And besides," she said, eyes flicking to the photo Helen had tried to destroy me with. "True friends are the families we choose."

I looked at her for a long moment before pulling her into a hug I think surprised us both. Taking in the scents of expensive bath oil and custom perfume, I smiled against her hair. "Sometimes *you* are shockingly profound."

She pulled back, eyes glistening as she smiled at me, then pulled Cher—the rest of my chosen family—into the hug. "Well," she said modestly, "I've skimmed a lot of life-coaching articles in my day."

It was perhaps the girliest moment of my life, but I didn't mind so much. There was no one I had to defend myself from here.

"So. Shall we go celebrate?"

I nodded, then dumped the photo in my bag. I didn't want to leave it behind and let Helen think she'd gotten to me, so I'd dispose of it outside of the mansion. I refused to let that woman make a difference *or* an impact on me.

Cher accompanied Suzanne downstairs to help attend to her adoring guests, Lindy left me alone, and Mackie wasn't lurking behind my shower curtain. The night was looking up.

I made sure to don my "hand flower" bracelet, and joined them within the hour to find the secondary dining room transformed.

Into a gothic bordello.

Terry, winner of the now infamous treasure hunt, sidled up to me almost immediately.

"What's all this?" I asked, gesturing at the unapologetic red and black scheme. Sure, the party was being held in "my" house, but like all good social debs, I hadn't a thing to do with the planning. Besides, if there was one thing that could give me away as Joanna Archer, it was my inability to juggle a menu and a seating arrangement.

"I know." Terry had a camera in one hand, a red cocktail with an onyx-stemmed glass in the other, and was dressed in the basic black the invitations had requested. "It's just one big juicy pot of pornography, right? Arun wanted to show off some of his more intricate textiles, and these are done in the colors of the family coat of arms."

"Indians have coats of arms?"

"Compliments of the British. There weren't any fire hydrants to piss on in the old days, so they had to mark everything with a sword and a lion."

I glanced at the silks lining tables and chairs, the tapestries hanging from the walls and their matching footstools, the double-wide lounge chairs with their red brocade. Crystal tassels set practically every inanimate object to sparkle. I guess nothing said "home sweet whorehouse" like black teardrop crystals. I blinked until I could focus properly again, turning to Terry. "You're the photographer?"

"Unofficial," he sniffed, casting a glance over his shoulder. Two small dark men were snapping photo after photo of the room's focal point, a moon-shaped table where Suzanne sat, arms linked with her groom.

"So that's Arun Brahma." My initial impulse to revile him upon sight reared again, but I dampened it, not wanting it to affect an accurate reading of someone who could be worse than merely slick. He could be dangerous.

For a moment I thought he also might be sleeping with his eyes open. While Suzanne laughed gaily, tossing her hair before the cameras like it was an Olympic event, he just sat there, merely altering his profile every once in a while so the photographers had to move for him rather than the reverse. Yet when Suzanne said his name, brushing her hand against his shoulder in as intimate a gesture as one could get while still clothed, his response was immediate. His regally dull expression didn't brighten, but it altered, like one of those paintings that seemed to follow your progress across the room with a knowing gaze. He leaned toward her with such fierce attentiveness that I wanted to slap him with a restraining order.

That wasn't love, I thought, watching him drink in her every feature as if it were the first time . . . and he was very thirsty. That was just creepy.

"You haven't met him yet?" Terry sounded surprised.

I shook my head. "He's suspiciously private. Does he move from her side?"

Terry sipped from his bloodred drink. "Only when eye-fucking her from afar."

Also creepy, but then who could blame him? The bride-to-be looked fantastic, blond hair set in siren's waves, lips as red as the tapestry behind her, eyes glowing. Still, there was something about the way he responded to Suzanne that just felt wrong. She tugged on his arm and he swerved toward her like a weight on a chain. A few months ago I would have closed in and tried to sniff out the problem— maybe he was drugged, maybe he was *Shadow*—but now all I could do was keep an eye on him, alert to even the smallest movement.

Or could I?

Easing back a step so I was out of Terry's peripheral vision, I lifted my glass to my lips. From behind it I whispered in a voice so low only those with access to other realities and realms could hear it. "Hey, Arun . . ."

His head swiveled before he caught himself. Eyes meeting mine, now narrowed, he paused only a moment before looking away. But he'd swallowed hard before he did it.

Suzanne sensed the absence of his attention as clearly as if she'd moved from sun to shade. She caught the arc of his quickly averted gaze, and brightened when she saw me. Her crimson smile widened as she waved, and she pointed at her wrist to indicate my bracelet.

I gave her a big cheesy thumbs-up while Arun watched her with an intensely glowing gaze. Most women would kill to be looked at like that. But some had been killed *after* being looked at like that. Now that I knew that he was something *other* than he claimed, I worried for Suzanne. I had no clue what his angle was, if he'd left me protective weapons on a scavenger's hunt, or if he was an ally. All I knew for sure was I didn't want her marrying him.

"Well, she looks radiant," I said to Terry, almost forlornly. Damn. She always had such bad taste in men.

"Yes. Jewels on every digit, and each one a testament to the power of blow jobs."

Time to extract myself from *this* conversation, I thought, brows raised. I turned away, caught Helen lingering in the doorway, and turned back. "Um, where's Cher?"

"Here, I'm here!"

"All done having bulimia, darling?" Terry asked as she joined us.

Cher shuddered delicately. "This ethnic food is hell on the American digestive tract."

"Told you to stick with vodka," Terry singsonged, holding up his glass.

"You should at least give it a try. I practically killed myself putting this party together," I said, knowing Helen could hear. I'd done nothing but throw the name and number of Suzanne's preferred party planner on Helen's desk, and I smiled, seeing her back go ramrod straight before she stalked from the room. Good. The less time she spent around my mortals, the better.

"Seriously, Olivia." Cher's gaze followed my own. "What does your housekeeper do other than skulk in doorways?"

"That's pretty much it."

Oblivious to my frown, she patted down her streaked hair with alternating black and red nails. "You should can her ass. Just because your father put up with that behavior doesn't mean you have to."

"No, no, no." Terry fisted one hand on his hip. "You need to look at her contract first. Otherwise she'll go straight to the press and reveal all your nasty little secrets."

"I don't have nasty little secrets." I just had nasty big ones.

"She'll just make it up," he said, jerking his head. "Don't you read *People* magazine? Celebrities' nannies do it all the time. And that bitch doesn't like you."

I wasn't surprised Cher and Terry had noticed . . . or that they didn't care for Helen. Mortals might be ignorant of otherworldly battles and politics, but everyone had intuition. Supersenses were just extremely well-developed extensions of that.

"Oh, here. I forgot this before . . ." Cher reached into her ample cleavage and withdrew a rolled up photo. "It's the one you made me take on that awful scavenger hunt. I didn't know if you still wanted it, or if you'd rather forget the whole thing, but it was developed along with all the other party pictures, so I made you a copy."

I held the photo in front of me, shocked at the crispness

of the image. The flash had caught the intricate etchings on the old treasure chest perfectly, along with the symbol that had been stalking my waking hours. I traced it with my fingertip, wondering aloud. "But what is it?"

Terry tossed a glance at the photo and finished the rest of his drink. "A snake. Duh."

He set his glass on a passing waiter's tray, wiped his mouth with the back of his hand, and turned back to me. Seeing my surprise, he leaned closer. "It is. See? Wrapped around a stick or some sort of staff."

Studying the photo more closely, I decided he was possibly right.

"What?" he asked, clearly offended by my pursed brow. "Snakes are present in practically every mythological system out there. Google it. You wouldn't believe the shit they represent."

"Such as?"

"Guardians of sacred treasures and sites—"

"Like in *Indiana Jones*?"

"Yeah, temples and stuff." He sniffed, tossing his head. "And, like, medicine and healing. Renewal and regeneration—shedding skin, get it?—and vengefulness, sometimes deceit . . ."

But my mind had snagged on the temple connection. A stupa was a monument containing Buddhist relics, which could be loosely interpreted as a sort of temple. As tulpas had derived directly from Tibetan Buddhism, the connection seemed more than coincidental. Because there was a stupa, or an extremely realistic rendition of one, in this very house. Not a definitive clue, but it was a place to start. "Thank you, Terry," I murmured, refolding the photo.

"Sure," he shrugged, then brightened. "Come on. For your sake I will risk death by Naga chili pepper."

Which would buy me time to think, not that I needed a lot of it. It was clear I was going to have to put the problem of Arun Brahma aside and canvass the stupa while I still could. If anything out of the ordinary occurred at

this rehearsal dinner—and a homicidal attack by a creature escaped from another world certainly qualified—
Lindy would immediately alert the Tulpa. Then every
action within these walls would be catalogued like a foren-
sic exam. So I'd investigate tonight just to be safe, maybe
during the soup course, before making sure all the guests
got home safely. Tomorrow I'd stop one of my best friends
from marrying a man who made her unabashedly happy
despite both his stalker and otherworldly qualities. After
that?

I'd gather up the arsenal my mother had left me and go
kill myself a tulpa.

20

Dusk still came early in February, so night's fingers slipped into the mansion before the main course was even served. I glanced surreptitiously at my watch, knowing it would be well into the midnight hours before this party was over. Suzanne hadn't stopped beaming since I'd arrived, and damned if I was going to be the one to wipe the smile from her face by cutting the festivities short. Even Arun had eased up on the devotedly deranged husband act, swaying in his seat as Bollywood films played merrily on the wall screens.

Deciding a round of raucous toasting was needed to slip away unseen, I passed the suggestion into the ear of a bald man who'd been bouncing along enthusiastically in front of a one-dimensional Aishwarya Rai. It was akin to holding a match to a water-starved field. The idea blazed through the crowd, and a microphone suddenly appeared. Some people were sincere in their toasts, some elicited hoots of laughter and a public dialogue, while others simply vyed for the attention of a man who ruled over his own Indian principality . . . and for the favor of a woman who would soon be a princess. I made my escape halfway through one of these.

Footsteps light, I slipped through the heart of the house, ears pricking at the occasional bursts of laughter from the dining area, though within minutes it felt like the festivities were in a separate home altogether. This side of the estate was crypt-quiet, and just as cool, as if all the body heat and warmth were confined to the proximity of the human activity.

And here you are, I thought wryly. Baiting not-quite-dead things in the dark. Somebody cue the too-stupid-to-live music.

But I was almost there. Another corner and I'd gained entry to a room made entirely of smooth white marble, bare of floor coverings but with tiny spotlights set low on artifacts Xavier had deemed precious. Stupas, essentially aboveground tombs, traditionally housed the bones of great lamas of the past. Xavier's stupa didn't contain bones—not as far as I knew—but it did house a thirteen-hundred-year-old *Tibetan Book of the Dead*, a recessed dais complete with gold throne, a phalanx of traditional prayer wheels, and a half dozen animistic masks. Crafted of varying metals and woods, each of these featured mouths open wide in silent, monstrous screams.

Spooky. Shit.

Three medieval-style windows popped from their casements along one wall, mere eye slits compared to the giant leaded windows overlooking the front lawn. Unadorned, they also seemed to follow my progress across the cavernous room. The rest of the marble room was sparse, making the giant gold dais and throne stand out all the more. With no interest in waking the dead, I avoided the prayer wheels, my attention on the masks spaced along the white. All were antique, all mystical, and I knew all contained a spirit trapped inside the hollowed space.

I put a wide swath of space between myself and a mask I'd worn before, even while squinting at the design work, looking for the telltale depiction of a snake. The spirit residing in that mask had once tried to take over my mind.

When donned unwillingly, it trapped a person's breath inside the concave form, effectively suffocating them without ever allowing their death. I half expected it to leap from the wall, secure itself to my face, and never let go.

Finishing with the masks, I turned my attention to the etchings on the *Book of the Dead*, bending low so I could view the spine of the book, propped open in its protective casing. Nothing. A closer look at the dais, carved and lacquered with geometric designs, proved it absent of anything resembling a snake, and the ornate throne was covered only in faceless whorls and endless knots. Sighing, I turned around in the room's center, trying to see the place anew, then stilled as my gaze locked on Xavier's office opposite the stupa's entrance.

My office now, I reasoned, eyes narrowing like those slitted windows. And one containing a hidden room where he'd ritualistically, incrementally, given up his soul to provide power and strength to his benefactor, the Tulpa. Resisting the urge to spin a prayer wheel on the way, I left the aboveground tomb for a room buried even deeper.

Pressing my back against the office door, I took in the scent of leather and old books, a faint stale whiff of the cigars Xavier had liked to smoke, and something like invisible iron lying in the air—heavy, but not readily there. Any other mortal would dismiss it—and the chill it induced in the spine—as skittishness induced by a dead man's room. Yet I knew it for the scorched remnants of a soul, leaving Xavier a dead man even before his body had given up the fight.

Pushing from the oak door, I made my way to the giant desk, where I flipped on a banker's lamp and sent the shadows scurrying like rats. The chocolate walls were still lined with bookshelves, their contents still untouched. Smoked mirrors and crown molding slipped along the coffered ceiling, and everything else was dark mahogany, rich and shining, yet utterly without warmth. I left the heavy burgundy curtains drawn, not wanting the light from the study to spill out and reveal my location.

Now to discover the hidden room's entrance.

I tried all the places you see in the movies—a latch under the desk, the wall lamp shaped like a candle, individual books lining the back wall. Nothing. Yet in going through the desk drawers I discovered the giant folder Xavier had handed over to me while on his deathbed. It detailed every boring financial aspect of the family business, which is why I hadn't missed it, though I had no idea how and when it got shoved back into his study.

Helen, I thought wryly, dropping the folder onto the desk. She must have removed it during that bleak period I'd been convalescing in the mansion. Like I said, I had no interest in its contents, but I hated when someone made assumptions about what I could or couldn't do. I'd decide for myself if I were interested in the family business, thanks very much. So I left the binder on the desk for later and went back to my search.

"C'mon, Jo," I whispered, looking for some freaky little symbolic mark. Everyone in the Zodiac world loved that shit. Hearing a muffled sound just outside the door, I fell still, but after a full minute I resumed my search. It was probably just one of the masks yawning in boredom.

I was about to do the same when my gaze caught on the fireplace . . . and more specifically the tool set perched next to it. Interesting, as I'd never seen a fire burning inside it. Then again, Xavier had been built like an ox, and had probably run hot, at least before his illness. Which made the stoking tools even more of an oddity. Bending closer, I found hinges attached to each wrought-iron tool. "Bingo," I whispered, yanking on one.

It wasn't that easy. They obviously had to be pulled in a specific order, and with four tools, the combinations were endless. I tried a variation of the most obvious ones, glanced at my watch, then began a second, more hurried round. By the third I was sweating. By the fourth I heard another sound outside the office door.

"Think," I cajoled myself, closing my eyes, trying to figure out what combination Xavier would find meaningful. The man had been neither sentimental nor superstitious. He'd only gotten involved with the Tulpa out of a desire to make a boatload of money. But while that told me he was a stupid, greedy bastard—things I already knew—it didn't help me ferret out the combination leading to his secret room. Frustrated, I yanked on all four tools at the same time, like I could force the damned thing open.

A latch handle shot from beneath the middle shelf.

I couldn't hold back my surprised laugh. Of *course* it would be all four at once. Xavier Archer always had wanted it all. Grabbing the handle and yanking it up, I pulled the heavy hinged door wide and entered the secret room.

Dual scents of sandalwood and soot hit me, the molecules and motes still heavy with remnants of the rituals Xavier had performed here. Obviously no one had aired out the room since his death, and for once I was thankful I'd lost my overly keen sense of smell.

After locating and lighting a thick, squat candle—the room lacked both electricity and contemporary furnishings—I shut the false wall behind me to prevent the scent's escape, then gave the odd room a long once-over.

It's like a movie set. Though all the furnishings— the pillows and throws, the incense and gold Buddhist statues—had been imported directly from Tibet. Xavier's fetish for authenticity, and undoubtedly the Tulpa's insistence on it, was apparent in every carefully chosen item. Colorful rugs in primary colors were rolled like yoga mats in the corner of the room. Bowls of bronze, silver, copper, and wood were stacked on a shelf above those, while another held an astonishing array of incense and candles, caught in stark relief against the whitewashed walls. I held the candle and the photo out in front of me and began comparing objects.

Intricate singing bowls, originally meant to worship the Buddhist gods, sat next to simple mallets lined on a rough-hewn shelf. I compared my photo to those, again coming up empty.

Dropping to the rug I'd once seen Xavier worshipping upon, I remembered the way Helen had stood at his back, forcing him to his knees and holding him there. The look on his face had been one of fear laced with agony, and while shock and lifelong animosity kept me from feeling sorry for him then, when I knelt on the very same pillow and viewed the room from his perspective, I couldn't help feeling a sympathetic twinge.

The air was cooler and less cloying on the floor than when standing, so I crossed my legs and reached for the sole item still propped in the room's center, a handheld prayer wheel. I'd researched the things after watching Xavier chant with one, and I gave this wheel an experimental flick of my wrist. Its weight surprised me as the metal cylinder inside clicked and the ballasted chain whirled to release the universally revered sound "Om" into the room.

I flicked my wrist again, then again, finding it strangely soothing. A mortal mind focused on the ritual of worship would easily fall into a trancelike state, bringing them closer to the object, or personage, of their worship.

In return for a few slivers of their soul.

Despite the thought, I flicked the prayer wheel again. The tonal notes sat up in the air, not loud but with an even hum, but since I wasn't worshipping anyone, I was safe enough. One thing I'd discovered in my year with the agents of Light was that intention was what gave a person's actions, and life, meaning. If one lived focused on their greatest desires to the exclusion of all else, then the Universe would move and redirect energy to provide the desired results. I flicked the wheel again and caught a rhythm. The chain reeled around, sending the magic out into the Universe.

So what was my intent? My greatest desire? Certainly not to ration out what was left of my soul to the Tulpa.

But seeing him dead? Yeah, that would be nice. I'd love to watch all the negative energy responsible for the Tulpa's powers spiral out—whirl, whirl, whirl—dissolving harmlessly into the Universe. But then what? I frowned. Leave Warren free to run this valley the way he saw fit? That no longer seemed right either.

The prayer wheel whirled steadily now; I'd caught my rhythm.

Finding my mother was an obvious driving need, maybe because her desertion hadn't been absolute. Zoe Archer straddled the divide between here and gone, super and mortal, truth and lies. She was like oxygen to me, invisible but vital, and as long as she was out there, I would want to find her. I could admit that much—whirl, whirl—at least to myself.

And then there was Hunter.

I shut my eyes, flicked my wrist and recalled his face. "Hunter . . ."

Why was it so hard to let go of someone who'd so carelessly released me? It hadn't been done in a void after all, not like Zoe, her whereabouts unknown. No, he'd left me for another woman—one he'd courted against troop rules, one he'd married, and one he'd chased after for years, even after meeting me.

So why?

Because he'd regretted his decision. I'd seen it in those underground tunnels, lurking in him like an undiagnosed disease. At the last, right before he abandoned this world, a small part of him wanted to stay, wanted me to understand. Wanted *me.*

There is absolutely nothing wrong with you. Not even in the darkest corner of that beautiful soul.

Yes, Hunter had known my darkness, tasted it, and even taken it on when sharing the aureole. But ours wasn't a onetime connection. It was a magic that reared its head every time we touched, when we made love, both of us willing it to grow stronger.

That was what Trish meant when she'd spoken of a soul connection.

So would it have lived between us if not for the aureole? How beautiful would he have found me without it? Would I even have had a chance of capturing his interest in my current fragile, *mortal*, state?

Whatever the answer, it neither changed the past nor the one thing that kept bucking whenever I mentally tried to say good-bye: *Hunter* had offered up his body as a soft place for me to land in a season where everything was hard. I'd been on my heels in my new role as the Kairos, part of a world I hadn't known existed. My sister's death had rocked me back further. And, in the hours before the first time we made love, the shock of finding my childhood lover locked in the embrace of a mortal enemy had flattened my will to live.

For a while Hunter made all of that better, if not okay. And it hadn't been a one-sided seduction. I could own up to my part in it all. I hadn't turned to him as much as I'd fled, finding solace in his strength and peace in his acceptance. Hunter had helped steady me in my new life.

The magic of the aureole connecting us? That was just fucking *icing*.

"Jo?"

My hand came to an abrupt stop as I opened my eyes, the sacred sound from the prayer wheel breaking into two syllables, then down into silence. I was on the floor of what looked and smelled like a Babylonian garden.

"Oh, hell no." The syllables scratched the air like stencils.

"That's what you get for flinging around a prayer wheel," I muttered, standing cautiously and trying to blink away the reality before me. But there was no blinking it away.

I was in Midheaven. Again.

21

I couldn't tell who'd called me. Between the whirring of the prayer wheel's chain cutting air like newly sharpened shears, it had been a fractured sound, like a computer getting a hard boot. But at least I knew where I was.

Another elemental room, I thought, glancing about, my breath echoing hollowly in the tinny air. What else could it be? It was both as shockingly ornate as the odd water room, and as mysterious as Solange's fire room, yet singularly different than both. Weighed down beneath the scents of verdant foliage and humidity, it would have also been as dim as a late-lying sunset were it not for the twinkling lights strung across drooping boughs by the hundreds. A tentative, almost playful breeze pressed against me, and I shivered as I glanced up at a ceiling hidden by viny whips and a cover of evergreen and pine. More lights winked like stars between the branches, and I shivered again, recalling Solange's sky of soul-encrusted stars.

But how the hell did I get here? Shen had told me on my last go-round with the elemental rooms that drugs were what allowed incorporeal passage into this world.

Apparently incense and a prayer wheel counted.

And what about calling forth the world in my mind? I hadn't called Midheaven to me; I hadn't even been thinking about it.

No. Just about someone living here. Rolling my eyes at my own stupidity, I searched for some other sort of exit while trying to forget Diana's helpful addendum: that I needed someone to pull me back out of the world in case Solange found me here.

Flat, stone-topped lanterns were tucked amid the greenery, while topiaries and pyramid-shaped shrubs popped up like the heads of curious gnomes. Centered was a small lawn with a gravel pathway cutting the middle, while a small pond sparkling with refracted light sat to my right. Moss in every shade of green climbed boulders slick with algae, and a cluster of wild roses burst brightly from verdant thistle where berries also glistened with dew.

Yet all was not nature and silva. Curving chaises and concrete lounge chairs dotted the small space, and baroque chandeliers swung from the lowermost branches of the accommodating pines. Seductive statues cast inquisitive glances my way, and wrought-iron side tables were layered in lace and pastel spun silk.

The coup de grace was the giant stone table tucked beneath a Japanese cherry tree caught in full bloom. A tiered tray held finger sandwiches, scones with clotted cream, quiche, and tiny pastel petit fours tucked between slivers of white cake. A mirrored side buffet sported crystal goblets and flutes, and a perfect mismatching of gorgeous bone china.

"A fucking tea party." My metallic mutter skipped sound waves like a rock.

"You'd prefer a latte from the drive-through, I suppose?"

I'd been anticipating an appearance by the dangerous rulers of this pretty little world, and whirled to run smack into the chest of an all-too-real, and apparently bemused,

Hunter Lorenzo. He quirked a brow, and steadied me with one hand.

"Of course." I pulled away, trying to hide my shock, my alarm. My *pleasure*. "I'm American."

He merely motioned to the tea set. I looked around, waiting for ambush or at least to wake up. Nothing happened, so I inched past a fern floor and moved farther into the garden. "Tricked-out pad," I said lightly, though my heart was pounding, making my throat tight.

"The earth room," he said, confirming my prior suspicions. His voice was as leaden as mine. "Whatever you used to induce the dream state must have been from the dust."

I'd been right about the incense then, I thought, frowning. And the drugs Carlos had given me the first time were disguised in drink . . . thus calling forth the water room. I didn't even want to know what I needed to bring on fire.

I tried to meet Hunter's gaze, but after working so hard to push even the thought of him away, his sudden appearance was jarring. His eyes were warmly intense, destroying the illusion that I'd let go of this man emotionally. I hadn't. Not even a bit.

As usual, I covered my discomfort with attitude. "So why are you here?" I asked, crossing my arms.

He took in my body language, blinking fast like he too was making a mental adjustment, and lifted his chin. "We're both a part of this world now," he said softly.

"So that means what? I'm at your mercy? I'm trapped and have to wait until you and your *wife* decide to let me go."

He tilted his head. "Don't you have an anchor grounding you back home?"

"I didn't mean to come here."

"No wonder she's so angry." His brow furrowed, and for the first time he looked unreal, as if the expression was pressed upon his face like putty, altering a moment after he willed it. Did I look the same? "We really are connected . . ."

His gaze flitted to my lips, then back to my eyes. I thought about the way he'd strung me along, pulling me in until the very end. Even in the moments before forever leaving Las Vegas for Midheaven proper, when trapped in a tunnel before the rushlight that would ferry him to Solange—his wife, his grail—he'd played on our intimacy.

There's absolutely nothing wrong with you. Not even in the darkest corner of that beautiful soul.

No, I thought now. There's not. But there's something wrong with someone who could equally want, love, two women. I didn't believe that was possible, and getting my life back meant letting go of every impossibility. If friends were the family we choose, then it was time to let Hunter go completely. He'd been no friend to me.

"No, Hunter," I said coldly. "We're not even from the same world."

His jaw clenched at that. His nostrils flared. It was a wonderful display of masculine pique. "Who's Carlos?"

I drew back. "What?"

"Carlos. You called out his name the last time you were here. You called for him to help you." His voice was so strained it almost made me laugh. Was he jealous? While biding in another world, locked in his new/old lover's embrace?

"Carlos is a friend." A real one.

"How—" He broke off and cleared his throat. I thought he was going to ask how long I'd known Carlos, but he switched it up on me. "How long have I been gone?"

"Ten weeks." And three days.

A shudder moved through his entire body.

"Over here?" I asked, because time passed differently in Midheaven. It ran backward or sideways . . . by some other means than that which flipped the earth around its axis.

"I've counted only two days." And the strain in his voice meant he'd been counting hard, almost as if the loss of his life on the other side of the tunnel system—the one he'd so freely left behind—pained him. It made me frown.

It made him irritable. When he opened his eyes again, the worry had already been shuttered. "Ten weeks, huh? Shit, the weather probably hasn't even changed, and you've already found a new 'friend.'"

"Well, I'm just like the weather, *Jaden*. You just don't know when it's going to change."

"So what's the forecast now?"

"Cloudy," I said. "With a good chance of fuck you."

"So, the usual," he said dryly.

It made me want to smile, so I bit my lip against it.

Hunter stared a moment longer before his expression cleared, and then he strode to the table . . . and poured me some tea.

O-kay, I thought, still casting glances into the surrounding rain forest as I followed and lowered myself to the stone bench opposite him. Inhaling deeply, I scented cloves and leaves and flowers, pressed and steamed into a pulpy death, and realized my sense of smell was still powerful over here. The strong mixture was almost as relaxing as chanting.

"Don't you have to ask permission to enter the earth room? Get a hall pass or something from the wifey?"

His face hardened as much as it could in its strange putty state. "I stole your gem from Solange's planetarium. All I had to do then was wait for your return."

I gave him the same look I would have had he told me Santa was real. He'd stolen from a woman even the other matriarchs in this world feared? "And what would be worth that risk?" I asked coolly.

His returned gaze was funeral sad. It made me feel like I'd been the one to trample what was between us underfoot, which was ridiculous. I should have blurted out then what had happened to me in the time since he'd left, but for some reason I didn't yet want to confess to him my mortal state. Maybe I'd just have some tea first.

Hunter returned his attention to his cup, but instead of pouring black tea as he had in mine, the same pot spit out a hot, sugary brew of cardamom and ginger and creamy milk. One side of his mouth quirked at my astonished stare as he returned the pot to the table's center. "You can have anything you wish when you're dreaming, right?"

"Is that why you look like you?" I asked suddenly, lowering my cup. He was the Hunter I'd known, lithe and coiled strength beneath burnished skin, glossy black hair pulled into a low, blunt club. Jaden Jacks was more imposing, with his shock of bleached hair above a frame so large it almost burst. He was more like what you'd think a superhero would look like. Except, I thought, for those sun-spun eyes. Those hadn't changed at all.

"In dreams you become as you wish to be."

I didn't know what that meant, and it made it sound like this was as much his dream as mine. So I concentrated on what I did know.

"You should have told me who you were," I said, setting down my cup so suddenly it clattered against its saucer.

"I told you what truth I could."

"Which part was truth, Hunter?" The part where he made love to me but was thinking of Solange? When he claimed he could tell me apart from any other woman by touch alone? Or was it when he told me the Light inside me was magnified because of the Shadow?

I waved my hand in the air, dismissing the subject before he could answer. It no longer mattered.

Not looking at me, Hunter took a deep breath, then paused. A moment later he tried again. "I once told you drinking almost killed me a decade ago, remember?"

I nodded, but didn't tell him that I'd read the manual called *Dark Matters*. That I already knew about the night Solange nearly drove a tomahawk through his chest.

Solange then. Solange *now*.

"Well, it was really only three years past my metamorphosis. I was twenty-eight, in my prime. I was seduced, blindsided by . . . *her*."

He shot me a meaningful glance, which told me he didn't want to say Solange's name. Names had power no matter what realm you inhabited. They could call a person to you, and alert them to your presence. Since he'd stolen a gem from her sky of stars, and was now having tea with the woman whose soul he held, I didn't blame him.

My own voice fell to a whisper. "And why couldn't you tell me that much?"

"Warren forbade it. And no one else in the troop knew. Warren wiped the memory of what I'd done from all minds but mine." Eyes unfocused, he ran a hand over his head, pulling loose a few strands. "That was my punishment for succumbing to a Shadow."

I believed that. On the night I'd given up all my powers, Warren told me he'd known Hunter would be attracted to me. He said that I, a half Shadow, was just Hunter's type. Saying nothing, I glanced around the garden—the strange amalgamation of English Victorian and Asian chic—and sighed.

"Does it help at all to know I'd have told you the truth if possible?"

I jerked my head. "It only makes me wonder what else you were lying about."

He bit his lower lip, eyes saying, *Not us*.

To refute, I motioned around the room.

Hunter leaned on his forearms and closed his eyes. Opening them again, he looked resigned. "I need to tell you about . . . it. About that night. I have to tell you all of it."

"Over scones?" I asked acidly before shaking my head.

"I must. I—"

"I saw it!" I pounded the pretty stone table with my fist. "I read the manual. I saw the way you met in the bar, the fight"—the *lovemaking*—"atop the car. Everything! It was all there."

"It's recorded now?" He winced, the expressive cringe a half second behind the impulse creating it. It made me wince in return. "Of course it is."

The events were over, and the open knowledge wouldn't affect either the Shadow or the Light. Thus Hunter had no more secrets to hide, though somehow it made him look vulnerable. He ducked his head, nodding to himself, then dared a glance up. "And what about . . . the rest?"

Slowly, I licked my lips. "What do you mean?"

"Doesn't it make even a little difference?"

"I didn't read the whole fucking manual, Hunter." He opened his mouth to protest and I held up a palm. "I don't want to know what happened, okay? I don't care about your reasons."

"But—"

"I don't need to know why you left me, only that you did!" It was out of my mouth so fast I jerked backward. Damn it!

Hunter's gaze softened. "Jo—"

"No!" My turn to shake my head, and I did so. Hard. "We had another conversation once. After you kept me from slaying Regan in front of Ben."

I stared down at the dark warm liquid cupped in my palms, remembering Regan, dead and harmless now, though she certainly hadn't been then. She'd taken on an appearance similar to mine in order to seduce my childhood love. She'd known their lovemaking would kill me. Yet the only way to stop her would have been to put an arrow through her chest during the act . . . and that would have destroyed Ben. Hunter saved me from the decision by spiriting me away. And that night was the first that we'd made love.

I glanced back up at him, knowing we were remembering the same thing. "I told you then that I hoped someone, someday, would feel as strongly toward you as I did for Ben."

And Solange was rabid when it came to him.

"But that wasn't the truth," I went on, pushing my cup away. "What I meant was I wanted someone to feel that way about *me*. Strong enough to put me first. To stay. No matter what."

His voice softened, his eyes turned pleading. "It wasn't that simple."

I cocked a brow, voice flat. "So you've said."

And I'd heard enough. I stood, wanting out of the earth room, or the jungle book, or wherever the fuck I was. My gaze momentarily caught on a flickering movement behind a flowing willow but the tree fronds only swayed in a soft breeze, sparkling with little lights and tiny chimes.

"Just finish the manual." He stood too, pleading with his eyes. "It will make a difference. It will matter."

It was a *dark matter*, I thought, jaw clenching. And I was gray. "Here's what matters. You told your wife I'm the Kairos, and now she's sent Mackie after me."

"She's the only one here in full possession of her soul. You, me, the other women. We all have less than her. We *are* less than her."

"So your wife is invincible?"

His jaw clenched again at *wife* but he jerked his head. "Yes."

I raised my brows. "All-knowing, all-seeing? As close to a goddess as you can come?"

"Over here she is *the* goddess."

I tilted my head, thought about it a little more, then held out my hand. "Give me my gem."

"What?"

"The one you said you stole from her sky. I want it."

He narrowed his eyes, and there was that strange shifting of expressions again, one below the other. "I can't."

"Because the goddess will know if you do?"

"Yes," he whispered.

"Then how the hell did you manage to steal a gem from her beloved soul sky without her knowing?"

Hunter froze. And laughter bubbled in the trees, ringing bells, sending the lights to sway. "Very good, Archer."

I wasn't the Archer. But Hunter didn't know that . . . and therefore neither did Solange. She sauntered from behind an elm like the goddess everyone thought she was. I *knew* I'd seen movement there.

She was dressed in low-cut silver or gray, it altered depending on how she moved through the light, and swept the ground cover as she walked. She held up something misshapen and tiny that winked bloodred in the meager light.

"Hold her," she told Hunter, and before I even had a chance to bolt, he had my arms pinned to my side. Yet his grip was gentle, like a caress, which made it worse. I got a whiff of his skin as his breath rustled my hair, and an image flashed through my mind, his naked legs folded like wings over mine. Cringing, I pushed it away.

"First Regan. Now Solange." I could almost make a paper doll chain with all his betrayals.

He drew closer, as if his touch was an embrace.

"Your boner is trespassing," I said roughly, bringing my heel up and back. He grunted, doubling forward, but didn't let go.

Solange's laugh sent the bells to tinkling again. "Darling Joanna, as feminine as ever. But what on earth have you done to your aura? You look positively gray."

I am a gray.

"You can see that?" Just keep her talking. Talk . . . and maybe someone would find me.

In a dead man's hidden room. Yeah, that was likely.

Rolling my soul gem in her fingertips, Solange lifted a slim shoulder. "One's aura is both protection and an indication of their life energy. It's like a cloak thrown about the shoulders. You look positively naked."

"It's my chakras. They're all out of balance."

She closed a fist over my soul. "Maybe it's the Shadow overtaking the Light in you."

I shook my head. "I'm no longer an agent of Light. Warren kicked me out of the troop."

Hunter jolted. Solange scoffed. "Warren would never do that. After all, you're the Kairos, right? A perfect balance of Shadow and Light."

And she smiled sweetly, like it made me special.

Like it made me a target.

Hunter tensed, as did I. Solange held her smile as she lifted my misshaped stone to her lips and placed it in her mouth, and with it held between her teeth, blew me a kiss. Yet it was the siren waves of *her* mahogany hair that blew back over her shoulders as the starlight on her breath hit me. I inhaled involuntarily and her wordless voice whistled in my lungs. It said I would die. It promised immediately. And on the exhale, I screamed.

A crack sounded overhead, drowning my voice and shaking the trees above us. I didn't know what I'd done, but the foliage trembled and stone lanterns toppled. The lights above winked violently, the bells clanging like funeral tones. My heart caught its rhythm again . . . and immediately started pounding.

Hunter looked up. "That was on your side."

Another crack, followed by a thundering rumble. The sky darkened to opaqueness and the garden grew misty, blurring around us.

"No." Solange stood, fists clenched as if to beat the fog away. "You won't escape that way again."

"I've got her," Hunter said, strengthening his hold and yanking me to him so hard my newfound breath was again lost. He put his forearm around my neck, and I knew I'd be unconscious in seconds. When he leaned in to squeeze, though, the sky splintered again, and in the wake of the reverberating rumble, he whispered, "Run."

Solange straightened, eyes alight with black fury. She lifted another stone to her mouth, and I bolted, burying myself in greenery, but not before I felt the wind lash my back . . . and heard Hunter's deep wail.

I saw nothing between the mist and deepening sky. I tripped over roots and rocks, but kept sprinting in one direction. If it was a room, it had to have walls, right? Meanwhile, Solange's blown kiss chased me, surrounding me like the waves of a dozen oceans, pushing and pulling me at the same time, seeking entry to what remained of my soul.

Hitting the ground, I kept low as the alive, seeking air blasted overhead, and moved beneath the verdant ferns until I found an ancient poplar. It was so dark now that even squinting as I pivoted around the trunk I was unable to see my body below me. So I squealed when I found myself face-to-face with Hunter.

"Listen," he ordered, darting a glance over his shoulder. "I need to choke you out. Unconsciousness is the fastest way to get out of here. Whoever's trying to get to you may not have an anchor, but they've got willpower and your corporeal body next to them."

Did I *want* to go back to someone like that?

Hunter wasn't offering me a choice. "Once you're on the other side you can't ever come here again. Not for anything. Not at any cost. It won't be worth it."

"Why?"

"Because your soul is in her sky, Jo . . ."

No, it's in her mouth.

"It's just a sliver, and imperfections abound, but it's enough to control you."

I filed that information away for later, if there *was* a later, and shook my head. "I mean *why* are you protecting me?"

He was close enough that I saw the sadness spring up, outlining his irises. But Solange called out to him then, and though it sounded like she was still in the clearing, her voice was a bullet. It bowed him over. He fell into the mist and onto an earth as black as the sky above.

That's what happened under Solange's control.

I joined him, diving to where he'd disappeared. I thought he'd be unconscious himself, but his hands immediately found my neck. I startled, my first instinct to pull away, but Solange had used him to lure me here, and he'd defied her to get me back out. As his fingers tightened around my neck, I realized he was going to pay for freeing me.

And as long as he was going to pay, he was going to make it worth it. His mouth found mine like it was a target, and my eyes fluttered shut, the last strangled threads of my breath lost to his lips. The trees and bells blurred my name overhead, while Hunter's mouth moved against mine without sound. Then his expression shifted, separated, and dissolved. Yet his final words chased me back into my world. "Don't ever return. She wants your power, your ability to—"

A hand touched my shoulder and I located the floor beneath my back. Gasped for air.

And smelled burning sulfur.

When I opened my eyes, I froze, and thought about ignoring Hunter's advice and calling back out to Solange. Because I'd just woken up in a tomblike room, bereft of weapon or help . . . and with the Tulpa looming over me like I was already dead.

22

"What are you doing here?"

The Tulpa's tone was ice, his eyes narrowed, and if I could still have seen auras, I knew that his would be bright red.

When in doubt, I thought, the taste of tin still sharp at the back of my throat, answer a question with a question. "What happened?"

"You tell me, dear." He straightened, leaning on a cane, his voice still sharp. "I walked in and found you sleeping in the middle of the floor. I had a hard time rousing you. In fact, you seemed to be in some sort of meditative trance."

The last two words were said in the same tone a judge might use on a defendant . . . one he'd already found guilty.

Pushing the fear away, I stretched and yawned loudly. "Too much wine, I guess. I was missing my father, so I came to his office to be—I don't know, near him somehow. I was thinking how much he'd like to be at this dinner . . ." The Tulpa's brows arched, and I quickly amended my statement. Xavier would have loathed the festivities and not allowed it on his grounds. I shot the Tulpa a knowing smile. "I mean, everyone who is anyone is here, and he was so smart he could probably get Arun to put up the capital for some new business venture . . ."

The Tulpa twisted his cane handle thoughtfully. I hurried on. "So I was looking at the pictures on the mantel when I brushed up against those poky things out there, and found this." I motioned around the room, suddenly no more spacious than a honeycomb cell. The Tulpa's eyes following my fingertips certainly made me feel like I was about to get stung.

I dropped my hand to my side . . . too fast. A shift in expression and suddenly the elderly visage he'd donned for "Olivia's" benefit grew into points and angles. Shit. I started speaking quickly. "So I came in, picked up one of these old toys, and suddenly I was out like Kim Kardashian on a Saturday night."

He didn't laugh. In fact, the word "toys" had the dark brow lowering further. I tried on an innocent smile, but it sat forced on my face. The Tulpa stilled like an empty beach minutes before a tsunami.

Kill him, Joanna, I thought, swallowing hard. Kill him, gain the aureole, free the rogue agents in Midheaven. *Turn his own weapon against him.*

I glanced at the singing bowls and mallets. What was I supposed to do? Bonk him over the head with a handheld prayer wheel?

"H-How did you get here?" I asked, pushing to my palms. "I didn't see you at the party."

Meaning I hadn't invited him.

"I stopped by on a whim. The guard at the gate knows me. Then Helen told me you were here."

I recalled the scraping noises earlier at the door and fought not to sag. There was simply no way a mortal could escape these people's notice.

"It's an interesting room," the Tulpa said, pretending to look about. "Do you remember your father as being particularly . . . religious?"

I tilted my head, pretending I didn't know what he was

asking as I continued my search for a weapon. A prayer flag up the nose? Stab him with incense? "No, of course not. He was a Christian."

He didn't laugh. But he didn't strike me or smite me or, like, *eat* me either. Instead he held out his hand to help me up.

I rubbed a hand over my face like I was clearing the cobwebs, then accepted his offer with the other. He lifted me so smoothly it was like taking a magic carpet ride to my feet. When I looked up, the Tulpa's gaze was also smooth . . . and boring into mine. His fingertips played beneath mine as he traced my prints. I prayed Io's handiwork held up under the soft scrape of his fingernail. If not, I'd next feel my bones cracking beneath his palm.

But the charming smile from the boardroom had returned, if sporting an edge it hadn't before. "I think, my dear, that I can be a significant influence in your life."

I almost laughed. He already had *that* pretty well covered.

"I have enough people telling me what to do, thanks." I inserted a little pout in my tone, petulance topping it off like a sticky sweet cherry. "The board of directors wants me to hand control over to them, my secretary tries to hold me to my father's rigorous work schedule . . ." the Tulpa snorted. Xavier hadn't done a whole lot of work in his waning months. "Even my housekeeper keeps badgering me about responsibilities."

There. If I got through this alive, if he thought I was becoming suspicious or annoyed or fed up at Lindy's perceived place in this household, maybe he'd tell her to lay off. It would buy me the space I needed to inspect the mansion for more of its secrets. Sure enough, the Tulpa's top lip thinned.

"Now what in particular would a housekeeper be badgering you about?"

Inching toward an ornate gold-plated blade on a triangular base in the corner, I gave him a look that said, *Exactly!*

"Household budgets and stolen cars and moving back in here."

"But you live in the Greenspun Residences, don't you?"

Though anyone would know that, the Tulpa wasn't asking out of mere curiosity. Regan Dupree, the Shadow Leo, had been meting out information about me to the Tulpa by the spoonful to advance her own precarious position and get back in his good graces. She'd told him the Kairos was residing in the same building as Olivia before I managed to kill her.

The Tulpa leaned against the wall. "I'm assuming you have friends there? Neighbors? People you greet in the hallways . . . who help you with your groceries?"

"No one in particular," I said, and was about to say more, then thought better of lying. "Though one woman has been particularly friendly since Daddy's death . . ."

"And what's her name?" His voice smoothed out even further, tugging on my consciousness, so my head teetered on my neck. It was the same fizzy loss of control one had after doing shots on no sleep and an empty belly. I didn't even have to feign dizziness as I struggled for words.

"I don't think she ever told me. Odd, huh?"

"But she lives there?" The dream state intensified, and though I could fight the mind control—*somehow* I could fight it—I slouched a bit more. "Oh, yeah. She couldn't gain such regular access otherwise."

"And what does she look like?"

"She has red hair . . ." I frowned, pretending to think on it further. "And blond, and brown. Once even blue. But the red is best on her."

"A disguise, then?" he muttered, as if to himself. I reached for the gold knife, folded my palm around the upright handle.

"Wigs, anyway." I yawned loudly, feeling the buzz lessening. Good. His suspicion was lifting. "Big party girl," I added, and pulled upward. The knife didn't budge. It was welded to the base.

To hide the homicidal movement, I caressed the ornate bell propped next to the knife, before letting my hand drop.

He jerked his head. "Come with me."

And a giant pulse, a vibrational flash, had me stepping forward before I could stop it. I went with the impulse, though reminded myself to be more on guard as we returned to Xavier's office. If he really suspected me, I might end up grabbing hold of a knife and thrusting it into my own belly.

"Ever see one of these?" He pointed with his cane to a booklet lying on Xavier's great dark desk. A comic book. A *manual*.

I fought to keep my expression neutral. If the Tulpa was asking me about it, the people in my building, and what I knew of Xavier's religious habits—all while attempting to hoodoo me into eliciting the truth—then I wasn't even close to being off the hook.

"Yeah," I said as calmly as I could. "My sister used to read those rags."

"Did she ever show you one?"

"Joanna knew I'm loyal to *Vogue*."

"Not her," he said through clenched teeth. "The girl. In your building. Did she ever try to give you one of these?"

"Of course not. I mean . . . she's cool."

The Tulpa lifted his chin. "There are cool things in there. Look for yourself."

I glanced down and recognized the Shadow Pisces, Adele, caught in profile on the cover. Her face was iron, black smoke billowing behind her as she stared back at me. I feigned a shudder. "Her outfit is atrocious."

"There are other pictures."

He wasn't going to let up, so I sighed and took the manual. Opening it, I demonstrated what he was really interested in. The manual didn't come to life in my hands. No thought bubbles appeared above the heads of the featured Shadow agents. No cracks of battle or death cries lifted into the air. An agent of Light would have been zapped by the Shadow manual with the first touch.

I flipped through the pages faster, and the tug on my mind lessened. I finally threw it back onto the desk next to Xavier's folder and said the one thing I hoped would have him backing off. "This is a very strange conversation."

The Tulpa, never one to want to appear odd in front of mortals, broke with that desire and stared straight into my eyes. Another pulse of thought energy throttled through me, this one so violent I saw white. "Well, I think you have some very strange questions, Olivia. Some strange suspicions of your own. I think you came in here to discover the answer to one of them in particular."

And he withdrew the photo Cher had given me earlier, clearly stolen from my body while I was having a tea party with Hunter in the wild forests of Midheaven.

That alone would be enough to have my head swimming, grasping for an answer. But the additional mental tug and weight returned, like he'd captured my gray matter on a hook and was pulling me to an unknown shore. Flipping open Xavier's binder to a marked page, he slid it in front of me, and there, beneath Xavier's infamous tight-assed script, was the haunting symbol I'd been searching for. The one on the chest that had borne me paranormal weaponry.

The same one the Tulpa grasped tightly in his hands now.

23

I abandoned the idea of killing the Tulpa in lieu of finding a way not to *get* killed. But he wasn't going to make that easy.

"Tell me what you know of this emblem," he ordered.

"You're right—I saw it the other night, my friend took a picture of it for me because it looked familiar, and now I know why. It was in the binder."

He remained unmoved. Literally. "Why?"

"I don't know."

"What did Xavier tell you?"

I blinked. "Teal and lavender are my best colors?"

The Tulpa's eyes narrowed into slits while his nostrils widened. "Let me be clearer, Olivia. What has he told you about this image?"

I opened my mouth to reply but nothing came out. I stretched my vocal muscles but they only thinned in my throat, aching like the worst case of strep I'd ever had.

The Tulpa's eyes flashed, sunlight burning over onyx, and his voice lowered about five octaves below Barry White's. "You are dreaming, understand? When you wake, you'll remember nothing of this conversation. But you will, always, tell me what I want to know. Now. What did Xavier reveal of the Serpent Bearer?"

I let my gaze lose focus, though my mind was as sharp as his tone. Serpent Bearer? My genuine confusion seemed to infuriate him. He moved a fraction of an inch—really just an extension of his neck—and willed his personal energy forward. I went airborne, sucking in a breath just in time for the fireplace to knock it back out. Muscles cringing around my spine, my legs shorted out, dropping me to my ass on the stone hearth. The next inhalation brought me no relief, but it did bring me a big fat wallop of mental manipulation. My eyes drained of moisture, the lids refusing to shut. I then rose like a marionette willed from above to slump before the Tulpa, while the power holding me there snaked like fingers in my brain.

"What do you know of the Serpent Bearer?" he repeated, voice rumbling, hypnotic and infuriated.

"Nothing," said the probing power slipping out in my voice. But even through the tingling mental fog, I could see he didn't believe me. There were too many small coincidences, things that didn't add up—or worse, that *did*. Olivia shared a father with Joanna Archer, a penthouse in the same building, she had stumbled into this hidden room, possessed this symbol both in a book and a photo. Taken all together, it was probable I knew something. The Tulpa was intent on figuring out what.

His refinement was gone, replaced with an aggressive warrior's stance, and the illness that forced him into a wheelchair last week, and to carry a cane today, shed like a cast-off blanket. His aura flickered and bulged, and his true visage flashed: the barbed shoulders and spine, the whipping tail, the teeth like daggers and eyes of fire.

"Tell me what you know!" The too-low baritone thrust like shrapnel, pinning me back to the fireplace. The leaded windows shattered behind their heavy draperies. Yet he didn't whip the door clean off its hinges a second later.

No, that was done by another monster altogether.

Fear hit me like a natural disaster, and the cry that burst from my mouth echoed through the room to thrust the Tulpa's probing power from my body. Seeing the direction of my petrified stare, the Tulpa whirled just in time to avoid Mackie's viciously curling blade. Clearly mistaking him for some sort of defender, Mackie ignored me for the moment and faced off against someone who also wanted me dead.

I doubted the Tulpa had ever seen anyone like Sleepy Mack before . . . I wasn't even sure he knew who he was. But he bared teeth as sharp as Mackie's were jagged, and power burst like an A-bomb as he tackled him. Smoke poured from his malleable body, and vibrations whipped at me in waves, not threatening to smash me against the wall—I was already there—but to send me right through it. Mackie soared backward too, body half catching on the door frame before the power flipped him back outside. The Tulpa strode forward, but paused to shoot a warning growl at me.

It cost him. Mackie plowed into his stomach like a linebacker, and the thing that was my father distended to absorb the blow like putty. Mackie's face twisted and he wailed like a tornado siren before redoubling his efforts. Feinting like a madman, he flicked the blade from one hand to the other before swiping upward in an unlikely blow.

The Tulpa was fast . . . but he lost two fingers.

I screamed again involuntarily, not out of any sort of empathy, but because a magic that could injure a tulpa was that frightening. The Tulpa's fingers twitched on the ground, before steaming and dissolving into nothing. All that remained was black blood streaming from his left hand. Then the Tulpa's own surprised and infuriated cry joined mine.

Mackie leapt away, hunching his back like a startled caveman, his head jerking with quick, audible sniffs. He had no eyeballs, so they couldn't widen, but his mouth did, and a dried and blackened stump of a tongue licked air.

He scented out me, my father, and our shared bloodline. Again, mistaking the Tulpa for my guardian, he lunged.

He struck at the knees this time, and while the Tulpa could morph, there was little he could do about being swept completely off his feet. Mackie literally bowled him over before he pivoted to thrust the Tulpa through the air and onto Xavier's thick antique desk. In the same motion, he swiped at me. I could only watch as his weapon appeared before my face, the sharp blade cutting air, the last of his soul singing in the iron.

It struck . . . and an invisible wall sparked with the blow. Mackie screamed as the blade sent sparks scratching over the wall. Lowering his head, he whirled with a snarl. Skamar, framed in the doorway like a diminutive devil, quickly calculated the situation—the Tulpa clamoring from his back on a destroyed desk, Mackie's knife still singing my death—and I breathed a sigh of relief.

Then she turned away and lunged for the Tulpa.

Mackie's head rotated on his shoulders and he offered me a skeletal scream. My back again hit the fireplace as he began stabbing at Skamar's wall, impaling its center over and again, causing sparks to fly and the wall to thrum with pulsing light. In the moments it took his rotted brain to understand this wasn't the most effective approach, and I realized Skamar had chosen her beloved vendetta against the Tulpa over helping me, I found the levers leading to the secret room and pulled. The secret entry clicked open, but I couldn't lunge. Mackie was too fast, and wall or not, he'd find his way around it if I forced a chase. For now he struck horizontally, intent on finding the edge. I inched the other way with each stroke, already knowing I wouldn't be fast enough.

Meanwhile, the tulpas brawled. For the first time I saw Skamar's full power, the advancements she'd received from having a recorded name in the manuals of Light, all the power that had been thrust into her body when I brought the fourth sign of the Zodiac to life. The individual movements were too fast and blurred for mortal eyes, but when a punch landed—and she delivered twice as many as the Tulpa—light burst from her body in blinding waves, covering the Tulpa like dust, momentarily freezing his dark movements.

No wonder he was exhausted. It was like pushing the pause button on his ability to morph, and the flashes showed an uncontrolled muddle of body parts disjointed from powerful blows, his unnatural length and limbs and talons torqued into even more sickening poses. She'd blast him with light, and while he was still breaking, strike him again.

But the Tulpa was experienced, crafty, driven, and crazed. What he lacked in power he made up for in fury, reminding me in no little way of Mackie. Snarling and swiping, they punched body-sized holes in the walls before careening across the room. Then they were out the door.

I had no time to rejoice. Mackie's blade called my name again, found the wall's end in a squeal of sharp delight, and I bolted. Then, as expected, an explosion of weight hit my back. I cringed reflexively on the ground, but the pinning weight didn't shift. I couldn't hear a thing. Lifting my head, I realized there really had been an explosion behind me, and I shifted quickly to climb from under Mackie's dead weight. Then I turned.

Harlan Tripp stood in the middle of the room, a look of fierce pain stamped beneath his ever-present Stetson. Smoke rose from an archaic conduit, the grocery bag of weapons at his feet. "Go," he croaked out, voice strained. I frowned even as Mackie stirred at my feet, yet my expression quickly turned to horror as I realized the smoke wasn't coming from the weapon, but from burning hands as Tripp grasped the barrel tight.

"Let it go!" I yelled, though as Mackie pushed to his hands, I thought, But plug him first!

Tripp shook his head, grimacing. "Can't." He blasted Mackie again so he fell flat. More smoke, and Tripp's hands were suddenly one with the gun, his flesh sliding like molten wax before hardening, the weapon instantly a part of his body. A part, I saw, pulse hammering, that was killing him.

"Oh, my God. Oh, my God."

"Go, for fuck's sake!"

I bolted for the shattered windows, leaping over Mackie's body. I had to salvage what I could of this, which meant protect my own life . . . yet I skidded to a stop, one hand on the heavy curtain. *The binder.* It was flung open on the floor from when the Tulpa's body hit the desk. "Wait!" I yelled, already running back behind the invisible wall, past Mackie, who was stirring once more.

"Hurry!" Tripp didn't want to fire again. I couldn't imagine the agony each shot cost him, and I didn't want to be the cause of any greater pain. Picking up the binder, I folded it tight to my chest and turned . . . into Mackie.

My eyes widened at his low, whirring growl. This close, I smelled old sweat overlaying decay, and saw every sinew in his muscular arms tense as his hand squeezed his knife. Behind him, Tripp was shaking his weapon ineffectually, gaze whipping to meet mine, helplessness etched on his brow. His skin had melted beneath the trigger. He couldn't fire another shot.

Mackie leered, poised like a king cobra, and Tripp shot forward. All accomplished warriors have an awareness when someone is behind them, and Mackie was no different. My own warrior's nature had me sprinting while he turned, but I wasn't so fast I didn't see that slim, deadly blade find a home in Tripp's chest. It pierced the leather vest, sent a black button flying, then found his skin, and his heart. He fell still, eyes going dead while still on his feet.

Mackie ripped the blade from his body, listing toward me. We both yelped when Tripp miraculously lunged for one last blow, the butt of his gun ripping air to land on Mackie's temple with a resounding crack. The monster went down again . . . and I plowed into something as hard as his petrified skull.

"Archer!" Strong hands steadied me and kept me from struggling.

I whirled, tense . . . and then slumped. "Carlos! Help. Tripp—"

"I smell it," he said, motioning behind him. "Get her out."

Fletcher and Milo stepped forward, but I pointed behind me. "No. Get *Mackie* out."

Carlos saw instantly what I meant: if I fled, my Olivia Archer identity was forever lost. The Tulpa had been forced from the room before Mackie attacked me, and his bitch, Lindy, had no doubt followed to assist with Skamar. If I disappeared now, leaving the scents of rogue agents and Mackie behind, they'd put all the pieces together and know exactly who I was.

If I stayed, pretended to be an unwitting mortal whose mind had played tricks on her in a moment of stress, I'd still get my shot at the Tulpa. I had a hidden room I could take refuge in, which was a damn good cover for making it out alive. The Tulpa couldn't say any different; he'd had his hands full upon leaving the office.

Assessing all of this within seconds, Carlos's next order sent everyone in motion. "Attack."

They ignored the weaponry in the grocery bag Tripp had dropped, clearly wishing to avoid his fate, and attacked Mackie with their hands, boldly pitting fists against blade—a suicide mission if done one-on-one. Yet together it was an effective example of the power of numbers.

They drove the crazed man from one side of the room to the other, the incessant whining in his throat rising to a pitch only dogs could hear as he was herded away from me. He gave one last desperate lunge—a move I didn't even note until the men clustered around him formed a wall in front of me.

Then Alex cried out and an entire arm fell to the floor. Mackie squealed in delight, and the others continued punching, though more carefully . . . which wouldn't work.

Panicked, I whirled as the men lost ground and Mackie inched closer. Lunging for the grocery bag full of weapons, I didn't care what I withdrew as long as it was lethal.

It was the saber, with its side firearm. Yet, the cluster was too tight, the movements too fast, and I couldn't be sure I wouldn't hit one of my men. I backed all the way across the room, heels braced against the bookcase behind me, then yelled for them to clear. No one heard. But Tripp, now propped against the far wall, rolled his head, saw the weapon in my hand—one no one else could touch—and my braced stance. Fingers to lips, he let out a piercing whistle, then collapsed into himself.

I caught Gareth's dazed expression, before Carlos yanked him back. Mackie scented me, spotted me, and lunged in the time it took to blink, and though I was ready, he was halfway across the room before I plugged him. He dropped a foot from the bookshelf and lay still.

"Eat lead, you rancid prick." I depressed the trigger again . . . and the fucking thing shorted out. Pissed, I flipped the weapon around and used the flat end—and all my mortal strength—to hammer his skull. This had the surprising effect of reviving him. His head whipped up, bowler hat still perfectly affixed, and he growled.

His leap never reached me. It must have been Carlos who caught him from the side, because they were the first two out the shattered window, the others following, pummeling Mackie like schoolyard bullies in the moonstruck night.

Chest heaving, I ran to watch for a moment, catching only a glimpse of the dervish, a mass of limbs and fury, but one headed away from me, rather than toward. Within seconds the sound faded, leaving me alone with breath arrowing jaggedly from my chest, my mind numbed but whirling. Somehow, despite having been enclosed in a room with both the Tulpa and Mackie, I was also alive.

Adrenaline coursed through me, banging against the thoughts already careening through my head. How to hide what I knew? How to explain what had happened here? How to convince Lindy and the Tulpa that a sole human woman could have made it out of this room alive?

Yet every question fell away when I whirled to spot Tripp's tortured body propped against the wall, eyes fixed on me. They were bright with the kind of pain that drained rather than sharpened the senses. He hadn't much longer to live.

Look what he did for you. I crossed to him, tears instantly welling. More than Warren had ever done. And it was so unexpected—a fucking former *Shadow*! A man raised to both despise mortals and murder the Light. And he lay dying because he'd protected someone who'd once been both.

"Archer . . ."

"Shh . . ." I knelt beside him, earning a pained grunt when I accidentally jostled him, but his gaze remained on mine, aware, coherent, and unwavering. His cowboy hat had come off when he fell, and it was the first time I'd seen him without it. It made him appear naked somehow. Dark sweaty hair plastered itself to his skull in thinning strands, and I swept them back before resetting the hat on his head. His hands were still melted around the silver gun's barrel, still steaming on his lap too, though it looked like the nerves in his palms had finally shorted out. His chest was another story.

"Oh God, Tripp. I'm so sorry."

"I'm relieved." His mouth quirked as I jerked my head up, and he motioned downward with his chin.

I frowned, but released his head gently, then pulled up his pant leg to reveal a bubbling mass of flesh so infected it was nearly writhing. Grimacing at the redness, I covered it again, careful not to touch it. "Mackie's blade," I said, suddenly understanding why he'd fought to save me, heedless of his own life. I'd seen the wound before, but hadn't put the two together. It was already predetermined. I hoped none of the others, once outside, were struck tonight.

"Better to die fightin'."

I thought so too. Tripp, knowing this, let his head fall back. But just when enough time had passed that I thought he was slipping away, his fevered eyes slitted back open. "Carlos believes in you."

I averted my gaze. I didn't want him to feel like his actions had been for nothing, but I couldn't lie either. I didn't believe in myself.

Despite his pain, his impending death, Tripp moistened his lips and kept talking. "I got something for you, girl. Been carrying it around with me for when this time came. If you'd please . . ."

He angled his head at his chest, unable to get to whatever was inside his inner vest pocket. I tried not to look at his smoldering, melted palms, and carefully unbuttoned his vest. Mackie's inflicted wound already bulged red, like Tripp's chest was some sort of science experiment gone wrong. His eyes were on my face, so I kept my expression unreadable as I reached inside his pocket to withdraw a plastic bag of slim brown cigarettes. I looked back up into his sweaty, rugged face. "'Cause you don't think I'll live long enough for lung cancer to kill me?"

"Them are special cancer sticks. Quirleys. Got 'em from Miss Sola herself." He frowned at some memory, one that had him drifting off before he jerked his head. "I earned those babies one by one, each costing me a chip she could use to thread the constellations in her night sky."

"Is this—"

"What I bartered your powers for?" He'd been anticipating the question. "Hell, yeah."

Cigarettes, I thought as he began to cough painfully. I felt the old anger begin to rise, but there was no real life to it, and it resettled quickly. What did it matter? I'd have given up those powers in order to save Jasmine shortly after anyway. Besides, Tripp and I hadn't been allies in Midheaven. Over there, it was every soul for himself.

"And it was worth it too," he continued, anticipating

an argument. "I knew one day I'd be coming back here. I knew I'd see my vengeance met . . ."

But now, fading, he'd seen no such thing. I didn't correct him, figuring a man should be allowed his dreams in his dying minutes.

"What do they do?" I asked, slipping one from the bag. It tingled against my fingertips, and I released it so it slid back into the bag where bits of loose tobacco glowed.

"You'll find out when you light one for yerself. Or you could ask your ol' friend, Micah."

I glanced at him sharply, hands going still over the quirleys. "This is what you used against Micah? What blackened his skin from the inside out?"

"It festers there, a constant burn beneath the skin. It's a reminder that even intangible things can be dangerous." Tripp's top lip lifted in a sneer, and for a moment all I saw was Shadow. "Just be sure 'n' blow out, don't suck in. You can hold the smoke in your mouth, but let it into your lungs and all that mean intent'll turn on ya, burning you from the inside out."

I glanced back down. I had a coating over my organs, a protective spray over my skin, and magical ciggies. All due to Tripp. "Why?" I finally asked, eyes lifting to meet his.

"'Cause I believe in you too," he said, falling still. "You can do what I cannot. I knew it the first time you stepped foot in Midheaven. It was confirmed when I learned of your dual nature. My goal after that was to keep you alive."

Because *I* was his best chance of killing the Tulpa. I fingered the quirleys in their protective pouch, though I didn't answer.

"Ah, I see." Tripp's air let out of him as if through a hose. It rattled as he sucked it back in. "You got nothing to live for, is that it? Or at least nothin' to fight for? Well, I can help with that too. Though it'll cost you."

I lifted a brow. "Cost me what?"

"Nothing too terrible, don't worry. But first would you like your reason?"

Not *a* reason. But *your* reason. Something specific, then. The obvious answer would be yes, but a reason also meant a care in this world. Care meant risk. And risk meant something could be taken from me again. I sighed. "Will it hurt if I lose it?"

"Not as much as if you lost it without a fight."

And despite a buried unwillingness, curiosity burst inside me. He was right. I leaned so close his breath mingled with mine.

"Solange was pregnant when she first entered Midheaven. She'd been havin' relations with an agent of Light, you see."

I held up a hand, wanting him to save his breath. "I already know all this."

"Well did you know that she even fancied herself in love with him? 'Course, love is relative. Solange knew the story would soon be revealed in the Shadow manuals, 'cause them pregnancy pheromones were about to give her away. It'd make her a target from both the Light and her own kind, especially the Tulpa, who don't abide deceit. So she plotted a way to flee, and there's only one place to go when hiding from a man who can rule your mind."

Another world entirely. One tailored to the whims of deadly, plotting women.

"I learnt the whole story during my time with her beneath those murdered stars."

Gaze lost to memory, Tripp's top lip quirked. "Oh, she did so want to talk with someone familiar with our world."

"So she escaped this world and gave birth to a child there?"

"So she said. Never saw the babe myself, but every so often we would hear a cry . . ."

I thought back, because Hunter had spoken of his daughter once, just after discovering I had one as well. As proof that I could trust him not to tell Warren about Ashlyn—because even then I'd known the troop leader would use the child for his own purposes—he gave me the name of his child, whom Warren also didn't know of. "Lola," I whispered.

Tripp licked his lips, wincing. "Never learnt the child's name, but I do know this. She sacrificed the soul of a mortal child to ferry her and her unborn into Midheaven . . ."

The same way Hunter had used Regan's so his soul wouldn't be sliced into thirds. I shook my head, pieces of knowledge shifting, threatening to realign reality as I knew it.

It wasn't that simple.

"Your man, Hunter, is being tortured, Joanna. Calls himself that throughout it all, too. *Hunter*. It infuriates Miss Sola, but he won't answer when she calls him JJ or Jacks or Jaden. Not even when she insists."

I swallowed hard, knowing how painfully insistent Sola could be.

Tripp's head dropped in a nod. "He's been through the mill since Warren locked him up tight."

"He entered Midheaven of his own accord."

"True. And he openly told us all how your troop turned you into your sister. But even the big 'uns open up under torture."

"Bullshit." He wasn't being tortured. He was being made love to beneath a ceiling of stars, by a woman revered as a goddess.

"No, it's true. Said you was somethin' pretty special. Well," Tripp paused to catch his breath. "He screamed it, anyway."

I winced and whispered, "Why are you baiting me now?"

"Even if I were, it wouldn't make the information any less real." His head lolled. "Trust me, right now your former ally is beggin' mercy from the merciless."

I licked my lips. "Hunter searched for Solange for years. He had identities he hid even from the troop, all so he could look for a dark-haired woman. Dark-eyed. A type."

"'Cause she stole his child."

Just finish the manual. It will make a difference.

Thoughts fractured in my brain like a puzzle, the pieces thrown at me so fast I was having a hard time making them fit. I could believe in wacky cigarettes and demons wearing bowler hats, but I was having a hard time wrapping my brain around the idea of Hunter seeking Solange out not because he loved her, but because he was hunting her. His real goal? Keep his child from being raised as a Shadow.

"Your man Jaden Jacks," Tripp rasped, "didn't leave you for her, Joanna. In fact, he confessed his love for you *to* her, and refused to recant it, even under torture."

There's absolutely nothing wrong with you. Not even in the darkest corner of that beautiful soul.

"Oh, God."

"Goddess," Tripp corrected, head rocking slowly to the side, eyes slipping shut. "Ain't nothin' I wouldn't confess under torture. Not to her."

I glanced back down at the quirleys in my lap. Solange had jigsawed pieces of me into little bits once, throwing my spirit and aetheric spine down a staircase, sending my body spiraling after seconds later. And I'd only seen a fraction of her power. In her world, Mackie was a lapdog, I was a beetle to be crushed underfoot, and men were little more than batteries. But my mind had already clamped down on the idea of Hunter, *my* man, being tortured.

"I'll fucking kill her," I whispered, and I believed it. All I had were cigarettes and spray-on defense, but I suddenly wanted her death as much as I'd wanted anything in my life. "I'll carve up her heart and fasten it to her beloved sky with pushpins."

"Now *there's* a reason to live." Tripp managed a half smile. "So for my little present . . ."

I studied the speculative shine in his eyes. His last wish before death. He'd just turned my mental life on its head. His gift would have to be equally valuable. Something as rare and unique as the quirleys. Something only I could give, like . . .

"One kiss."

I wrinkled my nose, but immediately replaced it with a placid face. Still, I let my eyes roll. "You're a lech, Tripp."

Now he did smile, damn him. "I'm a dying man."

Because of me. I couldn't stop that. But I could give him a kiss.

"Happy Valentine's Day, Harlan." I bent forward and pressed my lips to his. He tasted like tobacco, sweat, and smoke. It was as chaste a kiss as I'd ever given, something that would pass between siblings, and that delivered the comfort of mortal touch, understanding, kinship . . . and forgiveness. It was a kiss of absolution, and it cleared the worry from Tripp's furrowed brow.

"So that's Light . . ." he replied wonderingly, and let his head drop back, knocking his hat forward again. I lifted it, moved it aside, and still he didn't move. After the horror and messiness and pain of death, there was ultimately only silent acceptance, and stillness.

But Harlan Tripp, the stubborn bastard who'd long survived two worlds, wasn't quite done yet. He laughed, loopy, not feeling much of anything anymore. "You're a high roller, girl. Still sittin' at that table. Still in the game . . ."

I palmed his head when it fell to the side. "What?"

His eyes didn't open but he managed a humorless smile. "Still got them chips?"

"The ones from the warehouse?" I kept speaking so he wouldn't have to nod. "Yeah, but you said they're useless. I gave all my powers to Jas."

"But you can still cash in the ones you won." Like Shen's sense of smell? The albino's aether, whatever that was?

"How, Tripp?" My heart bumped in my chest. *Still a player. Still in the game.* "How do I cash in the chips"— the powers—"I won at that table?"

But Tripp was nearly gone, mouth barely moving, mind already skipping to some other final thought. "You said your troop kicked you out," he whispered, without force. "'Cause you weren't useful to them anymore. 'Member?"

I nodded.

His eyelids lifted one last time, and in the stillness of the room where he'd die, he wrapped me in his gaze. "I been fueling a matriarch's world for years, an' one thing I learnt . . . a woman ain't put in any world for her usefulness. You got purpose beyond the things you can do for others. And everyone's got a right to their own damned reasons."

Was that why he'd told me about Solange and Hunter? So I'd act on the truth, and make a choice reflecting what *I* wanted? I'd never know. The short speech had cost him too much. "The chips, Tripp . . ."

He didn't even hear me.

"I ain't a good man, Archer. Don' mistake me for that. But I'll tell you this much," Tripp slurred, eyes closing a final time. "Someone's tryin' to keep you from your reasons? You'd damned well better question *theirs*."

24

I knew the Tulpa had survived Skamar yet again when Helen returned to the compound, acting as if she'd never been gone.

I knew Mackie had also escaped when Carlos didn't.

Of course, with a force equivalent to a small tornado having swept through the mansion, neither Helen nor I could pretend nothing had happened. So I tucked Tripp's words about still being a high roller aside and used my cell to call the police while moving the quirleys and weapons and binder back out to the guesthouse. Then I returned to wait in the secret room for Helen to find me. I hated leaving Tripp's body where it was, but Helen would never let it be discovered by mortals. Sure enough, as she and the first officers on the scene led me blinking like a newborn back into the destroyed office, both Tripp and Alex's severed arm were gone. Not even blood marked the floor.

"I think they were after my father's financial information," I told the investigating detective, aware Helen was listening intently from over my shoulder. "They tore the room apart, and the only thing they stole was a binder he'd given me upon his death. It contained everything he wanted me to know about his affairs, the company, and its financials. That means the money," I explained earnestly.

There. That would get back to the Tulpa, first thing, and I'd be off the hook for the missing binder. As for the rest . . .

"I hope you have a copy somewhere," Officer Greenlaw replied, jotting in his notepad.

"And how did you get away?" Helen butted in, earning dual glances of irritation from both Greenlaw and me.

"I hid in the room where my father apparently liked to pray," I said, shifting to train my gaze on hers. "I stayed there even after the noise outside had stopped, just in case the scary man was still there."

"And you said he was wearing a bowler hat?" asked the cop, again taking notes.

"That's right, a dusty one. In fact, everything about him was strangely musty." I shuddered in the girliest move I could think of. The officer gave me a sympathetic nod. Helen didn't look as convinced. So as the interview continued, I shivered and sighed, explaining I'd gone to the office because I was missing my father, that I'd been alone the entire time—in keeping with the Tulpa's hypnotic suggestion, which Helen would also relay—and remembered very little after hitting my head. Then I started crying, switching subjects to mourn Suzanne's ruined rehearsal dinner, nerves making it easy to produce the tears that had the detective planning his own getaway.

Yet enduring an interrogation wasn't all bad. For one, it got me out of the sleepover. The other guests were methodically interviewed and dismissed, including Cher, who had left her dinner at some point to come looking for me. The police interviewed her separately, but came to the conclusion she'd gone upstairs to my bedroom and seen even less of the destruction left in the tulpas' wake than the guests mingling off the foyer.

Suzanne, meanwhile, was beside herself. She left in tears, bottom lip quivering, apologizing to me as if it were her fault, and wondering aloud if the dinner's interruption was bad luck in either American or Indian culture. In contrast, Arun simply looked unaccustomed at having anything upset the natural order of his world. Yet he did his best to soothe his distraught bride, one arm draped protectively over her shoulders, whispering soothing platitudes in her ear as he guided her to the door.

"Let's hope the wedding goes more smoothly tomorrow," she sniffled before kissing my cheek, tears staining her worried and worried eyes.

"I'm so sorry," I said, squeezing her hand, and I truly was. No bride should have to remember chaos when marking her wedding anniversary. I caught Cher's glance over her shoulder, and she nodded, signaling she'd accompany her stepmother home and remain with her through the night.

As for Arun, there was no opportunity to corner him, and no reason we should be seen conferring alone. So I followed the trio out onto the steps of the marble entryway and waited until Cher and Suzanne had their backs turned, arms tucked consolingly around each other's waists. Leaning against a white pillar, I whispered, the words immediately lost to the night-soaked air. Arun still turned at his name.

"I'll kill you if something happens to her."

Arun merely tilted his head and smiled up at me. Then he replaced Cher's supporting arm with his own, and allowed Suzanne to lean into him. I made sure their car had been whisked away before I allowed my sigh of despair to perfume the air. I had to stop that wedding.

After the guests left, and the household crew was busy whispering among themselves, Helen excused herself, muttering something about a migraine. I knew she'd be desperate to discover the status of her leader—that nasty unrequited love again rearing its head—and seek instructions on what to do next.

So I disappeared as well. Throughout Cher and Suzanne's whimpering concerns, the police's questioning, and Helen's looming suspicion, Tripp's final words kept rattling through my mind. *You're a high roller, girl. Still sittin' at that table. Still in the game . . .*

Because of the other men's chips.

Also because I was headstrong, stubborn, and I was *right*. So his final sentiment took hold, grew roots, and sprang up fully formed in my mind.

If someone's keeping you from your reasons, you'd do damned well to question theirs.

And more than Mackie, more than the Tulpa, more than Solange and everyone else who would have me caving to their whim, one man had kept me from being anything more than *useful* in this world. Warren, the leader of the Light, the man who saved, introduced, and initiated me into the world of the Zodiac, had also consistently manipulated me into doing his will. Instead of telling me the truth, instead of trusting I'd want to do all I could to advance his goals and the goodwill of the troop, he kept me in the dark. In *shadow*. And he'd done it all while holding his own reasons tightly to his chest.

He'd *known* of Solange's deeds, that she had stolen a changeling's aura all those years ago to safely cross into Midheaven, thus he also knew it was possible to use another person's soul for that purpose. Yet he kept me in ignorance, allowing and even *encouraging* me to give up mine in thirds!

Worse, knowing Hunter had been pursuing Solange, he shared nothing of Midheaven with him. He could have prevented Hunter's defection and disappearance step by aching step, but had driven him to that ultimate decision instead, then banned him from the troop.

"And locked away the man I love."

The one, I'd just learned, who still loved me.

So I changed into head-to-toe black, crossed to the guesthouse by the light of an uncertain moon, and encased my body with weapons. I removed safeties, cocked back hammers, and sharpened blades. I took Xavier's fastest

Ferrari to the warehouse Tripp had convinced me to leave unlocked and unguarded, picked up one more vitally important weapon, then raced directly to the tunnel where Skamar had sucked the sentience from Luna's pulpy body.

Then I called that bitch out.

The way you call a tulpa to you, the way you direct them like a satellite tracking enemy warheads, is to think upon them and their looks, their actions, and especially their name. The Tulpa gained power from his followers in this way. He demanded an around-the-clock rotation of meditative prayer and ritual, all focused on providing him with greater life force. Hence, Xavier's hidden room.

But Skamar had a *given* name, and a person's mind could latch more easily onto a being with a name than without. It was hard to pinpoint something's relevance in the world without knowing what to call it. That was the Tulpa's main problem . . . and it was the reason I screamed Skamar's name at the top of my lungs now.

With a bunch of curse words interspersed in between.

I heard her first, though the blast of energy accompanying her flight thrust me back against the curved, mildewed wall. When I opened my eyes, she was caught in the flashlights I'd brought in from the outside—in case cursing her wasn't enough to lead her to me—and glaring like I'd interrupted her midnight nap. Like I was a minor nuisance, I thought, even more pissed. Without warning, I lifted the saber, and used its small, antiquated side firearm to take out a chunk of concrete beside her.

"What the—"

"The last time we spoke, you told me I smelled of despair." I reloaded, tilted my head, and caught her in my sights again. "What do I smell like now, Skamar?"

The skin over my face no longer thinned to allow my skull to rise eerily to the surface, my eyes no longer burned tar-black like my birth father's, but the bile in my belly surely still stained the air, and my heart pumped wildly, overriding my fear.

"Put it down before you hurt yourself," she said, meaning before she burst forward and yanked it from my grasp.

I redirected the barrel on the center of her chest. "You chose to chase the Tulpa over helping me. After you told me you'd watch over me."

"I said I'd help when I could."

"You could have helped me tonight! And your choice cost a man his life!" The image of Tripp's bubbling chest and melted palms angered me all over again. "An independent agent who was finally about to claim his life on his own terms. He had a right to that, Skamar. Instead he gave it to protect me because you—someone who is practically immortal—would not."

"Hey, you came to me for help!" Unused to being challenged or questioned, she was angry now too. "If you've a bone to pick, first remember I'm not obligated to assist mortals at all."

"A 'bone' to pick?" I said disbelievingly. "Obligations? Skamar, I'm talking about weighing your options and then doing the *right* thing. Even if it means you don't get what you want."

She laughed harshly, though the sound was hollow, and not entirely because of the tunnel. "You want me to grow a conscience?"

"Since my mother clearly didn't imbue you with one, yes. It's a basic personality trait in a friend and ally."

She sneered, perfect teeth almost radiant in the spotlights. "Well, I'm not burdened with such bad habits."

I lowered my chin and voice. "You mean you're not *blessed* with them, you bitch."

A quiver went through her body, like the words actually stung. And that was where *I* was the more powerful. Maybe I'd just given her another name. I grinned as evilly as she had a moment before . . . and found I couldn't stop. "You think you have consciousness? Why, because you can breathe and move around freely in this world?"

I didn't have to smell her anger to know it stained the

air. Her eyes bulged, wide and wild, like her gaze wanted free of her body. Her body stiffened like a petite petrified board, fingers making fists without her willing it. "I can control people! I can break things on whim."

"So can a toddler," I retorted, and had the satisfaction of seeing her face fall slack.

She tilted her head gently, dangerously. "My every action reflects the noble purpose *your* mother created me for."

"Exactly my point."

"Which is?"

"You mistake animation for a life." My saber was heavier, so I readjusted, refocused on her. "You might as well be Mickey-fucking-Mouse because right now you're just a clump of walking tissue, and always will be unless you let *something* touch you."

"Like *what*?" she demanded, fisting her hands on her hips. "A knife with someone's soul inscribed in the blade? Because this is what happened two days ago when I kept Mackie from following your mortal ass!" And she lifted her shirt to reveal a screaming red scratch on the soft white flare of her hip.

I regarded the injury coolly, though dialed it back a bit since she had, at some point, tried to assist me. So Mackie's blade could even injure a tulpa. It made him the most dangerous being I knew, at least on this side of Midheaven. And that was saying something.

"I'm not talking about that."

"Then *what*?" she screamed, causing me to jump, and the tunnel to shake. "The Tulpa? The Shadows? Who do you think I should allow to touch me?"

"How about letting a poem touch you, Skamar. How about a song to lift you up and reassure you that you're alive. How about love?"

"Weakness!"

"Life!" I screamed, because those were the things she, and everyone who wanted to point me in a given direction like some wind-up toy, were trying to take from me.

"You're not really alive, Skamar. You know things because my mother knew them. You think you know me because you've mined her thoughts and come up with your own emotionless conclusions about what makes me tick. You think because you have stolen memories, because you *ruminate,* that you're entitled to walk around this world as you fucking please."

Her vocal cords stretched in her throat as she leaned toward me. "I'm entitled to that and more! I was birthed to reign over the underworld. I'm a tulpa!"

"You're a leech."

A scurrying behind her drowned out her gasp—a sound that could have been anger, injury, or insult—before another figure, followed by more still, slipped up behind her. Warren stepped into the circles of light.

"Oh, good. I'm glad you're here." I turned my weapon on him and recocked the hammer. "If you haven't already heard, I'm in the mood to pick some bones."

"Where did you get that?" Warren, thinking me harmless, jerked his head at the aging conduit in my hand.

"Some new friends gave it to me. You like?" My voice was cold, hard, and unwavering. "Admittedly not as shiny as the ones Hunter used to make, but since he's locked up tight in another world, you won't be getting any more of those either. Too bad, huh?"

Warren's eyes narrowed and he licked his lips. He knew I was getting at something, but not yet sure what. Gratifyingly enough, the Taurean glyph on his chest began to glow faintly. "You've been keeping things from us again, Jo," he had the nerve to counter. I almost laughed, except there was nothing funny about this man's need for control. "You failed to mention the appearance in the valley of Sleepy Mac."

"Oh, you know how Midheaven is, Warren." I shrugged the concern away. "You can't speak of things or people in that world to someone who has never been. In fact, there's no explaining the absolute and debilitating horror an agent—and a man, especially—has to endure once there." I clenched my jaw. "I mean *how* could you possibly understand the pain of being reduced to an object for someone else's use? How could I begin to even tell you what it costs in terms of mental and physical anguish to enter that world? Or," I said, widening my stance, "the myriad of ways it might be achieved?"

I was depending on the troop at his back to regulate his composure, but if I thought my words would have him on his heels, I miscalculated. He was suddenly in front of me, a breath away though I hadn't even blinked. I suddenly realized, as I unexpectedly stared into a face of controlled fury, that here was the being without a conscience. "Let me see your fingertips," he whispered, lips barely moving.

When I stayed still, he grabbed my palm so roughly the bones rubbed together.

"How sweet," I said, matching his tone. "You want to hold hands."

We held the stare as he rubbed the smooth pads of his fingertips over my newly printed ones. "The fuck you playing at?" he hissed harshly, pushing my hand away. It forced me three full steps back. "You're mortal."

"And no use to you, right?"

A woman ain't put in any world for her usefulness. You got a purpose beyond the things you can do for others.

"Well, I count," I told him, and raised my voice so Skamar and the agents behind her could hear me clearly as well. "And Hunter does too. We may not be agents of Light, but we have our own reasons for existing."

Warren sneered. "Tell me your reasons, Joanna. I'd love to hear them."

I smiled thinly. "Why? So you can strip them from me too?"

If someone's tryin' to keep you from your reasons . . . you'd do damned well to question theirs.

"It's enough that you know I can still touch magical

weapons." And while Warren pondered that, my expression brightened as though I'd just remembered something, and I gave a signal behind my back. "And speaking of weapons, there's one other thing you might find of interest . . . animals love me."

Buttersnap's low growl throttled through the tunnel and Warren jolted. His eyes darted from mine to the warden I'd retrieved from the warehouse, suddenly at my side and baring canines sharper than switchblades, salivating as she waited for my signal. Now his glyph fired like a lit wick.

"Don't," Warren warned, barely daring to breathe.

I lifted my saber so the tip was touching his chest, and his heart thrummed through the long blade. Power pulsed through me in a heady rush. Sure, I'd probably die in this tunnel. Buttersnap could take Warren, but there were half a dozen other agents fanned out behind him, and a tulpa who'd already proven she didn't overly care what happened to me. But Tripp had told me to honor my own reasons, and if revealing the truth about Warren's actions wasn't a reason, I didn't know what was.

"I'm not afraid to die again, Warren," I told him, weary as someone who'd just climbed from a car wreck. "There's nothing more to strip from me in this world. An unstoppable demon wants me dead, and not even one of those who call themselves Light—not even the tulpa created by my own mother—will lift a finger to help me. So *my* finger is on this trigger, poised there because *you* brought me into this underworld only to throw me away. In a way, as much as my mother and the Tulpa did, you created me."

"Not for this."

I tilted my head so a blond lock fell over my eyes. I blew it away. "No, because this is out of your control. You wanted someone you could manipulate, which makes you no different than the Tulpa."

"Bullshit," he said roughly.

"Really? How else would you explain why you erased the memory of a man—an agent of Light—from the minds of an entire troop, just so you could reinvent him into a superhero more to your liking?"

"I discussed it with them ahead of time. They agreed it was for the best."

"Though no one would remember *that*."

His weather-beaten face hardened, the lines deepening. "You're making shit up, Joanna. I suggest you be careful."

"Or what? You'll alter my memory too?" I laughed, and its harshness surprised even me. "What you—and the Tulpa, for that matter—don't seem to realize is that while thought can be manipulated and controlled, emotions cannot. They're willful. Unpredictable. They're what you really wish you could dampen and tame. Emotion threatens your authority. It inspires change."

"Nothing's changing," Warren replied, but his teeth were again clenched.

"You set Hunter up."

Warren's eyes slitted, his nostrils flared, and his mouth went flat. *"Don't."*

"You let the troop believe Jaden Jacks was another man entirely, a Shadow even, and that he'd disappeared years ago. You arranged the Hunter identity, kept his past from everyone who trusted you to tell the truth, and ordered him silent as well. And when you found he was still searching for Solange, you decided to rid yourself of him for good by locking him in Midheaven."

"Jacks cost a mortal child his life!" he said, protesting way, way too much.

"Solange tricked Hunter." I raised my voice, using the name the rest of the troop associated with the man they'd once counted as their friend, ally, and brother. "She stole the child's aura from him, knowing he would never destroy an innocent. She used it to escape into a world the Tulpa could never follow, but let Hunter live."

"Why?"

The voice popped up behind Warren, surprising us both. He half turned to shoot a warning look at Vanessa, who was frowning like a kid trying to puzzle out a word problem. Her dark eyes darted from him to me. "Why wouldn't she just take Hunter . . . I mean, Jaden's life?"

"Because she really did love him, inasmuch as a Shadow can love anyone beyond themselves."

And recalling Tripp and the lengths he'd gone to attain vengeance for his own family, I knew it was possible. Which made me fear for Hunter all the more. And to get to him, I was going to have to get others to believe it too. So I delivered the final truth. "And because she was pregnant with his child."

Gasps rocketed into the air—even Skamar hadn't known that—and in the glare of the dimming flashlights, faces bloomed with shock. But none was more jarred than Warren's, and I was glad. It was nice to see the man who hoarded secrets outwitted by Hunter. It was fucking poetic.

"That's right, Warren. There's a girl child on the other side of your *impenetrable* lock." I snarled those last words, letting him know it was anything but that. "A child who is, by all accounts, both Shadow and Light. And you know what that means."

"Another Kairos," Tekla whispered, and even in my weakened mortal state, I felt the shift in the troop. This was something they should have known, if Warren had trusted them enough.

"The *only* Kairos," I said, before returning my flat gaze to Warren, who was still focused on me, though he'd gone unnervingly still. "After all, I'm just a useless mortal. Right?"

"And not even that for much longer," Warren whispered, and I didn't even see him pull back his fist. The image was imprinted on the air in front of me, however, because that's where the impact between him and Carlos occurred. If I lived through this, the homicidal fury in Warren's frozen gaze, burning like a negative before me, would haunt my dreams. Then the image melted away and chaos overtook the small tunnel.

Rogue agents whizzed past me so fast the only way I

knew they were grays and not Shadow was because I still lived. Conflict sounded, face-to-face, hand-to-hand, because the rogue attack was sudden and unexpected, the agents of Light too crowded to even lift their conduits, much less fire them. But their chests were lit down to the last.

Without weapons, all the rogues had were their bodies, and those—visible during the spotlit collisions—were coated in Micah's protectant, which he belatedly realized when he plunged his surgeon's blade into Vincent's chest, only to receive an unexpected blow to the jaw in return.

The action was jammed, like dust devils banging into each other, so when one of the agents of Light wrested free—a sole glyph lit up in the foreground where the spotlights shone brightest—I saw only the lift of a deadly blowgun in my direction. Kimber, the Libra of Light who'd always hated me, sucked in a deep breath.

"No!" Vanessa screamed, pushing the weapon aside. The impact developed, then dissipated, before my eyes. A scrape against the curved wall behind me—Kimber had actually fired!—and I scurried behind Buttersnap, though it would've been too late had Vanessa not intervened. "It's Joanna!"

"She's not ours!" Kimber countered, pushing her away, pointing again.

Vanessa punched her so hard I expected the word "Pow!" to appear over Kimber's blond, dreadlocked head. "She's not theirs either!"

"Somebody just shoot!" Warren ordered, his voice choked beneath Carlos's tensile fingers.

But Buttersnap reared up in front of me and let out a ripping, ragged howl. Nobody shot, though I didn't know if it was because they were afraid to hit her—making her even stronger and larger than she already was—or reluctant to hurt me. I wasn't about to split hairs either way, and neither was Buttersnap. Lowering to all four paws, she corralled me backward in the direction the grays had appeared, and away from the Light. The fight continued in front of me, sweeping gusts and flashing images, though the accompanying sounds of battle were constant.

But one thing stood out clearly: Vanessa, still immobile where she'd knocked out Kimber, grays on the defense around her, the stunned Light battling a foe they hadn't known existed. A curious look of pity and wonder marred her lovely face, and remained that way until I disappeared from sight.

At the roll of the dog's muzzle, and the accompanying rumble in her throat, I straddled the giant back, holding tight to the skin where a bitch might scruff her pup. Buttersnap raced forward, breaking from the tunnel like a Kentucky Derby winner. I kept my head low until I was sure we weren't being directly followed, then relaxed enough to look behind me. I tried to make out the tunnel entrance, the chaos inside, but it had vanished. Fleeing on the warden's back, the entire city was reduced to a blur of colorful outlines. Streetlamps whizzed by overhead, before smooth pavement gave way to rough, and then to the packed desert floor.

I felt good, I realized, as the cold winter wind numbed me. Sure, Mackie was still out there, and my threats against Skamar didn't amount to much more than a temper tantrum, but it was gratifying to know I'd finally tallied a mark in my favor against Warren's manipulative scheming. From the look on the faces of the rest of the agents of Light, he was finally going to have to provide some answers.

No, I wasn't a lot better off than I'd been that morning, I admitted, escaping into the desert, cactus and rocks reaching for me beneath a vast dark sky. But in a world ruled by beings who only paid attention to those who could move and manipulate and control events and outcomes, who had power and the means to use it, and who undeniably *counted*, I had come out of this altercation alive and on top.

And they were certainly paying attention to me now.

25

Of course, the agents of Light followed. Once over their initial shock, once they realized these were not Shadows they were battling, but rogues—also enemies, according to the law of Warren—they were human Scuds on our trail. My revelations about Hunter weren't enough to stop their pursuit, and I hadn't expected them to be. Mistrust of rogue agents was too deeply ingrained for them to dismiss us automatically, but eventually what I'd revealed would give some of them pause. For now, the weaponless rogues fended them off with a mixture of crafty defense and a good head start, though they made sure I was safely away before falling back.

What really saved us, though, was the troop's shock at our numbers. Almost a dozen rogues existed in the valley? For the agents of Light, this revelation was akin to discovering me a year earlier. There were as many rogues as agents of Light . . . and they didn't even know of the other four who'd left the valley. Thus, we numbered more than even Shadows, who boasted a full troop, one agent for each star sign on the Zodiac.

So, with a head start, and clear knowledge of where we

were headed—whereas the Light had to fan out, cover and cut off all angles, and try to anticipate our direction—we made it over the city line, crossing the invisible boundary so abruptly I didn't even know we'd done so until Buttersnap's gait slowed and she circled widely to return to Carlos's side. He was breathing hard but his face was alight. One by one every gray who'd entered the tunnels returned, safe, and Carlos laughed so long and loud the sound threatened to rip the sky.

I climbed from Buttersnap's back, giving her a tight squeeze around the neck, earning a giant, sloppy kiss as the others joined Carlos, whooping wildly into the night as Warren and company paced the invisible barrier like they were straining against leashes. I listened to the joyous laughter ringing about me and could almost scent the perfume of their giddiness at this unexpected victory. It would smell like fresh baked meringue, I decided with a small smile. Bright vanilla, morello cherries, a dessert served first after a miles-long marathon.

When Kimber fired a dart in an attempt to reach us despite the known boundary, I laughed along with the other rogues as the little missile dropped harmlessly to the desert floor. In fact, fatigue, relief, and the spent embers of righteous anger had me so wound up that I found I couldn't stop. I knelt on the desert floor, arms wrapped around my core as I tipped over. Gareth found this hilarious, and together we howled into the night, almost burping up jagged laughter as the agents of Light fumed only feet—yet miles—away.

Eventually, Carlos and Gareth helped me up, and I sent a final giggle spiraling over the invisible barrier while giving a fury-pale and trembling Kimber the finger.

Sure, the hubris might cost us all dearly later. But right now? The giddiness was amazing, the satisfaction at seeing Warren thwarted and fuming complete.

However, the celebratory mood was quelled once back at Frenchman's Flat. Io met us in the atomic anteroom with reports of Alex's deteriorating condition. Sure, he'd only lost an arm, and sure, even mortals recovered in time from such an injury. But Mackie's magical blade was working quickly, and by her estimation, he wouldn't make it through the night. I thought of Tripp's leg wound, festering like gangrene. Maybe Alex was lucky.

"He wants to see you," she told me, brows raised over those full-moon eyes. "All of you."

So we proceeded to his sickroom in a funeral march, spirits dampened, the silence weighty. Yet we found Alex sitting upright in bed, a meal of chicken and rice on a tray before him while candles burned around and above him like he was in a cage of flame.

"I understand the Tulpa and I now have something in common," he said, glassy-eyed, but with enough bite to allow he knew how drugged he was . . . and that he would soon die. For now, though, it seemed he'd decided to feast.

And so we all did. With the candlelight casting shadows over the beaten floor, we pulled chairs to his bedside, using it as a table as we told tales of the full battle in Xavier's study and of in the stinking tunnels where the grays faced off against the Light. Roland and Gareth re-enacted particularly good blows, while Vincent fended them off with a plastic spork, pretending to be Mackie. When they settled, Oliver mentioned his surprise that Vanessa would stand up for me against Kimber. I shrugged, uncomfortable with talk of my old troop, and it wasn't long before the subject returned to Mackie and his rampage as they led him away from the mansion. There was also collective awe expressed at the injury he'd inflicted on the Tulpa's hand. What kind of magic could defeat the most magical being of all, a tulpa?

Alex was drinking as well, throwing back tequila and beer chasers faster than any of us, and why not? He didn't have to worry about the hangover. He howled with laughter, doubling over as Gareth mimicked the reactions of the Light when the grays rushed the tunnel in my defense.

Oliver, in particular, did an award-winning imitation of Warren's face as Carlos pinned him against the wall, and though Carlos professed not to be their leader, their affection and regard for him as such sat bare on each face.

I looked around at the roomful of outcasts and outlaws, awed how a group of people who were so powerless, and who had so little compared to those aboveground, could find joy in the smallest victory. Yet the feeling was addictive, probably because I too had been living in lack. So I smiled and, as I licked the warming beer from my lips, enjoyed the moment. We were like medieval warriors come back from war—Vikings anchoring in some great northern port, celebrated as heroes by our loved ones, and returning with stories of battle and adventure.

"To Tripp!" Alex yelled, and the others took up the toast, lauding a man who'd been a part of this rogue group for mere weeks. Carlos had tears in his eyes, and even Vincent sniffled in the corner, head tucked against his broad chest. They didn't see Tripp as separate from themselves, I realized. His struggle as an outcast, a rogue, was theirs . . . and so was mine.

It was how the agents of Light should have treated me. I sank back into my seat, trying to tuck the emotion away before it could taint the air—Alex deserved to celebrate in his last hours among friends—but once the despondency took hold, I couldn't shake it. Maybe because only weeks earlier I'd lain in bed as helpless as he. Maybe it was because my troop had never gathered to celebrate my battles and heroism and *life*.

Maybe I was drunk.

I picked up my bag, and mumbled something to Io—closest to the door—about the bathroom as I backed from the room. Then I grabbed an oil lantern, and as Carlos and I had done only a day earlier, exited the rogue lair to seek privacy upon the desert floor. This time it was night, and I was as alone as I felt, so when I looked at the sky, wounded with stars, tears welled.

I couldn't figure out why I felt so deflated as I wandered across the brutalized terrain, but I wanted to sit down in some radioactive crater and be swallowed up.

Instead I found what looked like a moon rock, though it'd probably once lived deep beneath this desert floor, and was as surprised to find itself sitting upon this ablated surface as I was. The lantern wobbled atop it, then steadied, and I got right to business, doing what I knew I'd come all the way out here to do. I pulled out the manual with Hunter on the cover. He was penciled in silhouette, a hulking figure outlined against the tunnel that would ferry him to another world. I flipped it open to where I'd left off and read the rest.

The story Tripp had told me was all there, so obvious in black and white that it made me wonder how I hadn't seen it before. Solange had put scales on all our eyes, I supposed. A too-pretty face could do that. But the real reason this manual was stripped of color was because Solange had moved through Hunter's life—or Jaden, as he was known then—like a Nordic winter: dark, cold, fierce, and relentless.

After they'd met as children, after Solange tried and failed to rectify that night's choice to let him live, and after becoming his lover instead . . . she decided to use him. Love him or not, he was Light and she was Shadow, which meant a child between them would be this world's prophesied savior: the Kairos. Of course, in a matriarchal society this person's mother would be exalted.

How ironic that to bring the child safely into the world, she had to leave it. The Light would want to destroy it, the Tulpa would use it, and Solange wanted the power solely for herself, and so she used Hunter one last time.

Entering Midheaven required payment—a third of an agent's soul . . . or all of a mortal's. The manual didn't say why she didn't use Jaden's soul—maybe she thought it too risky. He was too big, too strong. Maybe she really did love him in part. However, the other part stole the soul of a child who'd trusted Jaden, using it to cross into Midheaven. She killed the innocent, escaped from everyone else, and had been ruling Midheaven in the way the mother of the real Kairos would—utter omnipotence.

Meanwhile Hunter had lived with the guilt and consequence of her betrayal, just as he must now be living with the consequence of helping me escape.

Don't ever return. She wants your power, your ability to . . .

I glanced back down at the closed manual and rubbed a thumb over his profile, then closed my eyes and imagined Solange sucking on a sliver of his soul; cold and diamond-shaped, like a sparkling lozenge.

Then I took a deep breath, picked up the lantern and headed back to the bunker, shaking. Yes, it was cold, but that didn't bother me. If things went my way, I'd soon return to a realm where this cold, blasted patch of desert would be as dreamy as a day at Laguna Beach.

Because Midheaven wasn't done with me yet.

And after reading this manual, I wasn't done with it either.

I was guided back to the rogue bunker by another hurricane lamp. It was a beacon leading me closer, and though the night hid all but his outline, there was no question who stood there. Yet I was surprised to also find a bistro table set up right behind the cell's cavernous mouth, complete with two battered chairs and a softly fluttering tablecloth. Less surprising were the two shot glasses and half-full tequila bottle perched atop, and when Carlos caught me peering at the bottle's glass bottom, he laughed as heartily as he had when escaping the Light. "Not this time, *mi molcahete*. Not this time."

I took a seat. "A candlelit dinner in the middle of a nuclear blast site. Carlos, you do know how to romance a girl."

He pretended to flip back the tails of an invisible tuxedo

as he settled across from me. "I'm trying to make up for the state of the place. Maybe entice you to stay . . ."

I looked away as his voice trailed off. He thought I might want to run after being attacked by a tulpa, a madman with a soul blade, and the entire troop of Light in the same evening. Shows how well he knew me. Though I had to admit, a fresh start elsewhere sounded good. But that wasn't my life. I turned back to him. "Alex will die."

Carlos inclined his head. "By morning at the latest."

"Faster than Tripp."

"A more severe wound. Plus, I suspect Harlan picked up some vital immunities during his time spent in Midheaven. One can't go through a heated kiln without being changed. Strengthened."

He raised his glass for a toast, brows lifting meaningfully at me as well. I ignored that. I didn't feel any stronger for having been in Midheaven. That place had stripped me raw. I also, for once, ignored the drink.

"Will they stay long, do you think?" I asked Carlos after he'd sipped.

"Of course," he said, jerking his head in the direction of the city. "They'll pace the barrier until morning, trying to figure out a way around it and into our hideout. They are stunned by the bright new knowledge of our existence. It upends the world as they knew it . . . along with your own timely revelations, of course."

So he'd been in the tunnels long enough to hear about Hunter, I thought, gazing at the tequila. Well, it only made sense. I ran my index finger along the glass rim, dipping my finger into the golden spirit, but still didn't drink. "Did you know the Jaden Jacks story, Carlos? I mean, had you ever read about it in a manual or even heard the rumor before?"

He shook his head, and sipped. "The ways of the written word are mysterious, *weda*. As great a magic as any power we possess."

"But why are some things in the manuals while others

aren't? The open knowledge that Hunter was really Jaden Jacks could have saved him from having to enter Mid-heaven."

"Maybe," Carlos said, with less care than I'd have liked. "Or it could have led to his death. You can only trust that such information is revealed in its heralded time."

Just like life. I leaned back on the chair, parked on the desert floor. I was nothing special out here on the edge of a crater. Another speck of dust piled on top of the rest.

"For example," Carlos said, breaking back into my thoughts. "Take a mother in possession of a child's biological makeup. Maybe she waits some time to tell the babe of her alcoholic uncle, or the cancer riding rampant over her mother's side. It doesn't determine a person's entire fate, but it certainly marks their life. Yet are they to worry of it before misery even visits them? Or are they meant to live well, making the best choices they can, no matter what is fated in the future?"

I could feel my emotions passing like storms in my expressions. Doubt and bitterness and anger all made appearances in sweeping succession. It made me want to hide my face in the tequila until my lips were numb. But there was something—someone—else I wanted more. "So you're saying it's for our own good?"

"I only *trust* that it's for our own good."

"So what about now? The Light knows where you are. It won't be long before the Shadow does too." Because Warren would let the secret out. The Shadow and Light were enemies, but rogue agents were a common one. A third party would upset the balance between the two warring factions, and the Tulpa wouldn't welcome that either.

"It doesn't matter." Carlos said, again with that shrug. "*They* can't cross the line."

"But Mackie?" I asked, because that's where the line blurred.

Carlos set his glass down. "And now you have come to the reason we're here."

Because as a rogue, Mackie could cross into Frenchman's Flat as easily as the rest of us, and with the Light stalking the perimeter like wolves, it wouldn't be long before he pinpointed my location. My mind—so recently settled, and spinning with joy—cringed. This was why I wasn't drinking. Best to face fated truths sober. "Where is he?"

"We led him to the California state line. He's probably still in Barstow somewhere. Maybe he stopped at the outlet mall."

My mouth quirked upward, but only at one side. "Can we stop him?"

"Sleepy Mac is our bunker buster." Carlos gazed at the stars and blew out a deep breath. "He will plow through anyone and everything standing in the way of his quest to murder you."

"Comforting, Carlos. Thank you."

"I wish I could say differently." He shook his head. "But I've never met a being so single-minded and strong."

Yet he sat with me, sipping tequila in the starlight on the edge of an abyss, even though Mackie couldn't be stopped. It was forlornly comforting . . . and made me think again of Alex and Tripp and the rogue agents forming a family out of a bunch of paranormal misfits. Carlos should be running from me, but instead he was sitting. *Dining.* And the men downstairs were celebrating, even though fate might have plans as heinous as Alex's for them.

"So then what do you say we speed things up a bit?"

Carlos's eyes dilated, and I knew that beyond the liquor in his glass, he smelled something that excited him. "What do you mean?"

"I don't think we should allow Mackie to even attempt to breach the cell's crater." It was the least I could do for those who'd stood, and sat, and lay dying, for me. "You guys need this place. It's your home."

"And you suggest?"

"A show of boldness verging on the insane," I said grandly, pouring him more tequila.

"I like it already," he said in his liquid, rhythmic voice, though for the first time he looked uncertain.

Smiling, I reached over and squeezed his hand. "Tomorrow is Valentine's Day, and more importantly, the date of the grandest, most lavish wedding this city has ever seen. The papers have been announcing it for weeks. Dignitaries from all over the world are expected to attend. I'm a bridesmaid."

He cocked a dark brow. "Which Mackie surely knows."

"*Which*," I emphasized, "means I'll have to stick very close to the Tulpa."

The irony in sticking close to one enemy to avoid another had one corner of my mouth lifting, but Carlos's considering exhale was a teakettle's hiss. "This is your grand plan? Kill the Tulpa in front of hundreds of guests, gain the aureole, then escape Mackie for Midheaven?"

And stop Suzanne from marrying a freakishly obsessed man with ties to a paranormal underworld. After that?

I was going to fucking ferry Hunter away from Solange and back into this world. Unless I died trying, I thought, shrugging. "You have a better one?"

"*Wedita*," he said, laughing humorlessly, "I never thought we would get *this* far. I have no plan at all."

"Okay, then."

Carlos reclined again, one arm over the back of his chair. "Of course, you're forgetting one grave detail. You can only attempt public patricide by first getting past one very pissed off leader of the Light."

Ah, yes. Warren. I sighed and attempted Carlos's careless shrug, but he didn't smile. Instead he pursed his lips and stared off into the distance. "I don't think the other agents of Light will move to hurt you," he finally said, voice a mere whisper. "Their confusion was obvious tonight, both at our appearance and your revelations about this man, Hunter. But what you couldn't sense was their flashing anger and mounting frustration. I know this tangled knot of emotions. It will turn them against one another."

Yes, but would they move to *help* me against Mackie? Because none but Vanessa had done so during the tunnel fight. I frowned, mentally canvassing the scene at the border. I couldn't be sure, I'd been too giddy with laughter to notice, but I didn't think I'd seen her there. And if *I* noted her absence, along with her violent opposition of Kimber, Warren had too. A fist-sized worry unclenched in my belly, one I hadn't even known was there, as I realized one person in the troop remembered me.

I silently thanked Vanessa.

"You could still head that way, you know," Carlos said, jerking his head in the opposite direction of the city. He was right. With Olivia's money I could change my mortal identity a dozen times a year, alter my locations at whim, and still never make a dent in anything but the interest.

But Suzanne's words on the night of Mackie's first attack swung my way like a pendulum marking the moments. *No gossip or naysayer—and certainly no asshole—is going to keep me from love.* The next moment brought Tripp's voice back to life, words so recently spoken I could almost feel the warmth of his breath on my cheek.

Everyone's got a right to their own damned reasons.

I glanced down and tentatively rubbed my printed fingertips over Carlos's. "There's no freedom in flight, Carlos."

His smile took a long time to spread over his face, but when it did, it lit up the night. "And now you've discovered what all rogues eventually do. It is why at some point we settle somewhere, and battle for the right to remain where we choose."

Which settled *that*. Tomorrow I'd head back into Vegas, risking Warren's wrath, the Tulpa's suspicions, and Mackie's blade, all because what I really wanted, my *reason,* was as valid as anyone else's. I wanted to get the aureole, enter Midheaven, and take back what was mine. More than anything? I still wanted Hunter.

"You still offering your full resources to protect me from Mackie's blade?" I asked, tilting my head.

"I'm here, *verdad*?" And the shrug was back, as was the gleam in his eye. What a fatalist. What a dreamer. "You should get some sleep."

I nodded, then stood, and waited for Carlos to accompany me back into the cell. When he only held out his hand for my lantern, I realized he was standing guard.

"And while you're sleeping," he went on, graciously ignoring my sudden tears, "send up a prayer that we find a way to get past your former troop leader. He's pretty pissed."

"I'll take care of Warren."

"Really? So again, you're going to take on Warren, the Tulpa, *and* Sleepy Mac?"

"All in a day's work."

"You must be some sort of superhero."

In response, I stepped forward and kissed both his cheeks, scented the slim vein of tequila coming off his breath, then briefly pressed to my lips to his. If I weren't in love with another man, and if Carlos didn't know that, we might have deepened the kiss into something more. I pulled back and saw that knowledge in his eyes too.

"No, *chilango*," I said, cupping his cheeks. "But despite all odds, I'm alive, and that's enough."

But it wasn't all.

So with my failures piling aboveground like a funeral pyre of mistakes, I headed off in search of Io instead of rest. I had an idea which might just set a torch to that pyre, but what the hell . . .

One way or another, life as I knew it was about to go up in flames.

26

"You sure you want to do this?" Io asked when I told her what I wanted. She remained ambivalent at my answering nod, those wide eyes searching, but ultimately shrugged, agreeing to put me under with the same drugs Carlos had previously used to send me to Midheaven. As long as she stayed nearby to pull me back out again, I assured her I'd take care of the rest.

She placed a condition on the favor, though, claiming she wanted to work on my body again since female anatomy had become more or less a novelty to her since joining the cell. Remembering Hunter's final, desperate kiss, I relented, telling myself her curiosity was professional, not unlike a doctor keeping up on her skills, yet I was still nervous about her fondling my organs . . . not to mention a little skeeved now that I knew that's what she was doing.

"Interesting," she muttered after placing my pancreas back into its natural resting spot. Swallowing hard against the rise of bile in my throat, I rolled my eyes. Really, was there anything this woman wouldn't touch? "But what's that doing there?"

"What?" I asked, lifting my head, but she shifted her body to block my view.

"Let's see if we can't work it out . . ."

She rolled her fingers atop, along, and then into my lower abdomen, and I winced as she pulled and stretched in little striated motions, as if plucking harp strings. The motion caused me to alternately tense and relax, and while Buttersnap was lying passed out in her regular position at my right side, one particularly odd movement had me letting out a nauseated groan, causing the giant hound to lift her head and growl—almost like I was an agent of Light.

"Shush, you beast," Io said, shooing the dog with one hand.

"Ugh," I said, as she found the center harp string again. "Stop it!"

"No? You want it to stay?" Io asked, though she wasn't addressing me as much as she was my stomach. "Well, never mind then."

She then began administering a more traditional massage, the magic of her fingers making fast friends with my fatigue. "Ready?" she asked, and I managed a nod. There was a needle's pinch at my upper arm, and suddenly I floated, like oil atop water.

"I'll be right here," Io whispered from some far-off place. My fingers curled around the object that was as much a part of Midheaven as I was, clutching it to my chest like it was a life preserver. In some ways, I knew, it was.

My soft, velvet thoughts veered sharply then, a roller coaster downslope that plunged my veins into fire. My ears took on a frantic buzz, like I'd stuck my head in a hive as I dropped farther . . . and then suddenly I was sailing upright, walking on my own two legs through a heavy fog, like a spongy night in London or some other place that wasn't arid with desert heat. The haze was disconcerting, and I waved a hand before my face to push it away, still "walking" until lights appeared in front of me. The liquid boil of my blood evened out, and my footsteps took on the scratchy reverberation I remembered from my last two mental visits in Midheaven. Once I spotted the outline of a pagoda lantern, the haze dissipated and static electricity whipped around me, the fabric of the world being unzipped.

"Home sweet home," I muttered, each syllable skipping like a stone, my mouth lined in copper.

The saloon was exactly as I remembered. The long, polished bar stretched before me like a lazy feline, the staircase leading to the elemental rooms to the left, and the board with the myriad Most Wanted posters still staring eerily at me from the far right. Closer to the wall of pagoda lanterns, where I was standing, Sleepy Mac's piano sat in dust-covered silence, waiting for its owner's return.

As before, the entire room was devoid of color. Instead a sepia-toned coating washed out everything—the glossy bar, the mirrors reflecting back my hard gaze, the dozen poker tables eating up the room's middle. The sole exception to this ashen uniformity was a bright, glossy red door with a scrolled gold handle, rimmed in a fierce glow. It was the only thing holding back the heat siphoned from the sun's core on the other side.

Not that it helped much. Even in my dream I began to sweat. The bartender, Bill, was nowhere to be seen, but a single glass of elegantly cut crystal sat brimming with golden liquid on the otherwise empty bar. Even knowing how the liquid slowed actions and thoughts and time, catching it as if in molasses, I still couldn't help licking my lips.

There was absolutely nobody else in the room. No washed out men curled about the dozen or so poker tables, bartering for chips containing their personal powers—speed, strength, and soul.

You can still cash in the ones you won . . .

Tripp's words mocked me because I still didn't know how.

"Back so soon?"

Solange appeared like a Vegas stage magician, absent one moment and there the next, though I didn't applaud. Her face was what romance novels would term dewy, her hair pulled back into a slick brown plait, revealing the only adornment I'd ever seen her wear—simple gold chandelier earrings, ones she obviously cherished. She wore a long black coat with gold fur at neck and wrists, shining buttons lining the front to land at mid-calf, where black stiletto boots disappeared beneath the soft hem.

"You learn quickly. Already able to move about in the aetheric of your own accord." She clapped her gloved hands once. "Bravo."

"Forgive me if I don't take a bow," I said evenly. "That would entail taking my eyes off of you."

Her jaw clenched, prettily of course, and she tapped her chin with a finger. "I distinctly recall telling you, in no uncertain terms, to leave the Rest House and never return. Did I not?"

"Well, you have something that belongs to me."

She lifted one slim brow then leaned back on the glossy bar, pushed with her palms, and was sitting cross-legged in an instant. "Just as well. We have some accounts that need settling. Join me for a drink?"

She blinked prettily. I crossed my arms and stayed where I was. The last time I drank something this woman provided, I awoke to her holding a sliver of my soul between a jeweler's tweezers. "I owe you nothing. You're the one who threw a shit fit and crushed your pretty glass room. Believe me, I had no desire to be there."

"Of course you did," she snapped, and her boots hit the floor. Fuck, she was fast . . . and her fuse as short as ever. I made a point of staying within reach of the pagoda lantern. "Our truest desires are always revealed in Midheaven."

Exactly what Shen said. Where the hell had the little bastard gotten to anyway? "Yeah? So how many times *has* Hunter asked to leave?"

She pursed her lips prettily. "You mean my husband?

Jaden?" Her face rearranged into a sweet smile. "Joanna, he came here to *find* me."

No, he'd come to find Lola, the daughter she'd saved from the Tulpa and stolen from Hunter by destroying another child's soul. But no reason to allow I knew that much. Solange's knowledge of me was already too great, and her next words proved it.

"How're things in Vegas?"

"I think you know," I said, jerking my head toward the piano, but not taking my eyes from her.

"Jaden and I have been talking about going back. He's asked me to marry him again, you know."

"Before, after, or during the waterboarding?"

She put a black-gloved hand to her chest. "You think he's here against his will? Dear Joanna. Or should I say Olivia? Look at you and then look at me."

"Looks are deceiving."

"Sure," she agreed, eyeing me narrowly. "But I'm talking about power. It's what attracted him to me in the first place."

"Hunter's not driven by the need for power."

"But Jaden always has been."

I shook my head. "No, he wants autonomy."

She smiled beautifully. "He wants to be ridden into the next world."

My jaw clenched. "I'm not going to argue with you over who knows him better."

"Good, as you've no grounds to." She lifted her chin. "He's with me, isn't he? Crossing over of his own accord? And don't forget, I tasted him first."

Maybe it was the way she said it, her tone as she bit off that final word, or the quick jerk of her chin as she tossed her hair, but by the time I caught my reflection grinning fully from behind Solange's back, I knew. "But I'm the one who tasted him *last*, and that's what's got your silk thong in a bunch, isn't it? He doesn't love you. He doesn't even want you. Probably the only man in Midheaven who ever turned you down."

"The only man anywhere," she corrected, the bite alive in both her gaze and her voice. "And he didn't turn me down. Not before you. You have a hold on him, a connection the past can't sever. And it has nothing to do with who he prefers."

A *soul* connection. The aureole tying Hunter to the last third of my soul, then—even between worlds. "And that's why you wanted me dead."

"And because freeing the rest of your soul will finally finish my sky."

I thought about leaving then, just calling out to Io and getting the fuck out of the O.K. Corral because Solange wasn't just batshit crazy—she had the power to back up batshit crazy. "And what does Hunter think of that?"

She didn't bother to correct his name this time. "He's going to love the idea. Soon."

"I'd like to hear it from him."

The almost beautiful smile visited her face again. "He's tied up at the moment."

And there wasn't a thing I could do about it.

"Juden told me they believe you are the Kairos in your world," she said, like she'd never belonged there. Of course, she'd been here a long time, and despite her earlier taunt, had no desire to return to Las Vegas. Why would she? There, she was a rogue, on the run from both Shadow and Light. Here? A goddess. *The* Goddess. She crossed her feet at the ankles as she leaned back on the bar again. "It's why you once told me that you and Tripp were natural enemies, though you weren't exactly an agent of Light."

"I'm not the Kairos."

"Oh, I know." She smirked but stopped short of saying she had birthed the fabled child, now hidden somewhere in the folds of this alternate reality. "Though there's something about you. Some power you possess which others don't. You should have died the last time you were really here."

"You mean when you threw me down the stairs."

Solange nodded absently. "You were somehow protected then . . . and when I tried to sliver away your soul to augment my beautiful night sky. That stone's deformed. It won't ever fit."

"Guess you should give up."

"Why? I get at least one more try."

"You're not getting the last third of my fucking soul," I said, widening my stance.

"Because you're still protected." She sighed, and the sound grated like sandpaper against my spine. "I can feel it."

Well thank goddess for small miracles, though I remained close to the lantern. She smiled like she found my wariness endearing. "By the way, learn anything more about the constellations since we last met?"

"I've been kinda busy," I replied flatly.

"Then let me tell you about my favorite, Canis Major. It contains a star called Sirius, the brightest in the sky. It's part of a pattern we call the Winter Triangle."

"Does this boring diatribe have a point?"

"In gemology," she continued, shooting me a sly wink, "and you know I'm a fan . . . in gemology an asterism is an optical phenomenon reflecting the shape of a star on a precious stone's surface. So you see, I've decided a star as remarkable as Sirius needs just such a gem to do it justice in my rendition of the night sky. Something with the right amount of power and heat to fuel that Big Dog. The soul bits you gave upon crossing here twice came close to what I was looking for, but another third and my masterpiece will be completed. And I will finish it, Joanna. Once I do, my sky will hum with enough power to fuel multiple worlds . . . and I'll rule them all."

"I told you—"

"I know what you said! But Mackie will either bring me your soul pierced on the tip of his blade, or I'll flash-cook 'Hunter' until the connection between you burns."

And waving her hand over her head, the pressed tin ceiling disappeared, the heat fell away with it, and I was suddenly gazing directly into her sky of souls. No denying it, I thought, breath caught in my chest. It was stunning.

"Don't look for the Big Dog . . . you're not there yet. But can you find Ursa Major?"

The Big Dipper. I traced the luminous handle, gaze catching on the two stars comprising its scoop. They were bright but not completely luminous. The gems and the soul she'd stolen to form them contained some sort of impurities that made it appear like honey had hardened inside a crystal casing. Like her aforementioned asterism.

"Check out that dreamy nadir, those golden depths. They're perfectly identical, which is rare. Aren't they beautiful? Don't they remind you of . . . someone?"

And she beckoned the night sky down so the twin stars of the Dipper's bowl unhinged from the sky and lowered in a dizzying and unnatural 3-D display, the other stars fading until all that remained were . . .

"Hunter's eyes." My voice cracked.

"The windows to the soul," she agreed, motioning again. The gems lowered some more . . . and blinked. The rest of his body began to form out of the dark matter comprising the faux universe, like he was his own constellation, though his golden eyes remained fixed on me.

Solange was suddenly whispering in my ear. "The planets and stars are constantly evolving, Joanna. The universe is not a fixed entity, and it's not as gentle as it looks from afar. And the requirement of any phenomenal birth or death is a wild chaos. Do you know what my favorite kind is?" She smiled at me with a beautiful sweep of those lips. "Violence."

And Hunter blinked. Reaching up, Solange levitated, but then paused midair to look back at me. My hot blood suddenly ran cold. Her intention was written all over her beautiful face. She couldn't touch me . . . so she was going to touch him.

"Take a good look at your one true love, Jaden." She spoke softly, but every word was honed. "Because now you see her. Now you don't."

I whirled, lunging for the lantern closest to me, but knew I'd never make it in time. Sure enough, Hunter screamed. One hand cupped around the flame, the other poised in front of it, I could only glance up. Solange's laughter cut the air as she returned her attention to Hunter . . . and plucked out his left eye.

He screamed again, the lone remaining eye blinking furiously, and I sucked in a deep breath as Solange turned back to me, hand lifting.

"Don't you dare put that in your fucking mouth." My voice was strained. My breath was held.

"Or what?" she said, pretty mouth twisted like a snake. But then she glanced down, recognized what I held in my hand. I'd have smiled as shock blunted her pretty features, but there wasn't time.

"Suck it, Sola." And I blew out the air in my throat, aiming for her face, fixed on that mouth.

The quirley was as savage as Tripp said. The smoke took on a life of its own, forceful as a rapist, and Solange screamed as she put her hands to her face and throat, eyes bulging as tar-black death whipped around her. Hunter's gem fell from her hands, and I yelled even as I dove for it. "Io!"

Solange fell atop me, screaming and tearing at the air with her hands, smoke still ripping at her pores, but I held my breath . . . and made damn sure to keep my eyes closed as her hands scraped over my body. When icy palms wrapped around my shoulders, I bucked to free myself, fighting like a mental patient strapped to a gurney.

"Come back!"

I lunged upright, Io suddenly beside me, the night sky just a memory and Hunter gone. I sucked in a breath of air so cold I coughed, the ache burrowing to spread like a fissure in my lungs. Buttersnap licked at my arm, and I pushed her away so abruptly the great dog whimpered.

"Ugh," I managed, keeping my breath shallow so I didn't puke.

"Shh," Io said, an arm around my waist, holding me close.

I shook her off too, needing to be untouched, alone, so the rage I was feeling wouldn't zap anyone else. My breath rattled harshly in the too-still room. "She needs my power, my soul, to finish her horrible sky."

Yet Midheaven was the one place I needed to go. That's where my army was. That's where *Hunter* was.

Io inched closer again but was careful not to touch me. When my breathing had calmed somewhat, she said, "How do you feel?"

"Truthfully, Io?" I asked, hand over my queasy stomach. "I'm pissed."

She stared at me with her wide, lidless gaze before nodding once. "That could work."

Sure it could, I thought, the fresh memory of Hunter's scream sending a shiver through me again. It ran through my body, down my limbs, and zipped to my fingertips, where I shook it off . . . and sent Hunter's soul gem clattering to the floor.

I cried out and dove as I had in Midheaven, this time to save the gem from Buttersnap's inquisitive nose. Cradling it to my chest, I looked back up at Io. She gazed back, as dumbfounded as I'd ever seen her.

And looking at the gorgeous jewel in my hand, recalling how Hunter had warned me never to return to or for him, I swore an oath to every star in the heavens above: the blow I'd just dealt Solange wasn't even the beginning of it. Fuck the universe; fate wasn't a fixed entity. Mortality or not—Mackie and the Tulpa and my other numerous enemies aside—I was more than happy to show Solange a wild death.

"I'll give you the phenomenal violence you seek," I said, cupping the gem in my palm as gently as I would a baby bird. "I'll deal it to you like a hand of soul poker."

I'd deal it out in fucking spades.

27

Winter's dawn along the Mojave flats was as beautiful as a tea ceremony. The outlines of the scraggly Joshua trees were backlit in baby blues, a precursor to the pastels soon to sweep the sky. Mountains loomed in lavender, and the soft desert scents were still in evidence, though like all shy desert things, they too would soon go into hiding. I'd avoided watching dawn or dusk in the last weeks because those moments broke my heart. The veil between this world and the Zodiac's alternate reality was thinnest then. That was when troops crossed from their sanctuary back into mortal reality, so it was poetic to be leaving Frenchman Flat at this time, returning to the city coiled like a bright snake, waiting for my return.

Just like the agents of Light, I thought, spotting Felix and Micah still lined against the invisible border just beyond rogue territory. I walked toward them in the new day's chill, the rocky desert crunching beneath my boots while eggshell and pink warred with one another in giant, silken swaths across the lightening sky.

"A pretty day to die," Carlos remarked, watching the sparse, wispy clouds evaporate with the last tendrils of night. I gave him a sidelong look and his hands went up. "What? I didn't mean you. Just in general."

I adjusted the holster at my waist, and the agents of Light drew in tighter on the other side of the invisible line. In addition to the two men, there were only Tekla and Kimber. Warren probably had them guarding the border in rotations. I ran a hand over my hair, slicked into a low bun, then dropped it, aware of how much nervousness the movement contained. The Light stood across from me, widelegged and still, and I tried to imagine what Carlos and I looked like as we approached in the cold dawn. Probably pretty ragtag. I was an outcast, with only mortal fighting skills and a mutant hound tethered to my side. Carlos was just plain disreputable in his shit-kickers and dusty jeans, the scruff shadowing his cheeks a good couple of days beyond sexy.

I halted only feet from the barrier, letting the day fully claim the sky before speaking. "Micah. Tekla."

Felix gave me a little wave and I smiled at him, but before I could get too comfortable, Kimber made her presence known. As usual she was pumped and pissed, kohl-darkened eyes narrowed, chipped, black nails poised on her dart gun. Following my gaze, she smiled evilly. "I won't miss this time."

I considered giving Buttersnap some slack. Kimber's glyph took on a faint glow, as if she read my mind, but I wouldn't do it. I'd never get Buttersnap's muzzle off quickly enough.

"Finished hiding?" she asked, tossing her long blond dreads.

"I was just taking a little siesta. Right, Carlos?" He nodded, and I nonchalantly kicked at some bramble. It tumbled over the invisible line, right to the toe of Kimber's boot. "After all, I'm going to need my full strength to face Sleepy Mac."

Kimber huffed so hard I doubted there was any air left in her lungs. It didn't keep her from speaking. "In your mortal state? Better to stick to your siestas on *that* side of city limits."

"Well, you'd think so, wouldn't you?" I forced out my own mock sigh and patted Buttersnap on her great black head. Her body thrummed beneath my touch. She could barely stand being this close to the agents of Light without attacking. Io had done some sort of hypnosis on the dog, though, a mental prescription not to move from my side unless I expressly commanded it. "But unlike you, Mackie can actually get to me here. So going after him in Las Vegas is the lesser of two evils."

She jutted out her chin, a nasty smirk widening her face. I hated smirks. "You have to get past me first."

"Okay."

And Carlos shot her with a tranq gun. We high-fived as she dropped like A-bomb fallout. It'd been my idea to plug her with a mortal weapon, and I'd have done it myself but this was more gratifying for us both. He never got to fire things, and looked pretty jazzed about his shot. Even Buttersnap was wagging her tail so hard her whole body shook.

Felix snickered, then sobered under Micah's dark look. They could smell the drugs in the shot, and knew Kimber was fine. In fact, troop members routinely did worse on April Fool's Day. It would be humiliating for her when she woke, but what was she going to do? Hate me more?

"Do you have an actual plan here, Joanna?" Tekla gazed up at me with soft eyes, her tiny frame lost in the folds of gray silk, her hair pulled back like mine, but more severely. Her voice was authoritative—she was shitstorm powerful—but permissive and fair. She wasn't angry with me like Warren. And though I couldn't scent their emotions, I didn't think anyone besides Kimber was either. "Or are you going to drug every moving thing?"

"The plan," I said calmly, mirroring her folded hands, "is to kill the Tulpa, gain the aureole for myself, thus preventing Mackie from killing me and allowing me to enter

Midheaven without stripping away the last of my soul. Or, you know, dying upon entry, since I'm mortal." I looked around. "Any other questions?"

"You're going after Hunter." It wasn't a question. It was Felix at his most serious . . . and it sounded like he wouldn't mind coming along.

"I'm going after Hunter."

"We're not going against Warren's wishes, Joanna," Micah said, shooting Felix a hard look before gazing down at me from his seven full feet. The soot and black fire festering beneath his skin shifted with every syllable, causing him to wince, but his eyes were still kind despite the agony. The look nearly brought tears to my own. "I know he can be brusque, but he has reasons for everything he does. And he's kept this troop together for a long time."

I wanted to say the Tulpa did all of those things too, but had no desire to antagonize Micah. At least he seemed to have given himself something for the pain. His eyes were a bit too glassy and his words slid into one another where they didn't cut off abruptly. I fought back a wince when he swallowed hard. So he'd turned his back on me. I still hated to see him like this. "I'm not asking you to go against him," I said softly. "I'm just asking you to let me pass."

"You mean defy his wishes."

I yanked the old silver gun from its holster with my free hand and pointed it at Kimber, now sitting up. The liquid green vial atop the chamber caught the morning sun like it was drawing the light in. "I mean, live and let live."

Tekla eased in front of Kimber. "There's no need for that."

Despite her gentleness, it reminded me whose side she was on. I used the gun to motion her aside. "Yes, Tekla, there is. Because a man is being held captive and tortured in another world, and he was driven there because of the things Warren didn't tell him . . . just as he didn't tell any of you."

Micah shook his head. "I told you he has his reasons."

"Yeah?" *That* reason was sounding more and more like an excuse to me. "Well, if circumstances were different, it could easily be any of you over there."

"Hunter made bad choices."

"We all make bad choices." Most people made them in a vacuum, acting on what was known and doing the best they could. But if someone kept the truth from you, forcing you to act in its absence, then even a bad decision was a false negative. But again, it wasn't the time. They'd come around to the same thought eventually. If they hadn't already, I thought, noting Felix's silent frown.

"Look, I know you have a job to do, you're still in a troop, and Warren's your leader. I get it. But I could use some allies."

The ensuing silence almost sizzled in the air, and despite the coolness, it reminded me of a scorching summer day. Finally, Micah spoke up. "Where are you going?"

Tekla looked at him sharply. He continued watching me, sooty shadows sifting beneath his skin like black clouds.

"Valhalla. Noon. The wedding of the decade." I smiled wryly, but none of them smiled back. "All the major players will be there. Show up. Help me."

Only Tekla's mouth moved. "No."

It wasn't said cruelly. No more animosity in the refusal than if I'd asked her to get me a pint of milk at the store.

"Then just let me pass."

Nobody moved, and in that frozen moment, I unexpectedly began to feel sorry for them. Sure, I was the weakest, the outcast, the one most likely to be dead by day's end. But I made my own decisions now, calling and controlling my own shots, and unlike any of them—dependent upon Warren's whim and "reasons"—I could no longer be used.

Maybe they sensed something of my thoughts, because Tekla and Micah simultaneously stepped aside. Both silenced Kimber's protesting whine with a sharp look. Felix only watched me.

"We'll tell Warren," Tekla said. "Immediately."

Of course. "Thank you."

Carlos and I started forward, shifting so we were back-to-back with Buttersnap taking the lead, but Micah veered as well, and shook his head. "Only you."

I stared up at his looming frame from the distance of only five feet. It felt like miles. "The rogues are not your enemies, Micah."

The liquid ash below the surface of that first layer of skin wavered as his jaw clenched. "They aren't allies."

"They could be." The plea was in my eyes, if not in my voice.

Tekla cleared her throat. "Not today."

Glancing from one senior troop member to the other, I decided not to press my luck. Rome, I thought, hadn't been overthrown in a day. But I stared back into Micah's kind, destroyed face. "I'm so sorry you've been injured, Micah. I'd never wish it for you. And I'm . . . I'm just sorry."

Tears must have already been waiting because they spilled over his cheeks in light black streaks. "I'm sorry too."

And he wasn't talking about his own pain.

I nodded, then turned back to Carlos. "Wait until they're gone. Warren will pull them all to come after me. There's an employee entrance south of the parking garage at Valhalla. I'll make sure someone knows you're coming."

He frowned, not liking it. But I had to go, and even though the rogues were more committee than troop, he still needed to keep their best interests in mind. Finally, he touched my cheek with one hand. The warmth made me realize how cold I'd actually been. "Be careful."

"You mean the opposite of careful." Because what I needed to be was effective. I had no idea how those two things could possibly coincide.

"*Sí, mon*, but be careful doing that."

I smiled, then turned back to my former troop. "Oh, yeah." I looked at Tekla, who raised a brow, and I shrugged. "I could use a ride."

* * *

Well, I couldn't very well walk the sixty-five miles back to the city, could I? I wouldn't even make it to the wedding in that time—and the cell didn't have cars. So despite the declaration that they wouldn't go against Warren's wishes, Tekla offered to accompany me, and no one dared go against her. Maybe they thought she'd kidnap me and turn me over to Warren as soon as we were out of sight. She easily could, but I didn't think so. Otherwise she would have grabbed me as soon as I stepped over the boundary. There was something else at play here.

Yet Tekla said nothing as she drove in the waxing light, just sat at the wheel of a stolen truck, as if she wasn't blowing down the streets like a hurricane. I needed to grab a shower and my bridesmaid dress before the wedding, but despite the speed of the trip, I was actually surprised when Tekla pulled to a stop a block from Xavier's home, mindful of the mansion's surveillance cameras.

Facing her as the truck idled, I searched for the woman who'd taught me about Ophiuchus and told me to make a difference. She looked childlike in the cab of the great truck, and had to sit forward on the seat just to touch the pedals.

"You're choosing a dangerous path, Joanna," she finally said, staring straight ahead.

I was about to say that it had been chosen for me, but stopped myself. I could have chosen differently a number of times. I could still do so now. Instead I fingered the gem in my pocket, one as warm as the heart in my chest, and shook my head. "I was born to this path."

She glanced at me sharply, the stare growing long, before she finally nodded.

"You believed in me once, Tekla. You wouldn't have spent so much time working with me if you didn't. You wouldn't have been so hard on me." I glanced out the windshield. The daylight was now spread around us like a stain. "You believe in me now too. That's why you drove me today. When you know that Warren will be furious."

"Warren—"

"Has a reason for everything he does. Blah blah blah." I jerked my head at her. "What about your reasons?"

She lifted her chin. "They are the same. We work in tandem, always and only for the best of the troop."

I'd have laughed loud and long at that, but it wasn't really funny. "And how does allying with Caine fit into that?"

I got a flash of her face inches from my own and wrapped in fury, and then she was facing forward again. It happened so fast I almost missed the movement altogether. Heart skipping, I didn't dare blink. "Caine is none of your business."

"Caine did more for me than the troop as a whole. He gave his life to help me."

"Why do you think I'm here?" she snapped, looking at me again, and I sat back, air whooshing from my chest. Well, that cleared things up a bit. Tekla wasn't here for me specifically, or to screw over Warren in general. She just didn't want Caine's death to mean nothing. But the brittle frown on her face kept me from asking what he'd meant to her.

"Warren's a control freak with tunnel vision," I said instead. "He manipulates everyone, especially those in the troop."

"He's still our best chance to preserve choice for the mortals in this valley."

"Well maybe the mortals in this valley deserve better than that." Maybe *I* did.

Tekla's nostrils flared and she straightened, her gaze again straight ahead. "Don't make him a scapegoat for all your ills, Joanna."

Now her imperious manner just pissed me off.

"He sent me to Midheaven knowing it would take something from me! I lost vital pieces of myself over there!"

Tekla turned a cold gaze on me. "And who do you think advised him to do that?"

My mouth fell open, but all that escaped was air. I

touched the gem in my pocket, trying to center myself. "I . . . you wouldn't . . ."

She hit the steering wheel so hard the truck rocked. "You're so sensitive about your parentage and past, so hell-bent on making sure we see you for who you are . . . and that a simple hair color or cosmetic enhancement won't change that. But you never afford us the same luxury. We are Light. *Pure* Light. We fight for one thing only, and that's against the Shadows. Always. Only. Period. *We* are not gray."

I nodded, swallowing hard. "And I've always been that, haven't I?"

She frowned, like she had to work to harden herself to me. But her words said differently. "It is in the stars."

These people and their fucking stars.

"Thanks for the ride, Tekla." I got out of the truck and slammed the door shut.

She rolled down the window as she pulled from the curb. "Good luck."

But she wasn't saying it for me. She was saying it because it would benefit her troop, her cause.

I thought of dream-Olivia saying Tekla was one of the people most directly influencing me now. I guess my T-Rex brain had known it all along.

You're not the only one doing the best you can to survive in a hard world.

"No, bitch," I answered the dream Seer as I began to walk. "But I'm doing better than you."

28

Despite my morning trek across the desert, I was the first in the wedding party to reach Valhalla, arriving so early the casino floor sported more patrons from the night before than those beginning their gambling day. Go ahead, chase your money, I thought, watching a bleary-eyed man battle a slant-topped bandit. *Someone needs to keep my food cheap and my taxes low.* He eyed me back, less interested in what my black roller suitcase contained than in the stretch of my T-shirt and jeans. A predictable response in a predictable environment, and just the annoyance I needed to calm me before attempted patricide. Gotta love Vegas.

But now I was dressed in an Indo-Western sari, an amalgamation of eastern and western influences, with a black sequined halter attached to a pink satin bodice and matching lily embroidery. The bottom of the dress was a soft lavender that lightened into pink and ivory as the body scarf swirled across my middle, ending in a dramatic drape over my left shoulder. It was an elegance that was almost impossible to pull off, even without rusted weapons tucked into every fold.

Meanwhile, Valhalla's pool area, spanning the hotel's center courtyard, had been turned into an outdoor cathedral with velvet chairs rimming the pool and a Plexiglas aisle leading to an equally translucent dais. Suzanne and Arun had worked hard to make sure both Indian and American cultures were well represented. Physically it wasn't much different than a traditional western wedding. Giant floral arrangements in the softest of pastels dwarfed stunted heaters dotting the patio surface, and silk banners threaded the entire area to create an enormous tent, more to shield the ceremony from the curious gazes of guests in the looming hotel rooms than out of any eastern tradition.

Arun's culture would be more fully represented in the ceremony than anywhere else. Prayers and hymns were explained in a wedding program, and garlands and embraces would be exchanged at preordained times. Though Suzanne would enter to the traditional wedding march, an artist would perform it on a sitar rather than a piano.

I sighed, wishing there was no need to plant weapons among the silks and flowers, but ordered the wait staff on a mandatory fifteen-minute break anyway. I had to be safe, though it wouldn't necessarily preclude me from being sorry. I placed the saber within the vase of the floral arrangement closest to the side of the dais where I'd be standing— and the bladed cane along the back of a pillar bolstering one of the soaring silks. The trident was perfectly holstered at the small of my back, one quirley hidden in the depths of my cleavage, and the gun with its bubbling green vials also disappeared beneath my sari's folds. If I had to be in an enclosed area with both the Tulpa and Sleepy Mac, I was damn well going to wear something that would make a more lasting impression than my borrowed tiara.

Yet, as the Tulpa was immune to all paranormal weaponry, and Mackie was both aware of my identity and that I was armed, my greatest weapon was offense. The defensive protectant would only shield me from one blow, but it might buy me enough time to pull the trident from my back or the cane from the bushes. I didn't anticipate using the quirley, as I'd need time to both pull it out and light it—though the sole candle in the dais's center might prove useful if given the opportunity. And though Io had reinforced the protective coating on my organs, my preference was to avoid even the tiniest of flesh wounds. I scarred now, I hurt now, and as evidenced by Luna's sad demise, I could suffer a worse fate on this side of Mackie's blade than mere death.

"Any second thoughts?" I asked the bride once I'd returned to her . . . probably because I was having so many. I did my best not to sound hopeful. We were ensconced in the elevated bridal chamber, as scented, soothing, and relaxing as the city's finest spa, and with a panoramic view of the pool area.

"A little late for that, don't you think?" Suzanne replied from in front of the vanity. Twenty minutes from showtime, and she looked like a living goddess. Her dress was a strapless lengha with a full underskirt of tulle, and done entirely in gold silk and threaded appliqués. Her veil, also gold, was more of a headdress encompassing the full of her forehead. Diamonds lined the sharp arch of her brows, the sparkle warring with the yellow gold earrings and glossed, flecked lips.

"Forever's a long time," I answered, still considering a forever spent with a consciousness encased in never-healing flesh. I shivered, causing Suzanne to laugh.

She folded ornately hennaed hands in front of her. "If you're lucky, you find the one who makes you feel like forever isn't long enough."

"If you're lucky, you don't puke when someone says something like that." Cher entered the room with a necklace so large I wasn't entirely sure it wasn't a breastplate. Now that she mentioned it, I did feel a little queasy. However, Suzanne's responding squeal helped take my mind off the crowd gathering like a storm outside, and I held up her veil as Cher fastened the gold clasp around her neck.

"You young women are so impossibly jaded," Suzanne said in a breathy sigh. "But I choose to be eternally optimistic. That's why I'm getting married on Valentine's Day. That's why red, representing the heart, and gold, representing my faith in love, are my wedding colors. That's why the little cupids, poised with bows and arrows, are featured in all my centerpieces. I wish this sort of love for everyone who witnesses mine."

Her words would have increased my nausea if they weren't so sincere. I bit my lip and privately swore not to let my red-blooded heart mess up her gold dress . . . though I wished even more that *I* were armed with a bow and arrow. Little cupid bastards.

But Suzanne wasn't done rhapsodizing. I supposed it was allowed on one's wedding day, though it did nothing to assuage my guilt over compromising her ceremony. Even if Arun was a freak. "Yes, I believe love's the greatest motivator of all. It's the reason the sun and moon chase each other across the sky. It's vital to the breath of the stars."

I huffed. Too bad nobody ever told that to Solange.

Cher, tilting her head, considered her stepmother. "You know, you should have gotten a boob job for the wedding."

Suzanne stopped cold, straightening like an affronted peacock. "Really?"

"Yeah, you're totally bossier than your boobies right now." Cher shook her head, eyes angled down.

"Well, shit." Suzanne looked down too. She pursed her lips, thinking. "Maybe we can stuff 'em with toilet paper."

"Oh, I'll go get some," Cher volunteered. "You didn't hear that, Ms. Board of Directors . . ."

"Didn't hear a thing," I said, pretending to cover my ears as she sailed from the room.

"I wish she would have told me this sooner," Suzanne muttered, bending over like she was flexing her pecs. It created a little channel in the front of her dress. From the way her eyes widened it must have looked to her like the Lincoln tunnel.

"You're gorgeous," I reassured, momentarily putting my life/death issues aside, and my hand on her arm. "Really. I didn't even notice your boobs—" I broke off, immediately realizing that was the wrong thing to say. "And it's the most beautiful wedding gown I've ever seen."

Suzanne relaxed enough to fluff her skirt, and twirled to face the full-length mirror. "Did you know white is the color of death in India? It's true," she said, not bothering to wait for my reply. "The women primarily get married in red over there, head to toe. Even their bindis. Arun and I compromised on gold, but I could tell it bothered him. Do you think it's bad luck? Am I going to be unlucky in love if I wear something on my wedding day that is only a shade away from a color some believe signifies death?"

"No," I lied, earning myself an uneasy smile. "Hey, aren't you the one who told me no gossip or naysayers were going to keep you from love? That's all superstition is. Gossip, but on a global scale."

After a long moment her expression cleared. "Darned tootin'." She nodded once, took a long, shaky breath, and slumped. "Then again . . . there's the whole *death* thing to consider."

"Ah, but you also said true love never dies." She'd also once said the reporter who uncovered the identity of Demi Moore's plastic surgeon should receive a Pulitzer, but I didn't bring that up. "Remember?"

"Even when love's gone, its memory keeps you safe." She closed her gold-dusted eyes, and after a moment opened them again and smiled. "Thank you for the reminder."

"You mean thank you for the toilet paper!" Cher declared, holding two rolls aloft. "Boy, they don't skimp on the quality here at Valhalla, do they? Open your shirt, Momma. This shit's four-ply!"

I watched them through the mirror, these two mortals who had ended up in my life by default, and knew this was why I'd brought the weapons today. I didn't expect to survive, not really. Mackie would attack me no matter where

I was, and the only chance of surviving was to gain the aureole by killing the Tulpa. And since I believed Arun was somehow abetting the Shadows in his quest to marry Suzanne—or at least advancing some sort of personal, paranormal agenda—compromising this ceremony was my best chance to stop them all.

Yet I also believed the agents of Light would show up and do the right thing—help me battle Mackie and protect these mortals. I might die at someone's hands today, be it Mackie or the Tulpa, but at some point on the trip here I'd become resigned to that.

But Suzanne and Cher would *live*. These women had done nothing more wicked in their lives than dream of love, and I swore—as toilet paper and giggles streamed across the room—that Suzanne's worries over bad luck weren't going to touch her. It might hit me with the force of a natural disaster, but it wouldn't strike her.

The whispered promise calmed me somewhat. I even laughed, watching Cher stuff the wedding gown of a woman with hopes of being an honest-to-goodness princess within the hour. I frowned when they tried to do the same to me.

And then it was time.

"The candles," I whispered to the nearest attendant. "You forgot to light the candles."

He hissed and rushed off, and I bit my lip as I canvassed the pool deck. It was full noon and a gorgeous winter day, the slim bite in the air negated by the heaters and bodies now packed around the giant pool. There were stanchions to keep guests from falling in, and as I scanned the pool area one last time, mentally marking all the places I'd planted the weapons, safety was definitely my greatest concern. How was I going to keep all these people safe?

The fact was, I couldn't. But the agents of Light could, if they chose. And so could the rogues . . . though I didn't see Carlos or any of the other grays anywhere. I wondered if they'd yet to leave the compound or had trouble entering Valhalla, but it was too late for me to check on either of those things. The sitar player was already in place, and I heard from the walkie-talkies that the groom was on his way out. Showtime.

Glancing up, I frowned at the looming hotel. Its size made the pool area resemble a lion's pit, and Shadow agents and Mackie could easily jump from the rooftop, yet there was nothing I could do about that. I only hoped the Zodiac's paranoia about avoiding human attention would keep them from trying. Unless Mackie showed his face. Then it would turn into a free-for-all. Meanwhile, I was the only armed person in the room.

"It's good to be queen," I muttered, with a small, private smile.

As the head of Archer Enterprises, Valhalla's COO, and an esteemed member of this wedding party, I'd ordered a metal detector and a small phalanx of security guards to check every bag and body entering the enclosed pool area. It was a precaution easily explained away by the august guest list, along with the groom's wealth and world prominence. Any agent wishing to enter would have to disarm, and most would not. The Shadows weren't even on guard because the Tulpa had no idea what was to happen here. And while there could have been some turnover in that troop in the weeks since I'd been expelled, only one agent I knew was patrolling the hotel's halls, and it was his usual post.

As for the Light? Well, that was answered once Warren sidled up behind me.

"It's official," he whispered in my ear. "Someone is going to die this afternoon."

I whirled, but he grabbed my arm before we could speak, forcing me into an alcove normally used to stock towels.

We faced off and his top lip lifted in a snarl. "Perhaps we can share a dance after the festivities, dear."

I pulled away, rubbing at my wrist. "So last night you

were a homeless man living off buffet scraps, and today you're a South Asian livery boy." I looked at his uniform, liveried for the occasion, stolen for the same. He was in white, distinguishing him from the guests, and his hair had been shorn overnight, shorter and cleaner than I'd ever seen it.

"Last night you were carrying a weapon you shouldn't even be allowed to touch, and today you're dressed like a South Asian Barbie. Also a dichotomy."

Like my entire life *wasn't*? "Well, you know. It's important to keep up appearances."

He crossed his arms and leaned against the wall, slouching as he stared at me. Most unliverylike. "You're making life very difficult on me."

"God forbid," I said, echoing his flat tone. What did he want, an apology? Nothing I said could make me any more of an outcast than I already was—or less.

He turned his head, squinting out over the crowd, eyes lingering on the sitar player as the first song began. I'd have to go soon. "The rogue agents can't be trusted. They're using you, and as soon as they get what they want from you, they'll either kill you or abandon you. Most likely the first."

"They took me in when I had nothing and no one. You introduced me to a world that wanted me dead, then practically ensured the fate by turning your back on me. They saved me from Mackie. Where the fuck were you?"

His nostrils flared, but all he said was, "They're using you for your knowledge of the troop, and the tools you can provide in combating us."

"I don't have any tools."

"What about the defensive compound protecting them last night?" he said, expression dead and tight. "The one you're probably wearing now?"

Oh, yeah. That. "I have a right to protect myself, Warren. Besides, maybe I had some protectant in reserve."

"I went to the warehouse, Joanna. It was unarmed, and your scent was all over it. Yours and *Tripp's*."

He spat the man's name out like it'd gone bad in his mouth, and I lifted my chin. I wasn't going to talk to Warren about Tripp . . . a man he thought of as an enemy, but one who'd died saving me. The urge to pull out the quirley and blow venomous smoke in this man's face was almost overwhelming. I refrained, but only because I was expecting a far greater threat than Warren. "The defensive protectant is not an offensive weapon. Again, I have a right to my own defense."

He shook his head in disgust, and I realized he was right; this was futile. Despite my ejection from the troop, Warren believed I'd betrayed him, and nothing was going to sway him from the belief.

I turned to walk away.

He raised his voice, "What I'm most concerned with is the other weapon you've so generously handed them. You."

I turned slowly, disbelief oozing from every pore. "How do you figure?"

"You can still touch the conduits, Joanna. You shouldn't be able to, not as a mortal. And not as a rogue."

"So how?"

Another look overtook his features, one both softer . . . and harder. "Come back into the troop, and we'll figure it out together."

"*Now* you want me back?" Like being thrust underwater, I could see his mouth moving, but his voice was distorted, the words that unreal.

"I'm holding out an olive branch, Joanna," he said, a tight smirk stretched over his weathered face. "You should take it."

I laughed so loudly a small clump of wait staff turned to stare. "You've found another use for me. Is that it?"

"You're making a scene," he said, jaw clenching so tightly I knew I was kicking off some potently bitter emotion. But I was just trying to figure out what about me would be so useful to him. I mentally ticked through everything he'd learned lately—the grays, their hideout at the

Test Site—but only one thing truly clicked as a matter of urgency. I laughed again. "Oh . . . I see. You know there's a child in Midheaven, and Hunter—a man you also discarded—is your link to that child. And I'm your link to him. Because we share the aureole."

"You don't share the aureole," he snapped so quickly I knew he wasn't entirely sure. "That's impossible with a mortal."

I'd done a lot of things in the past year previously thought impossible. Pursing my lips, I watched him another few seconds. "And I suppose my return to the troop is conditioned upon telling you everything I know about the cell?"

"Of course."

Wow. I shook my head at the hubris. This man wanted it all his way. "Not going to play out that way, Warren."

"Really?"

"Hell, no," I snapped, so angry I was shaking. "I might not be an agent, you arrogant prick, but I'm human and I have my rights. Primary among them? Freedom. Choice." I spat the words at him, remembering the ones Hunter had given me too. "The ability to create the world as I want it to be."

He lunged, his nostrils flaring wide, and tugged on my arm. "Not this one."

I jerked from his touch, but it was too late. A sharp pain pierced my palm, and he scored my hand all the way down to the newly printed tip of my middle finger, giving an especially hard yank. The print didn't come off as the blood welled, but my defensive protectant did.

"You wanna live by your own rules?" he said as the fine netting rippled, then dissipated. "Then you'll die by them too. Good-bye, Joanna."

And he left me defenseless in an open-air venue I was sure Sleepy Mac would find before the ceremony was over. Holding my palm closed, I winced and looked around to see if anyone had noticed. I told myself the wound was so shallow it wouldn't make a difference. Not when it came

time to grab a weapon. I'd even almost convinced myself
of it.

And that's when the Tulpa arrived.

He paused as he spotted me inside the entry of the pool
area, then angled his wheelchair my way. You still have
weapons, I thought, trying not to panic. But as the me-
chanical whirring of the Tulpa's chair grew closer, every
aging conduit seemed so far away. It was impossible to be
in this being's presence and not wish for protection—full-
body armor would do nicely—and I wasn't the only one
who felt that way. Even the mortals he passed straightened,
then slumped, his power making them squirm without pre-
cisely knowing why. The instinct of prey caught under a
predator's stare had been bred out of the mostly urban
population, but it still flickered beneath the cool, sophisti-
cated veneer, like a carp's tail catching the sun before
diving lower.

If you were watching the scene from a distance—or,
more likely these days, on a reality show—the knee-jerk
flinch would be hard to understand. The Tulpa looked
weaker than ever. He was confined to that chair, devoid
of the power he'd exhibited in Xavier's office, and the first
two fingers of his gloved left hand were unnaturally stiff.

Still, just like a cockroach, the menacing fucker just
wouldn't die. Afraid of telegraphing my intent to stomp
him in the very near future, I smiled like I was happy to
see him.

"Olivia dear," he said, holding out one gloved hand as
he pulled to a stop before me. "I can't tell you how happy
I am to see you. I read the news reports about the unfortu-
nate events in your home last night. I hope you weren't too
badly injured?"

"I—I bumped my head at some point, I think. I don't remember anything at all." Lindy had no doubt already told
him that, but his gaze still sharpened fractionally, and the
softest mental probe whispered over me.

"But you're fine now?" he asked, all concern and sweetness beneath the soft, and hard, pulse.

I smiled. "Perfectly. Ready for a wedding!"

His brows winged down and his gaze narrowed on my palms. "Then why are you bleeding?"

He inched closer, nostrils flaring. My heart jumped as he reached again for my palm, and a quick glance up revealed Warren smiling smugly over the Tulpa's left shoulder. Agents, including the Tulpa, could scent out their enemies through blood, though they all had olfactory blind spots when it came to their own. I had the Tulpa's blood running in my veins, so I was safe. Thus, my nervousness curdled into bile. "Thorns," I said, meeting the Tulpa's darkly inquisitive gaze. "The rose bouquets are enormous, and the florist accidentally left some of the thorns on mine, so I had to pull them off myself. See?" I made sure he got another good glimpse of my fingertips—printed, mortal, obviously harmless despite anything else he may or may not be smelling—and had the pleasure of watching Warren's face fall when the Tulpa released my palm.

"You should wash up quickly, my dear," he said, angling his chair away. "The ceremony's about to begin."

"Yes, but first . . ." But first I had an idea. Furrowing my brow, I let my gaze soften again as I stared into his eyes. It was easy to bring back the feeling I'd had last night in Xavier's office, and in the conference room when the board of directors had fallen so completely under his spell. I swayed, blinked slowly, and repeated his demand to tell him anything I remembered about ". . . the Serpent Bearer."

His expression shifted, skin thinning over the sharp bone. Even his vocal cords tightened. "What about it?"

Another pulse of thought energy had me swaying for real, and I swallowed hard before flattening my voice into a liquid roll. "A man . . . he gave me the photo of that symbol. He was so strange, talking in riddles . . ."

"What exactly did he say?"

"I didn't understand . . . but he said he planted the treasure chest for me. The bachelorette party was his opportunity . . ." I frowned, like the thought was escaping me. My next words slurred. "Because I'm an Archer . . . Xavier's daughter, which makes me somehow special." I tilted my head and let my gaze slide from his face.

The Tulpa squeezed my arm until I refocused. "What man, Olivia?"

Keeping my gaze liquid, I smiled softly, then pointed over his shoulder. "Why . . . him."

The Tulpa whirled in his chair. Warren's eyes widened and he visibly jolted and started backing toward the exit, but they'd shut the glass doors leading back into the hotel to keep the photographers and gawkers out . . . and the rest of us in. Warren licked his lips, considering his options. He finally settled against a faux pillar lining the groom's side of the pool. As if on cue, the preceremony music swelled.

"Well, I guess it's time," I said brightly, shaking my head as if coming out of a daydream. I smiled down at the Tulpa, who was overly still as he considered his own next move. I made it for him. "Oh, don't look so worried. I'm going to make sure you have the best seat in the house."

And before he could object, I motioned to one of the attendants. "Center aisle, front row, closest to me," I instructed, and while the Tulpa paused, what could he really say? I was smiling sweetly. Warren was in the same room, though he didn't know why. And as he was supposed to be Olivia Archer's advisor, appearances had to be upheld.

So he rolled away, and I headed back to the bridal chamber. This could all go very, very wrong. But the new seating arrangement would definitely keep the Zodiac leaders busy. Maybe, I thought as I headed back to the scrolled staircase, they'd be so busy watching each other that I would be a mere, and deadly, afterthought.

My foot had just struck the bottom stair when the gilt door opposite me opened to reveal Arun Brahma, looking handsome and rich and imposing in silhouette. He looked . . .

well, like a prince. Flanked by two bodyguards, one holding the door, the other at his back, he also looked nervous.

My mind winged back to all the home videos I'd seen of
brides bursting into giggles and grooms falling into faints.
If I had to put money on it, I'd bet the pot on Arun Brahma
going down.

Maybe I'd get lucky, I thought, shooting him a smile,
and he'd even do it before the vows.

Then a scream shattered my thoughts. It broke off as
I whirled, turning into a series of thumps before ending
in one hard crack. It took a moment for me to recognize
Cher, half airborne, tumbling down the marble stairs like
a helpless rag doll, but I was running before she even
stopped.

"God. Cher, you okay?" I cradled her face as Suzanne
wailed from the top of the staircase and began her dangerously hurried descent. She was covered in so much gold
tulle it would be miraculous if she didn't join Cher in a
crumpled heap. "Someone call an ambulance!"

"My arm . . ." Cher wailed, squeezing her eyes shut as
she turned in to herself, hugging her right arm to her chest.

"You, back in your room," I ordered Arun. He frowned,
probably some aristocratic response to being accosted by a
plebeian. "You're not supposed to see her," I said, jerking
my head at his bride, now crouched next to Cher, murmur-
ing and stroking her stepdaughter's cheek.

Suzanne lifted her head, caught his eye, tears in her
own. "Just go, Arun."

He hesitated, his desire to be by her side apparent even
despite the circumstances, before turning mutely. I inched
closer to Cher, now rocking and wailing in sharp stac-
cato breaths. We were beginning to draw a crowd, and I
scanned the faces, worried about Mackie, but it was all
hotel personnel and, moments later, medical staff.

"She fell down the stairs," Suzanne was saying as we
moved aside, her own sobs warring with Cher's for the lim-
ited airspace. "She was right next to me, but when I turned

to check my reflection one last time at the top of the stairs, she was gone."

"No," argued Cher, wincing. "I didn't fall! I was pushed."

I stilled. "Pushed?"

Suzanne leaned closer, smoothing the hair back from Cher's beautiful, red, pained face. "Darlin', there was no one near us."

"I know when I've been pushed, Mother!" Cher snapped. "I did not fall down those stairs."

Then she moaned, leaning over herself, and the paramedic edged Suzanne back. We gazed at each other over Cher's head, before I broke to canvass the top of the staircase. Anyone could be up there. Just because Suzanne hadn't seen someone push Cher didn't mean it hadn't happened. Agents could cover the entire pool area in a blink. But to a mortal mind, one used to making sense only of that which they could see and touch and sense, there had to be some other explanation. Suzanne searched for one now.

"Maybe it was my dress," she fretted, running her hands along the full skirt. "Maybe it pushed you with the force of its layered tulle, beads, and endless beauty."

Cher's head shot up, eyes hot. "Or maybe it was the hands planted on my back!"

Suzanne began to weep openly. "Somebody tell Arun the wedding's off."

"No!" Cher's anger evaporated as she lunged toward Suzanne, crying out when the movement jarred her broken arm. The attendants moved in closer, but she shooed them away. "You can't do that! You have to get married."

"But my baby is injured."

"No, Momma. I won't be responsible for ruining the happiest day of your life. So much planning went into it. And all these people are here—"

"All these people," I interrupted, "will be happy to come back."

But Cher wasn't hearing it. She grabbed Suzanne's arm, her face etched with pain, but her voice pleading. "Momma,

Arun is the love of your life. He is a prince. And I am going to call him Daddy. Please, please, don't call it off."

Suzanne let out a great sigh, turning her head to the vaulted, gold-brushed ceiling, then closed her eyes. "Okay," she whispered, though she was shaking her head.

The paramedics worked quickly, stabilizing Cher and picking her up when she refused a stretcher. It would make too much of a scene, she said. Yet even leaving via the back doors couldn't prevent that. The yells of reporters, the click of cameramen, and the surprised gasps of onlookers swelled as they realized it was the bride's stepdaughter being carried from the room. Then the door clicked shut, the security guard stoically planted himself in front of it, and a sniffle sounded behind me.

"Maybe wearing a color only once removed from white wasn't such a good idea."

I turned and grasped Suzanne by the shoulders. No, I didn't want her marrying Arun Brahma. But with both the Tulpa and Warren in the house, and Mackie surely on the way, it was the lesser of all present evils. It was also my best opportunity to rid myself of half that paranormal foursome.

"Nonsense," I said, squeezing until she looked me in the eye. "That accident had nothing to do with some eastern superstition. Besides, you'll have a weeklong Indian wedding next month, and Cher will be well enough to attend that. Right now, you're on American soil. White *is* lucky, but gold is divine. Now. Let's go back upstairs, touch up your mascara, and tuck in your toilet paper."

Suzanne turned and I placed one hand on her waist supportively, the other on the gun at my back.

"Oh God," she sniffled again. "Please don't let anything else go wrong."

I didn't say there were other wannabe deities involved in this disaster. She could pray all she wanted for nothing else to go wrong, but she'd be lucky if, from this point on, anything else went right.

29

I'd been thinking about weapons and fighting and blood, about chaos and death and battles that never seemed to end, about what it meant to be mortal and what it meant to be super, and how strange that all these forces were gathering during a ceremony of "this man joining this woman." Something both so ordinary and celebratory. Irony had such a dark sense of humor.

So when I stepped back onto the giant pool patio, with its white and gold runner draped over the floating Plexiglas aisle and dock, I blinked up at a blue, temperate sky with a sense of amazement. The air was utterly still, every color and object sharp, as if outlined in charcoal. Glancing at the front of this small arena, where the priests and Arun stood side by side, I saw that the candles signifying two people being joined as one were now lit, burning straight up as though lifted by strings. The still, perfect setting made me wonder if Arun controlled the weather in addition to a good portion of the Asian world.

The sitar player let the last haunting notes fade, and the full string orchestra used my appearance as a cue to begin the first song of the ceremony. Eight hundred of Suzanne's

closest friends—and two of my greatest enemies—turned
to watch me make my way down the floating Plexiglas
aisle.

The longest fucking aisle of my life.

I plastered what I hoped was a pleasantly expectant look
on my face and tried to keep my eyes off the water reflected
through the clear plastic at my feet. It was a beautiful
touch, light refracting against the undulating water, but it
combined with my nerves to nauseate me, so I lifted my
eyes, looked straight ahead, and steadied my breath.

I was also overly conscious of the trident at my back and
the gun at my thigh, and kept my movements small so the
sari stayed put, revealing neither. When I made it to my
position at the western priest's left without being attacked,
decapitated, or injured in any way, I gave both him and
Arun a nervous smile. The priest nodded back, but Arun
barely glanced at me before returning an anticipatory gaze
to the aisle. A second later the wedding march started up,
and the rest of the guests did the same.

The dress appeared first, full, but with the odd effect of
making Suzanne look taller. Or maybe it was pure bliss
doing that, because she beamed as brightly as the winter
sun, beginning that fateful walk down the center aisle, ac-
knowledging the oohs and ahhs with a slight inclination of
her head. She was beautiful for a woman of any age, but the
years had somehow come together on this day to make her
more solid somehow. She moved like a gift, wrapped in all
that jewel-encrusted gold. It was probably just the reflection off the walkway, but her glowing skin was bested only
by her eyes, dewy with emotion.

Arun, in turn, was thunderstruck. She reached his side,
unable to look away from him as well, blindly offering
me her bouquet before holding her hands out to him. He
took them almost by rote, staring into her face like he was
trying to adjust his eyes to some new phosphorescent light.

Oh yeah, this guy was *totally* going down.

I'd have found that more amusing if I wasn't preoccupied with stopping the wedding, Warren's hard attention, the Tulpa's paranoid edginess, and the small task of staying alive.

With all those concerns buzzing around my head, I barely listened as the western priest began to speak, the words unexceptional despite the bridal pair's status, the guest list, and the opulent setting. Even the eastern priest's melodious Hindi rang familiar. In the end, a wedding was a wedding. But at this one I kept my attention divided; half on a gently swaying Arun, half on the violent stare-down between Warren and the Tulpa.

Glancing back at the American priest, I tried to mentally nudge things along, but like Judge Ito, he was milking his moment for all it was worth. He was also beginning to sweat despite the coolness of the day, his eyes shut as if his words about love being the foundation of a marriage were a heartfelt prayer.

And his weren't the only eyes shut. The Tulpa had willfully broken the staring contest, and now he faced forward, a look of intent concentration petrifying his features. Well, why not? I thought, swallowing hard. His archenemy wasn't going to make a move with all these people about. Yet something about this panicked Warren, and his restless gaze darted between the Tulpa and me.

Then a muffled argument broke out at the back door. That confirmed it; the Tulpa was using his mental energy to call for backup. Fortunately, due to my preemptive security measures, the Shadows couldn't enter the room in the middle of the ceremony without an invitation, and—most importantly—without making a scene. Thus, at a particularly loud shout, the Tulpa's brows furrowed and he cracked an eye in the direction of the door. Suzanne, and most of the guests in the back row, glanced over as well.

Poor Suzanne.

However, the American priest only grew louder, speaking passionately about this most sacred personal union. Arun still stood starstruck next to his bride. That pulled her attention back to the ceremony, but the continued banging and shouts unnerving the crowd were working their way across the pool deck. Even the water below us seemed choppier, and though the Tulpa had to notice, he was the only truly still form alongside this sudden makeshift sea.

Well, I thought, breath catching. Not quite the only one.

The head was a black, unmoving abyss in the restless crowd, though the depth of that darkness lessened when Mackie lifted his empty gaze and threw off his stillness. He'd been slumped, lost in the crowd of hundreds, which was why I hadn't made him out before. Yet he straightened now, deeming whatever was happening outside those doors as his cue to move. He rose, knocking into the guests hemming him in, and edged his way to the center aisle.

I gasped, holding back a scream only because Suzanne stiffened and I needed time to inch my hands down to weapons at thigh and back. If I brought attention to my defenses before I could get to them—never mind draw them—Mackie's knife would open my aorta before you could say "Kiss the bride." Besides, was it too much to hope the Tulpa would wake the fuck up and intercept?

A giant pause in the priest's diatribe caught my attention, and I angled my eyes over to find him staring mutely as Mackie drew closer. Suzanne whimpered, distressed by the minister's loss in concentration, and I slowly tucked my hand in the hidden hem of my sari.

Where was Carlos? I wondered, heart pounding. Where were the grays? And why wasn't anyone in the audience screaming at the sight of a walking skeleton?

Because they can't see his face, I realized, gaze shifting again to his. Sure, they passed along quizzical looks after he'd passed, but he was walking so stiffly it was almost like he was a part of the ceremony—which was probably how he saw it. He only inched closer, drawing the moments out, a familiar low whine starting to whirr in his throat as he reached one bony hand beneath his dusty bowler hat. I found the trident at my back.

But why wasn't the Light moving against him? I wondered, sliding my bouquet hand down my leg. I risked taking my eyes off Mackie long enough to locate Warren, and found him leaning against the pillar again, face hard, eyes shuttered.

Damn him, he was going to let this happen!

The noise from inside the hotel increased, and a sharp bang made everyone, save Mackie, jump. That was when the Tulpa finally opened his eyes. His brows furrowed as he found me, no doubt unnaturally white and wide-eyed, and he finally turned to stare Mackie fully in the face.

There was no other way to describe what Mackie did next. Still believing the Tulpa was my protector, his head snapped so far forward it was as if he possessed an extra row of vertebrae. His beef jerky skin stretched over his neck and he hissed.

The guests around him gasped. The Tulpa stood, rising like a plank, free of his chair, and more horrified gasps sounded as the two faced each other across half an Olympic-sized pool.

Warren remained where he was, content to let the Tulpa and Mackie take one another out.

Suzanne's restless movement let me know it was time. I pulled out my gun as she turned toward the ruckus. Poor Suzanne, I thought, aiming at Mackie. She just wasn't meant to have the wedding of her dreams.

Someone screamed. Mackie tested the Tulpa, whose eyes were still locked on him, by taking another step toward me. The Tulpa responded by baring a mouth full of fangs, which only made Mackie yank out his soul blade, eliciting real screams.

Suzanne growled in frustration and yanked at her voluminous gold skirts.

"That's it!" To my utter surprise she reached behind her, pulled a sawed-off shotgun from a Velcro holster hidden somehow at her back, and aimed the barrel down the aisle. "You guys are fucking up my wedding!"

And she shot Mackie straight through the chest.

The crowd exploded into action, everyone running for the single set of doors like rats escaping a maze. Everyone, that was, but those who knew what was going on. Or, I thought, ears and mind buzzing, those suddenly finding out. I blinked as guests fell into the pool, swimming toward the other side to avoid the corpse now sprawled on the center aisle. I saw Warren straighten from the corner of my eye, but my gaze winged back to the Tulpa as the screams escalated.

"Hello, boys." Suzanne reached behind her without looking, and again I was surprised when she pulled out the saber I'd planted, the one I thought no one knew about. I replaced my gun at the small of my back as she handed me the shotgun, though kept my eyes on her. Everyone did. A smile like flint glittered on her gold-painted face. "Miss me?"

Warren and the Tulpa both froze, and their shocked expressions spoke volumes.

Warren found his voice first. "Zoe?"

"Fucking Zoe . . ." the Tulpa's voice rasped.

"Suzanne?" I shook my head. I seemed to be having the hardest time coming around to this. I shook it again. *"M-Mom?"*

The Tulpa's gaze rocketed my way.

Pivoting, we both turned our weapons on him, suddenly back-to-back on the floating dais.

"Get behind me or get out," she told me, her voice so wooden it didn't sound familiar at all. Warmth rose in my belly, an anger only there when my mother tried to tell me what to do. It felt foreign, strange, upsetting . . . and fucking good.

"Kinda bossy for a mortal, aren't you?" I said, resighting on Mackie as he tried to push into a sitting position.

"Must be the boobies." And we fired at the same time. I plugged Mackie through his chest again twice. She pulled the trigger on the saber's sidearm, sight steady on the Tulpa.

The unmistakable sound of gunfire and Mackie's graceless cannonball into the middle of the pool caused further panic, though the Tulpa caught the bullet in his hand. Zoe had actually aimed a bit high, not wanting to strike any of the still-fleeing guests. Meanwhile, Warren still had yet to move. *Nice time to go into shock, you asshat.*

The Tulpa began levitating. "Put the weapon down, or I'll kill every mortal here."

Zoe hesitated, then slowly lowered the saber to the floor. While there, she reached beneath the mounds of gold tulle and pulled out a paranormal bazooka.

I looked down at my puny shotgun. "I see you saved the best for yourself."

"Always hold a little bit back, Joanna," she said, jerking back on a loading lever. "I did."

Which I guessed, was how she could touch the conduits now.

The Tulpa wasn't interested in chitchat. He floated even higher, edging over the pool surface. "I'm warning—"

"Fuck yourself, *babe.*"

He stilled, floating but frozen. "Everybody underwater," he said coolly. "And stay there."

The chaos instantly calmed. Those already in the pool simply sunk to the bottom, those near the seats or platform—and there were still at least three hundred— slipped over the sides like a school of brightly colored, well-mannered fish. Silence descended, and when Arun made to follow the priest into the water, Zoe pulled him back with one arm, never taking her eyes from the Tulpa.

Warren finally found his voice, running forward, but was helpless to stop the mass drowning. "No!"

The Tulpa ignored him completely. "Give yourself over to me," he said, floating closer. "Or I'll kill your groom too. No prince, no happily ever after."

I licked my lips, and though the Tulpa spared me a glance, I was all but forgotten. It was Zoe he wanted; Zoe he'd always wanted. He hated her more than he loved life. More, even, than he loved death.

Zoe yanked Arun in front of us both.

"What are you doing?" I asked, confused, but the Tulpa whipped his arm around so fast the bullet Zoe had shot returned our way with twice the speed, and Arun's chest exploded like a Catherine Wheel on the Fourth of July.

Cringing, and covered in a thick layer of gelatinous goop, I shivered at the icy substance, wiped at my face, and looked over to find Zoe also masked in the see-through substance. She shook her head as she looked down. "Shit. I was almost done too."

"A doppelgänger?" I asked in disbelief. "You were making another one?"

She shrugged one shoulder. "It gets easier with practice, but no. I picked this one up off an old shaman in Bali. The transfer from his mind to mine laid me up for weeks, but it was worth it." She stared at the ooze, now edging into the pool, that had nearly been a life-form. "Well, almost worth it."

"Y-You were going to marry a tulpa?" Warren asked, just as shocked. All three of us turned his way. He sounded like a prejudiced nineteenth-century southerner.

Apparently Zoe thought so too. "Why it's every girl's dream, Warren. Who wouldn't want a man they could control?"

I couldn't help it. I snorted.

The Tulpa growled, floating closer, nearly to the center aisleway now. Bodies upon bodies were trapped beneath it, faces pressed against the transparent bottom like a macabre windowpane. "Why would someone just give you their doppelgänger?"

It was a good question. I kept my weapon on him, though my arms were shaking, and looked at Zoe.

She smiled. "I asked nicely."

"You mean you fucked him."

"Oh my gawd. Different note, but still the same fucking song." Zoe didn't sound one bit afraid of him, and he sagged so greatly with her words that his toes hit the water.

"I told his creator what I wanted him for. I'm not the only one who thinks you need to die."

"The weak," spat the Tulpa.

"The Light," said Warren.

"The righteous," Zoe said, arrowing a hard look at Warren, correcting them both. "I'm not Light anymore, and haven't been for a long time. I'm an independent, though independent even from the rogues. I like it that way."

"How can you say that?" Warren was at the edge of the pool, as dumbfounded as I'd ever seen him. "You dishonor your family by disavowing us."

"What would you know about honor? You've treated my daughter like shit, you bastard. So don't talk to me about who has failed to live up to their word."

Warren jolted as if slapped. "Zoe—"

"After I entrusted you with her care, no less. If I'd known, I'd have schooled her myself. She wouldn't be here now. The identity we secured for her would still be a secret from *it*."

The Tulpa dipped farther, and he had to fight, arms pinwheeling himself back into the air from his calf-high immersion. There was still no sign of Mackie.

"Why didn't you?" I asked hurriedly, because I didn't know if I'd get a chance again. The Tulpa might kill her once fully recovered. Or me. Or she could, so easily, just disappear again. "School me yourself, I mean."

"Because the agents of Light have conduits, a troop, and a sanctuary." Zoe spoke so quickly I knew she'd prepared this defense long ago. The speed also told me she shared my concerns. "But I contributed in my own way. I haven't stopped fighting since the day you were attacked. I haven't rested in years, not for a moment. I gave all my power, my family, and then stayed away. All I have left is this mortal life."

The Tulpa floated higher, looming at us from a forty-five degree angle. My arms shook almost uncontrollably as I forced my weapons to follow. "I can help relieve you of that," he said.

Zoe followed him too. "You'll have to if you want to get to her."

"Gladly," he said, and lunged.

"No!" Warren threw himself at Zoe, deflecting the Tulpa's blow . . . but not stopping it. Zoe flew backward like she'd been spat from his fist, without even getting off a shot. That was for the best—struck with a conduit, the Tulpa would only grow stronger. Her head hit the pillar behind us with a force that left her sprawling awkwardly on the floor. I raced for her while a battle I couldn't see raged behind me.

Zoe was flattened. I checked for a pulse and found one—fucking strong too—so moved her head to my lap, lifted her bazooka again, and vowed to blast anything that even hinted at coming our way. Was it too much to hope that Warren and the Tulpa would destroy each other? That they'd rip each other to shreds in the effort to get to the woman who had betrayed and left them both?

Of course it was.

Even at his weakest the Tulpa was more powerful than a single agent. The other agents of Light were probably on their way, drawn by the turmoil and the rising scent of battle, but so were the Shadows. I had precious few minutes to get Zoe out of there. I caught a rare glimpse of the fight going on over the water as the Tulpa rammed Warren into the platform. The impact must have momentarily severed his spine because all his limbs flew wide, like a starfish, and when the Tulpa kicked him over the side, he sank with a numb expression of horror and deep sorrow.

Then the Tulpa charged me so fast the sound was sonic. A flash of light, the impact of two powerful beings imprinting on the air, and I raggedly exhaled. Skamar had arrived. Finally. Their growls and blows were a sandblasting, and sent me scrabbling backward, pulling Zoe behind the giant floral arrangement.

"Mom?" I supported her back and neck as she struggled

into an upright position and tried to untangle her legs from her dress.

"I'm okay, I'm okay." She put a hand to her head as if trying to hold it on.

"Can you stand?" Because I couldn't carry her. Frustration at my mortal frailty rose from me in a low-pitched growl.

As if to underline that, Warren—dripping but healed—was suddenly at my side. "I'll take it from here," he said, reaching for her.

"No!" both Zoe and I yelled, automatically pulling into one another, voices and limbs locking us together.

For the first time since I'd known him, Warren looked injured. He could just take her from me, of course, but he wanted her to come willingly. Like the Tulpa, he very simply wanted *her*. "Please. Let me help you."

Some silent thing passed between them, some old conversation that had probably ended unresolved, because there were feelings there I couldn't understand. Slowly, Zoe shook her head. "Save Jo. That was the agreement."

Warren gazed at Zoe with a mixture of confusion and softness, and licked his lips, eyes on hers. Oh my God, I thought, surprise rocketing through me. He *loves* her.

Then, probably scenting my shock on the air, he looked at me. There was no confusion in that look, and certainly no softness. Just bitterness for causing his love story to come to this, as if it was both my doing, and purposeful.

"Warren . . ." Zoe's voice was a warning.

He lunged, and my hands were empty before I blinked. Zoe was suddenly gone—tulle and touch, strength and frailty—the only thing remaining behind were gold flecks and elongated screams. "No! Go back! Joanna! Jo! Help her!"

The cries faded quickly, Warren fleeing as fast as he could. I had a moment to wonder what exactly he was trying to outrun, but then the Tulpa froze, head jerking up.

Determination rode his face like a stampede, and he shot
to the sky like a reverse comet. Skamar didn't hesitate. She
followed in an equally earsplitting blast.

I slumped, dazed, to find myself alone on the dais, my
raspy breath breaking the eerie silence of what looked like
a mass suicide. Yet the Tulpa's absence released the mortals of his magic. They began popping up from the pool
bottom like colorful mushrooms, coughing and sputter-
ing as they swam to the pool's edge, helping others do the
same. The water, in turmoil, appeared shark-infested, and
sure enough, no sooner did I have that thought than a roiling pressure ruptured the surface.

Out of that—stiff, dripping, and bloody, but with bowler
hat firmly in place—Sleepy Mac rose like a specter. His
blind, mad gaze was already fixed on me.

30

Every person asks themselves how they're going to die. Most people wish for something gentle and in the night, a scant few petition the skies for adventure, to go hard and young, guns blazing—sometimes literally, sometimes not. Over the past year I'd faced the question a number of times, not because I wanted to, but because it presented itself to me like an unwanted hooker in a lineup. I mean, once the choices were narrowed down, you had to pick something, right?

So this was how it would happen: Mackie would lunge, carve into my mortal flesh with that blade, and what remained of my soul would join his, trapped inside that fisted iron, while my body finally fell to dusty silence.

Well, it wasn't *exactly* how it would happen, I thought, easing my hand around to the gun at my back.

But then, like a crosscurrent, she landed. Positioning herself at the point where the aisle met the pier, one foot on each side, she halved the distance between Mackie and me. Pointing her nose straight into the air, Skamar sniffed, then angled her head my way. "Smell that, Jo?"

I didn't move, fearing whatever I did would be wrong, she'd leave, and I'd be headed for the glue factory again. Yet I was screaming inside. *Scoop me up! Take me away! Deliver me from this particular evil, and I'll never take your name in vain again!*

But Skamar was preoccupied with something other than escape. "It's not your fury, nope. Not like the last time we met. That smelled like the aftermath of a traffic accident. It's got quite a nice hook to it, actually."

"Skamar . . . ?" I ventured, seeing Mackie list her way, and thinking it was an odd moment for philosophical musings.

"Nope, not even the despair I sensed when this walking miasma killed your cat." She ignored the grating metallic whine rising from Mackie again, but I couldn't. It was a noise associated with homicide.

"Skamar." Maybe intoning her name would snap her out of it.

Inexplicably, she closed her eyes and tilted her sharp, slim jaw up to the sky. "No, this is fresh and floral, like spring's blossoms and green wood. This," she said, turning her back on Sleepy Mac, "is *life*."

"What are you doing?" I said, panicked as Mackie's head lowered, blade lifting.

She continued to foolishly ignore him, opening eyes both determined and sad. "I've decided you're right. It is time for something to touch me. To prove I'm more than animated flesh. Not like this half-life behind me." The sadness left her eyes. "It's time, in other words, to pick some bones."

Mackie clearly had other ideas. He grinned so widely his black stub of a tongue showed between his teeth. His laughter was ground iron. Skamar's smile didn't meet her eyes, sincere, severe, and still fastened on mine. "But you might want to look away. 'Cuz when I pick 'em? I pick 'em clean."

She pivoted as Mackie lunged, and for a second's fraction pulled back, as if bracing herself. Then she dove forward so quickly it was like she expected to move clean through him. She didn't, of course. Sleepy Mac didn't give ground, had never needed to before . . . though seconds later I bet he wished he had.

His scream rose like a tornado siren, jagged and uncertain, but too late. I cupped my hands over my ears—countless people behind the dueling creatures did the same—but stayed focused on the whipping dervish just as Skamar bit down and ripped the nose from Mackie's face. She didn't spit it out, didn't even chew. Just swallowed it full and swung back down for another bite. First one bony cheek disappeared, then the other. She had his wrists pinned, and though he didn't let go of his blade—he'd never do that—he flailed in panic, jerking his head from side to side as he tried to avoid the tulpa's barbed teeth. He was struggling too hard for her to get a good bite, so I shook myself to my senses and shot him twice. That enabled her to find his throat, and his grunts and screams gurgled into silence.

That's when his arm started swinging.

Skamar lifted her head, blood blanketing her chin as she stared right at me. "Shoot me!"

I wasn't sure I'd heard right, and kept my aim on his body. "What?"

"Shoot me," she repeated, head lowering. "Quick!"

As she began shredding fingers from his free hand, I remembered what happened when you shot a tulpa . . . and lunged for the bazooka. Narrowing my gaze, I pointed the giant barrel at her middle and fired. She grew a foot with the first rocket, and another six inches with each additional shot. It didn't sound like a lot, but it was six inches in *circumference,* and after the first two strikes, Mackie sure as hell knew the difference. He turned his head on what remained of that sinewy neck long enough to growl at me, hate naked in his black-socketed stare, the skeletal face now missing so many of its features.

The warning movement cost him. I shot again and Skamar engulfed him with her jaw, crunching down on his skull like a nutcracker. His expression literally shattered before me. His black tongue lolled from his mouth, then fell, severed by his own teeth.

But his flailing blade finally found a home in Skamar's side. I shot him again, but it was too late. She twisted, her face scrawled in agony, but dove in once more. I turned the weapon back on her, causing her to jerk but also causing her to grow.

Her jaw was the size of my head now, and she easily engulfed the whole of Mackie's crushed skull, right down to the base of his neck. And she bit. After snapping it, after his muffled cries fell silent in her mouth, she jerked back, ripping it from his body. Mackie's shoulders slumped, his posture both defeated and confused, and from there it was an easy thing for Skamar to dismantle the rest of his body.

"Motherfucker," I whispered, lowering my weapon. She ate every bit of him, every bone, dried jerky muscle and gristle, and she licked her fingers when she was done.

"Old habits die hard," she finally said, offering me a bloody, lopsided smile. It was how we'd met. She had been a doppelgänger—*my* doppelgänger—and so hungry for life she was willing to eat me.

Then Skamar convulsed and let out an agonizing scream. Jerking back and forth, she forced herself to stop with visible effort. A moment of stillness.

Then, like a shark's fin breaking the surface, the knife burst through her belly.

"Spit it out!" I screamed, wanting to go to her, but knowing well enough to stay away. The man was in pieces inside of her, but he was somehow still alive.

Skamar winced, clearly wanting to, but slowly shook her head. "I can't."

And screamed again.

Because Mackie's soul was in the blade, I realized. She had to swallow him whole, masticating his body, blending it with hers until she totally blotted out his existence . . . which meant the blade too.

And *that*, I suddenly realized, meant Skamar would end up like Luna—a fully conscious being trapped in a body of flattened nerves and destroyed tissue. Sentient, but with no way of communicating with the outside world. A bright mind in a decaying body. It's why she'd hesitated, and I couldn't blame her . . . yet it was also why she'd returned. No one else could stop Mackie, and he would *never* stop.

"When he's done," she said, seeing my understanding, "suck the last breath from me. That's where the soul resides. Th-That should do it."

I swallowed hard. "But I'm mortal."

She winced. "You're alive. You . . . count. Please."

I nodded at first, unable to get any words past my thickened throat, but I owed it to her not to leave her to a fate of conscious death, just as she hadn't left Luna. "I promise."

Skamar's eyes were wistful and she was breathing hard. "Tell Zoe . . . I love—"

The blade reared up inside her throat then, severing vocal cords to poke through the white flesh, the shark's fin trailing blood behind it. The last bit of Mackie's soul fought for escape, but she punched her middle, breaking her own ribs as she pummeled him into submission. She gurgled loudly, defiantly, and finally, pitifully.

Simply watching was the bravest thing I could do. But I cried as I did so, choking down vomit numerous times, and at some point my knees numbly gave in. Mackie's frenetic thrashing gradually ceased, and after a while the deft flicks forcing Skamar to jolt and twitch turned into lethargic slices that only caused more blood to trail from her body. In desperation, or maybe his last hoorah, he gave a final energetic swipe at her heart, and the still-beating thing popped from her chest, pulsed over the top of splintered ribs, pounded a handful of times, then slowed.

The breath stilled with the blade. When neither Skamar nor Mackie moved, I climbed shakily to my feet and crossed to the pulpy mess. Hesitating, I licked my lips before leaning close. Skamar was flattened, destroyed. But her eyes, tucked deep but still whole, swung my way.

"Oh, God . . . oh, God . . ."

I fell forward, ignoring the squishing slide of destroyed flesh beneath my knees, and found the carved ruin of her lips. Mackie's blade had cut through the flesh of her lower jaw, but most of her skull was intact, which was probably why she was still able to exert her will over him. Knowing she was still there, thinking and feeling and simply *being* alive, actually made it harder to kill her, but it was also the only way to destroy him. Besides, she'd already forgiven me for the death. She wouldn't forgive me for letting her live.

So bending down, I placed my lips against hers, already cold, and I sucked. The dry coil of breath worked its way into my mouth like rising steam, surprising me and reverberating strangely in my throat, like it was someone else's voice . . . and it was. Skamar's dulcet pitch smeared my esophagus on its way into my lungs.

Mackie's black fanged timbre clawed at it.

I pulled away, coughing, the throbbing in my chest threatening to make me ill. Out went Skamar's soul, a taste of creamed blood, and out went Mackie's soured one. Skamar's consciousness thanked me as it sailed free, but when the last of Mackie's deadened soul was hacked from my body? It screamed.

A gelatinous shudder rolled along the entire pulpy mass beneath me then, followed by a long, gentle sigh. The whispered exhalation probably wasn't a whole lot different than the way Skamar first entered the world. Just the flip side of a lone, fateful breath taken by a woman begun as a vision. One given life by a powerful woman's mind.

My mother.

Zoe.

I sat back on my heels, wiped my bloodied mouth with the back of my hand, and closed my eyes.

Suzanne.

31

The soft ceremony of morning's birth in the desert is one thing. Yet the neon metropolis flourishing in the Mojave's middle creates its own dawn, and in the moments before the sun slams into the desert floor, the lights of Las Vegas shimmer, almost as if they exist in another world. Determined to leave an imprint on the valley's day, they fight for their right to burn air. It's a futile battle, of course. The first rays of morning exert their dominance, the city lights flicker, and then each snuffs out under the onslaught of the sun touching the valley like a kiss of gold.

Only three days after the catastrophe that was so-called Suzanne's so-called wedding, I was alone on a quiet residential street, with only the sun's kiss to keep me company. Well, that and a Beemer-sized dog stalking me from the shadows. I'd picked up the morning newspaper from the corner convenience store, glancing up at the security camera in the corner as the cashier sleepily rang up my purchase. If anyone happened to check those tapes—and there was no reason they should—they'd see an overage goth girl with soft hair in a sharp bob. The black shade was absolute, no high- or low-lights to warm it up, and it sat like a storm against my too-white cheeks. The nose stud and brown contacts were probably overkill, the ankh tattoo temporary, and the black clothing cliché, but I'd already been far too sorry. It was time to be safe.

I'd seen no television in the last thirty-six hours—reception was pretty shitty in a blown-out bunker within a top secret nuclear site—but my guess was it had been a continuous broadcast of what I was reading now: the wedding disaster recap, and a fabricated explanation of how a floating Plexiglas dock had collapsed, trapping the wedding party under the water. Also how Olivia Archer, the last living member of the Archer family dynasty, had disappeared.

At first it appeared to be an accident, but the prevailing theory now was that Olivia, the bride, and the billionaire groom, Arun Brahma, were all kidnapped by a South Asian terrorist group that had been targeting the textile magnate for years. They'd turned Arun's passion for a westerner into a weakness, reportedly the sole vulnerability to ever visit the pathologically paranoid prince. It was a lesson, some were saying, to the limitations of love.

"Assholes," I muttered, earning a second glance from the cashier. I grabbed my paper and a pack of reds—part of my new disguise as Olivia didn't smoke—and swung out the glass door.

Some belated crisis of conscience had the cashier calling after me as he angled his gaze at the cigarettes. "Those things'll kill ya, you know."

"I should be so lucky," I said to myself, and headed out into the reluctant morning. Not that I was overly concerned about being accosted by Shadow or Light. The Shadows were no doubt celebrating. The agents of Light were on their heels. I assumed my acceptance among the grays had brought the fifth portent of the Zodiac to pass, though Carlos said there was no way for us to know that for sure, or what the sixth sign would be. Grays, night crawlers, were always the last to know. What was painfully obvious to everyone was that Warren had his hands full with a newly invigorated Tulpa, once again the most powerful being in the valley.

"You're welcome," I muttered, gazing at the photo in the paper, taken mere minutes before Mackie's attack. The Tulpa was sitting straight-backed in his wheelchair, eyes shut. I thought of all his powers—mind control, the ability to morph into new shape and form, to enter dreams and steal breath, to create black holes and inflict pain without ever touching a person. Shaking my head, I consoled myself with Io's assertion that he hated the Shadows as well as the Light.

To be honest, it wasn't much consolation.

Meanwhile, the photo angle had also caught Warren leaning against his pillar, a hard scowl blighting his face as he stared straight ahead. If I'd only assumed he hated me before, I decided, swallowing hard, this picture certainly put the question to rest.

But that wasn't why I shuddered in the street's cold center. No, Mackie's bent head caused that, bowler hat propped atop as if on a peg. Another shiver went through me at the memory of his living knife carving out Skamar's chest, and I half expected his head to swivel on the page, his blackened tongue pushing forward as he hissed.

The next photo was a blurred shot of the ensuing chaos, and of all the people the Tulpa had ordered into the water via mind control, piled atop one another like battling carp. I'd told Carlos the entire story while he dyed my hair in an old paint bucket, which had him more convinced than ever that I was not only immune to the Tulpa's mental manipulation, I would be the one to stop him entirely.

"You may be a mortal," he said when I protested, "but you're still a part of him. You can still kill him by turning his own power against him, even that of his mind."

I'm sure he meant that to be reassuring, but his words had the opposite effect. Didn't that mean the Tulpa could do the same to me? Wasn't it possible it worked both ways?

And I still had no idea why the Tulpa was so concerned about the symbol of a snake wrapped around a stick. What was the Serpent Bearer—its purpose, its meaning—and why was it so important to a man who could already manipulate others with his mind alone?

All I knew right now was that I was mortal, and the Tulpa was all-powerful, and that was yet one more thing Warren could blame me for. At least the agents of Light were too busy battling back the newly invigorated Shadows to patrol the city's invisible border. For now, the grays were free to enter and exit the city at will. Yet I knew Warren hadn't forgotten us, *or* the child of Shadow and Light living in Midheaven. *Hunter's* child.

Tucking both the paper and those particular worries away for now, I arrived at my destination, but froze short of the property line. The house where Ashlyn, another child of the Zodiac, had lived was vacant. The grass was already browning, there was a lockbox on the handle, and the window where my daughter's gaze had found mine was bare.

"Shit," I said under my breath.

"I moved her after you shot out the living room window."

Turning, I saw a woman dressed in gray running sweats, a walnut ponytail as freshly dyed as mine pulled through a ball cap shielding most of her face. Though obviously fit—and now I knew why "Suzanne" had always treated fitness, and running in particular, like religion—she walked steadily, carrying a stainless steel toolbox. Odd enough to earn her a second glance, I thought, but probably not a third.

"Oh, that?" I said lightly, like my heart wasn't threatening to jump through my chest. "I was just trying to get your attention."

She set the toolbox on the ground, tucked her hands into her jacket pockets, and gazed at the house where her granddaughter used to live. "Well, all kids act out sometimes. It frees them emotionally from parental control, or so I've read."

I didn't bother answering. It was small talk, and had nothing to do with where we were today. "Dare I ask how you got away from Warren?"

"Do you need to? I fucking walked." Lowering her chin and voice, she stared at the house like it was her enemy. Like it was Warren. I'd never seen that look on her face before, not in person, and it rattled me. Suzanne as Zoe. Zoe as warrior, as Archer, like me. I swallowed hard, and changed the subject.

"How's Cher?" I asked.

"She's in L.A. They decided she needed a specialist for her arm. I don't think she'll be coming back for . . . a while."

I nodded once. "And the arm?"

"Clean break."

"Lucky," I said. "Whoever pushed her must have known what they were doing."

She turned her gaze on me then, and it was afire. "She is lucky. Had she been in the front row of that marital shitstorm, she probably wouldn't have survived."

I nodded again. So I wouldn't be seeing Cher for a while. My initial pang of regret surprised me, but I wouldn't have seen her anyway. I was no longer Olivia, and Cher was no longer safe in Vegas. Not with the Tulpa pulling every possible thread to get to me. Maybe someday I could visit her on the beach. Still, I sighed. Cher's companionship was the loss of something I hadn't even known I'd valued.

Glancing back at the house, I decided I was glad Ashlyn was far away too. "So is that it, Mom? Hurting someone is okay as long as it's for the greater good?"

And just like that we were no longer talking about her stepdaughter, but her real ones.

If Zoe felt the same storm of emotions, she didn't show it. She appeared almost defiant in her mortal flesh, a woman who'd made hard choices under hard circumstances and wasn't about to apologize to anyone for it. That was okay. I knew what that was like, and I wasn't looking for an apology.

But Zoe didn't know that yet. "I wouldn't ask anyone to do something I'm not willing to do myself," she said woodenly, staring down at the tool chest.

I nodded. "Like become mortal?"

She glanced at me sharply. "That was your choice."

"Ah, but look who I had as an example." A friggin' superhero. And one who'd given over all her powers to save me. So had there really been an alternative? Was there any way I could have simply allowed a little girl to die in a flooded tunnel while I stayed relatively safe, and very much alive?

Sure, I thought, huffing lightly. But as Zoe Archer's daughter, I think the guilt would have eventually killed me.

Zoe, not one to take any criticism without a fight, argued back. "But you had an advantage I didn't. You spent your formative years outside the troop. I, on the other hand, was raised inside it, groomed for a position in the Zodiac, primed and nurtured to become the Archer of Light." She laughed humorlessly. "I mean, I had no idea you could actually bleed just by knocking into something, or that it would hurt to stub your toe, or get a paper cut. I even had to alter the way I had sex—"

"Too much information," I sang, cutting her off.

She smiled thinly, as I wanted. God, there was history behind us. There was so much to ask her, so much to say. A part of me wanted to rail, to ask questions I'd agonized over all through my teen years, while I was punching nylon bags and sparring mitts. But now didn't feel like the time for hard words, and I wasn't as angry with her standing next to me. I remembered my back against hers as we faced off against Mackie and the Tulpa. How we'd clung to each other when uniting against Warren.

No. It wasn't anger at all. It was sympathy. And sadness. And a boatload of understanding. Life was not a straight shot. It veered dangerously. Sometimes all you could do was hold on tight and hope for the best.

"Do you want to know the hardest thing of all?" Zoe

asked, voice soft as she frowned into the distance again. "Worse than the physical weakness, far worse than the loss of powers, was the emotional isolation. Always before, I'd been a part of something. I'd acted independently, of course, going undercover for months without contacting the troop, but that was different. I was doing it for them. It counted, and they were counting on me. But all of that disappeared along with my powers. For a while I wished I was dead rather than mortal."

She winced at how the truth sounded when spoken aloud.

I winced because I understood. "And now?"

Shrugging, Zoe tossed me a lopsided smile. "I've mellowed with age."

I whistled through my teeth. The woman who'd pulled a bazooka on the Tulpa, and put a round through Sleepy Mac, was "mellow." Yeah, and I'd been a natural blonde.

"I like it now, though. Mortality, I mean. The anonymity is almost soothing. What I do can't be recorded, and doesn't really matter. Not on a global scale."

I quirked a brow. "You mean outside of little things like creating doppelgängers, plotting the Tulpa's downfall, watching over me, and acting in support of the rogues who wish to overthrow both the Shadow and the Light."

"Yes. Outside of that."

I smiled hesitantly, wondering if it should be this easy after so many years. Sure, she was my mother, but she was so many other things too. So many other people. It was hard to be sure who I was talking to: Zoe? Suzanne? The Archer? A legend? My mother? Someone Warren once loved? Someone else entirely?

But looking at her shifting her weight in the early morning light, I decided it didn't matter. Right now she was just a woman standing on the street . . . and one who was saying good-bye.

So my questions could wait a bit longer. I'd probably kick myself for it later, but I decided to treat her as gently as I'd like to be treated, and as too few people had bothered to do in the past. Besides, there was too little time as it was.

"What will *you* do next?" she finally asked, dark hair swinging over one shoulder. She looked nothing like the golden goddess at the wedding. Even her stance and carriage were different. I wondered if she'd miss being Suzanne.

I rattled off my to-do list. "Figure out how to cash in on some soul chips. Build an army. Free the rogues from Midheaven." *Retrieve my boyfriend from the arms of another woman.*

She tilted her head. "Even those who don't want to be free?"

"Everyone wants to be free," I said, still thinking of Hunter.

"Don't be so sure," she cautioned, sighing. "And your fight won't be solely against the Shadows this time."

No, it would also be against the Light.

Maybe.

Because now everybody knew Warren hadn't just been treating me like shit, but jacking with the whole of his troop. Knowing them as I did—good, smart, strong people—and remembering Vanessa's shocked face in particular, I still hoped they'd call him on it. Either way, something had to give. He'd said in the tunnels that nothing was changing, but he was wrong. It already had.

"Well, no self-respecting democracy was ever born without a solid fight," I muttered, trying to keep my voice light.

"True. Just plenty of bloodshed."

I shot her a wry look. That wasn't helpful. Besides, true freedom was worth fighting for, both as a group and an individual. My work now was to gather people around me who believed that. I might be mortal, but I'd returned to the paranormal world. All in, more than ever before.

"I could use some allies," I said, shooting her a sidelong glance. "As many as I can get."

Something old and lethal sparked in her eyes as she considered it—and I knew she too remembered standing atop that dais, back-to-back, weapons primed, adrenaline running like napalm in our blood. She smiled at the memory, but slowly the light in her eyes died. "I have another task now. I'm more focused on the good of a particular individual than a whole troop."

"Ashlyn," I said, and we both pretended my voice didn't crack.

She nodded, then said brightly, "But you have Carlos. The rogues can provide you with more protection than I can. I, uh, don't have much left."

I didn't argue or agree. Both would be true.

"She knows about me, doesn't she?" I said instead, remembering the look the girl had shot me from the parted curtains of her bedroom window.

"Not you in particular, no. But us. Them," she said, motioning out into the world, the underworld. "I couldn't let it happen again."

Meaning allow a young girl to enter her second life cycle without training, knowledge, or defense.

"I've been putting her through an augmented form of training." She sounded almost sheepish about it. "Don't tell her adoptive mother, okay?"

I gave her a flat look, which caused her to grin. I also tried to work up some jealousy just to see if it lived inside me, or at least some pique that she'd spend so much time and energy training a young girl while I was out there figuring it out, mostly through error, on my own. But the anger wouldn't come. I guess I was mellowing too. "Subversive, as always."

"It's when I'm at my best."

I smiled. Yes. *That* was my mother.

"I've missed you." The words slipped from me, and the welling tears were equally unexpected. I choked them back, a proud woman crying in front of a proud woman, waiting until I could again look her in the eye.

She stared at me, my mother's eyes still locked in Suzanne's face, fighting not to blink lest her own tears fall. "I was here all along."

What broke inside of me then was primal, like a child's need to cling to something warm and soft. A fractured wail escaped me even while I told myself to shut up. I bent at the waist to hold it in, then at the knees, curling into myself even as I ordered myself to stand. And my mother, *my* mother, Zoe Archer—once the Archer, agent of Light, who'd nearly toppled the Tulpa, and who had a mind strong enough to form doppelgängers and control other people's tulpas—she tented herself over me, wrapped her arms around what was both my and Olivia's body, and held me together.

It bloomed then, an unexpected lemon-herb mixture that had nothing to do with supersenses and everything to do with family. My body recognized my mother, even though my eyes had failed to all these years. And, as she shook holding me, I knew my pores were crying out to her too. I knew she loved me.

And she'd never really left.

"I miss Olivia," I said at some point.

"I do too," she replied, and we wept for my sister as well. That pain was still shockingly acute, though it didn't take long for our sobs to lessen. After all, we were each used to holding ourselves together. So when only harsh sniffles were left to cut the silence, Zoe pulled back and helped me rise. We swayed, but steadied each other, and finally looked up. Were my eyes that red too? Was my face that bleak? Was there really so much of my mother in me after all?

"We should go," she said, wiping at her face and pulling her ball cap lower. "They'll scent this soon."

I didn't have to ask who. Whether the emotion was ferried to Shadow or Light, the results wouldn't be good.

"When do you leave?" I asked, wiping at my eyes.

She only smiled, closed-mouthed. Panic struck me, but

I knew better to ask where she was going. "Well, will you call? Let me know how she's doing?"

"When it's safe," she said, meaning not a moment before. It could be years. "And you'll know when she's *ready*."

An Archer. But would she be Light? I frowned, then realized Zoe was saying something, words tumbling as fast as a chip hustler's dice roll. "You could come with us. The three of us could start over, maybe create something entirely new."

Grandmother, mother, daughter. Three Archers battling side-by-side, back-to-back. But I thought of Warren, running this city like a game board. The Tulpa, all the pieces once again stacked in his favor. I thought of the valley, its inhabitants, *my* city, and I only smiled.

She dipped her head in understanding. "That's my girl."

Leaving the toolbox at my feet, she turned and walked away.

I don't know how many moments passed. Eventually Buttersnap shifted restlessly between two cookie-cutter houses, and an old woman in a tattered bathrobe and toeless slippers slipped outside to pick up her paper. I gave a wave that had her scurrying back inside, then picked up whatever new lethal baubles my mother had given me, and left before the nosy neighbor could call the police.

As I walked, I thought of what Zoe said about the anonymity of mortality, and how what she did no longer mattered on a large scale. I wished I'd spoken up then. I wished I'd told her that everything a person did, big or small, really did matter. It mattered to the ones you loved. Or, at least to the ones who loved you.

In fact, I thought, sucking in a breath of the sharp, cold air, when you were mortal your actions probably mattered even more.

32

The run-in with my mother settled something inside of me. Sure, I had a boatload of pressing things on my mind—survival, the loss of my life aboveground, Warren's race with the Tulpa to see who could kill me first—but Zoe and Cher and Ashlyn were all still alive, and the knowledge that they were finally safe was like a salve on my consciousness.

Also safe, at least for the time being, was the family that remained behind . . . those who had chosen me.

It was because of them, and that choice, that I wound my way through the passageways beneath Frenchman's Flat at three o'clock the next morning, running my hands along the walls of caked candle wax, careful not to set my newly dyed hair alight. I was searching for a blank smooth spot on the wall, finally locating one about three feet before entering Marge's anteroom. I went straight to work, wiping it down and then filling it in with the plaster I'd gotten from Io. Then I took the family photo in its expensive silver frame, the one Helen had thought would flatten me on a night devoted to families, and pressed it until the cement and glue overtook its sides.

It was my talisman. The past I'd escaped. The connection I was giving up now that I was a part of the cell.

I looked at the lost family I'd once been a part of, wondering at the path that had led me from the grandest home to a blown-to-shit crater radiating death. Then I thought about all the other mortals who went it alone in the world. Most people didn't have another family to turn to where life leaned on them, cold and hard.

I fingered Hunter's soul stone, which lay ever in my pocket, and it suddenly didn't matter how I got here. Those reasons were now a part of someone else's life: I was no longer the Archer, the Kairos, or even Olivia. Yet each of those things had made me the Joanna I was today, and for that I was grateful. Despite the hardships I faced, I had a reason to get out of bed every morning.

Sure, my *reason* was sitting in a world of heat lightning, and my mortal body was nothing more than a dangling electrical wire. True, women waited for me over there, the strongest being a sadistic monster obsessed with my demise. But what could I say? The memory of Hunter's pained scream made me want to clean my blades, take up all the arms I wasn't supposed to be able to touch, and show Solange the true meaning of obsessive violence.

Which brought me back to the conversation with my mother: after all these years, I finally knew exactly who I was.

I was Joanna Archer, a mortal with some extra benefits. I had a family of chosen friends, who had also chosen me. I was gray, an amalgam of light and shadow, which made me both dawn and dust, and in the world of the Zodiac, that was where the web between reality and its flip side was at its thinnest . . . and open to pure possibility.

The box my mother had given me contained things she'd clearly spent a long time collecting, including instructions on how to live a dual existence, plainly hidden in the cache of letters Cher had believed were left by her birth mother.

There were some baubles I didn't yet know what to do with, and makeup I assumed was more than it seemed. The box was, indeed, a catchall—a life literally objectified—and one I'd certainly pore over later. I also had Xavier's binder, which if I wasn't mistaken contained information on something called the Serpent Bearer, a little tidbit the Tulpa was so desperate to discover he'd openly attacked a mortal.

Then there were Zoe's more obvious gifts—the old conduits that no one could explain why I could still touch—which I had to confess gave me a thrill. I also possessed a weapon no one else knew about, one I'd handpicked myself from a cooling body, and wore it always on me now. The curve of Mackie's knife was constantly warm, too, as if the souls of the dead still lingered inside.

I was starting to gather my army around me, my weapons and resources . . . all the things I'd need to take another world by storm.

Meanwhile, Io was charged with changing, or fixing—I wasn't really sure which—the inside of me. The rogues, I was coming to understand, believed a person's inner balance was the most important factor in both their actions and the reactions those provoked.

"Your chakras are still blocked," she chided, leaning over my prone form, the light behind her framing the black cloud of her hair in the now-familiar thin purple halo. She pushed my ribs aside, and still unused to that, queasiness welled inside of me. I swallowed it back and closed my eyes. "You're already getting yourself a new shape here, though. Even without the outer alterations. Look at all these deformities. I wish you could see them."

Her obvious fascination made me glad I couldn't. "So, if they were visible on the outside . . . what would I look like?"

"Hunchbacked. A mutant. Something new."

Then why did I still have a connection with Hunter, one so strong even Solange couldn't break it? One that called to me through the wall separating our worlds? Io, who specialized in such connections, was aching to find out. That's why I was lying here like a science experiment, trying to keep an image of dissected frogs out of my mind as I rested my hand atop Buttersnap's tar-black head.

"So what about Hunter?" I wasn't shy about asking how we were connected. Not when Io could so clearly feel or see or sense it anyway. But I was self-conscious about how I still thought of him, and corrected myself before she could. "I mean Jaden."

"No, you were right the first time." Her haloed head lifted softly, gaze pinned to mine. "He is Hunter to you, and always will be."

Yes, I thought, swallowing hard. That felt right. "Hunter, then."

Her hands did some invisible work over me, mouth pulling tight while her lidless eyes remained wide. I was growing used to her appearance, and had even begun to find some beauty in the giant eyes. They were like two black moons reflecting back a bruised earth.

Wonder what that made me?

After a few long, silent minutes, she turned to me with a sadly wistful smile and confirmed what I'd already known. "There is nothing left of the aureole you once shared with Hunter. Only the ghostly imprint of its presence."

Disappointment visited me at that, a small sinking that went under without a fight. Feeling it, Buttersnap licked my hand, but Io put her hands on my shoulders. She leaned so close the opaque orbs of her eyes turned into an eclipse, and then told me there was a connection all the same.

I left Io's table feeling dazed, drained, but strangely peaceful in a cloudy fuguelike state that only energy work—or extreme trauma—could achieve. I'd just experienced both. Needing to be alone for a bit, I bypassed the main hall and headed up the packed earth ramp leading back to the surface. Carlos's words about night crawlers and how they lived on long after those mightier had fallen, revisited me.

Pausing to pull one of Tripp's quirleys from my pocket and pop it in my mouth as he used to do, thought about that. Olivia, and her aversion to slithering analogies, must have rubbed off on me because I decided she was right. It was disgusting.

"I'm not a night crawler," I said to myself as I emerged into the cool night. "I'm a high roller, baby."

With chips in my pocket, and a few cards still held against my chest. Still in the game. I searched the vast, black sky, ignoring the burning stars, eyes finally locking on the moon. Of all the gaseous orbs suspended in the bosom of the sky—of all Solange's talk about stars and power—I preferred this gentle planet best. It was malleable, pliant, welcoming. Tonight's was smeared at the edges, though vibrant at the center, at least until a tier of paper-thin clouds swept over its face. Within minutes they'd wiped it from the sky, leaving behind only a promising glow.

It was a reminder that something you thought you knew well could alter its appearance in a blink, and surprise you with entirely new features. If it could happen with a planet, then it could easily happen with a life.

It had just happened to mine.

And it made me wonder if you could ever know anyone well at all . . . including yourself. I did know this much. I didn't want defenses so strong that I remained untouched over the course of my lifetime. Watching Caine turn physical contact into a perversion, one requiring pain just to feel anything, had taught me that much. Watching Warren's stubbornness, even at the expense of the troop, underlined it. I didn't want to be alone or inflexible either, not physically or in my mind. Instead I'd listen to Io, lean on her a little, maybe on Carlos too, and for the first time allow myself to feel even *more* because of my losses.

Glancing up again, I found Sirius in the sky, the star Solange wanted to craft with the remainder of my soul. I thought of the chips, and soul bits, I'd won for myself in poker, and wondered how I was ever going to cash those in, and if it was really even possible. Tripp hadn't trusted me enough to say how at first, and in the end he'd been too busy dying. But he'd known. Which meant someone else did as well.

Footsteps sounded behind me, closing in, but I didn't turn. I was fixed on that bright star again, feeling the loss of Hunter so greatly—and opening to that loss—that it moved inside me, deforming me yet again into something new.

"You know what?" I said, gaze still fixed on the Big Dog as I rolled the quirley between my fingertips. "I don't believe it's an agent's job to preserve choice for the mortal population of this world."

Carlos reached my side. He looked solid, smelled good, and felt safe. I shifted closer to him. "Then what?"

"We're not meant to defend it. We're meant to create more of it."

For the mortals. And for us. We all had the right to choose.

Carlos inhaled deeply beside me, which made me wonder what exactly he was smelling. Probably red pepper, brine, and diesel oil, the earmarks of determination, stubbornness, and righteous anger. "Io told me."

I nodded, waiting to see what he'd say next.

"So, even with this new information, you haven't changed your mind?"

"Bitch has my man."

He inclined his head. "It will be even more dangerous for you now."

Every life gets sideswiped at one time or another. Sometimes even more than once. The question is, what do you do after that? Do you build something new out of the shrapnel . . . or do you just stay safe?

I knew what my mother's answer was as surely as I knew she was still tunneling and plotting out there in the world. I turned my head and smiled at Carlos, sharing my answer with him. "Shows how much you know about women, Carlos. This will make me more dangerous."

Carlos stared, face and scent unreadable to me, but he finally returned my smile before jerking his head at my quirley. "You'll have to stop smoking, *mi morena*."

"Oh, it's okay." I pulled the odd brown cigarette from my mouth, thought of Tripp, then shrugged. "I don't inhale."

Carlos gestured to the underground entry then. I nodded, he slipped a protective arm over my shoulders, and we headed back to my temporary home beneath the pock-marked craters of Frenchman's Flat. The other rogues, he told me—the grays and the night crawlers, my new allies and troop—were waiting to offer up their congratulations. I placed one hand over my belly, where Io had told me the real connection between Hunter and me lay . . . and dropped the other over Mackie's blade. No, I still wasn't super. But I had breath, a blade, and I had choice.

It was enough for now.

NEW YORK TIMES BESTSELLING AUTHOR

VICKI PETTERSSON's

SIGNS OF THE ZODIAC

THE SCENT OF SHADOWS
978-0-06-089891-5

Joanna Archer prowls a different Las Vegas after sunset—a grim, secret Sin City where Light battles Shadow—seeking answers to whom or what she really is...and revenge for the horrors she was forced to endure when she was brutally assaulted and left for dead.

THE TASTE OF NIGHT
978-0-06-089892-2

A deadly virus is descending on Las Vegas—a terrifying plague unleashed by the powerful overlord of Zodiac's dark side: Joanna's father. Death reigns supreme—and Joanna stands at dead center of an epic and terrible war, the last hope of a damned world.

THE TOUCH OF TWILIGHT
978-0-06-089893-9

Stalked by an enigmatic doppelganger from a preternatural realm, Joanna can feel the Light failing—which is propelling her toward a terrifying confrontation with the ultimate master of evil, the dark lord of Shadow: *her father*.